MY CURSED LIFE

BEVERLY DOW

PublishAmerica
Baltimore

First printing

ISBN: 1-4137-7107-6
PUBLISHED BY PUBLISHAMERICA, LLLP
www.publishamerica.com
Baltimore

Printed in the United States of America

DEDICATION

I would like to dedicate this book to my loving, understanding husband and my two wonderful children, who brought more light into my life than the sun itself. They had many upsets and have been in situations that I would not wish upon any individual. But with our love and determination, we struggled and achieved happiness. I want to thank them for being a major part of my life.

MY CURSED LIFE

ONE

Winters are never really nice in Nova Scotia. The winter of 1958 was no different. On the evening of the twelfth of March, two low-pressure systems were making their way towards the Atlantic coast of Canada. They first seemed to be aiming straight to Cape Breton; however, in a bizarre twist of fate, they fused together into a double-low and veered to the south, feverishly heading toward the Halifax peninsula. When Halifax woke up that morning, it was as if Satan himself had come up from Hades and orchestrated the whole scene. Two feet of snow had fallen on the city, soon to be followed by sleet and freezing rain. The emergency workers who were able to get to work that morning were running off their feet everywhere, plowing the streets and repairing power lines. It was pure mayhem. This was the day I was born.

I grew up in this little hamlet called Mussel Cove. If you blinked driving through you would miss it. It was twenty miles from civilization, surrounded by trees and a lot of water. It had one thing going for it—its scenery. The traffic in the summers was horrific since it was the main drag to Peggy's Cove. Tourists came from everywhere to see that place. It had a beauty all of its own. The sunsets were breathtaking, and the view of the bluish white-tipped waves was spectacular, though on stormy days, the swollen, blackened waters were frightening and very unforgiving. There was more than one life swept off the great, white smooth rocks over the years. I personally could never understand why people drove from all over North America to see water splashing up over those huge white rocks.

We had a beautiful home perched on a hill overlooking the cove. It was quite beautiful. Of course, when I was younger I never paid much heed to the scenery. What a place to raise a family. It had recreation written all over it. There was water for swimming, fishing and skating and lots of woods for making tree houses and hunting. What more could a child ask for? My parents were not your typical parents. My dad, Alexander, was a bit of a hyper sort. His fuse ran pretty short, though he had a warm side to him, and regardless how tortuous we were, he was always there for us. Not only did he work full time in the city, he also was the village's barber and plumber. He is a very respected man throughout the village. He has a great sense of humor like no other dad I ever met. My mother, Sheila, was full of life. She was not only the best cook in the village but also a very creative artist. She loved painting flower arrangements, moose and deer. When she didn't have a paintbrush in her hand or dough hanging off her fingers, she was dealing out cards. At least once or twice a week, the ladies would gather at our home to play cards and sip on tea. She always had the counters full of bread, pies and cookies. That was one thing in our home: No one ever went hungry. It was a good thing I was athletic to keep that fat off my ass. The people in Mussel Cove adored my parents, even to this day. My parents were like " the cool parents" in the neighborhood. The front door was always opened to every kid. I don't think there was a kid in Mussel Cove that didn't have a meal or two at my parents' home over the years. I had quite an imagination living out there amongst the woods and water. I was very much a tomboy. I preferred to climb trees or play with dump trucks in the dirt rather than play with dolls. My mother tried her best to pour my ass into a dress and shiny leather shoes. I swore she wanted me in the movies. I look back at some of the photos, and some of them resemble Shirley Temple. They were the days the men dressed in white shirts, ties and felt hats. I don't think I ever saw my mother in a pair of pants. And soon as she walked into the kitchen, before touching anything, she immediately tied an apron around her waist. I can still see that big bow sticking above her butt. I had few friends while growing up, but the ones I had were genuine and honest.

I never really got to know my oldest brother Patrick until much later in my life. He was either in university studying or off in the summer working. But on the other hand, there was Mark, my second brother. He was a different story.

We hated each other's guts. We fought continually. Today, he probably would be in jail for child battering. We were constantly at each other's throats. He would either be pounding on me for wearing his pants or throwing something at me. Mark and I mixed spelled trouble. Of course, being the only daughter, I often got away with murder. But poor Mark usually ended up getting a crack over his back from the broomstick or a slap on the ass from the leather belt. Today, that would normally be called "child abuse." In those days, it was basic, good old-fashioned discipline. That horrible belt, I remember that all to well. Mom used to hide it in the flour bin in the closet. Whenever we got a wack with it, there was a perfect outline of flour. At least growing up in those days I knew who was boss.

Over the years, Mark and I grew to love each other very deeply. Then there was my younger brother Justin. We were so close in age we ended up being best buddies as kids. We did everything together. The trees became our second home. We shared our trucks, dinkies and our tree houses. I never had a lot of dolls. In fact, I never even owned a Barbie doll. What girl in North America did not own a Barbie? My dad had bought me a doll the day I was born. I still have her in my closet. She is a little beat up, with nail holes in her ass and chopped off hair because I thought, of course, it would grow back someday. I still have the sad-looking thing sitting in my closet.

Justin and I were feeling our oats one day up in our tree house. We were getting quite a chuckle over the fact that he had a little weenie, and I had none. It was directly in front of my parents' bedroom window. My mother caught her eyes on us while cleaning her bedroom window. The expression on her face was frightening. We knew we were in trouble. We knew exactly where she was headed—right for the flour bin. That's where she hid that dreadful leather strap. She ran to the tree and yelled, "Get down from there right now, you two devils!" as she stood there waving that strap in the air. We tried to avoid the swings of the strap by shimmying down the other side of the tree, but my mother had long arms. There was no getting around it. We got a good wallop when we crawled down.

Those days were so different than today. There were only two television channels to watch, and we'd never heard of VCRs or computers. Mother had a cowbell that she used to let us know when it was mealtime. It didn't matter where I was, either in my boat or climbing a tree, I heard that thing ringing through the air, loud and clear. If I didn't see a meal on the table, then I knew I was in trouble for something. It was like ringing in the herd.

One of my most treasured possessions was my old rowboat. I would spend countless hours riding the shores of Mussel Cove, across the bay to the big island. I'd make a lunch in the morning with homemade bread and jelly and fill a mason jar with diluted lumpy powered milk and headed for the cove. By the time it was lunchtime, the milk had turned warm. But you know, I didn't care. Back in the day, a juice pack was never heard of. I was just thankful I had something to drink. I spent so much time on and in the water that the village nicknamed me "Fish."

One of my gloomiest days in my younger years was watching my old boat sink to the bottom of the cove. This terrible rain and windstorm came rapidly up the coast with little warning. It destroyed anything in its path—wharfs and boats. The shoreline was full of debris. Within seconds, it swallowed my boat in one quick swoop. My eyes filled up with tears. I never realized how unforgiving the ocean could really be until that day. Mark and I were sitting in the living room window watching the storm progress. The waves washed up over the road, carrying with it pieces of wood, dead fish and garbage. Had I known in advance, I could have hauled it up to shore earlier that day. It took me days to get over the loss. That boat and I were best buddies. Part of my life was swept away from me that day. I could never understand why Dad didn't buy me another boat. Maybe he thought it was time I did more girlish things.

One of the biggest events in Mussel Cove was Sunday church. That church was packed to capacity. The men all dressed in their finest suits, and the ladies decked out in their flowery dresses and overwhelming hats. It was also the biggest day of the week for the kids. After church, weather permitted, we would all hurry home, change into our old clothes and head for the wharf. Our neighbor Bill owned a large fishing boat. Everybody would squeeze onto the boat and head for the sandy beach just outside the cove. The night before the big event, the women would prepare baskets of food to take on the community picnic. We had so much fun. We ate like pigs and played in the water until we were shriveled up like prunes. The men all gathered on one side of the beach, drinking their beer, and the women on the other, keeping busy preparing the food for the picnic. The women had to stay sober to make sure none of us drowned. It was like their motherly duty. We never heard of a life jacket. Those were the days when there were few rules, and the ones that were there were kept simple. God, the fun we had on those boat trips! That tradition stayed within the community for years and years.

In those days, we had a bus that would take us into Halifax for fifty cents. When it was a rainy day, my best friend Barbara and I would hop on it early and head into the big city. I never had any money, so I packed a lunch to take with me. Instead of the community calling me Fish, they should have called me Huckleberry Finn. I swear that old bus had no shocks. It would bounce us all over the road. It was a rough, long ride, but it got us out of Mussel Cove for the day. We would spend hours window shopping. One day, I never made the trip. I was standing by the back door. The bus driver was making his final stop before entering the city limits. He opened the front and back doors to let the passengers in. Forgetting to shut the back door, he took off like a maniac. I took a jolt backwards, flew out the door and rolled into the ditch. My legs were scratched from the knees down to my ankles. The bus stopped immediately. One of the passengers ran out to help me up while another one called my parents. I was laid up for a week. Barbara didn't know whether to cry or laugh at me.

Barbara always had money on her. She had this thing called an "allowance" every week. I never received any money until my mother went back to work. My allowance was called "hard earned money." While most young teenage girls were out playing, I was home making dinner, ironing or vacuuming. I squeezed sports and my social life in between chores. Sometimes my brothers were made to help in the kitchen to dry the dishes or make the lunches, though even those times were rare. They were boys and did not have to do household chores. That was women's work. They kept their room like pigsty. I not only did their laundry but also kept their room clean.

Mark got so fed up with sleeping in the same room with his two brothers that he built a room down in the basement. It was his realm. That's where he would strum out loud horrendous music on his guitar. That music would blast up through the floorboards and drive me crazy. I hated his music. I was more into the Helen Reddy or Ann Murray style of music. He was quite the character. He was categorized as the black sheep amongst the rest of us.

Dad had bought a stereo from an estate sale. It was a beautiful piece of furniture—a turntable and radio built in to an oak cabinet. He cherished that thing. Until supper was served, he'd spend time listening to Nat King Cole. He'd sit back in his big old La-Z-Boy chair, mellow out with a cigarette and stare out at the ocean. It was his pre-dinner ritual. But my brother Mark was soon going to destroy one of Dad's few sacred moments.

One day, Dad walked into the living room, grabbed his favorite album, and as he turned to place it on the turntable, he saw nothing but a bare floor. He shook his head and looked around the room, thinking my mother might had moved it to a different location. He yelled out, "Where is my stereo?" As he spoke, we heard sawing noises coming up from the basement. Justin and I were crouched down on the highest step in the dining room, looking down on the situation. We knew there would be hell to pay. I looked at Justin and said, "Guess where he got the wood!" Mark took the liberty of removing the stereo cabinet from the living room to saw it up for shelves. Dad flew down those basements steps so fast there was a breeze when he flew by us. Dad was not a happy camper that night, and Mark had one sore backside. He had paid dearly for those shelves. It would be years before my dad would get another stereo.

Saturdays were the days I hated the most. My mother always worked, so Dad and I were left to make the bread for the upcoming week and do a ton of laundry. Dad and I spent the morning kneading large quantities of bread. We'd pump out at least two dozen loaves. After lunch, I'd roll out the old wringer washer and start doing the laundry. I could only use cold water, and in those days they didn't have detergent that worked well with cold water, so the water usually had clumps of soap through it. Often, my clothes would have lines of dried detergent on them. There were times I thought I was living back in the eighteen hundreds. It would take forever to do the laundry. While that old wringer was twirling relentlessly, I would stare out the kitchen window, looking up at the sky, wishing I were somewhere else. We never had a dryer until much later on in my life. My hands used to freeze hanging the clothes out on those cold winter days. When I would take them off the clothesline, they were as stiff as boards. The ironic part was they would have to be hung up again in the basement to dry. No wonder the windows rotted out. Talk about doubling up the workload. Laundry was one thankless job.

My dream was to be a dancer and a member of Girl Guides of Canada. Those activities meant driving into Halifax, and that wasn't about to happen. My piano teacher lived in Mussel Cove, so I could walk to my lessons. She was one strict lady! She was more concerned with posture than my actual playing. For an hour, I'd hear, "Sit up straight! Straighten out those fingers!" She was so annoying at times. The thrill I had from those lessons was when they were over. I detested every minute of them. And I might add my playing was dreadful to listen to. Even Feebie, my cat, put her ears back when I played. I had to practice that piano for thirty minutes every day. Didn't I curse that. If anyone were to touch me while playing, I would have snapped in two.

The annual beauty pageant was coming up for the Huntington Fire Hall Queen. Since I was of age and a resident on the road, I could submit an entry. I did it for more of a joke than anything since I was such a tomboy. My mother had bought me a gorgeous, long, red polka-dot backless dress for that evening. When I arrived there that evening, I realized I was the only girl from my community. The rest of them were from the village that was hosting the event. There were twelve of us in total. When I walked backstage, I had daggers thrown at me from behind from the other participants. They gave me the cold shoulder immediately. When I met with judges, they were very impressed with me. My parents were so proud of me that night. I answered all of the questions properly and managed not to trip while wearing those damn high-heel shoes. I must have done something right because they crowned me queen. The emcee approached me with a dozen roses and proudly placed the crown on my head.

I cried with happiness. I looked down at my parents, and they were standing in front of me throwing kisses towards me, but since I was not from the community, the entire audience began to boo at me. The emcee rapidly presented me with the remaining gift certificates and quickly escorted me through the back door. The crowning, photos and gift presentation took all of ten minutes. I was not long getting out of that place. The next morning, I made the front of the newspaper. It read, "Our New Huntington Fire Hall Queen," with my picture displayed below it. It was sure a proud moment for me. One of my obligations was to sit on the back of a fire truck on the Halifax Natal Day Parade, waving my hand to the city residents.

I was very athletic through all levels of school, so I had to juggle my time between household chores, homework and sports. My only bonus was to receive a ten dollar bill for taking care of the house all week Wow! Today, that would be classified as child labor! I was always trying to earn and save money. One summer, I landed a job at a millionaire's home. Their mansion overlooked the ocean and was built on a bed of white rock. The place was massive. When I walked through the front entrance, I saw this huge pipe organ. It went up so high my neck got sore looking up at the thing. The windows were massive, and a dining room sat easily twenty or more people. My first impression of the place was, "Wow!" I stood there in total amazement. I could smell money as she walked me through each room. Every bedroom had its own bathroom. I said to myself, *I guess there are no line-ups here to use the bathroom!* It was like stepping into a movie star's home in Hollywood.

After I cleaned it a couple of times, there was no more wowing. It became one big house that I had to clean for these filthy-rich Europeans. She would pick me up every Sunday morning in her Bentley and drive me home just before supper. That was the only joy I had working in that house. The couple that owned it were from Germany. He was one mean old son of a bitch and grumpy. I hoped he would one day die an awful death, and I had good reason to think that. Every Sunday, I had to wash the floors on all three levels. Every time, he would flick his disgusting stinking cigar ashes on the floor, and as he walked by me, he would grunt and groan. He was not only rich but ignorant. His wife, on the other hand, was much younger than he was and somewhat pleasant. She was quite particular on how she wanted her house cleaned. The floors had to be swept, washed, rinsed and dried all by hand. By the end of the day, my knees were two beet-red joints and were sore as hell. I worked my butt off for a measly ten dollars. I knew I would never become rich that way. I did almost anything to earn money; note the word *almost*.

I not only spent my teen years being a maid but also waited tables, cooked a lot of meals and took care of the house while my parents worked. I had a couple hundred dollars saved in the bank and was proud of it. My brother Mark wanted to go to London, England, with the school one year. My parents didn't have that kind of cash, so they used my hard-earned money. Trust me, I wasn't too thrilled! The only compensation I got was that my mother bought me a long, leather burgundy coat.

I finally gave up the millionaires job and took up the paper route. The route was from one end of town to the other. It might not have seemed big when you drove through it, but when you walked it every day without a bike, that was a different story. I was living the life of Cinderella wondering when my fairy godmother was ever going to show her face. Her boss probably had her in shackles, so she wouldn't have to deal with the likes of me. I developed leg muscles on me like a pit bull. My paper route job was short lived. What I didn't know when I took that route was that there was this man who I had known all my life. He turned out to be a terrible monster. He was a well respected resident of the community. Each day, he became friendlier with me. Being young and naïve, I thought he was just a nice person.

I thought that until that one awful day when I went to his door, and he invited me in. At first, I declined, but he said, "Come in, I have lots of candy for you!" Being the innocent victim and trusting him, I went into the kitchen. He grabbed me and with his strong arms, pulled me into the living room and threw me on the couch.

I started crying, "What are you doing? Let me go!" I started yelling out his wife's name. "Nancy, Nancy, where are you?" I was scared to death. I didn't have a clue what he was doing to me. Every bone and muscle in my body trembled. I was helpless. Before I had a chance to breathe, he jumped on top of me, fondling my entire body, kissing my neck and my tiny breasts.

As he was panting, he whispered into my ear, "You feel so good!" I could feel his saliva dripping down my neck. When he got through with me, he made me promise not to tell anybody, or he would hurt me. When I crawled off of the couch, my knees were shaking uncontrollably. My eyes were red from crying, my nose running with snot. He stood there like a proud peacock. I quickly ran out the door. As I was leaving, he put his finger to his lips, "Remember—hush hush, little one!" I was never so glad to get the hell out of there. I ran up to my favourite tree and cried and cried. It had started to get dark, so I ran quickly home. When I arrived, my parents were worried sick about me.

They could tell that I had been crying. My mother held me in her arms and asked me, "Where have you've been? We called all of your friends." I wanted to tell her so badly, but I was too afraid. I kept remembering that awful word in my head, *Remember*. His words are still embedded in my brain today. I couldn't even eat dinner that night. I had a hot steaming shower. I felt so dirty I scrubbed my skin until it hurt and then went to my room and cried myself to sleep.

The next day, I stood at the end of his driveway trying to figure out how I could deliver his paper to him. I was terrified to go near his door. I bravely started walking towards the house. I threw the paper at the front door, and as I turned around to rapidly escape, he grabbed me from behind, covered my mouth and carried me into his house. The creep had been in the backyard doing some gardening. If I only had known. I was shaking and kicking him furiously while I was in his arms. Before he had a chance to throw me onto the couch, I kicked him so hard in the groin that he almost threw up over me. I dug my nails into his neck until I saw blood under them. I made a beeline to the front door and ran so fast I never even once looked back. I had on these cheap sneakers that didn't have any ankle support. When I ran down the road, my ankles rolled, and I tumbled down into the ditch. I arrived home with swollen ankles and dirt all over my body, and I was shaking with terror. I never felt so dirty—not only on the outside, but on the inside. That was the last day I ever delivered papers.

The sad thing is that that person is still alive today and living in that same house. I often wondered why I never said anything. I think it was out of sheer fear. Over the years, I always hoped he never molested anyone again. That guilt still remains with me every day I wake up. I have hoped with every breath I take each day of my life that he would die a slow, painful, ghastly death from a cancer eating his guts and intestines out. And even that would be too good for him. To this day, I never told a soul. He turned a sweet, innocent country girl into a terrified abused wreck. When I used to hear the girls at school talking about sex, every hair would raise on my body, and I would run away from their conversations. I would almost vomit at the thought of it. That perverted sick monster ruined a large part of my life for a very long time.

TWO

There was a trip to Switzerland coming up at school. It would be a trip of a lifetime, and I wanted to go so much I could taste it, but I didn't have the funds. So, since they had robbed me blind a few years earlier for Mark's trip, my parents felt obligated to let me go and paid for most of the trip. They knew I had worked so hard to earn the little bit of money I had in the bank. I earned every cent of that trip in more ways than one! A group of twenty of us went on the trip and traveled by train throughout Switzerland. What a beautiful country! My friend Barbara and I couldn't afford luxury meals or accommodations, so we took knapsacks, a tent and the standard Canadian Tire outdoor cook set. We cooked most of the meals over open fire. The days were spent climbing mountains and sliding down glaciers.

One day, I was chased by a mountain goat. I threw a snowball at him that hit him directly in the head. He didn't take to kindly to that. I came within inches of a horn up my butt. The days were hot and the nights cold. One night, we had a terrible rainfall. It washed out the entire campsite. We managed to gather up all my wet things, stuff them into our knapsacks and, luckily, find an old dirty barn to sleep in. We nestled in amongst the hay and the smell of cow manure. By morning, we smelled as bad as the barn. There was no such thing as hopping into a shower. On our way into town, we found an old rusty water pump. We each took turns washing ourselves down. At nighttime, we often went to a pub to have a couple of beers. They loved Canadians so much, it was a rare occasion when we had to pay for it.

On my way home, I had a stopover in London, England. It was a treat to stay in a hotel room. I took the longest shower I ever took in my life. I had hoped to go shopping that evening to pick up a couple of souvenirs to take home, but that wasn't going to happen. Just down the street from the hotel, a bomb had gone off. They claimed it was set by a group of IRA protesting against the British government. It was certainly a trip I have never forgotten about. I hope that one day I will return to that beautiful place and enjoy the magnificent scenery and people once again.

You can now get a good picture of how my life was unfolding. I was born under a star of misfortune, worry, turmoil, bad choices, bad news and confusion. I've had more downs than ups. I've made more wrong decisions than right ones. When I was born, that star burnt its way through the atmosphere and buried itself far into the bowels of the earth so that it would never be found again.

During my school years, I was very active not only in sports but also with the student council. I was a very outspoken individual and was liked by my peers.

I also won several awards while attending school—everything from sports to achievement awards. When I graduated from twelfth grade, I didn't have a clue of what I was going to do. Talking about my career in my home was never mentioned. I managed to get a job at a bookstore in Halifax as a cashier. It wasn't something I wanted to spent the rest of my life doing, but it was something to do until I could decide what I wanted to do with my life. I eventually enrolled in an evening course to take English 101 since I had enjoyed English immensely during my high school years.

I eventually saved enough money to leave home and got myself a sweet apartment in Halifax. I had to share the kitchen and bathroom with another girl, but that didn't bother me. Just the fact of having my own place was great.

I couldn't afford a car, so I used the bus to get around. Life wasn't so bad after all. I made great friends and finally felt my life was getting back on some track. Which one it was, I didn't know.

I had just moved into my new place. I had ton of things to do. The new books we ordered had arrived. That meant a lot of lifting, dragging and carrying books down into the basement. I'll never forget that particular day. I had a lot of errands to run; I was going to eat on the go. I grabbed my lunch and left the store in a hurry. I no sooner stepped outside the door than I ran smack into a man who was on his way in. Books went flying into the air, and my lunch ended up all over me. I apologized to him a thousand times. It didn't seem to faze him that a hyper, skinny broad just ran head on into him. He was one nice-looking man, tall with an athletic build and a sexy smile. In fact, he was very nice about the whole thing. On the other hand, I looked like an idiot. I had tuna salad dangling from my hair, my eyelids and even my clothes. Now I was going to smell like I hadn't had a bath in a week. *Great!* He introduced himself as Dustin Ryan.

For the next couple of weeks, I saw him at the store almost every day. When passing by my desk, he would modestly say, "Hi! Have you worn any tuna salad lately?" with a genuine smile. At first, I thought I might have scared him off. Maybe I had, "I need a man. I'm desperate," written all over my face since it took him so long before asking me out. Then my next guess was that he was involved with another woman and didn't know how to unload the witch. I'd muttered to myself, *Christ, a guy as good looking as him must have something hanging off his arm.* But I found out through a girl in the office that he was just an incredibly shy person. He walked over to my desk, laid his books down and asked me if I would like to join him for a slice of pizza the next day. I replied with a smart-ass remark: "Just a slice? Why not the whole thing!"

It's a wonder he didn't turn around and run for his life and never return. If he had half a brain, he would have. He looked at me as if I were serious. The next day, I met up with him at the pizza joint just around the corner. He looked so studious with his worn-out leather bag. I discovered over lunch that he was a student at St. Mary's University, studying to be an environmentalist. He was in his fourth year.

I thought to myself, *Environmentalist.* That impressed me. At least that would get him another date. I dove into that pizza like there was no tomorrow. I was so hungry! All I had in my apartment was one light bulb and a carton of sour milk, so whenever I was treated, I took full advantage of it.

I was the kind of person that took all the creamers, sugar packs and salt and pepper packages. My purse usually weighed more leaving the restaurant. He might have been a little put off watching a grown woman looking over her shoulder before ripping the condiments off the table. It was called survival. I hadn't heard from him for a couple of days. I knew damn well I had frightened him away.

A few days later, in strutted Dustin with his leather book bag. He was smiling from ear to ear. He had received his marks and was quite proud with the results. He aced the main subjects and averaged the others. I could tell by the look on his face he was in the mood to celebrate. He walked over to my cubicle and invited me out to supper. He apologized for not phoning or dropping by, but he had been so busy studying for his exams. I quietly murmured under my breath, "Thank god, I thought it was my eating habits!" That guy must have been a sucker for punishment, wanting to take me out again.

He told me over dinner that in his earlier days in university he was no better. In fact, he often took the utensils. The restaurant was pretty classy, so I knew I had to behave. The tables actually had linen tablecloths. Boy, it was a step above my league. When that waitress showed up at our table with a basket of rolls, Dustin looked right at them, then instantly at me. I reached across the table, tapped him on his hand, and said, "My purse isn't big enough." He sighed with relief.

After dinner, I invited him back to my place to have a beer and watch a movie. It was *To Sir with Love* starring Sidney Poitier, one of my favourite actors. Suddenly, Dustin heard a noise coming from the bedroom. He quietly got up, grabbed my personal protection dog (the baseball bat by the front door), and slithered along the wall to the bedroom door. He signalled to me to move behind the chair. The next thing I heard was a man screaming at the top of his lungs. I ran to the bedroom door and peeked inside to find blood flowing down the window sill onto the floor. In a low voice, I said, "What in hell happened here?"

Dustin whispered, "I hammered the baseball bat on this creep's hands." As I was walking towards the phone to call the cops, out of the corner of my eye I noticed a man running down the street with his hands tucked underneath his arms.

I yelled at Dustin, "He's running into the woods, come quick!" But by the time Dustin got outside, the guy had vanished.

There was no way Dustin was going into those dark, eerie woods with a half-crazed man bleeding to death. The cops were at my door within minutes. They investigated the area and came up with nothing. Today, they could have taken a sample of his blood and checked out his DNA to compare it with their records. The only reassurance they gave me was, "Well, ma'am, secure your windows and make sure your door is locked at all times." They were such comforting words coming from those donut-stuffed cops. After that eventful evening, my nerves were dancing around my brain cells. Dustin decided to stay, just in case the creep returned. He slept on the floor with the baseball bat under his arms, and I took the couch. The next morning, we cleaned up the blood and secured the window with large nails and a large piece of wood. That still didn't comfort me, so I started looking for an apartment that was at least three or four floors up.

After that evening, we started seeing each other on a regular basis. I guess you would have classified us as a couple. Dustin landed a summer job playing his guitar at a local jazz club in downtown Halifax. The money and tips weren't too bad. Man, he was great on that thing! Most of my weekends were spent listening to him playing at the club. I was also entertained by the starry-eyed girls ogling him. Often times, I would have the crew from work meet us there. On the odd occasional Saturday evenings, he would manage to get off work early so we could go to a party. Even though he wasn't working at the club, he could never escape the guitar. We would get invited to a house party just so our friends could listen to him play. He was one talented man. We got along great. He owned this old, beat-up, five-speed dark green truck.

Over the summer, with a lot of patience (and guts) he taught me how to drive that thing. I'd grind those gears so hard he'd cover his ears. I don't know yet how in hell I got my driver's license. It probably was because the driving instructor had focused more attention on my legs than my driving. That summer flew by so quickly. The leaves were falling, and the nights were getting chillier. Dustin was back at the old grind. He had to spend every ounce of energy on his studies that year. He was shooting for high marks to land that job up in northern Alaska. I too started to consider going back to school again. In time, I enrolled into a night class to study people management development, a course for which was held at St. Mary's University. I thoroughly enjoyed it. I didn't get to see Dustin as often as I hoped for, but when we did it was certainly quality time!

We dated throughout the year. He got along great with my family, especially my brothers. They not only loved his disposition but also his fabulous guitar playing. No matter where we went, the women were constantly staring at him. I guess I could have classified him as a womanizer. He graduated from university, but not with the marks he had hoped for. It was not from lack of trying. He had put his heart and soul into his last year.

I think he set his expectations too high.

His graduation was quite the affair, with seven courses to enjoy. Dustin was the prince of the ball, and, of course, I was the belle. God forbid there was someone else that looked better than me. I would have to go to extreme measures, which usually meant intentionally spilling a drink on their gowns. After the meal, we had the pleasure of dancing to the tunes of Canadian Brass. What an elegant evening. Dustin couldn't dance to save his life. He trampled my feet to a pulp. When I arrived home, the first thing I had to do was to soak my aching feet.

The next day he said to me that he wasn't going to return to university that fall. He was tired of studying and hungry for money. I had completed my course, and since I did so well, I was promoted to assistant manager, which gave me an increase of five thousand dollars more a year to play with. I never gave it a second thought to save any of it. That would have been too sensible. I was now supporting the both of us since Dustin wasn't working. We started seeing each other every night. I didn't know if it was because I was a good lay or because of my cooking. Either way, we were in love and decided to move in together. We found a cozy two-bedroom apartment right in downtown Halifax, overlooking the harbour. It was ideal for me, as I was only minutes from work. Dustin spent his entire days pounding the streets looking for a job. The problem wasn't what he knew. It was the lack of who he knew.

The snow was beginning to fall, and the hint of Christmas was in the air. Christmas was, and still is, my favourite time of the year. It brought smiles on everyone's faces. It was a time for family and friends to share in the season's festivities. There wasn't one particular thing I loved about Christmas, it was the whole package. My friends had bets that he was going to ask me to marry him on Christmas Eve. He phoned me up at work a couple of days before Christmas Eve. All he said was, "Be ready for seven o'clock and wear something beautiful. And if you need me, I'll be at my mom's place." At lunch that day, I went out and purchased a pair of sexy panties, a three-hundred-dollar low-cut, dark green dress, and a pair of slingback black shoes.

When I tried it on at the dress shop, I walked up to the mirror, took a couple of twirls and said, "God, I'm good, I can't get much better looking than this." I knew what that mindless, short, stubby clerk behind me was thinking of me by the expressions on her face: *That egotistical bitch, wouldn't I like to slap her silly. That would make my day!* and all within the same breath, smiling! I didn't give a damn. I knew I was better looking than her, and she was just plain jealous. I nicknamed her "Double Cheeseburger Queen."

When I arrived home from work, I began the preparations. I worked from my toes up. It wasn't much of a challenge since I had the right equipment to work with. It was just a matter of prioritizing where I wanted to spend most of my energy. My priorities, of course, were my face, hair and nails. If I had had the guy in front of me who designed the G-string panties, I would have shoved them up his butt and pulled them out through his mouth. They should be outlawed. They were the most uncomfortable piece of clothing I ever had on my butt.

He arrived in that old truck at seven sharp. That was one thing about Dustin—he was always punctual. He had made reservations at the finest and most expensive restaurant in town, The Sky Is The Limit. I knew that was going to be the night. We arrived at the restaurant to find our table had a beautiful arrangement of flowers. I wasn't used to that kind of treatment. For one thing, I wondered where he had gotten the money. He told me over dinner that he landed a great job at the laboratory at Dalhousie University in the research department that day. Boy, that guy was just full of surprises that night! Meanwhile, his mom had loaned him some cash to carry him through until he received his first pay cheque. Little did she know, a lot of her money was being spent on that glamorous evening. The flowers and the atmosphere were fabulous. He ordered a bottle of champagne. As the waiter was pouring the wine, Dustin kept staring at the flowers, and I couldn't figure out why. I knew they were gorgeous and must have cost a lot of money, but come on! So I said to him, "What's with you and the flowers? Did you hand pick them?" He never replied.

He lifted his glass and made a toast: "To us for now and forever, my love!" It actually brought a tear to my eye. Now I was getting really antsy. The anticipation was driving me to down the wine even quicker than usual.

The waiter showed up to light the candle and offered us the menus. By now, I was so nervous the crack of my butt was even sweating. He ordered another bottle of champagne to have with dinner. Any more of that stuff, and I would have had three Dustins to go to bed with that night. When I think about it, that wouldn't have been such a bad idea! I was beginning to doubt that he was going to pop the question at all. Every time he would reach across the table to hold my hand, I thought that was going to be the moment.

He asked me, "Do you notice anything special about the flowers?" These flowers were getting the best of me now. I took a good hard look at them.

My mouth opened wide. "Oh my god!" A little glimmer came from a pink bow. There was a diamond ring dangling from one of the ribbons. Now that was romantic! He untied it, placed it onto my finger and, in front of the entire restaurant, got down on one knee and said, "Will you marry me?" Not only did we get a standing ovation, but there was a plus side—we got a free bottle of expensive champagne. I wasn't embarrassed at all. It took an awful lot to embarrass this girl. I was so happy. What a night! We had tears of joy. If only life could have remained that way. After all the excitement, we headed back to our place, cracked open a bottle of cheap screw-top wine and began phoning our family and friends to tell them the good news.

It wasn't long after that the two mothers started making their wedding plans for us. It was a fairy-tale wedding. For some reason, Dad spared no expense, probably because he thought it was a one-time deal. Everything from my custom-made dress to the food was fabulous. The entire village was invited plus people neither one of us knew. In a small town, you either have them all or no one. Uncle Ross loaned Dad his Mercedes to take me to the church. There was a lot of cursing going on in that car. The car simply would not start. Everyone else was at the church, and since we still hadn't shown up, they got a little antsy. Finally, Uncle Ross showed up in another car. He looked at us and started laughing his butt off at Dad.

By now, Dad was furious. His face was beet red. He started banging his hands on the steering wheel, yelling, "You damn piece of European crap! Start! That's it, get out, we're walking to the church!" I couldn't stop laughing at him. He totally lost control.

Just as Dad opened his door, his brother knocked on the window and told him, "Do up your seat belts!" It was a safety precaution in that car model. In those days, you never heard of wearing a seat belt. The only way the Mercedes would start was if one or more of the belts were locked in place. It was too funny. He raced that sucker down the hill and smoked it to the church.

The church was packed to capacity. When the service was over, we all paraded to the legion. I looked over my shoulder to see the most unusual site—the headlights of all the cars were reflecting off the ocean as if a giant string of Christmas lights was outlining the shoreline. It looked awe-inspiring. When I walked into the legion, I could have brained the decorators. They couldn't have been more tacky if they tried. The ceiling was covered with streamers and big white bells. The bar was literally outlined in mini white bells. I looked at Dustin and said, "Were they drinking when they decorated this place?" The good thing was that gifts were piled high and laughter filled the room. The men lined up at the bar, itching to get their hands on a cold one, while the women gawked around the room to see who was wearing what.

I didn't have the customary bride and groom on top of the cake. Instead, I had chosen a sweet pair of cats on top. There was no particular reason, just that I adored cats. I detested that dim pair of plastic idiots that everyone and their dog put on their wedding cake. When it came time to throw my bouquet, the women swarmed into a large circle. I could see their greedy little mitts flying in the air with the anticipation of grabbing it. Instead of my bouquet landing in the crowd of women, it hit the ceiling. Flowers sprayed throughout the room. The women hit the floor, grabbing what little flowers were left. I guess that meant there were going to be a lot of weddings in the near future. Dustin's parents had given us a gift that we would remember for the rest of our lives. It was an all-inclusive trip. Since we were flying out early the next morning, we didn't stay long at the reception. His parents were wonderful—they treated me as if I were their own daughter.

Dustin had arranged for breakfast to be sent to our room that morning.

I was so excited about the trip I could hardly eat. I had the typical whore's breakfast—a cup of black coffee and a cigarette. I quickly dove into the shower. Dustin was feeling a little under the weather, so he didn't have the same high level of energy. When I got out of the shower, Dustin was sound asleep on the bed. I stood over the bed and began to pour a glass of cold water over his face. He leapt off that bed like a flea. "What did you do that for? Damn! I don't need water, I need a cold beer!" That got him up.

"If you don't get your butt off that bed, we're going to miss our flight!" I knew it was going to be hot when we stepped off that plane. I slipped on my bikini and wore a trench coat to the airport. Dustin thought I was nuts. We just made our flight.

When we arrived in Puerto Rico, the heat was incredible. As soon as the airplane door opened, a gust of hot air blew in. We got into a cab to take us to the hotel. I asked the driver, "What time is it?"

He chuckled and said, "Why? You're in Puerto Rico!" I guess he made sense. The streets were full of kids riding bikes on and off the sidewalks. And the local derelicts where bumming for money on the corners of the street. The sun was intense; it was heat I had never experienced before.

When we stepped out of the cab, the hotel staff greeted us with a drink topped with a pink umbrella. The outside of the hotel was surrounded by a brilliant array of flowers. Tropical music filled the air. It was magnificent! The pool looked so appetizing. It had a bar shaped like a coconut with numerous waiters running their butts off serving drinks. Our room was amazing. It not only had a panoramic view of the ocean but also had a sunken hot tub next to the huge king-size round bed. The table in front of the television had a complimentary bottle of champagne circled with a tropical arrangement of flowers and fruit. I thought to myself, *I have died and gone to heaven!* I was in an awe state of mind. Dustin poured us a glass of the champagne and walked out to the deck. The scenery was captivating. The calmness and peace was indescribable. I looked up into the sky and took a deep breath of fresh air. There was a fresh smell that filled the insides. It must have come from the fruit hanging from the trees.

I didn't even unpack. I couldn't wait to dive into that tantalizing pool. The pool had stools in it, so we could have our drinks while enjoying the beautiful blue water and absorbing the hot sun. Dustin told the bartender, "Dos cervezas, por favor." We watched the bartender, who was a little portly, fill two small six-ounce glasses of beer, put them on a tray, and awkwardly walk down about ten steps to serve us. "Gracias," said Dustin. By the time the bartender got back to the bar, we had downed our beer. So Dustin asked again, "Perdonne me, señor, dos cervezas, por favor." So again, we watched him go through his routine. Again, "Gracias."

The third time we asked for beer, the bartender got the idea. He reached into the fridge, got four quarts of beer and gave them to us, gasping for air and saying, "I hope this will satisfy you for a few minutes?"

Dustin looked up at him with a sly look, "Don't get too comfortable!"

The pool was refreshing for the moment, but the minute I stepped out of it, the heat sucked up every bit of fluid off of my body. During that afternoon, we met up with other couples who also were on their honeymoon. We sat around the pool drinking their famous rum cocktails and talking about our weddings. The more we drank, the more elaborate the weddings became. Booze was cheaper then drinking pop, so we couldn't afford not to drink! "My god, what a first night on our honeymoon!" It introduced my liver to a whole new program. The next morning, my pores were sweating out beer, rum and orange juice.

We had been told to go this nightclub, the Banana Boat. That place rocked. I could hear the music three blocks away. The waiters gave us a menu of special house drinks, ninety-nine percent of which were made from bananas. "Why not!" After a couple of cocktails, we started to dance. There were black lights in the ceiling. As we were dancing away, Dustin started laughing his butt off. I didn't know what was so funny. I was getting a little annoyed with him. Then I looked around the dance floor and noticed everybody was laughing at me! Dustin was in hysterics. He quickly grabbed my hand and wrangled me through the crowd to get me outside. Dustin stood in the parking lot, trying through his laughter to explain to me why he was laughing. He finally spilled the beans. "You should have seen yourself up there tonight, it was priceless!"

I pulled out a cigarette, sucking it to its limit and angrily yelled at him, "What was so damn funny? Do you mind telling me the joke?" Finally, after he stopped laughing his butt off, he told me that when I was smiling, I looked like I had no front teeth.

I used to play hockey in high school, and in this one game, a player shot the puck right on my face. I lost all my front teeth, and I've worn a partial since then. Those damn black lights made it look as if I had no front teeth. I must have looked like a total fool!

Speaking of having no teeth: We were on a beautiful day sail just off the coast, and there were a couple of obnoxious guys from Boston with us. The food and booze, of course, were included. These guys were loud and ignorant. They would lift their butts and fart and burp to their hearts' content. They drank like fish and ate like pigs. They were so annoying. Dustin and I ended up moving to the other side of the boat.

Then, all of a sudden, one of the pigs starts to choke. This one servant starts to yell, "Help dis' man, he cannot breathe!" I run to the front of the boat, get behind him and start squeezing his stomach upwards. Within seconds, a tiger shrimp flies out of his mouth along with his false teeth. I stood back and watched these morons with their hands in the air waiting to catch the pig's teeth. They bounced on the deck and landed straight into the water!

He then looks at the servant and yells, "What are you standing there for? Jump in and get my teeth!"

The waiter replied, "No way man, unless you want to see me eaten alive by smilin' shark!" We all laughed so hard we almost cried! That shut him up instantly. He sat on his deck chair and never said another word until we got back to the resort. He was going to look so cute at the Banana Boat tonight! He deserved every bit of it.

The food at the resort was fabulous. They served everything you could think of from seafood to stuffed pig to baron of beef! The fruit display was simply incredible. I ate so much fruit that I always had to make sure there was a toilet within range.

We joined up with another newlywed couple to have a game of golf. I teed off first. My ball soared into the bright sky as Dustin and the other couple struggled to see where my ball was going to land. We did find the ball along with a dead bird next to it. I nailed that bird dead on. That was a great way to start off the game, killing off the wildlife. The couple we were playing with didn't make it past the second fairway. Her husband took a sharp cramp and ran towards the trees. We waited for him for about ten minutes. Since he never came back out, we figured he didn't make it. His wife was a little embarrassed, so she quietly left the scene. I said to Dustin, "No more fruit for him!" That made for an eventful game of golf.

The night before we left to go home, the hotel put on an enormous beach party. Live music, free drinks and barbeques lined along the shoreline cooking everything from lobsters to steak. I saw these meatballs, and since they looked so appetizing, decided to give them a try. I sank my teeth into these tender balls. They were literally melting in my mouth. I went back for seconds, but before doing so, I said to the cook, "This is delicious! What is it?" He looked over at the next cook and started to laugh.

He replied, "Do you really want to know? Or would you just like another piece?" I was curious now.

"Seriously, what is it?"

He came close to my face and said, "I take the finest goat balls and stuff them with curried lobster meat!" Well. My golden tanned face instantly turned snow white, and I started spitting out any fragments that were still lingering in my mouth. Dustin laughed so hard.

He looked at me and said, "You look like you've seen a ghost! Or maybe a goat?"

I said to Dustin, "I just ate *goat balls*!"

As I was storming towards the bar to disinfect my mouth, I heard Dustin behind me muttering, "Gee, I wish she would gnaw on my balls once in awhile!"

I turned around. "Dustin, it will be a cold day in hell before that will ever happen!"

I immediately went to the bar, gargled some dark rum and spit it out. I had kind of lost my appetite. We headed back to our room to pack up our things since we had an early flight in the morning.

THREE

When we arrived back at our apartment, we found several messages on our answering machine. Dustin tended to the messages while I started to unpack our things. Dustin walked into the room with a long face. "I have some bad news. The lab is cutting back their staff, and since I have little seniority, I'll be the first to go!" Apparently, the grant they were supposed to receive never pulled through. Oh well. Between my salary and my savings account, we would be able to manage awhile. I knew one thing: There wouldn't be any lavish parties or eating out for a while. The honeymoon was over in more ways than one. He had to find a job, and fast! He eventually found a job in Truro, working with the town planner in developing ways to create better waste management. Since it was a forty-five minute drive, he decided to get an apartment close to work.

The position wasn't exactly what he wanted, but the money was great. There was no way I was quitting my job until he knew it was going to somewhat be a permanent position. After a few months, the traveling on the weekends became tiring. Since Dustin was enjoying his job, I decided to join him. I would look for work once I was there. It was a difficult day when I had to say good-bye to my job and all of my friends. The gang had a farewell party for me. They showered me with parting gifts, an elegant dinner and wine galore. It was certainly a sweet and sour evening. They assured me that if I ever returned, there would always be a job waiting for me.

Dustin had rented out a two-bedroom apartment minutes from his job.

Since I had all of the furniture at our place in Halifax, he was left to sleep and eat on the floor. He was delighted to see that moving van pull up to the building. When I arrived, the place was a typical bachelor joint—boxes of pizza on the floor complimented with empty beer bottles and a sheet nailed to the front window. He turned the place into a pig sty! It didn't take me long to transform it into normal living quarters. I told Dustin, "Another couple of days, and I would have had to hire exterminators to come in here!" Men can be such pigs at times!

We did a lot of entertaining with his new colleagues. Dustin was always the centre of attraction at the parties because of his great guitar playing. He could bring a room to a total silence when he played "Classical Gas," or fill a room with laughter when he spoke like Donald Duck . Dustin loved life to the fullest! I landed a job at the local newspaper company as a proofreader. I must say it was a rather interesting job. There was a lot of crap happening in that small town. It was one job where I definitely had to keep my mouth shut. A lot of the things I proofed never hit the papers. They were filed in the "shredder cabinet." In other words, it never happened. There were times I wished I was the Editor-in-Chief. I would have added some nasty spices to that newspaper. There definitely would have been a downside, though—I probably would have been assassinated the first week on the job.

We often drove to Halifax on the weekends to visit our old friends and drop in on the family. I swear they thought we were poor as church mice. They would load us up with food, and though I had a good job, Mom would always slip me the occasional twenty dollars. Sometimes we would go to the legion on Saturday night with my brothers and their wives. There wasn't a big selection of places to go on the old beat-up road, so we made the best of it at the legion. We danced to the oldies and drank a lot of beer and wine. Our weekends were fun. We didn't have a care or worry in the world. As long as we had enough money to pay the bills and party on the weekends, that's all that mattered.

After, we would return to my parents' place and eat Mom's homemade pizzas. They were then and still are the best pizzas in town. I never realized until much later in my life that pizzas generally were made up of cold cuts and mozzarella cheese. Mom only used homemade meat sauce and cheddar cheese. Boy, they kept me in the closet! Our parents made sure that our truck was full to capacity with food when heading back home.

That thing had a terrible heating system. During the winter months, our feet would literally freeze. To stop the wind from blowing into our truck, Dustin had to tape the windows shut with green gun tape. At least it matched with the colour of the truck. One trip back home, one of the wipers stopped working. Of course, it was pouring the sea out. The only bonus was that the broken wiper was on my side. Dustin's eyes were glued to the windshield like a splattered bug.

Dustin loved homemade donuts. He was constantly buying them at the local bakery. I had never made a donut in my life, so one stormy Saturday afternoon, I thought I would surprise him and make a batch. I didn't have a clue on where to start. I finally found a recipe in one of my mother's cookbooks. When he opened the door, he smelled the aroma of deep-fried donuts cooking. He flew down the hall, tripped over his own two feet and ran to the stove. He could hardly wait to sink his teeth into one. He quickly sat at the table, anxiously waiting for his donut to arrive in front of him. I can still see him sitting there licking his lips.

He took one big bite into the donut and chipped the front of his tooth off. He threw the donut down and started yelling in pain, "That donut broke my tooth. Great!" I ran into the dining room to put a bag of peas on his mouth until I could figure out what to do. To top it off, I could see smoke coming from the kitchen.

"Oh my god, now what?" I ran into the kitchen to find the pot full of donuts on fire. The lard boiled so hard, it had sprayed on the hot burner. It reminded me of a witch's pot overflowing with unforgiving heat. I took the fire extinguisher and blasted the pot. "Oh my god, oh my god, I'm going to burn the place down!" I had the walls, floor and ceiling full of foam. The fire alarm was dancing off the ceiling. I was running frantically between the dining room and the kitchen. Dustin was basically useless, whining over his broken tooth.

I stood at the kitchen entrance, overwhelmed with the mess and shaking my head back and forth, and Dustin yelled out, "Where in hell am I going to find a dentist in Truro on a Saturday afternoon?" I didn't have to worry about that for too long. One of our nosy neighbours took it upon herself to call the authorities. Within seconds, there were firemen, ambulance attendants and policemen standing at our door. They pounded at the door. It was a good thing I got to the door when I did. They were ready to axe it down. By now, Dustin was in terrible pain.

While the firemen were taking care of the situation in the kitchen, the ambulance attendant gave him a shot in the ass to subdue some of the pain. They carried him through the mess on a stretcher. He was muttering to the ambulance attendants, pointing his finger at me. "Don't eat her donuts, they're deadly!" When I finally made it to the hospital, Dustin was as high as a kite. I took him home a few hours later. There wasn't a dentist to be found anywhere until Monday. The apartment reeked of smoke, and the kitchen was a total write-off. Thank god we had insurance. Dustin stuck to the bakery's donuts from there on out.

He started getting bored with his job. He found it wasn't challenging and could see no promotion in the near future. He needed something more rewarding and daring. One of his buddies had his private pilot's license. Flying always fascinated Dustin. When they would go up flying, that's all I'd hear for days. I couldn't understand how anybody could have a fascination for flying; I detested it. I preferred to have both feet on the ground at all times. But flying gave him a sense of freedom. The sky was the limit. He knew we couldn't afford for him to get his commercial license, so he started to investigate other avenues, one of which was the military.

I arrived home from work to find him sitting on the living room floor, sipping on a beer and looking through a bunch of brochures he picked up from the recruiting office. Other then winning the lottery, which never would have happened, his only other choice was to join the military and hopefully become a pilot. Personally, I thought that was a little drastic, but he was very determined to do it. Before he made any solid decisions, he went to the recruiting office in Halifax.

They accepted him immediately. Since Dustin had a master's degree in Environmental Studies, they had wanted Dustin to be an engineer, but he said no. Pilot was the only career he wanted.

It wasn't long before we were packed up and on our way to Halifax. We had enough money saved up to get ourselves an apartment in Clayton Park. It was funny; my oldest brother and his wife lived in the same apartment building just around the corner. Dustin was off to basic training in Borden within weeks. I landed a great job working once again with the newspaper. I started taking night classes in advanced business communications. At least my classes kept me out of trouble in the evenings.

Dustin aced the basic training course. The first three weeks there, he lost twenty pounds. The athletic part was grueling. When he graduated from Borden, my parents and I flew up to attend the ceremony. We were so proud of him. I hardly recognized him with his short hair and weight loss. It was just the beginning. He had a long road ahead of him with a lot of rough uphill battles. We didn't have a clue what to expect in the future. He had a bit of time off before his next course, so we headed for Niagara Falls. We had such a grand time there. Everyone was happy there. Of course! Why wouldn't they be? It's a honeymoon town! There was more tack there than you could imagine. I sure had my fill of Elvis Presley. There was no way you could escape his image.

Upon our arrival back home, there was a letter notifying Dustin that he would be leaving for Portage La Prairie, Manitoba, in the following month to start his basic flying training. He had been warned by his peers that it was one complex course. There was no in between. You either passed or failed. He thought that I should have a dog to keep me company while he'd be away. I didn't agree, but it made him feel better knowing I had a vicious miniature bulldog. I named him Clyde. That's the only dog I ever knew that liked beer. I could never lay a beer bottle down on the table. He would jump up on the chair and, with his front paws, kick it off onto the floor and lap it up. I got so tired of cleaning up his messes, I started putting half of my beer into his bowl. He lapped it up so quickly his eyeballs bulged out. Afterwards, he'd lie on his back, display his groin, let out a disgusting fart and start snoring. He was such a pleasant thing to look at. He was certainly entertaining. When I had company, I'd have to lock him into my bedroom, so people wouldn't think I was raising a "porn dog." He chewed up shoes, furniture and even the upholstery in the truck.

Once Dustin knew he was going to pass, he thought it was a good time to join him in Portage. I had no idea what the place offered other then what Dustin had told me, which wasn't much. I had to finish up my night course before leaving. It was one difficult move. Every time I turned around, I was ripping up my roots. I was very close to my family and friends. My parents drove Clyde and I to the airport. By the time I arrived in Portage, Dustin was acing the course. He had rented out a mobile home just outside the base. I arrived at the airport and was greeted by Dustin's new friends, Peter,

Douglas and Jason. They drove to the airport in Jason's new sport GTI Rabbit. Clyde was so happy to see Dustin, he peed all over him. For the next hour, we smelled dog piss, and since it was so cold out, we couldn't even roll down a window. I'd look out the window to see nothing but barren land and the occasional barn or silo. I said to them, "There's nothing here! It's so flat!" The wind screeched across that highway with blowing snow, causing almost whiteout conditions.

Life in Portage La Prairie was simple and at times extremely boring. Dustin spent countless hours studying with the other students. There was absolutely no place I could work. I asked him one day, "Why did you bother bringing me out here to no man's land? There is nothing here for me!" He knew I was ticked off with him. My highlight of the day was getting the mail and taking Clyde for a walk. The town didn't have much to offer. There was one main drag that carried an array of shops consisting of grocery, liquor, drug and clothing stores. The town had two pubs: one was for the derelicts, and the other was more of a classier joint. It had tables you could actually put your drink on. Right smack in the middle of town was the legendary City Hall. There was a man-made lake with a beautiful park on the other side of it. I often took Clyde there for walks. Thank god I had Clyde to keep me company. I had really lowered my standards, having a dog as my only form of entertainment.

I should have stayed home until he finished that segment of his course. I would have been a lot happier. There was this local bar called Harvey's Inn. Given that it was the only lounge in town, it usually was standing room only on the weekends. The student pilots would generally hang out there on Friday and Saturday nights. It was their place to unwind after a drilling week of test and studying. The local girls showed up dressed like sleaze-bags. I often wondered how they squeezed their asses into those tight jeans. Some of them were so tight you could count the wrinkles on their butt. I don't think their mothers ever showed them how to wear a bra. They would let their breasts bounce freely. Their only goal was to nail one of the student pilots. It was their one ticket out of Hickville. I might add that they were very unsuccessful with their tricks. The student pilots were forewarned before arriving in town. They were well aware that the town was crawling with horny single women.

After his graduation, which I might add was pretty low key, the commander handed them each a piece of paper acknowledging that they had completed their basic flying training. We had a huge party that night at our place. When I woke up the next morning, there were bodies laying everywhere. I cooked them up a huge pan of scrambled eggs and pancakes. It took me half the morning to gather up all the beer bottles. The mobile home reeked of cigarettes and stale booze. Not very appetizing! There were a lot of sore heads that morning.

The next part of the course was in Moose Jaw, Saskatchewan. It was the advanced flying training course on the Tutor jet. Moose Jaw was a booming little town. It had a large steel industry that employed fifty percent of the population. That's where I found a job as an administrator. We lived in a beautiful apartment. The building was hardly broken in when we moved in. It was close to all amenities. There were a few other student pilots who were married also living there. It wasn't long after we moved in that we discovered the town whore was living upstairs in the building. That made life interesting. There was a lot of action coming and going up those stairs on the weekends. You would never know her occupation by looking at her. She was so sweet and innocent to look at. Now there's a case where you couldn't tell a book by its cover.

We attended a buffet and dance at the mess one evening. As we entered the mess, they were selling tickets for door prizes. We noticed our apartment building's whore when we walked into the bar. She was sitting around a table with a crew of new student pilots. She was in her glory. When they started drawing for the prizes, much to her surprise, she was one of them! It was, of course, a joke. She stood up, took a bow and accepted the joke quite proudly. I guess she really was a nice person after all.

The weekdays were nothing but studying, testing and intense pressure. Dustin sure had his tough moments, especially with meteorology. There were times I didn't think he was going to make it. He took it one week at a time. He knew he would need a lot of determination and willpower to pull through. The weekends were times to party, and party it was. The philosophy of the students at that time was that if you were still on course by the end of the week, you celebrated by getting inebriated. On Friday night at the Officers' Mess, there were so many instructors and students, you had to hold your glass of beer over your head so you wouldn't spill it.

One night at the mess, I got really tipsy. Dustin and the boys dared me to get up on the table and dance. I always enjoyed a good dare, so I boldly got up on the table and started to dance, but not for long. The mess manager pulled me off the table and, within seconds, kicked my butt out the door and banned me from the establishment for two weeks. There were parties up your ying-yang. You couldn't turn a corner on any Friday or Saturday night without seeing student pilots drunk and laughing their butts off. The single pilots were always hounded by local girls hoping to nab one of them and get married.

There was one night when we were all sitting around the bar. We noticed on the other side of the bar that one of the student pilots, who had a few too many, was making the moves on a very attractive woman. Even though he was quite drunk, she didn't seem bothered by that. As Dustin went to the bar to refresh our drinks, he took a good look at the woman then quickly came back to our table and said, "She has an Adam's apple! She's a man!" We were laughing so hard, we almost split our guts! Dustin went up to the student pilot and whispered into his ear, "She's not what she appears to be!"

The student pilot looked at him. "Get out of here! Look at her, she's beautiful!"

Dustin replied, "Don't say I didn't warn you!" It wasn't long before the student pilot and his pick up left the bar. He had his arm around her shoulders and turned around and gave us a big wink. The following Monday, that student was the laughing stock of his course. Rumour had it when he sobered up the next morning, she was not quite what he had expected to find next to him. And his course never let him forget it.

One Friday night, I came home from work to find Dustin in the bathtub with the shower curtain wrapped around him. I looked down at him and remarked, "He must have made it through another week!" I put a blanket on him and left him there until morning.

The single guys always enjoyed my home cooking. They had named me the "Course Mom." I always had a crew around our table. A bunch of them came over one Sunday afternoon to watch a football game. I decided to play a prank on the boys. I made two huge lasagnes and a dark chocolate cake for dessert. They dove into that cake like a bunch of hungry animals. Little did they know that the chocolate cake was partly made with Exlax. When the boys went up flying the next day, they basically were filling their flight suits with day-old chocolate cake. They had to come home early that day, and did they ever curse me! Today I would be fined and most likely be sued. It was a long time after before they would touch anything that resembled chocolate in my house.

One of the girls I worked with was having a party and invited us to go. She lived in a trailer court on the other side of town. When we arrived, there was a bouncy half-grown Doberman dog that came running to our car. I was a little nervous at first. She came to the deck and said, "It's alright, he's harmless!" I took a large salad along with some beer. The men, of course, were all standing on the deck, and the ladies congregated in the kitchen.

All of a sudden, we heard screams coming from outside. "No, no, you stupid mutt! Oh my god, no, don't!" I ran outside to find that the men were in the next door neighbour's yard. There was hair and blood everywhere. I ran over to the fence to see a kitten bitten in two.

I said, "What a disgusting mess!" I turned around and threw up every last bit of food I had in my stomach. That poor kitten didn't have a chance. The dog stood there with cat hair and blood hanging from his teeth. Dustin and the other men cleaned up the mess while the owner took the dog to the vet to put him down. That was a sweet ending for a lovely barbeque. There was no way I was having my steak rare that night.

Dustin and I had planned to start a family after he completed his flying course. However, that wasn't going to be the case. I became pregnant during his flight training. He was so excited. He called over his flying buddies to share the great news. They weren't long coming over with beer to celebrate the occasion. At first, I found it very difficult to come to terms with the fact that I was going to be a mom. I wasn't overly thrilled in the beginning, but as time went on, I realized how precious it really was. I knew it was a very special time for us. I didn't know if I was capable of taking care of a baby. I could barely take care of myself. I had to take a crash course in motherhood.

Over the months, there were a lot of sweet and sour moments. We watched a lot of friends get the boot. They called it "CT," ceased training. Dustin, after long and stressful days and nights of hard work, finally graduated. The graduation was an elaborate affair. People came from all parts of the world. They weren't just Canadians on these courses. There were also men and women from Europe and Jamaica. In fact, Dustin's course was the first one in Canada to allow women to enter the program. Dustin had requested to be sent to Shearwater, Nova Scotia, to fly Trackers. But since he was older and more mature than the other pilots, they posted him to Portage La Prairie to be a flying instructor.

The move was difficult for me since I was eight-and-a-half months pregnant. There wasn't much of a choice of housing, so we moved into a PMQ—housing provided by the military. They were an eyesore. The houses had absolutely no style or design. We basically lived on top of one another. It was one big fish bowl, and everybody knew everyone's business. The one good thing was that Dustin could walk off his beer gut while going to the flight line.

Shortly after we arrived, I gave birth to our son, Adam Dustin. What a proud moment. I was exhausted. I had been in labour for eight long, painful hours before he decided to enter the world. He was then, and still is now, an adorable creature. The question was, was I ready for him? I looked down at him and said, "We'll have to teach each other along the way, little buddy!" He had these beautiful blue eyes. We nicked named him "Big Blue." The pilots who remained in Moose Jaw as instructors got wind of our new addition, and they flew to Portage to see him. They showed up at our door with gifts, food, flowers and beer. You'd swear that baby was theirs, the way they went on. Some of the outfits were pink with flower designs on them. I could tell they didn't have a clue what to buy.

We both tried to live the same carefree party life we had before Adam was born. That brought several complications to our marriage. Dustin would think nothing of bringing over a complete crew of airmen from the United States for dinner on a Friday night, without any warning. They would party all hours of the night. The next morning, my living room not only looked like a morgue but smelled like one. We were burning the candle on both ends. It started to take a toll on both of us. He still wanted to attend TGIF every Friday night to mingle with the students and instructors, and often times, they were very late nights. I was itching to go back to work. Somewhere in between all of this, there was Adam.

Now when I think back, our demands were selfish. We became very frustrated with each other. We were constantly at each other's throats over the smallest things. Dustin was away a lot on cross-country trips with his students, and I was left behind with a newborn and no family support. I finally landed a job at the curling club as their administrator and payroll clerk. I had a lot of juggling to do between Adam, work and entertaining, not to mention my marriage.

I joined the Officers' Wives Club so I could start socializing with the local women. What a bunch of cats. They sure had their claws kept sharp. They were a fine group as long as I didn't get too comfortable with them.

We had organized a bingo party at the Officers' Mess to raise money for a local charity. It was opened to not only military people but also to the local residents. The bingo caller was a French student pilot. He was so funny, half of the time he called out the numbers in French. He was there learning to fly helicopters. During the game, he kept one eye on the ball and one on me. When the game was finished, he immediately came over to talk with me. His name was Daniel Leblanc. He didn't hang around too long once he found out that I was an instructor's wife. I ran into him a couple of times after at the gym. I found out later through the grape vine, which was rather large, that he had graduated and been posted to Shearwater to fly Sea Kings.

Every week, the Officers' Wives Club had a meeting. It not only got me out of the house, but it was also entertaining. We organized everything from food fairs to live theatre. Every week, a couple of us had to bring a dish. One week, I made a delicious German coffee cake. I took great pride in making it. While I was getting ready to go, I asked Dustin to keep an eye on Adam.

Thirty minutes later, I came in the living room to find Dustin sound asleep on the couch. I could hear this little voice coming from the kitchen. It was Adam sitting on top of the table with both hands buried into the cake. He was covered in cake and icing! I couldn't get mad at him. I yelled at Dustin, "Come in here to see what our son has done to my cake! So much for keeping an eye on him for me!" I picked him up very gently and put him in the tub. While he played in the tub, I said to him, "You liked Mommy's cake, didn't you? Next time you see Daddy sleeping, you go into your special cupboard, get one of your favourite cookies and shove it down his throat! That's a good boy!" Adam was too little too understand a word I was saying. He sat there with his priceless smile, looking at me and splashing the water. I didn't have time to make anything else, so I ordered a pizza to be delivered directly to the mess.

I was so glad to hear that my parents were coming out for a visit. I was hoping it would take some stress off us. It was not only a relief but also so nice to see some of my family. They had planned to stay for a month. Since there wasn't much to do in Portage, we planned a trip to Banff, Alberta. One of my dearest friends offered to take care of Adam. At first, I was reluctant, but she convinced me that everything would be all right.

We toured around Alberta for two weeks. We had a fabulous trip. Even though we were on a magnificent trip, I could feel the tension between Dustin and I. We were both unhappy, and it was easily detected.

After my parents left, things became awkward at home. As much as I hated to acknowledge it or face the fact, that marriage had taken a rapid downhill slide. Dustin started staying out all night, and I was no better. I would meet up with my friends and hit the local bar in town. In those days, I never worried about drinking and driving. As each day went by, our marriage deteriorated more and more. Often times, Dustin wasn't there for meals. The love we had for one another shattered quickly.

As much as I hated to see the marriage come to an end, it was for the best. I came to the conclusion that we were married too young and didn't give each other any space to venture out. I couldn't blame the breakup over Adam, as he was only the innocent bystander. I knew deep down we didn't give it much of an effort to keep the marriage alive. It wasn't long before the rumours were flying through town. It seemed they all had their own versions of our breakup. We parted with no animosity, which made the divorce civil.

FOUR

I started a new life in Halifax. I was afraid at first, but I had my family there to give me the support I needed at the time. Since I had no money and not a clue what I was going to do, I moved in with my parents. Once I had my head on straight, I decided to go back to school and studied to be a medical assistant. Even though I passed it with honours, I found it wasn't really my niche. It wasn't challenging or rewarding enough for me.

One afternoon at the mall, I ran into a guy who I went to school with for years. We went for a coffee to catch up on all the local news. Over our conversation, he briefly mentioned that the company he was working for was looking for a branch administrator for the Maritimes. He said, "Let me see if I can get you in for an interview sometime this week." He warned me that the manager was a religious freak and extremely picky.

I looked at him and said, "Great, just what I need. Some uptight, soul-searching, closet perv!" Early that afternoon, I received a phone call from him telling me I had an interview the following afternoon. That night, my brother Patrick and I went out on the town to do some partying.

This was the norm for him and I. We hung around a lot when I returned back home. We hit all the hot spots downtown. We were having such a great time that we lost all track of time. It was kind of like a "pre-you-got-the-job party," but more like, "Let's see how many brain cells we can kill in one night!" I was one sore puppy the next morning. My head was a time bomb ready to explode. With a long shower, several cups of coffee and half a bottle of Tylenol, I started to feel somewhat human again. I wanted to kiss the guy's ass who invented Visine Drops. He was my saving grace that day. Since I was forewarned about the manager, I decided to wear a short skirt with a classy blouse. I wanted to test him out. Before entering the office, I inhaled a mouthful of Tic Tacs, took a deep breath and stuck my chest out proud. I found the office to be warm and friendly. The staff were around the same age as me. The secretary introduced me to everyone before I went in for my interview. The moment the manager opened his mouth, I knew he had an anal disposition. That perv couldn't keep his horny eyes off of me. Instead of the normal interview where the boss sits behind his desk, he pulled up a chair next to me. I thought to myself as I moved back into my chair, *Christ is he going to jump my bones! He's going to smell the booze seeping from my pores, or if he catches wind of my breath, it will knock him backwards.*

I observed he was frequently putting spray up his nose. Each time, he would apologize and say to me, "I have terrible allergies and find it hard to breathe sometimes."

That didn't bother me at all. I thought to myself, *Shove those chemicals up there all you want, buddy.* Those nose spray definitely saved the day for me. After an extensive approximately hour-long interview, he, without any uncertainty, hired me on the spot. He introduced me to the lady I was replacing. She had one hell of a demanding job. By now, my head was doing some serious hurting. Every word she spoke went into one ear and directly into my gut full of wine-induced acids. She had one week to train me for the position. What I had comprised on my resumé and what I actually knew were two totally different things. I needed a crash course in computers, and fast. The next day, I enrolled in a night course to study basic and advanced computer studies. It literally was a crash course. Even though my boss was a bit of an uptight ass, the job turned out great. The other staff members and I turned out to be best friends over the next couple of months.

I traveled extensively throughout the Maritimes and sometimes to Montreal and Toronto for product and equipment upgrades. It was high-energy and fast-paced, and that's what I needed. It wasn't long before I was promoted to Senior Branch Administrator. The job was not only great, but so was the money. The office ritual was often to go downtown to have a couple of cocktails before going home. There were more times than once where we covered each other's butts over the years, either because we were hung over or because we managed to get lucky. One guy in the office we all loved dearly was Ricky. He was the office's joker. There was never a dull moment when he was in the office. He was something else. Some nights, he'd party so much he'd sleep in his car next to the office and walk in the next morning the same suit and tie on. Even though he was married, he tried every trick in the book to get into my pants. I had to eventually break his heart and tell him he meant more to me as a brother than a sex object.

Adam was growing like a weed. He was the core of my life. I always put him first, before anybody or anything. He had energy galore. If I could have found a way to hook his energy up to a plant, I would have been a very rich woman today. He was making great new friends and loving spending time with his grandparents. As sad as it was, I decided it was time to move out from my parents' place to get our own nest. I also bought myself a little car to run the roads in. Life was finally looking up again! It wasn't long after I arrived that Dustin was transferred to Shearwater to fly Trackers. That was great for Adam. He could spend quality time with both of us. I was making new friends and actually bringing in a decent pay.

Dustin started dating again. It didn't bother me in the least. I knew then I didn't love him anymore. I was just happy for Dustin that he found someone to love again. It wasn't long before they were married. Dustin saw Adam as much as he could. He was away a lot flying on the ships. He was a great dad but didn't have a lot of spare time on his hands. Dustin's marriage had taken a turn for the worse.

He called me up out of the blue one Saturday morning to ask us to join him for the day at the beach. I thought, W*hat the hell? I'd love to. Besides, I have nothing better to do.* We filled the trunk with toys and food. My brother Patrick, who also had been divorced, had his daughter that weekend, so I invited them to join us. We were sitting on the beach enjoying the sun and pounding back some beer. I was nestled onto my blanket half asleep, enjoying the sounds of the kids playing in the sand. Patrick and Dustin were sharing old stories and enjoying their beer.

It was a perfect day until, all of a sudden, we heard, "Dustin! Dustin!" He looked over his shoulder and saw his wife standing on a hill in a beautiful white cotton dress, shouting out his name. Dustin tried to hide behind Patrick but was unsuccessful. She must have had eyes on her like a hawk because she spotted him a mile away. To this day, I haven't a clue how that woman managed to find him at that particular beach. So much for a day at the beach! They temporarily got back together, but it was short lived. Within a couple of months, they were divorced. I was really heartbroken for Dustin.

One of the staff members had resigned from his position at the company. We all met downtown at his favourite lounge to say our farewells and wish him well. The place was packed with pinstriped horny men; single or married, either way they had their end-of-the-week success stories. After a while, they sounded like a broken record. The women were just as bad, only they had better control over their drool.

I had gone to the bar to get a refill of wine and noticed this man across the room. He was sitting sipping on his beer and eyeing up the female species. I recognized him from somewhere but couldn't put my finger on it. He recognized me immediately and waved me over. He kept giving me hints of where we had met before, but I just couldn't clue in. Finally, the word Portage La Prairie rang a bell. He started to laugh, and said, "*B* un, *N* trente-deux, *O* soixante-dix..."

I gasped, "*Daniel*? Oh my god, it's you! You look great!" We got so enthralled in the conversation, I never made it back to the office crew that night. We spent the entire evening catching up on all the news over the years. His charm and wit swept me off my feet. He was tall, handsome and had an extremely good sense of humour.

The one thing I noticed about him the most was that he wasn't wearing a pinstriped suit. In those days, it was a rare thing in the bars to see a guy dressed in cotton casual pants. He dressed like a country boy, which portrayed his boyish characteristics perfectly. I had mentioned casually over the evening where I worked. When I arrived home that night, I realized I hadn't given him my home or work phone numbers. Within the next couple of days, he showed up at the office out of the blue.

The secretary came to my desk squirming in her pants. "There is a handsome man out front to see you!" I told her to pick up her jaw and go back to her desk. I peeked around the corner to see him pacing back and forth.

I quietly said, "Yes, it's him, he found me!" He apologized for not calling me sooner and blamed it on his lack of English. He didn't understand the exact spelling of the company. He had gone to three other computer companies before finding me. I thought to myself, *That was determination!*

He invited me out for a stroll along the waterfront and a light supper.

It was so beautiful on the waterfront that evening, though whenever it was nice, the rats and bums came crawling out from under the slimy rocks. The poor with their dirty hands were out begging for money and cigarettes, and the filthy, infested water sprayed up smells of sewer onto the rocks. That always gave me a hearty appetite. It sure added that extra touch of class to our lovely scenic oceanfront.

We ended up going to a quaint little café just up a few streets from the waterfront. I ordered my favourite, French onion soup. It came to the table pumping hot. I dove in like there was no tomorrow. I not only burnt every taste bud, but I damn near choked to death on the cheese. Instantly, my face turned beet red, and my eyes began to water. I leapt from the table and ran to the washroom. There was a lineup to get into the stalls, so I put my head over the sink and stuck my finger down my throat to haul out this hot ball of mozzarella cheese. It was disgusting. The women in the lineup were saying, "Ugh! Yuck! Geez!" shrugging their shoulders and turning their heads away. You would have thought they would have offered some frigging help. I returned to the table to find a very concerned Daniel. Trust me, I never took another bite of that soup.

He called me at work to invite me to his place for supper that upcoming Friday. I arranged for one of the girls at work to take care of Adam for me. While driving over to his place, I was anticipating a mouth-watering, succulent, buttery, cream-rich dishes from Quebec to be served. He greeted me at the door with a gentlemanly kiss on the cheek. There was an arrangement of wild cut flowers on the living room table with classical music playing in the background. A small fire was slowly burning just to give the room that perfect ambiance. I could smell something cooking but couldn't detect the smell.

The table was set up in quite a manly fashion. There was a fork, a knife, a tossed salad and an empty bottle of Mateus wine with a drippy candle stuck in the hole. I thought to myself, *This is going to be good.* He poured me a glass of French red wine, room temperature. I preferred cold wine, but what the hell. What could I say, it was free! It was so dry that the insides of my cheeks met and said, "Hello!" I almost choked on my first mouthful. He left the room to check on dinner. I was like a hound dog in the living room, sniffing the air looking for clues to see what I was going to be eating. He had one lonely little plant in the window. I quickly poured my glass of wine into the soil and managed to swallow the bit I had left in my mouth. It was god-awful wine! Within seconds, that poor plant curled up in the fetal position and died. He yelled out to me from the kitchen, "Come in and eat!" As I approached the table, he noticed my glass was empty. "Oh, so you like my selection of wine, do you?" I put my hand over the glass and asked for a cold beer instead. He put a pot in the middle of the table. I couldn't make out what kind of slop it was. It had a layer of butter sizzling on top and bubbles of fat oozing up around the sides of it as if to escape from the inevitable.

I pointed to it with a half smile. "What is this?"

He smiled at me and rubbed his hands together, "It's Shepherd's Pie! One of my most favourite dishes in the world. Help yourself!"

I thought to myself, *You don't get out much, do you?* He scooped a huge clump onto my plate. I looked down at it and remarked, "It certainly is colourful!" as I took a big swig of beer.

I took my fork, and with great hesitation, I slowly slid it into the hot, sizzling butter. Once it swam through the fat, it eventually made it to the meat. Well, at least I had one thing right about the dish, it was buttery! I wonder how many arteries I clogged over that dinner. I figured if I was going to make it through dinner without having a heart attack, I needed to inhale large portions of salad and drink some of that battery acid he called wine to dissolve some fat! Though the dinner got off on a rough start, the rest of the evening was great.

We ate out a lot after that evening. You can certainly understand why. If I were to continue eating like that, I would have turned into beached whale with a massive heart problem. The dinners, movies and parties became more frequent. I introduced him to a whole new way of eating, or he would never have made it past thirty.

Daniel had met Adam on numerous occasions at my place and at family get-togethers. They got along extremely well. Daniel treated him like his own son. Life couldn't have gotten much better than that...unless, of course, I won the lottery. It actually scared me a little because it wasn't a normal practice for me to have something "normal" in my life. After several months of dating, he wanted me to move in with him, but there was one major ingredient that had to be added: Would Daniel accept Adam on a full time basis? It's a totally different ball game to see someone else's child only on the weekends. It was going to be a permanent change for everybody.

I didn't want Adam to be hurt in any way. I asked Daniel, and he was delighted to raise Adam on a part-time basis. In fact, Daniel said that it was, "a package deal. You can't have one with out the other." We moved in together in a luxury liner harbour-view apartment overlooking Halifax. The kitchen was a chef's delight, full of all the bells and whistles. On the deck was a hot tub covered with hot lights to keep us warm on cold winter nights. It was paradise! Adam played in it like it was a pool. Why it is when you move, something that you love always gets smashed. I had a beautiful bamboo couch. It was fairly expensive. The first thing they did was rip the arms off it taking it in through the front door. Then they stood there like a bunch of morons and laughed! For the first time in a long time, I was at peace with myself.

Daniel spent a lot of hours in the evenings teaching Adam how to make model airplanes and gliders. One night I arrived home from work to find candles everywhere. There was a bottle of wine chilly on the table by the couch. Adam was across the hall, playing with his friend from school. Daniel was busy in the kitchen preparing dinner. I had him trained by now to cut back on the death dishes. He didn't hear me come in, so I stepped quietly into the bedroom to put something more romantic on. A couple of weeks ago, I had bought a beautiful, soft silk housecoat with wide, flowing sleeves. It still had the price tags on it.

I refreshed my makeup and put on some expensive perfume. Before leaving the bedroom, I looked into the mirror, lifted my breasts into the air and said, "Oh yeah baby , he'll eat these up like a starving pip on Saturday night!" Once I stopped admiring myself, I pranced out of the bedroom and, within the blink of an eye, hit one of the candles with the sleeve from my new housecoat. I started screaming, "Fire! fire! Daniel, help!" Of course, he was bewildered because he didn't even know I was home. Within seconds, he turned around with his beer in his hand and saw my sleeve on fire. He threw the beer all over me.

He couldn't believe his eyes, "What in hell are you doing? When did you get home?" I was very lucky I only burnt the hair off my arm and burnt a hole into the carpet. He stood there totally amazed.

So much for a romantic evening. The smell of burnt hair was rotten. He bathed my arm and applied ointment. He told me to go to the couch, sit there and not move until dinner was ready. He wasn't long putting the rest of the candles out, shaking his head back and forth while returning to the kitchen to finish cooking dinner. We didn't want a late dinner because we were leaving on a trip the next morning.

We had each taken a couple of days off and decided to take my niece, Heather, with us on a trip to Prince Edward Island. Beforehand, Daniel had rented out a cottage. He knew my idea of camping was a hotel without a pool. Tents and insects where not one of my ways of a trip. After the eventful dinner, we started loading the car up. Mark dropped off his daughter later on that evening. We were set to go. I put Adam and her to bed early so we didn't have any crazy, strung-out, hyperactive imps on the trip the next day. We were up before the kids. While the coffee was brewing, we jumped into the shower to get a head start on the day. We stood in front of the window admiring the ocean view. The sun was radiant and the view magnificent.

Daniel all of a sudden dropped his coffee cup all over the floor. He ran out the door to find that someone had smashed the side window out of his car. He came running back in. "Call the cops. Some bastard ripped my stereo out of my car."

I looked down at the floor. "What a way to start our trip!" I said to Daniel. "Luckily enough we didn't put the booze in the car last night or they would have taken that too!" He really didn't want to hear that, especially not now.

He wasn't long getting it fixed. When he returned home, we were anxiously waiting by the door with our suitcases. The day had started out hot and sunny, but as we got closer to the ferry, the sky became cloudy and dark. By the time we reached the island, it was pouring rain. We were a couple of miles from the cottage, and the car started swerving towards the ditch. Daniel held on to the steering wheel with all his might and managed to pull the car over to the side of the road. He ran out to see what the problem was. In the pouring rain, he yelled out to me, "We have a flat tire!" Have you ever heard a French man standing in the pouring rain cursing and swearing in French? It was extremely funny. I was cracking up, and the kids were giggling their heads off in the back seat. I had never seen him go on like that before.

Every now and then, he would throw his arms up into the air, shaking his fist at the sky. We had so much stuff in the back of the car, we all had to get out. When I got out of the car, he kept staring at me and said, "Are you jinxed or something?" I had to pee so badly, I ended up going into the ditch to relieve myself. As I was peeing, the rain poured down my crack to wash away the remains. At last, the donut tire was installed. We were soaked to the hide. It rained so hard, we had difficulty locating the cottage. We had been driving for hours. Finally, Daniel stopped at a local garage to get the tire fixed and ask for directions.

He showed the attendant a brochure of the place. The guy started to laugh. He passed the brochure around the room to the locals sitting around drinking coffee. It wasn't long before they all were having a good laugh. Daniel asked what was so damn funny. He said, "That's no cottage, sir. You've been had. This happens every year to some unlucky poor bastard. Once she rents out her luxury cottages along the coast, she rents out the apartments above her home." He gave Daniel the instructions to the place. When he came out of the garage, I could tell by his face it wasn't good news. Those two little monsters in the back seat had turned into laughing hyenas when they saw him.

He slammed the car door and gave me a disgusted look. "It's not what I reserved, but we're here now, so lets make the best of it." The two monsters in the back seat had their faces buried into the hands. We drove for no more than five minutes when he parked the car and said, "Here we are." No one dared to remark. We all looked around. There was no ocean view, no sandy beach and no place to barbeque—just an old house with flapping shutters. We knew we had no other choice but to take it since it was prime season on the island. I knew somehow we would make the best of it.

Daniel managed to get the place for fifty percent less than normal, mainly since she lied through her teeth. The entrance, of course, was located outside. We lugged our stuff up a hateful flight of stairs in the pouring rain. We were all exhausted when we were through. The place smelled of musk. We were all soaked to the hind. All of our heads, in sequence, turned to the VCR on top of the television. Now just to find a movie rental place. The first thing I needed to do was have a shower. The shower was so small, I couldn't turn around in it. When I tried to reach the shampoo, I banged my elbows up against the faucets. I hit my left one pretty hard, and it started bleeding quite badly. Of course, it didn't help that I was left handed. I came out of the bathroom with a towel wrapped around my arm and blood dripping off it.

Daniel didn't seem surprised at all. Actually, he told me he was expecting something to happen anyway. At that point, nothing would have taken him by surprise. He had Adam run to the car to grab the first aid kit. It mainly was designed for the children's injuries. He wrapped my elbow in heavy gauze and hoped it would clot during the evening. Boy, that sucker bled like a chicken with its head cut off. I became useless within thirty minutes upon our arrival.

I had packed enough food to get us through one day only. Daniel and Adam headed out to rent some movies. Heather remained with me to help prepare some lunch and be my other hand to operate in the kitchen. I began to get worried about them. Lunch was getting cold. They returned after driving almost an hour. Since they were out of province, it was difficult to find a store that would allow them to rent movies. Finally, one storeowner took pity on them. Daniel was wet, tired and frustrated. Before changing into some dry clothes, he sat in the kitchen chair and inhaled a beer. "What a terrible day this has been!" he said as he was sucking back on his beer.

This vacation was not turning out to be what we had planned, at least not at that point. Later on that afternoon, the rain let up a bit. Daniel noticed on his travels in the quest for movies that there was a grocery store near the old bat's home. One hundred and fifty dollars later and with three bags of groceries, we had baloney, eggs, milk, some fruit and a pile of junk food. Those tourist traps really have you by the short and curly. They gouge you from every rotten angle they can. They are hungry and want to rob you blind before they legally can suck the last drop of blood out your system. I call them the Tourist Trap Mafia. After dinner, the rain picked up again, only this time it brought company—thunder and lightening. We had no other choice but watch movies. It wasn't like we could take a stroll down a sandy beach and make a raging bonfire to have a weenie roast.

The winds had picked up during the evening. The howling, screeching noises were like a whorehouse on a Saturday night. The two kids had curled up in their sleeping bags, watching a movie on the living room floor. Daniel and I went into the kitchen to play some cards and indulge into something stronger than beer. After the day we had, we could easily justify a good sniff drink of rum and coke. Listening to him pour that poison into my glass was music to my ears.

The first one went down pretty fast. That was to get me motivated. The second was for trying to forget the day we had, and the third and fourth were starting to put a pleasant edge on the evening. All of a sudden, the lights went out. There wasn't a candle in sight or, for that fact, even a match. The kids came banging their way into the kitchen, their little frightened voices yelling, "Mommy? Auntie?" and echoing off the walls. We finished our drinks and snuggled up on the floor with the kids to fall asleep. When we awoke, we found that the power had been restored during the night. My arm felt a little better, mainly to do with the rum I drank the night before.

Adam pulled the drapes to find sunshine blasting into the window. That sun meant one thing only—beach. After breakfast, we weren't long making a large picnic and getting our swimming gear ready. We hit the beach around midmorning. I noticed that when we arrived, there was hardly anybody there, thinking maybe it was too early. We found a nice place to lay our stuff. Every now and then, the wind would come up, and there would be this rotten smell of dead fish. As the morning went on, the smell worsened as the wind picked up. The kids were checking out the shore and playing in the sand. I was quietly reading my book while Daniel was busy assembling a lightweight portable barbeque he had purchased for the trip.

I looked over my shoulder to see the kids nowhere to be found. Within seconds, I was in a panic, but not for long, though. They came ripping around the corner with their hands covering their mouths. They told us there was a bunch of dead fish immediately around the corner. We went over to verify their story. Sure enough, there were thousands upon thousands of dead fish with swarms of sea gulls and flies hovering over them. All I could say was, "This is incredible!" When we got back to our spot, the wind was so strong, it had blown Daniel's barbeque into the air. There was charcoal everywhere. The sand swirled into the air and felt like needles being driven into our faces.

I had made some sandwiches in case the kids got hungry before lunch. Unfortunately, the sand had beaten its way through the picnic basket and destroyed everything. I gave up. I looked up at the sky to see dark, rolling clouds just ready to piss all over us again. Without any hesitation, we headed back to the "cottage." On the way back, we found a little diner. I was frustrated to the limit and full of sand from head to toe. The waitress came over to our table and gave us the menu.

She came back a few minutes later, took one look at me and said, "Would you like something from the menu?" She realized by my eyes that I was a time bomb ready to explode.

All I could say was, "No, I would like a nice glass of wine, and *keep them coming*!" while spitting sand out from between my teeth. We arrived back at the so-called cottage early in the evening. We were as dirty as rats and full of sand. Each one of us hit the shower, and I cautiously warned each one of them not to make any sudden moves. We flicked on the television weather station that night and heard that the next couple of days were going to be nothing but rain and severe wind with a possible chance of thunder and lightening.

It didn't shock Daniel at all to hear this. He grabbed a beer out of the fridge, sat on the couch and looked at me. "Is there something I should know about you before this relationship goes any further?" he said with a half grin on his face. I bent over and stared right into his eyes.

"Yeah, Daniel, I'm the devil's daughter, live and in colour!" He just sat back on the couch, drinking his beer and hoping that the rest of his life wasn't going to be so miserable as the last couple of days had been.

We decided that if the weather didn't improve by morning, we would return to Halifax. The next morning, it was foggy and dam. The old lady reimbursed us for the remainder of the week. She actually felt sorry for us. That was one horrible vacation.

FIVE

I was never so glad to get back home. The next day at work, I was fit to be tied. The secretary looked at me, and asked, "How was your trip?"

As I was sipping my extra strong black coffee, I looked at her and said, "Have you ever been to hell?' She never commented any further. When I arrived home that night, Daniel was sitting at the table dressed up in a suit. I ran to him, dreading to hear awful words. "Who died?"

He looked at me. "No one died!" He asked me to get dressed up so he could take me out to my favourite restaurant that night. I thought that was rather odd since it was the beginning of the week. As I was walking into the bathroom, I muttered, "Who's he screwing behind my back?" As I was on my way to the shower, I stubbed my big toe and started cursing to high heavens. I bent over to check out the damages on my toe, and on my way up, I hit the back of my head full force with the bathroom doorknob. The pain was quite unpleasant!

My toe was throbbing like a toothache. Daniel came running down the hall to see what all the commotion was about. I was lying there on the floor with a bleeding toe, holding the back of my head. He carried me to the couch. He thought someone was down the hall beating the living crap out of me. He wrapped my toe with gauze and put a cold compress on my head. He said, "How do you manage to do this all the time? It's really unbelievable!" He cancelled the cab until my toe stopped bleeding and the lump shrunk a bit. With Daniel's assistance, I hopped my way into the shower . It's a good thing people can't hear what I think about while having a shower. My thoughts would land me in jail for the rest of my life.

He sat on the toilet seat so if something were to happen, he would be there to witness my self-abuse. I put on a sexy black dress and wore a pair of sandals since my toe was so swollen. While waiting for the cab, he poured us a glass of wine. I knew it was serious business when he ordered a cab.

He took me to La Cuisine de Paris, the top-rated restaurant in Halifax. It was the place where all the bigwigs from out of town entertained and where the elite proposed. The suspense was driving me nuts. The maitre d' showed us to our table. That restaurant was so cold, I could have hung Christmas ornaments off of my nipples. Obviously the owner was too mean to turn up the heat. That's the thing about these rich pricks—once they have made it big they get greedy.

Daniel ordered a bottle of wine. I asked the waiter, "Could you serve that warm, please?"

He lifted one eyebrow and replied, "Excuse me, ma'am, did you say warm it up?"

Under my breath, I muttered, "What an butt!" I guess he didn't get the joke. I swear, some of these waiters would go on their knees to please. They are hungry little bastards! Daniel held up his glass.

"I love you very much, but there is something I have to tell you!" At first I predicted that he was breaking off with me because of all the mishaps over the last couple of months. My stomach turned into a dried up sponge, and I developed a third tit in my throat.

He began to say, "Regrettably, I will be going away for a couple of months to Europe!" That put a damper on the evening. When the waiter showed up with the wine, I told him to keep them coming. It wasn't what I wanted to hear, but it was better than what I had predicted. All I could think about was being without him. We were like two peas in a pod. I knew our relationship was too good to be true. The thrill of eating disappeared quite rapidly, though after the second bottle of wine, Daniel going away didn't seem to bother me as much. I soon learned that Daniel was full of surprises. A couple of days later, I arrived home from work, and there was a large envelope in the mailbox. I opened it and found an airline ticket to Amsterdam, Holland. I jumped up and down; I almost peed my pants I was so excited! Adam and he were standing in the living room watching me make an butt out of myself on the street. I was jumping up and down kissing the airline ticket. No one had ever done that for me before. I looked up to see the pair of them laughing their butts off. I ran in that front door so fast to leap into his arms and wrap my legs around him. I couldn't thank him enough. He found out he had a couple of weeks between jobs, and that would be the perfect opportunity to see each other. I was beside myself.

On the day he left for Europe, it never rained harder. We were soaked just running to the car. Adam and I dropped him off early in the morning. Our chins were chapped from dragging along the ground, and our tear ducts worked overtime. After dropping him off, I had no intentions of going to work. On the way over the MacDonald Bridge, I flicked the radio on. As god is my judge, the song they were playing was, "Every Time You Go Away." Perfect timing! Daniel told me later on that week that while he was unpacking his stuff that morning, he randomly grabbed a cassette and popped it into the player. The first song that played was, "Every Time You Go Away." Talk about odds!

We ended up going to the mall and spending a lot of money. When we returned to the apartment, it was so empty. The welcoming committee had left. He had it all planned for me to meet him in Amsterdam in November. When I looked at the calendar, it seemed a lifetime away. I came to grips pretty quickly after he left. I had enough to think about between Adam and my job. At the same time, Dustin phoned me to tell me he was moving to Cold Lake, Alberta, in January.

Adam took the news pretty hard. He adored his dad. The only good side was that when he left, Daniel would be back to give Adam some fatherly support. Time was moving in slow motion. My calendar was locked on October! Daniel called continually. He didn't want to sound too enthusiastic about his trip, though I could tell by his voice that he was having the time of his life. One of Daniel's best friends, who also was a pilot, had to be flown home for a funeral and called to inform me that Daniel was going to be in Boston a couple of days in September.

I thought to myself, "Now I can surprise him for a change!" I wasn't long buying an airline ticket. Now, that had to be love because I detest flying with a passion. I arranged for my parents to take care of Adam. The day I arrived, the weather was beautiful and warm. I was walking through the terminal, and from afar, I noticed this handsome man all dressed in white. That was enough to make any women drop her panties! There's something about a man in uniform! It was a Kodak moment. We ran into each other's arms and caressed like two porn stars who hadn't had it in years. We loaded my things onto a shuttle bus to take us to our hotel.

The bus driver had a rude disposition. He looked like an over-sized bulldog. As we were entering the bus, he was stuffing his face with a chocolate-coated donut. Daniel told him what hotel we were staying in. As he looked at Daniel, I could hear him mumbling under his breath, "You gotcha self a nice whore for the weekend!" When I heard that, I was pissed!

I went right up to him and said, "That's right, you fat bastard, but I'm better than 'nice'!" He gave me one nasty look.

We barely were sitting in our seats when he started gunning it down the street like a maniac. He was so busy jamming that donut down his throat, he slammed right into the back of a transit bus. We were sitting in the front row. Everything went flying towards the windshield. Daniel had a tight grip on me to stop me from flying through the window. Other than a couple of bruises and a lot of cursing and swearing, no one was hurt. That ignoramus bus driver never so much as apologized to anybody. After an hour and a half, we finally made it to the hotel. I think back now we could have sued that fat-ass bastard. What a great way to begin our weekend. When the valet opened the front doors of that establishment, I stood there in amazement. That place was captivating! For the first couple of minutes, I didn't move.

I stood there eyeing every detail from the floor up. My leather shoes instantly turned into glass slippers. I was in Cinderella's world. I wanted to treasure that moment for the rest of my life. I marveled at the expensive surroundings, the colossal chandeliers hanging from a twenty-foot ceiling. The walls were engraved with Greek goddesses. The flooring was covered in radiating marble, and that staircase was mind-boggling with its brass rails and cherry mahogany steps. It was one classy joint, and I was going to lap every ounce of it up.

Our weekend was full of romance and very little fresh air. Daniel would get up in the morning, open the drapes and say, "Nope, it's pretty shitty outside. We better stay right where we are." It's a good thing they had room service, or we would have starved to death. Once we peeled our butts out of bed, we managed to do some sightseeing.

The first place we hit was "Cheers." That was awesome! The whole time we were there, I kept my eyes open for Ted Danson. We went shopping in the Quincy's market. It was right in downtown Boston, on the water. What a place to party. There were shops and restaurants galore. It was a little pricey. We popped into a pub to have a cold one, and it was over four dollars a glass—a lot of money back then. We were having so much fun, I hated for the weekend to end.

Daniel had made reservations at a posh restaurant. It was nestled right on the ocean. He had arranged for a table overlooking the water. The view was astounding until these two punks stuck their faces in the window and spit at me. The snot slowly made its way down to the sill. By the time the waiter got to the door, the twits were long gone. That was an appetizing moment! I certainly didn't order mussels that night.

That weekend flew by. What a memorable time we had. We arrived at the airport and headed to the bar. There are only two ways I can fly: one is by having a couple drinks, and the other is by popping a few Atavan. Daniel left the bar for a few moments and returned with a dozen long-stemmed roses. I had full intentions of drying them out when I arrived home.

The flight home was one of the worst trips in my entire life. Within seconds of hitting the air, the Captain came over the speaker and informed us we were returning back to Boston due to an in-flight emergency. There wasn't enough booze or Atavan to get me through that one. I was scared shitless! I looked directly into the man's face sitting next to me and yelled out at of the top of my lungs, "Oh my god, we're all going to die!" I started crying hysterically. That innocent man's eyes bulged out of his head. It wasn't long before I had all the kids bawling their eyes out.

I think I destroyed every nerve ending he had. I had my finger nails imbedded into his hand. If he hadn't drunk before that day, I well imagine it wasn't long afterwards he started. Later, I found out he was the maestro for the Boston Symphony Orchestra, which was playing in Halifax that evening. A flight attendant leapt down that aisle fast to shut me up to some degree. I was frantic! I could see it in her eyes that she wanted to slap me silly. Everyone was staring at me. I don't know if it was out of pure pity or if they all wanted to have a crack at me.

Those poor roses took an awful beating. By the time we returned to Boston, I was carrying nothing but thorns. There were petals everywhere. They escorted me off the plane first. I went directly to the bar, along with a lot of other passengers. I was pretty reluctant to get back onto another plane. Finally, after several hours, I boarded another flight. I sat the entire trip all alone. No one would even talk to me. I was categorized as the "crazed bitch." That wasn't the grand finale of that trip either. When we approached the Halifax International Airport, the fog was so thick that the pilot had to make five attempts to land the plane. When that god forsaken plane landed, we all clapped our hands.

SIX

The remaining time at home flew by quickly. The trip to Holland was approaching. I wasn't overly enthusiastic to put my butt back into a plane again. That time, though, I went to the bar, inhaled a couple stiff ones, and shoved some Gravol down my throat before getting into the sky tunnel. I no sooner sat in my seat than I was out cold. The flight attendant had to wake me up when I landed in Holland. At least if something did happen, I wouldn't have to know about it.

Daniel was anxiously a waiting for my arrival. I had a carry-on, so when that death trap opened, I wasn't long getting out of there. He had rented out an Audi, the reason for which I later found out. They drove like maniacs over there. Once you are on the Autobahn, it's pedal to the metal. The minimum speed was one hundred and forty kilometres an hour. I was terrified. I spent half of the trip with my head between my legs saying the Lord's Prayer. I swear, one wrong move, and we would have been mincemeat!

It was such a relief to get on a nice country road. First, we stopped in Hidelberg, Germany. When driving into Hidelberg, you could sense the warm ambiance. The buildings were ancient but very well maintained. They had so much character, and some looked like they had seen many hardships. We visited a castle. It overlooked the entire city. I never climbed so many stairs in my entire life. No wonder the queens were slim back in those days. As soon as we made it to the top of a massive, billion-brick building, it started to pour rain. It rained so hard that within thirty seconds we were soaked to the hide. We quickly headed back down to the car.

While on our journey down, I slipped and landed right on my butt. Daniel turned to see me crying in pain. He helped me get up to find that I couldn't stand up. I had sprained my ankle. He ended up carrying me back to the car. When we arrived to the hotel, he had the hotel doctor have a look at it. He basically told me to keep ice on it for a couple of hours. I hopped my way into the bathroom to check out my butt. It was black and blue with bruises. You'd swear someone jumped me in the alley that afternoon.

That town will always be etched into my mind for its beauty and a lot of other things. Once I was mobile again, we visited some bars that were at least nine hundred years old. I imagined these husky, burly stinking men coming through those doors back then. "Check your axes here, please." We ended up at a restaurant that was nothing like I had ever seen. There were long, old wooden tables that spanned from one end of the room to the other with benches. Everybody sat together. It was great! The chef came out to the table to hand us the one and only menu available. The menu had to be at least four feet wide and three feet tall. The menu was handwritten in huge letters. The amount of food on our plates was obscene. The food was scrumptious, and the company around the table were very entertaining! They would raise their stein and cheer for anything and everything. The pastries were extraordinary. It certainly wasn't the place to be if you were on a diet.

Another enjoyable part of the trip was when we went to the town of Malmedie, in the Alsace region of Belgium. The countryside was breathtaking. The mountains and hills were picturesque, with homes nestled in amongst them. The area was noted around the world for its lace. It was so detailed and fine. It was recommended by the hotel reception to go to this fine dining restaurant down the street. It was rated the finest in the region. It was small and gave the impression of the old world. We had the hunter's special, which consisted of trout, wild boar with brandy sauce, and deer. The meal was accompanied with a lovely, fruity bottle of wine. The entire meal cost seventeen dollars! What a superb meal! A meal like that in Canada would have cost us an arm and a leg.

While driving through Holland, the fields of tulips were awe-inspiring. They looked like giant mosaics. The colours were of the rainbow only a thousand times brighter. The windmills were just like you would see on a postcard. They were vast and unique. We stayed at a four-star hotel in

Amsterdam. The room was so small! We had two twin beds that were made for midgets. Only one of us could walk between the beds, and you had to walk sideways to do this. There was one shower on each floor. If you wanted hot water, you had to buy coins at the front reception.

When the locals walked their, dogs they would let them do their stuff anywhere, although there was city law against that. It was hard to distinguish what I was smelling in the air sometimes. It was either the aroma of marijuana or the smell of the stinking canal. The canal wasn't far from being the city sewer.

One evening, Daniel arranged a trip down the canal to see the sights. We indulged in cheese and wine and enjoyed the scenery. Some of the sites were indeed incredible, especially the Red Light District. Women were literally posing behind windows wearing very little see-through lingerie. In the corner of the window, they had taped their price list. That gave window shopping a whole new meaning! The boat was a limo on water. The majority of the boat was in cased in glass. The first thing the Captain said to us was, "Don't open the windows. You won't want to eat the cheese!" He started to laugh. Our server waited on us hand and foot. The minute my wine glass was down an inch, he was right there to replenish it. "My kind of man! Keep it comin' baby!"

He said to us, "Drink, drink up! You drink your face off, it's on the Captain tonight!" He was like a little flea leaping throughout the boat.

The boat was swaying smoothly and slowly down the canal. It was a picture-perfect evening. I looked up to see stars and to my side to see hookers. Interesting view! The weather couldn't have been more perfect. The lights from the shops reflected onto the water. We had just passed by the prominent Red Light District. All of a sudden, right out of nowhere, Daniel proposed to me! I stood up and shouted to the other passengers, "He asked me to marry him!" Everyone stood up and clapped. I started to cry my heart out. The crew and passengers were so happy for us that we had wine bottles galore. Boy, could you get more romantic than that? Now that was an original marriage proposal! You have to hand it to me, I know how to pick them!

The next morning, we went to the hotel restaurant for a beautiful continental breakfast. As I got up from the table to call my parents, I grabbed the tablecloth, thinking it was my napkin. Our entire breakfast landed up on

Daniel's lap. When the hot coffee landed on his nuts, he jumped back so quickly he hit his head on the window. While he was holding his head, I said to him, "You know, Daniel, it's not too late to back out of this!"

In his charming way, he replied, "It was just an accident." We decided to get married before Christmas. That meant I had a lot of planning to do when I got back home.

After Daniel got cleaned up and we re-ordered breakfast, we went shopping for an engagement ring. We didn't have to go far. There were diamond stores on every corner. I don't know what the hottest item was on the street—marijuana or diamonds. It made for interesting shopping. You know how we sell baseball caps and sunglasses on the street? Well, that's how they sell diamonds and drugs in Holland. After visiting two diamond shops, I finally decided on a white gold, half-carat solitaire diamond. I was so proud of it that before showing the ring to people, I would hand them a pair of sunglasses.

One evening, we decided to eat in our room. We spent a couple of hours picking out cheeses, wines, pastries and chocolates. We were like two kids on Christmas morning. We placed the goodies onto a large blanket on the floor. We had the wine chilling in the bathroom sink. Daniel went to have a shower down the hall. I poured myself a glass of wine and went out onto the deck to look at the sites. The air was sweet, probably since there was a huge winery down at the end of the street. I noticed a crowd coming down. They were drinking, singing, laughing and dancing up a storm. I wondered what all the commotion was about. I called down to the front desk. Apparently, one of the local businessmen was buried that afternoon, and they were celebrating his death. I thought to myself, *He must have been one hateful prick when he was alive for them to be celebrating like that!* When I heard Daniel come into the room, I went in to join him. I didn't think to close the French doors. We sat on the floor and began to enjoy our sinful feast. As I was just about to pour Daniel a glass of wine, a beer bottle came flying in through the French doors, missing my head by inches. The wine bottle hit the floor with a smash, splashing wine everywhere.

Daniel looked at me as if he saw a ghost. He says, "That bottle did not hit you! Can you believe it? Oh my god!" I thought that finally my luck was changing for the best. The hotel felt obligated and offered us anything and everything on the menu free of charge. We took full advantage of the situation and drank and ate the best they had to offer. After all, we had to celebrate my newfound luck!

My trip was slowly coming to an end. In one aspect, I was glad. I was going to need a vacation when I returned. Daniel was getting a little apprehensive. His future wife was her own worst enemy. The night before I left for Canada, he wanted to take me out to dinner but showed some concern. He decided it would be best if we stayed in our room and ordered in room service. At least he knew that would be safer for me.

I eventually got back to Halifax safe and sound.

My first priority was the wedding. We didn't want an elaborate, costly event. We wanted family members and a few close friends. The last thing we wanted was a ten-thousand-dollar price tag hanging off of our foreheads for the next five years. I had planned a private ceremony on my parents' deck followed by a lovely reception in their home. My parents supplied the champagne, and my sister-in-laws took care of the rest. I kept my fingers and toes crossed all day hoping no mishaps would happen.

The limos arrived to take us to the restaurant. Just as I walked out the back door, a seagull flew over me and crapped all over my dress. It resembled rotten cottage cheese. Once I got cleaned up, I headed for the limo. Daniel had arranged champagne and roses in our limo earlier. We had the best sex ever in the back of that limo that evening. When I arrived at the restaurant, I was greeted with more flowers and telegrams from friends throughout Canada. We had the dinner in a private room. "Thank god!" There were times the conversation got a little raunchy. The food, people and surroundings were genuinely fabulous.

When we left the restaurant, there were a couple of hookers hanging outside the restaurant. They immediately noticed my brothers. One of them walked up to my brother Mark, flung her hand on his butt, and said, "Hey, handsome, let's go back to your place for a private party!" The others stayed in the background, feeling up their breasts.

I overheard one of my brothers' rebuttals. "No, thank you. I prefer to wake up tomorrow morning with my dick still attached to my body!" That got them fired up.

As my brothers were crossing the street, the hookers started yelling at them, fists waving in the air, "Ya, you're all nothing but a bunch of pussies! That's right, ya ole' go home and suck on your momma's breast!" That was one thing I could say about them: They were entertaining to watch! When we arrived at our hotel, Daniel insisted on carrying me through the door. He was somewhat more traditional than me. He flung me onto the bed. While he was pouring the champagne, I took a look around the room. There was only one word to describe the place: Magnificent! It had everything from a bar to a sunken hot tub.

The bed alone could have slept six people. We had a gorgeous view of the ocean. The centre table had a huge basket of fruit with a bottle of champagne next to it. "I could sure get used to this place easily! Oh to be rich!" When I awoke the next morning, I tried to focus my eyes so I could see where I was. For a few seconds, I was disorientated. "Jesus what a mess!" My panties were lying on top of a pizza box. There were wine glasses on the floor, and the table had cold, half-eaten pizza on it. It looked like a whorehouse. "Boy, that champagne must have been some kind of powerful!" I couldn't even remember ordering in the pizza. "It must have been one hell of a night!" Daniel was snoring his head off. I took the liberty of ordering in breakfast. I ordered everything from fresh strawberries to pancakes.

When that poor waiter arrived, I was a sight for sore eyes. I certainly didn't look like a honeymoon princess. If the truth be known, I would have fit in quite nicely with the whores on the corner the night before. The waiter had two full wagons of food. I woke up Daniel, and the first thing I said to him was, "Daniel, where is your wallet?"

He sighed. "We haven't been married for twelve hours, and you're already asking me for my wallet! This looks promising!" We had a good laugh over that.

After breakfast, we headed for the shower. There was one thing missing the suitcase. I left it in the limo. "Great!" We left the hotel room looking like two dead fish who were revived, and we were faced with a huge blizzard. When we looked out the lobby window, we couldn't see three feet in front of us. We called a cab, and finally, after an hour or more, he arrived at the hotel. There wasn't enough Tylenol or Gravol at the drug store to carry me through that hangover. Champagne and me don't mix well at all. After several near-death mishaps, we made it home safely.

Things were going too smoothly. I had a loving husband, an adorable son, a successful career and wonderful friends. *God when is this fairy tale going to end*? I would never let myself believe that my life was going to continue on that way because that only happened in the movies. On Valentine's Day, I returned home from work to find another one of Daniel's great surprises. From the front door to the back of the apartment were red and white balloons with "Happy Valentine's" written on every one of them. They must have spent hours filling those balloons up. In the middle of the coffee table, Daniel and Adam had placed a huge arrangement of roses into a crystal vase encircled with chocolates. It actually brought tears to my eyes. The two of them were standing way in back of the balloons, anxiously waiting to see my expression on my face. They were chuckling like two little kids. After fighting my way through the balloons, I finally was able to give them each a hug and kiss. On my travels, I had noticed that there were several lobsters in the kitchen sink. These guys had the entire evening planned out. It was one perfect evening. The fireplace was blazing in the background, the wine was chilled, there were roses, and the big bonus was having dinner with two of my favourite men in the world. Another Cinderella moment!

I have to say that was the best Valentine's Day I have ever had, and amazingly enough, it went off with no mishaps…other than when I was cracking my lobster tail open and cut my two thumbs wide open from the shells. That was a little nasty. There's nothing more appetizing than watching blood seeping through white lobster meat. I wasn't going to throw away perfectly good lobster meat. I just washed the blood off under the tap and ate it. It took a good month before those thumbs healed.

SEVEN

We sure didn't waste any time starting a family. Just over two months into our marriage, I was pregnant. I was like my mother, Sheila. If there was a sperm cell flying around in the air, I was guaranteed to get pregnant. After leaving the doctor's office, I picked Adam up at the day care early on my way home. I had no intentions of returning to work that day. I went home to prepare a gourmet dinner. I even put on an apron. Daniel walked into the apartment, and much to his surprise, he found me running around the kitchen cooking up a storm.

He asked me, "What are you doing?" I had every pot full of food. He came up to me and held me in his arms.

I looked up at him and said, "We have company coming!"

He was delighted and said, "Who's coming?"

I replied, "We'll know in eight months!"

He looked at me like he never looked at me before. "What are you telling me? You're pregnant?" He hugged me so tight I could hardly breath. He was in the celebrating mode. Right after dinner, he went out and bought a very expensive bottle of scotch. I could hear him on the phone..."I'm going to have a baby!" Not me, him!

We had previously talked about having children but not so soon. Daniel wanted to have at least four. On the other hand, I was happy to stop at this one. He spent the entire evening drinking scotch and on the phone telling everybody we knew from Nova Scotia to British Columbia that we were having a baby. I became deathly ill with the pregnancy. I couldn't keep an ounce of food in my guts. Instead of gaining weight, I lost it. I was nothing but a string bean with a tiny ball in front of me. I could barely make it through a complete day at work. I was doing a demonstration at work with some high-end clients. They were quite impressed with the company's latest technology until I puked my guts up all over the screen. I blamed it on the smell of the coffee and donuts. "That's one deal that went sour!" I soon headed home to rot on the couch for the remainder of the day.

I opened the front door to find Adam and Daniel on the living room floor looking at an atlas. "What's going on guys?" Adam ran up to me and told me we were moving to Gander, Newfoundland, in the summer.

I looked at Daniel. "Gander? Whose back door did you crap on to get that posting?" My life went into fast-motion. Let's cram a entire lifetime into a year. Marriage, baby and a move. Once I got over the initial shock of moving, I had to resign my position. The gang at work had a great going-away party for me at a very expensive restaurant downtown. I really hated to leave the gang. We had become one big family over the years.

It was late summer when we pulled into the little town of Gander. It was hot and dry! We arrived one day ahead of schedule, so we were put up in the local hotel. It was a brand new development just outside of Gander. The lobby was massive. I could smell the newness when I walked into the lobby. I took note of how posh the place was. They wasted no expense on the place. The entire lobby was marble and brass. I wondered what type of clientele they were catering to. After all, we're talking about Gander here—it's like a dot on the map. I could hear a lot of laughing. It was coming from the pool. I went over to the window to have a look. There had to be fifty brats screaming their brains out in that pool. That's not what I needed. The only thing I wanted to do was have a long, cool, peaceful shower. Daniel and Adam headed down to the pool.

While I was getting my housecoat, I turned the shower on. The cool mist from the shower was so refreshing. I could taste the salty sweat as it was running onto my lips. I hadn't been in there for more than seconds when a faucet blew out of the wall. It missed my guts by a centimetre. I started screaming. The cold water was literally spewing out of the wall with great force. As I hastily jumped out of the tub, I tripped and hit the base of the toilet.

Water was everywhere. I was able to crawl to the phone to have Daniel paged and have someone come up to shut the water off. The water had now made its way into the bedroom. The carpets were soaked. My head was throbbing with pain. I don't know yet how that baby survived. Within a couple of minutes, Daniel and Adam ran frantically through the door to find a lot of water and me lying on the floor. Daniel laid me on the bed, and he took a quick look around the room. "My god! What in hell happened here? It's a disaster zone! Your head—my god, you're bleeding!" He grabbed a towel to see how badly I was cut. It was just minor. Daniel asked, "Were you attacked or something?"

I looked up at him with a disgusted look. "Yeah, Daniel, the shower monster jumped out of the wall and attacked me!" There was so much water, we had to go out into the hall. A crew finally arrived with buckets and pumps.

The management felt horrible over it. They moved us into the executive suite, and anything we wanted was on the house. Once again, being sick and pregnant, I couldn't take much advantage of the offer, but Daniel and Adam sure did. They had room service running their asses off that evening.

The next day, we met the movers at our home. Our home was located on a quiet cul-de-sac. It was a great place to raise the kids. Our bedroom was as long as a bowling alley lane. There were hardwood floors galore and a dining room that could easily seat twelve people. The backyard was full of blueberry bushes. The blueberries were the size of grapes. The pervious owners had a large pond installed in the middle of the yard. At night, it was something to see. There were lights inside the pond. It would, in fact, light up the entire backyard. After we were somewhat settled in, we decided to go into town to get some groceries. We quickly found out there wasn't much selection.

There was one grocery store. We went over to the counter to see if we could get some fresh fish, but all they had was frozen fish. We asked the clerk where we could find some fresh fish, and he said that it was fresh. I replied, "No, it's frozen."

He looked at me like I was stupid and said, "It was freshly frozen!" How could I argue that point? Even though Gander was small, the people were a lot more liberal than in Nova Scotia. They sold cold beer in their grocery and corner stores. That was a treat! I was roughly seven months pregnant and irritable as hell. If you looked at me the wrong way, I would tear your face off. It's a good thing Daniel was patient. There were times I'd rip him apart for absolutely no reason. Between the heat and the extra weight, I was fit to be tied.

The heat was truly unreal. Every lawn in town was burnt to a crisp. There was no relief other than standing in the shower. Trust me, I had those faucets checked before my butt went in there. Since the beach was a four-hour drive away, we converted our pond into a miniature pool. Our neighbours were a little strange. I heard he was a local fisherman and spent a lot of time at sea. No one seemed to know much about her. They never bothered to welcome us on the street, so we took it upon ourselves to get acquainted.

I had made a bunch of apple pies one afternoon out of sheer boredom. I took one of the pies and grabbed Daniel out of his seat to head over to meet them. I knocked and knocked on that door, and no one answered. Their car was in the driveway, and there were lights on. I put the pie on the ledge of the deck and returned home. "That's strange." I looked out the kitchen window to find a damn dog chowing down my apple pie. *At least something was enjoying it.* Later, I saw her hanging out her clothes. I popped my head out the door and asked her to come over for a coffee. She put her head down, dropped the clothes into the basket and flew inside. *What's with her? What is she so afraid of?* I threw on my shoes and went directly over to see her. I stood on her deck for a good thirty minutes before she peeked through the window. I couldn't see much of her because she kept covering her face with her hands. I abruptly opened the door.

When I stepped inside, the smell was unforgiving. Dirty dishes were piled everywhere with flies swarming over them. I had to run back outside to get my breath. The door slammed behind me. Over dinner, I mentioned to Daniel what I had seen that day. He basically told me to stay out of it. "Mind your own business!" I never listened to him before, and I wasn't going to start then. The next day, I called social services. I did not want to tell who I was. Since I was her neighbour, I wanted to remain anonymous and explained to them what I had witnessed. They weren't long sending an agent over to investigate the situation. He stood on her deck for the longest time. There was no way she was letting him in.

In wasn't long before a cop car was on site, followed by a fire truck. This was getting interesting! I kept my distance. I didn't want to seem too nosy. The fireman came on the deck carrying an axe. With one big swing, the door was down. The cop entered the house first. The smell must have been appalling since he landed back onto the deck within seconds, grasping for air. He yelled out to the firemen to call for an ambulance. In the meantime, they put face masks on and reentered the home. The first thing they carried out was a medium-sized cardboard box. The cop was holding it from a distance. The curiosity was killing me. When I saw that little box, the first thought that came into my demented mind was, *My god, is it a dead baby? No, it couldn't be! This isn't New York, it's Gander for crying out loud. Get a grip!* Within minutes, the ambulance was pulling up the driveway. The attendants pulled out stretcher and quickly went into the house. By now, the entire street had encircled the area.

I took a quick look at the crowd. Some were dressed in housecoats and slippers, others in sweats and ball caps. I thought to myself, *What a bunch of winners we have here today!* Their mouths were moving a mile a minute. I could just imagine the level mentality there was in that group. *Scary.* They hadn't been long getting her loaded into the ambulance. That was big news for a town that size. Seeing as I was her neighbour, my phone started ringing off the wall. I let it ring. I had nothing to say to anyone since I didn't know what had happened. It wasn't until the next day it was revealed in the newspaper.

The story made the headlines on every paper in Gander and throughout Newfoundland. "Estranged Wife at Peace with Cat." I was saddened and mortified when I read the article. The woman apparently was a manic depressive who lived on caffeine and pills. She had a cat named Cleo that, for the past eighteen years, she loved more than life itself. The cat had died. She never disposed of it. The veterinarian came to the conclusion the cat had been dead for at least two to three months. She kept it wrapped up in a baby blanket and had it by her bedside. That wasn't the best of it. Her husband had walked out on her a month before that. No wonder she was one missed up bitch! They hired special crews to go into her home and fumigate before putting it up for sale. I had photographers up my butt, asking me numerous questions and taking pictures of the scene. *This town was starving for some action!* The RCMP had an all-points bulletin out to locate her husband.

As far as I know, they never found him. That sure was the talk of the town for weeks.

Adam started school and made a lot of new friends. I was due to pop any day. Mom flew up to give me a hand when the baby was born. I was in the kitchen making the boys their breakfast, and all of a sudden I soaked the floor. "Daniel, come quick!" He ran out the back door to get the car. We arrived at the James Patton Hospital to find I was the only person in the emergency department. It was a far cry from the QEII hospital in Halifax. The nurses ran to me with open arms. Probably glad to have a patient to care for. They wheeled me into a private area and made me quite comfortable.

My contractions were roughly ten minutes apart. Daniel reached over me and said, "I won't be long. I'm just going down the hall to grab a coffee."

With the little amount of energy I had left, I clutched onto his shirt, pulled him one inch from my face and, with a witchy tone of voice, said, "Your hairy butt isn't going anywhere!" It wasn't long after that we had a new addition to the family. She flew out of me like a greased-up cantaloupe. We named her Alexandria Marguerite. I remember calling Dad to tell him the great news. His name is Alexander, and he couldn't believe we named her after him. I knew soon as I hung up the phone, his fingers would be burnt to the bone calling up all the neighbours.

The hospital staff strongly recommended that I breast feed. I couldn't argue with that. The ironic part about that was they fed me baked beans and wieners for my supper that night. That poor little baby would have shit her bowels out if I ate that. There were no complications other than a sore butt, so I was released in three days. Mom and Adam were standing in the driveway, grinning from ear to ear, waiting for our arrival. She had the house full of homemade food. The flowers, gifts and letters poured in daily. I never knew how many friends I had until I had that little gem.

She sure was a pleasure to have around. She was a weird little creature. She never slept through the day. Alexandria was such a pig, I couldn't keep her in breast milk. Within five weeks, she was inhaling formula and mashed bananas with baby cereal. By Christmas, she was indulging in all fruits and vegetables. That girl gave eating a whole new meaning! She always reminded me of a baby bird waiting for the mother bird to shove the worms down their throats. I never heard a peep out of her until morning. For the first couple of weeks, I was constantly going into her room to make sure she wasn't dead. We got her used to loud rock 'n' roll music and lots of people around right away. We weren't going to pussyfoot around the house while she was sleeping.

Adam adored his little sister, though he was terrified to hold her for fear that he would drop her. Whenever he wasn't in school, he was usually by her side. He used to take her little hands and measure them up to his. I always gave the two of them equal attention. I didn't want any mishaps happening out of jealousy. Mom left for Nova Scotia, and we started to live a normal life, if that was possible. I guess it all depends on how you define "normal."

Daniel was away a lot on search and rescue missions, but when he was home, he made up for lost time with the children and I. I had made several new friends. We were all very active in the Officers' Mess functions. It was the core of entertainment in Gander. There was one bar up the street that brought in male strippers once a month. Now that was entertainment. I needed to be released from my motherly duties for an evening. A couple of friends and I headed up to the bar.

When they came out on stage, my mouth hit the floor. I yelled out, "They're hung like horses!" They certainly were first in line when God was passing out dicks, that's for sure. Get a few more drinks in me, and I would have been tempted to join them on stage. They weren't permitted to remove their G-strings. That wasn't a problem in my eyes. One could only imagine how much meat was coiled up inside of that! To think I had to go home and sleep with Daniel after seeing these guys.

There was an event coming up on base. It was going to be a Medieval Dinner followed by a dance. Since we were so heavily involved with the mess functions, they elected us to be the king and queen for the evening. The town didn't have a costume shop, so I had to put my thinking cap on quickly. It took me days to make those costumes. I didn't have a clue how to sew; in fact, I can't stand sewing. None of my friends sewed either. Thank god for staples and sewing tape. The crowns were made up of tinfoil, sparkles and cheap jewelry and were held together with hundreds of staples. I used old drapes for the costumes and used glue, safety pins and iron-on reversible tape to hold them. I warned Daniel not to stand near any heat sources that evening or his outfit would go up in flames. They were quite the masterpieces!

When the cab arrived, my crown hit the ceiling. Daniel looked at me and said, "You look very regal this evening, but do you know you have blood trickling down your forehead?" I borrowed the cabbie's visor mirror to check it out. It must have happened when I hit my crown getting in, and one of the staples got out of joint. As soon as I arrived at the mess, I went to the lady's room to check my head. I looked into the mirror to see little blotches of blood on top of my head. There was no way I could put my crown back on.

Being somewhat of a spontaneous individual, I took Daniel by the arm, flung open the dining room doors, put my hands between my breasts and announced, "I have been kicked, beaten and robbed on my journey to attend this festive dinner by King Nutless' thieves, please excuse my ruffled appearance." They all stood and starting roaring their butts off.

I waved my hands downward to allow them to be seated. Everyone sat around a long, old rustic table. Since it was the Medieval times, we weren't permitted any utensils, only fingers to pick up your food. No one was allowed to start to eat or drink until the queen gave the word. Several times, I would stand up and raise my glass, and of course, upon doing so, everyone had to stand immediately and bow and lift their glasses and say, "Here, here, to our great queen of Ganderville." I would lower my glass and sit down. After the fourth time in doing that, the crowd was getting a little restless, so I finally gave in. The food had been served. There were mounded platters of turkey and chicken legs.

During the meal we had a jester entertaining us. He was a lanky thing dressed in a ridiculous green costume with a pair of oversized slippers with pom-poms hanging off his toes. There was an accident waiting for a place to happen. The first part of his act was rather amusing. He would run and leap into the air like a bouncing nymph. His flying days were short lived. While running to do his grand finale, he tripped over his pom-poms and landed between the chicken and turkey legs. He hit with so much thrust that the platter of meat spewed into the air. The wine and beer glasses came pouring down all sides of the table. I sat there stunned, my mouth agape, covered in booze and greasy chicken. Since he knocked himself out, the medics had to be called in to take him to the hospital.

EIGHT

That winter, we attended several wonderful parties at the mess. My parents flew up to ring in the New Year with us. The mess was holding a dazzling New Year's Eve party. There was a DJ who liked to play Newfie jigs, which were a favourite with the local mess members. They would all laugh and dance; it was a real hoot. I remember the DJ putting on a record, saying, "And now I'm gonna play 'In the Swing' from Buddy McDonald!" Lo and behold, we heard "In the Mood" played on the fiddle.

So Daniel goes to the DJ and says, "You know, that's 'In the Mood' from Glenn Miller."

The DJ said, "Oh no! Buddy wrote that song!" What an event that was. The men were all dressed in their mess kits, and the ladies were dressed in stylish long gowns. Dad wore a dark blue suit with a red tie that evening. That evening, he was referred to as John Turner, the former liberal leader.

As the evening went on, the drunker people got and the fewer ties and jackets were worn. The up-do's started to become the down-do's. There was one cab company in town. He made his fortune that night! He didn't drive people home that night, he flew them home. The quicker he could get back to the mess, the more money he made. While my parents were visiting, we decided to take a trip into St. Johns. What a lovely city. I gave up counting the number of moose we passed. We only stayed a couple of days. On our way back, we stopped at a restaurant. One of the items on the menu was surf and turf. We all ordered it. We thought it was rather strange that the waitress didn't ask us how we liked our steaks. We soon realized why. Within minutes, our plates arrived. Oh, it definitely was surf and turf! It was cod tongues and fried baloney. We didn't know the locals called it that way as a joke. That's one thing we learned: Newfoundlanders love making jokes at themselves. Only in Newfoundland. We got a big kick out of that.

We all wanted a feed of lobsters, so we drove to a little fishing village about thirty minutes outside of Gander. We stopped at a corner store to get directions. The lady was hilarious; you couldn't make one word out edgeways. She told us to "go down dere at de botton o' de 'ill, turn a right, and you'll see 'im 'itting on the wharf chewin' on a cig!" We drove into his driveway, and we saw at least six kids playing in the yard, kicking a old tin can around. We soon learned he had three more inside. He was one horny old bastard! Either that, or she made the neighbours happy!

The house was really tiny and beat-up. It literally sat on rocks. The screen door flapped like crazy side to side from the cold wind blowing off the ocean. Sure enough, there he was, sitting on the wharf smoking a cigarette. He had two teeth in his head and reeked of either home brew or battery acid. We needed to buy five two- to three-pounders for a decent feed. He took us to the bins that were nestled into the icy water by his wharf. He said to us, "See them ther' sittin' side by each, ther' da best!" We got a deal of a lifetime. He charged us a buck fifty a pound.

As we were putting the lobsters into a box, his wife came out the door yelling, "Ya get yor butt in 'ere, it's suppa' time!" I could hear him mumbling under his breath with a cigarette hanging out the corner of his mouth. "Dam ole' bitch, I'm goin' to do 'er in some day!" As he walked up the hill, chuckling to himself, he continued saying it over and over again.

They were some of the best feeds of lobsters I had in a long time.

Daniel and I were involved in everything from sports to dinner parties. We were enjoying life to the utmost. I was the envy of most of the military wives because whenever he went away on a rescue mission for more than two nights, I would receive a beautiful arrangement of flowers at the door. He had me spoiled rotten, and I was loving it. My birthday was rapidly approaching. I kept getting little hints from Adam like, "You're going to be really surprised, Mommy!" I tried bribing him to tell me more, but Daniel was quick to put his hands over his mouth. The day had arrived, and the suspense was killing me.

They let me sleep in that morning. I came dancing down the stairs, singing, "It's my birthday!" They were busy in the kitchen whipping me up a heart-clogging breakfast. Over breakfast, I was told not to go into the bathroom downstairs. As far as I knew, Daniel was cooking me a gourmet dinner.

Daniel tried all day to give me excuses to get out of the house. That afternoon, I decided to take Alexandria and head for the mall. On my return home, while I was stopped at a red light, I looked into my mirror to see a car coming at us at full speed. There was no time to react other than fly as much of my upper body onto Alexandria as I could. There's nothing sweeter than the sound of metals crashing into each other. I was shaken up and tried to straighten myself out. Panicky, I felt Alexandria all over to make sure nothing was broken or bleeding. Thank god she was all right. A knock on the window startled me. It was a woman yelling at me, something like, "Are you okay?" I could hardly understand what she was saying. I found out why. When I lowered my window, the aroma of whiskey hit my nose. She told me she would go get help. I began to shake all over. Alexandria was screaming her lungs out. My head was splitting in two. I looked into my rearview mirror to see that that drunk was fleeing the scene of the accident. I was too shaken up to do anything about it.

The next thing I knew, I was waking up in the hospital in a neck brace. Daniel and Adam were holding my hands. Daniel said to me, "This isn't exactly what I had in mind for your birthday!" The injuries weren't serious, so I was able to go home with a prescription of Tylenol III to relieve the neck pains and headaches. Besides, I wasn't going to let a car accident ruin my birthday. I rested on the couch while they fussed in the kitchen.

Since I wanted to have some wine with my dinner, I didn't take any of the pain killers. I was going to leave the wine for that. He had cooked me a delicious king crab supper. Underneath my place mat was a little velvet box, and in it was an elegant pearl ring encircled with diamonds. I sat in the dining room admiring my ring while Daniel started clearing off the table. Adam came up behind me carrying my cake. He was so quiet, I didn't even hear him. As I turned around to ask Daniel to bring in another bottle of wine, I elbowed Adam right in his arms. The cake splattered onto the floor, and Adam went down onto his knees crying, "I'm sorry, Mommy, for dropping your cake!"

Daniel came running out of the kitchen. "Now what?"

I told Adam not to be silly. "It was my fault for elbowing you, Adam!" I bent over to help pick up the cake off the floor.

Daniel said, "Just walk away, move aside, don't touch anything!" Poor little Adam. I think he realized by now that his mom was a walking disaster. I went into the living room to put some music on. As they were cleaning up the mess, a knock came at the back door. Since they were busy, I ran to get the door. Before I had a chance to fully open the door, a bunch of my friends burst in and started singing Happy Birthday! The men kissed and hugged me. Daniel came running to the door like a little kid, swept me up into his arms and said, "Are you surprised? Happy Birthday, love! This is your night!" And what a surprise it was! There were at least thirty people that showed up.

I never realized how well-liked I was. They were loaded down with food, booze, balloons and gifts. The women took over the kitchen immediately to prepare the food. Before long, the house was rockin' with music and laughter. Adam was in the living room, bouncing to the tunes and keeping an eye on Alexandria. They soon were sent upstairs to play in our room. The booze that poured into our pores that night was sinful. The gifts ranged from chocolate-flavoured underwear to sex massage oils. *Nice bunch*! They knew me! The party finally came to and end when the cops showed up threatening to put us all in the slammer for the rest of the night. The next day, the house was a catastrophic mess. The smell of stale booze and smoke would have ripped your guts and eyes out. After helping Daniel clean up the mess, I spent the rest of the day recuperating on the couch. In other words, recovering from the night before.

My dearest girlfriend down the street whose boyfriend also was a pilot was getting married. I, being the ringleader within the group, was asked to hold the wedding shower at my place. Of course, I didn't have the traditional shower. I had every thing from a stripper to spiked punch to porn movies playing on the living room wall. Trust me, no one was bored at that party. I had even the stuck-up old broads feeling their oats that night. This stud I hired was the best. He knew he was dealing with a wide assortment of women. He basically went to the one level of crudeness he knew—right to the gutter. He strutted his stuff like it was his last performance.

There was a major's wife who was a little on the snobbish side. She always attended functions with the proper ladies' attire. This stripper had her eyed from the word, "Go." She had hit the punch bowl several times during the evening, so I knew she wasn't feeling any pain, but she still had to maintain her image. I turned on this raunchy music—you know, your typical skin flick crap—and he started. Without any delay, he bounced his tight butt over to the major's wife. He put his arms in the air and swung those hips so sensual back and forth into her face that she was almost was dizzy. She never took her eyes off of his crotch for one second. Who would? You would have had to be a saint. The bride to be was having the time of her life. She kept going up behind him and squeezing his cheeks, and those cheeks were not on his face!

I made a cake that was in the shape of a large penis with a set of large, black balls. We all gathered around the dining room table to watch her cut the cake. One thing they didn't know was that the nuts were baggies full of red food colouring and covered with chocolate icing. The first cut she made went directly into one of the nuts. There was a direct line of red dye that splattered over her face and the rest onto her clothing. The rest of the ladies screamed and jumped backward. Their drinks hit the floor, smashing the glasses. Most of them screamed, "Oh my heavens." The bride-to-be stood there with red dye dripping from her hair and was totally shocked!

One of the ladies asked, "Who made this repulsive cake?" I had sixty eyeballs immediately focused on me.

"We'll give you one guess!"

The bride-to-be came up to me and whispered into my ear, "You are one sick bitch. Don't ever change!" Some of the ladies found it hard to eat the cake afterwards! I didn't care if they ate it or not. The thrill for me was over.

I think we had more fun than the men did that night. Women tend to be a little cruder than men at these parties. That certainly was one of the highlights of the party! I gazed around the room to see a bunch of hungry, sex-deprived women drooling and twitching in their seats to only hope to have ten minutes with a guy like that. I watched them quiver and squeal in their seats. He had no idea how close he came to being raped that night. He was pawed, pulled, and touched. At one point, one of the ladies even got down on her knees and kissed his butt. When she got back up into her seat, she took a big swig of her wine and said, "There's nothing better than a fine wine with a prime cut of beef!" and then licked her lips. I knew that night I had sent a lot of women home with a totally different concept of partying. Daniel arrived back from his stag party. He was half in the bag. He was swinging me around the kitchen and dancing to the music. My butt hit the lamp on the coffee table in the living room, and it fell to the floor and smashed all to hell. Another mess! He could tell by the mess in the house that we had a pretty good time ourselves. I ignored it and headed for bed.

We just got into bed when we heard a roaring, loud, horrendous noise. We ran to the window to see what the commotion was all about. We could see lights coming from a huge commercial jet. I looked at Daniel.

"We're going to die!" As the jet was quickly approaching our house, we both ducked down and held our heads. I started saying, "Our Father, who aren't in heaven." The house shook as the jet flew over us. We were terrified. That was one way to sober up quickly. It sure beat a cup of coffee all to hell! It was a long time before we could get back to sleep. Daniel found out the next day that a European airplane had to deviate to Gander, and the pilot had to make a quick turn when he found out he was heading for the wrong runway. Nice.

The town was really lacking not only in style, but also in selection. The first thing I noticed was that there was only one furniture store in town. That furniture store was making a killing. I contacted my brother who owned a furniture business in Halifax and discussed opening up a franchise in Gander. It would be designed as a mail-order system. He told me it wouldn't hurt to try. The first thing I had to get was an occupancy permit from the town. That was not an easy task. I had to fight with City Hall for weeks. These little towns hate to make change. The town was afraid I would be taking business away from the local furniture store. I had to convince them it was called "competition." After several disputes and landing on the front page of the paper a couple of times, I finally received my permit. Even then, they were reluctant to give it to me.

The next step was a visit to the bank. In order to pay for the furniture I needed for my show room, I needed cash. I cashed in all of my RRSPs and most of Daniel's. Since my business was going to be run out of my home, I had to decide not only what kind of furniture to buy, but also what portion of the house to display it in. We started with the renovations. We worked from the floor up. The work and money that was involved was more than we had anticipated! There were days I was exhausted. While painting the stairwells down, I plunked my butt down on the steps to take a breather.

Alexandria was busily playing with her toys on the living room carpet. Within seconds, I recklessly fell to sleep. With the thud of my head hitting the wall, I woke up to find her covered in dark blue paint. She upset the can all over the new flooring. I hadn't been asleep for more than a minute. The first thing I did was open her mouth. Thank god there was nothing in her mouth! From that day on, her speedy little butt was put into a play pen. When the decorating was done, the furniture arrived. Perfect timing! Once it was all in place, I stood back and marvelled at how everything came together so beautifully. It was one great moment! I had to cherish it since those moments were so few and far between. That evening, Daniel cracked opened an expensive bottle of wine to celebrate a "new beginning." Now I had to promote my business not only in Gander, but also throughout Newfoundland. I was soon to find out that it was going to be another big expense.

I thought that before the business had its grand opening, I should take a week and visit my family back home. I figured it would be a long time before I could take a trip once the business took off. At least, I had anticipated it would be taking off. I couldn't wait to get home to show Alexandria off and brag up my new business. Daniel couldn't go with us because he had way too much work to do. Our flight came right out of a nightmare. It was the flight from hell. The military put the three of us onto a Hercules aircraft. They strapped us into hammock-like seats. The noise was unbearable! Since Alexandria was so small, I kept her on my lap. I was so hot, the sweat was dripping off of my forehead. I could tell right from the start that it was going to be one pleasant trip! The turbulence made everybody around us sick, including my two kids.

We weren't in the air for five minutes when Adam threw up all over me and the baby. It wasn't a pretty sight. Here I was strapped in, full of puke, with Alexandria screaming my ears off and Adam having the dry heaves. What a relaxing trip. I just shut my eyes and hoped that when I opened them we would be there. The only good thing about it was that it was free. I could sense the fairy tale about to end. That was only the beginning of what was lurking around that dark corner. The pilot made an outrageous landing. He hit that runway so hard that Alexandria's head drove right into my chin.

I could sense a warm liquid running out the corner of my mouth. I asked Adam to have a look at it to see what colour the liquid was. Sure enough, it was red! My parents met us at the airport grinning from ear to ear. Apparently, when I smiled, the blood had seeped in between my teeth. Mom gave me her compact to have a look at myself. "Jesus, Count Dracula just had a meal!" I couldn't wait to dive into a shower. We reeked of sweat and puke. Alexandria's diaper weighed a ton and smelled like I dipped her into a toilet bowl. The drive to my folks' home was endless. My parents, Alex and Sheila, have a retirement home overlooking the ocean. The view is truly magnificent. Mom had prepared enough food for an army. What is it with moms? I swear, they want us all to look like pit ponies. I was in heaven. The sun was glistening off the water, and there wasn't a cloud in the sky. It was the perfect day to sit and suck back on a cold beer.

As I was lifting my beer, a car came whipping around the corner at high speed, hit the dirt, flipped up into the air, and landed bottom up in the ditch. Without any shoes on, I beelined my butt to the accident. Dad was close behind me. I didn't know what to expect when I got there. For one thing, I detest the sight of blood. I was the first to arrive at the scene. I bent over and looked inside the smashed window to find a man mumbling, "Get me out of here," as he was pointing his finger to the floor! There were definitely traces of alcohol in his system, and I could see now why he was pointing at the floor—there laid an empty bottle of whisky. He had drooled all over my head.

"God, the smell!" I said to myself. Dad and I didn't want to move him in case he had spinal or neck injuries. I knew that when the RCMP got on site, that guy was finished.

Once the authorities arrived, we returned home. By now, my beer was warm. Instead of showering again, I took the kids to the beach that was right in back of Dad's house. Convenient, or what?

The entire family showed up for the big barbeque that evening. The crude jokes and bullshit stories were prevalent amongst us. They were like bookends to the wine and beer. They complimented one another! My younger brother Justin's wife, Courtney, could have been easily certified as a raving idiot. She frowned on him drinking. The more she bitched, the more he drank. Mom had bought a huge watermelon for us to have after dinner.

Mom asked Courtney to bring it to the deck. Oh, she brought it all right! She threw it onto the deck! Watermelon went flying everywhere. She stood in the middle of the pulp and rind with her teeth clenched together and spitted the words, "Enjoy, everybody!" She proceeded to walk off the deck and drive off.

We always knew she was a little off-the-wall. We continued on our conversations as if nothing happened. Dad hosed it off the deck for the gulls to eat. Dad had made a tee-off time early the next morning. We were a little seedy to say the least. We met at the clubhouse for breakfast. It was terribly hot amongst those trees that morning. There was a combination of aromas in the air. Everything was stale beer, rancid wine and rotten beef. It made for a pleasant game of golf!

I sure hoped they went home and changed their underwear. We had to cut the game short. The black clouds rolled in, and the heavens opened up. We made it back to the clubhouse before the thunder and lightning stuck. This hadn't even been forecasted. After we had a couple of beers, I headed home, but the boys stayed. When I arrived home, Mom came running out the back door frantically screaming, "It's Alexandria! I think she swallowed some pills!" I ran into the house to find her sound to sleep on the floor with my purse wide open and the Tylenol bottle empty. I started shaking her W*ake up, wake up*. There was no time for an ambulance, and since I had a couple of beers, I didn't want to risk driving. Mom called her neighbour, who was approaching eighty, if he could give us a lift into the IWK. He never drove past fifty the entire trip. I could have wrung his skinny neck. I was beside myself. In the backseat of his car, I turned Alexandria upside down and dove my finger down her throat. With one big gush, her guts were all over me in his backseat. The attendants at the hospital weren't long shoving a chalk mixture down her throat. Following that procedure, they took her blood. Everything was fine. When the neighbour dropped us off at the house, he said, "Excuse me, I'm a retired old soul. Do you think you could spare five dollars for my gas?" What a prick! Poor old soul, my butt! He had his first dime he ever earned. I threw him ten dollars and told him to keep the change. He was noted in the community for being one cheap son of a gun. His wife was no better. She could make a slice of pie feed six people.

When Mark's wife Jackie wasn't working, you would find her butt next to mine. They owned a large chalet with a pool overlooking the ocean just minutes from my parents'. Her kids, Heather and Linda, were around the same age as Adam. They all treated one another like brother and sisters. I hardly saw Adam. He spent every waking moment at their place playing in the pool. Jackie could fill a room full with laughter. We'd laugh so much that our guts hurt the next day. We were like sisters. Many a night, we'd sit on the deck dreaming of ways of becoming rich and solving all the world's problems. When Dad was around, though, it was hard to get a work in edge ways. He has a mouth that never stops. In fact, when he takes his teeth out, they still keep on moving up an down. He has nicknames that span everything from "Motor Mouth" to "Jaws." He certainly is a well respected and loved person throughout the community.

We were having such a wonderful time we hated to leave, but I had an investment to tend to at home. Plus, Daniel was getting a little lonely in that big house of ours. We were booked on a service flight, but every time I checked in with Shearwater, we were bumped. In other words, there were more important people that needed the seats. We were secondary. By the third week, I was getting anxious to return home. I not only had to tend to my business, but school was starting up in a couple of weeks. I was bumped so many times now that our names were at the bottom of the list. I realized the military flight wasn't going to happen. There was no way I could fly with the commercial planes. I didn't have the money. We had no other choice but to drive to Sydney, Cape Breton, to catch the ferry to Port-au-Basques, Newfoundland.

Dad and I loaded up the car, and off we went. Before we left, Dad called Larry McQueen, a life-long friend of his who he had worked with for several years. He had retired in Bras d'Or Lake, which was about an hour or so from the ferry. It was going to be a little awkward for me, as I dated him some years ago. And to make it more uncomfortable, I was the one who left him high and dry for another man. In all honesty, I had been nothing but a bitch to him! I used him and his money. I ran into him a couple of times, and he looked terrible. I felt terribly guilty for what I had done to that man. He treated me like gold and spoiled me rotten with gifts. I just wasn't ready for the commitment he was looking for at the time. It was a shame he never married, and to my knowledge, he still hasn't married. The only thing I could hope for when we arrived was that he didn't carry any long-term grudges.

He owned a charming cottage on Bras d'Or Lake. When we unloaded ourselves out of the car, he was standing with open arms in the driveway. He was so delighted to see us all. I didn't know whether to hug him or shake his hand. I noticed instantly that he was a little jealous over Alexandria. In our relationship, he mentioned on several occasions he would love to have a bunch of children one day. I think that's one of the reasons I left him. What a place he had! The view was spectacular! There were huge windows from the floor to the ceiling absorbing every ounce of the view. I think he thought we were staying for more than one night by the amount of food he had in the kitchen. We both were uncomfortable at first, but once we had a couple of drinks in us, things began to mellow out. I took a good look around and thought, *If I would have stuck it out with this guy, look what I would own.* And that was just his cottage! Oh well, it wasn't meant to be. I left Dad alone with him so they could catch up on the news. The ferry was leaving very early the next morning, so it was an early night for the kids and me. When we awoke that morning, it was pouring down rain and windy as hell. It was not going to make for a smooth voyage.

Though it was sad to say goodbye to everyone, it was going to be nice to be back home again. The ocean was angry that morning. I knew I was going to be in for one awful, long trip. Before I put one foot onto that ferry, I inhaled four adult-strength Gravol. I gave the kids some, though as quickly as they took it, they were throwing their guts up. The waves bounced off the sides of the ferry with no mercy. It was so rough that we were forbidden to go outside on the decks. That old ferry bounced up and down like a teeter-totter. The ferry swayed from one end to the other. The sitting area was soon full of some pretty sick people. Even my two were sick as dogs! The place reeked of puke! The cleaners couldn't keep up with the messes. Finally, after shoving more children's Gravol down their throats, they both fell asleep in my arms. I looked at the ceiling. "Thank you!"

To look out the window was horrifying. It looked like, between the heavy rain and the ferocious waves, we were being attacked by billions of furious demons. Alexandria woke up rather abruptly and starting screaming her head off to the point where I was considering throwing her overboard. She managed to wake up Adam. *Great, round two!* I shoved a soother in her trap to shut her up. I knew Adam was feeling better when he asked for some food. We went to the cafeteria to find the prices outlandish. These people who operate these ferries should be hung out to dry. They know they have you by the short and curlies. What other choice did I have? We had to eat. It cost me almost ten bucks for a pissy little lunch. I called it highway robbery, bunch of crooks! I told Adam to enjoy every morsel of it!

As we got closer to Port-au-Basques, the weather improved. We were all exhausted, dirty and bewildered by that unforgiving, merciless voyage. I swore on that day I would never get on another ferry during a horrific storm again! I stepped off the ferry to find Daniel sitting in the terminal reading the newspaper. He was very glad to see us, but I could tell there was something wrong. The first thing I noticed was that his eyes were hollow and dark. He also looked very tired. He just didn't look like himself. I knew he had a long drive from Gander to the ferry, but something wasn't right. My first clue was after we loaded the luggage in to the car, and he threw me the keys. That was the last thing I wanted to do was drive. The only thing I wanted to do was book into a hotel, have a shower and hit the pillow. He insisted I do a little driving to cut down the drive the next day. Daniel knew I hated highway driving, especially at night. I was so tired, I couldn't drive anymore.

I pulled into a run-down, seedy, low-life motel. It was a good indicator that it wasn't a five-star joint by the reservation desk. The bum behind the counter was sucking back on a cigarette, wearing a baseball cap and a ripped, dirty t-shirt. At that point, I didn't care. We arrived at the room to find one double bed, a single, and a lamp thats shade had cigarette burns in it. The floors were covered in orange and brown shag carpeting. The beds had threadbare bedspreads. The air smelt of stale smoke. That shower was going to feel so good. I turned it on while getting undressed. I couldn't hear a steady flow of water, so I opened the shower curtain to see water squirting out of three or four holes, spontaneously. *So much for that idea! Let's try having a bath.* I learned very quickly there wasn't a lot of hot water either when I put my head under the tap to rinse the soap off and found nothing but cold water. I had to save my dirty water to bathe the kids in. Alexandria's brain cells weren't developed enough to know the difference between clean or dirty. It was Adam who put up the fuss. I told him he had two other alternatives: the pissy little sink or the toilet bowl. "Make up your mind!" To really put the icing on the cake, we had only two towels, and one of them was a hand towel. I had had enough. I put my shoes on and marched over to the office. There was a sign on the door. *Closed.* I had no idea it was so late. My skin had a layer of drool and puke on it. Not exactly the Estée Launder fragrance I was hoping for when I met Daniel back at the terminal. As I was coming out of the bedroom, I could hear snoring sounds. Daniel was fast asleep. What an uncomfortable bed. It was not only full of lumps, but also broken springs. No matter which way I lay, they would dig into me. I ended up taking a blanket off the bed and sleeping on the floor. No wonder he only charged me thirty-nine bucks for the room.

The next day was hot and sunny. After I peeled my aching body off the floor, we hit the road. Daniel had complained of a terrible headache. In fact, his head ached so badly he couldn't see properly. I gave him some Tylenol and drove the rest of the way home. He slept the entire way. At the time, I brushed it off as the flu.

It was so good to be home again. Daniel had a elegant bouquet of flowers sitting on the dining room table, and the fridge was full of food. While I unpacked, Daniel cleaned up the kids. The scent of puke was engraved into my nostrils but not for long. I had a long, long, hot, steaming shower. As I was coming downstairs to start supper, I noticed Daniel and Alexandria sound asleep on the living room floor. She was lying on his chest with her arms wrapped around his neck. Now I was getting a little concerned. Daniel never slept like that before. The first disgusting thing that popped into my mind was that maybe he had a whore while I was gone who screwed his brains out every day. I decided that couldn't be it; Daniel wasn't that kind of guy. After dinner, the kids were exhausted, so they weren't long out of bed. The only thing I wanted to do that night was sit back, put my feet up and enjoy a couple of cocktails with the man I loved. I definitely deserved it after what I had put up with in the last twenty-four hours! I noticed during the evening that Daniel was somewhat preoccupied. He wasn't quite himself. He was constantly rubbing his eyes and fighting to stay awake. I couldn't understand him. He had slept the majority of the day.

While walking up the stairs, I detected something unusual about Daniel. His balance was off. When we hopped into bed, he was asleep in seconds. I was so worried about him I couldn't sleep. So I wouldn't wake him up, I went downstairs and poured myself a glass of wine. I turned on the television, and it wasn't long before I fell sound asleep on the couch. I awoke the next morning with wine all over my housecoat and broken glass on the floor. I must have dropped it when I fell asleep.

Daniel yelled at me from upstairs, "Where are the Tylenol?" I told him they should be in the medicine cabinet. I knew I had bought a large bottle of them just before I left on my trip to Halifax. *My god, was he eating them like candy?* He asked me to go to the drug store to get another bottle. I didn't argue with him; he looked like he was in pain. My worrying had jumped to an all-new level. It had started to trouble me terribly. I had a quick shower and headed out. When I arrived back, I asked him what was going on. The only explanation he could give me was that he had been doing a lot of long night flying before I came home. He figured he was just plain tuckered out. After breakfast, I had planned on arranging the advertising for my grand opening for my business so on Monday, I would have everything organized for the press. The advertisement ran for four consecutive days. I was so excited. The first day the ad was in, I had numerous phone calls. The response was so overwhelming, I knew that the grand opening would be a great success. I was so elated over it, I totally forgot about Daniel's headaches.

Daniel, being a search and rescue pilot, had long, unusual hours. It wasn't exactly an eight-to-four job. For him to be home early or late or not at all wasn't abnormal, except for this one particular day. He previously had called me from work to tell me he wouldn't be home for supper. There was a fishermen's boat and crew in grave danger. I headed into town to pick up some of the supplies I needed for the grand opening. When I returned, Daniel was sitting in the living room holding his head in his hands. He said, "I had difficulties handling the helicopter. I could hardly land it!" When he looked up at me, there were tears of fear in his eyes. All I could do was comfort him.

NINE

The phone was ringing off the wall. I let the answering machine take over for a while. Daniel's health was a more urgent matter than my business. One of the crew members drove him directly to see the flight surgeon. That was normal procedure when there was a mishap. He couldn't find anything unusual, but just to be safe, he wanted him to see an oculist. The day I drove him there, I wasn't too concerned. I figured he needed glasses. The doctor tested his eyes thoroughly and mentioned that Daniel had some signs of nystingmus possibly caused by a pinched nerve around the optic nerve or by something that was applying pressure on his optic nerve. Either way, it had to be checked out. The flight surgeon made an appointment for Daniel to fly to the QE11 Hospital in Halifax to have a CAT scan on his head. There wasn't a moment wasted. The base had arranged for him to fly out on Friday morning and return on the following Monday. They were being optimistic! I remember that morning he left just as if it happened yesterday. I had a lump in my throat so big I could hardly swallow. It was a sweet and sour day. My grand opening was scheduled for the following Monday. I even had the mayor booked to assist in the ribbon-cutting ceremony, and of course, the press had planned on being there. That was a big day for me. My list of things to do was a mile long. The only thing that kept my sanity in tact was my business and the things I had to finish up before Monday. I had to put my butt into rapid mode. No matter how busy and wrapped up in my work I got, I still couldn't keep my mind off of Daniel. The "what ifs?" were driving me crazy.

Adam came home from school to find me crying my eyes out in the living room. He asked me what was wrong. I just brushed it off as being really tried and anxious about the business. He thought Daniel was away on a business trip. The kids didn't know what their mom was going through that day. My nerves were on high alert, and my guts felt like a rung-out dishcloth. Every time the phone rang, my heart jumped ten extra beats. The anticipation was beyond. There is nothing worse than having to wait. Later on in the afternoon, I called some friends over to help take my mind off of things.

We cracked open a couple of bottles of wine and talked up a storm. They knew I was terribly worried about Daniel. Of course, you know what happens when you get a bunch of women in a room drinking. The conversation goes right to the gutter. I swear, we are worse then men. It was quite entertaining. It wasn't long before I started feeling better. "There's good medicine in wine, sometimes!" They cheered for my grand opening and Daniel's safe return home. The phone rang, and I froze in my tracks. The room became silent. It was Daniel. He didn't even say hello. I remember his words as if it was just yesterday. "They found a wart on my brain." I knew I had ten sets of ears glued to my back, listening to every word I spoke. I couldn't understand what he meant.

"What do you mean a wart?" He wasn't overly upset. Neither one of us knew what to say. I was speechless, sick to my stomach and scared. There was a long sigh before he told me about the days' events.

When Daniel had arrived that Friday afternoon, he was sent to the Infirmary Hospital for a CAT scan. Halfway through it, the radiologist said that he could see a lump on the back of his head. When Daniel heard that, he felt relieved. He had been in dreadful pain for the last six months (which I was to learn later), and finally, he knew it was going to be taken care of. When the scan was over, they put him into this tiny room and told him to wait. A thousand thoughts had rushed through his head! Then these hree men dressed in long gowns showed up. One of them, a neurosurgeon, told him he had a tumour in his head. The first thing they had to do was release a lot of the fluid around his brain. They put him on a drug called Decadron. He was soon transferred to the Victoria General Hospital, where he would remain until they performed surgery.

I got a call from Daniel that Friday night. I was so excited to hear from him.

And what does he tell me? "Don't worry, it's just a little wart on my head. It should be removed next week." At the time, it put my mind at rest, but only temporarily. Five minutes later, I got a call from the neurosurgeon.

"Listen, I know your husband doesn't want you to worry, but I have to tell you the real story. He has a brain tumour. I would suggest that you come down immediately to Halifax to be with him." My entire body turned into a delicate piece of crystal. One wrong move, and I swore I would have shattered. I started crying and shaking. I fell to my knees and put my head into my hands.

"Why? Why? Oh my god, why?" My friends helped me onto the couch and were very supportive.

Adam came over to the couch to rub my hair and said, "Mommy, what's wrong?" I couldn't even speak to him.

"Please someone wake me up from this terrible nightmare!" I took a good look around at all the hard work and money we had invested into the house and shook my head. "Why, why?" It didn't even faze me. My only concern right now was getting Daniel better. Once I had my wits about me and my friends were quite confident I wasn't going to slit my wrist, they left. They were going to perform a critical intense operation on him in one week. Within hours, I had to find someone to take care of our cat, Yogo, and call everyone from the mayor's office to the local newspaper to delay the opening due to a family illness. My heart was smashed to smithereens. My dream shattered! I thought I was going to lose my mind. Alexandria was too young to understand any of it, but Adam could tell by my behaviour that it wasn't a happy time. Before leaving the house the next morning, I stood in the doorway, took one last look around and said, "This was supposed to be a great day for us!" Life can sure throw some nasty curve balls at you. Here I was with two small children and a lot of our money invested into my new business, and I didn't know if I was going to have a husband or not.

I arrived in Halifax the next evening not having a clue what to expect. I was exhausted, worried and totally bewildered. My parents met us at the Halifax International Airport. They were delighted to see us but at the same time distressed over the news. I went directly to the hospital. Daniel burst into tears when I walked into his room. He was a scared little boy in a man's body. The back of his head was all puffy and swollen. His eyes were black and hollow. All I could do was hug him and tell him how much I loved him. His whole body trembled with fear. He said, "Why, why, why is this happening to us?" Immediately, his doctor wanted to speak with me in private. He explained to me that the tumour was the size of a small egg. Daniel's head was swollen due to fluid around his brain. They had put him on steroids to keep the swelling down. It would make the surgery less complicated. Within two days, Daniel was unable to walk. He had absolutely no balance at all. He was now trapped in a bed until he had his surgery. I remember the day they operated on him like it was yesterday. These memories are the ones that haunt you for the rest of your life. I remember looking out the hospital window, watching the Snowbirds (Aerobatic Flying Team in Canada) practising over the city for the upcoming air show in Shearwater. Daniel used to love watching them perform. Now he was fighting for his life! Since the operation was going to be long, I decided to go to my brother's home to spend the day with his wife Beth. She was a great help for me seeing as she was a nurse and could explain some of the medical terms in simpler terms.

The operation seemed endless. He was put into ICU after surgery. The doctors took me inside a tiny sterile office, sat down and began going over the surgery with me. I remembered being so cold in there, almost in shock. There was no mincing words; they were straightforward and blunt. On a scale of compassion, one being the coldest and ten the warmest, I gave them a one! He had a cancerous tumour, and he would undergo at least six weeks of cobalt treatments. They saved the best for last: They felt they got it all. What was I supposed to do when I heard that? Stand up and clap!? Basically, they finished with a have yourself a nice day. They didn't want me to tell Daniel that it was cancerous until he was stronger. These doctors have miracle hands but cold hearts. They were speaking, but I wasn't listening. Their words were muffled and distant. Their sterile white coats would fade in and out. I wasn't expecting such heart-wrenching news. My entire body was numb. I remembered I peeked my head out the door and saw Daniel lying there so peacefully. A huge lump popped into my throat. I didn't know whether to scream, cry or run away from the situation. You hear the word cancer, and you see your life being flushed down a toilet bowl. It's like your body goes into a freezer mode. I walked over to his bedside and held his hand.

He immediately woke up, gave me a big smile and said, "I'm hungry." I gave him a hug of a lifetime. He kept asking me, "Is it cancerous?" At that moment, I told him they didn't know yet, that they had to send it off to the lab. I hated not telling him, but apparently it was for his own good at the time. Both sides of the family were devastated. The word flew through the military like a wildfire out of control. I had received calls right across Canada. Everybody admired Daniel, not only for his sick sense of humour, but also for his outstanding flying abilities. Patrick and Beth opened their home to the family seeing as it was close to the hospital.

A couple of days had passed, and Daniel was doing extremely well. The swelling had gone down, his balance had improved, and he was eating better. The morning the doctor told Daniel that his tumour was cancerous, he broke down and cried. My god, to see a big, strong man bawling his eyes out was wrenching to the soul. I held him tightly and told him we would get through it one way or another. I looked him right in the eyes and kept assuring him everything would be all right. We had to be strong. I had a million questions swirling around in my head. I really didn't know where to turn. I felt like someone dropped me in the middle of the desert and told me to find my way back home. He was released from the QE11 one week after surgery and was admitted to the Stadacona Military hospital until he had more strength and stability. I spent numerous hours with him, bathing him.

Once he was discharged, I moved him into the guest room at my parents' home. The painful ordeal put everybody's stress at an all new high. His treatments were to commence the following week. It was awfully tiring, and some days everything seemed hopeless. I felt helpless inside. His treatments were at the Dixon Building, located in Halifax. What a depressing place! It is the cancer treatment centre for all of the local hospitals. They marked his head, neck and throat with red and black X's. Within the second week of treatment, he lost all of his hair. He developed the "moon face." My handsome husband was no more.

One morning, Mom and I were standing at the kitchen sink. Daniel came up behind me and tapped me on the shoulder. I turned around to see a monster looking at me. He had half of his gorgeous curly hair in his hands. He started to laugh, but I couldn't see any humour in that. I guess the tiredness had got the best of me. That's one thing he kept the entire time was his great sense of humour. I, on the other hand, found nothing funny about any of it. I guess it was his way of coping with all that bullshit.

I was always glad to see Friday afternoon arrive. It meant no hospitals or dropping or picking up children for a couple of days. It was quality time to spend with Daniel and my family. During the weekdays, I never had much time to myself. My life was put on the back burner. There were days I would be sick to my stomach and dizzy due to lack of sleep. I was worn to the bone. There were people constantly dropping in to see how things were going and to help out with food. Saturday nights were the night to forget and try to have a little bit of fun. It was my night not to worry about anything. We would normally play poker for small amounts of money. We had to find a drink that Daniel could enjoy. He used to enjoy rum and coke, but the treatments burnt his esophagus so badly that he couldn't tolerate the pain. If he ate food that was too hot, too cold or too acidic, he would literally fall to the floor and roll in pain. "All right! No more bananas!" he'd say. After several attempts, I finally came up with a drink I thought he'd be fine with: Kahlua and milk. When he took his first mouthful of it, he started to sing, "I'm in heaven, I'm in heaven! Yes, yes, yes!" I personally think he selected the wrong wording, especially at that time in his life.

Since his treatments were killing his immune system, Daniel would catch every little virus that was around. Some days he would be so weak. I once watched him crawl to the bathroom. He couldn't get up. One evening, I saw Daniel crying in the living room. Alexandria had come to him with open arms to be picked up, and he was so weak he couldn't lift her. "I can't even hold my own daughter!" He cried to me.

Every day turned into a new challenge. There was little or no relief in sight! My day started with a ball of fire up my butt. I got up first so I could get myself showered and dressed before the daily madness would unfold. Between getting Adam ready for school, feeding Alexandria and getting Daniel ready for the long journey to the hospital, it didn't leave much time to enjoy a cup of coffee. Even though there were days I was about to drop dead in my tracks, I could never cancel one of Daniel's cobalt treatments. That was priority one! After his daily treatment, he was exhausted. My evenings consisted of laundry, children's homework and preparing for the next turmoil-filled day. I was a bag of nerves running on two legs.

Alexandria had developed an acute ear infection. After several bottles of antibiotics, nothing seemed to help. I had made an appointment with a specialist at the IWK. The doctor informed me that she would need tubes put into her ears at once. "Great, just what I needed!" Between Daniel's radiation treatments and her ears, I was fit to be tied! *Who else wants to chew a piece of skin off my butt?* To me, it was just another helping of shit thrown on my plate. The pleasures and joy of normal living were gone. I often wondered if I would ever see any light at the end of the tunnel. I had to be so strong all the time. I could never let my guard down. I arrived home from the hospital to find a message that Daniel's parents were flying down to see how he was recuperating. Daniel's mother had life-threatening cancer many years ago, and his younger brother also had cancer but wasn't so fortunate to survive. Cancer was quite prevalent in his family.

During the week, I used to give him a drink called Barley Green. It looked disgusting and tasted just as bad, but apparently it was supposed to fill the body full of good stuff to fight off cancer. I remember Daniel almost vomited when he would inhale that horrible stuff. I do think there was some truth in it though.

Daniel had to continue taking steroids even after surgery and through his treatments. It was to keep any fluids from building up around the scar tissue on his brain. Daniel was a strong and determined man. He wanted to get better and fast. Oftentimes he felt he was a burden to me. Within a couple of weeks, he began to walk better. His balance was improving. In general, his health was slowly but surely improving.

Before we left for the hospital one morning, he told me to pack an overnight bag. He had it prearranged for my parents to take care of the kids that night. He had made reservations at the Sheraton Hotel for a romantic evening. Before checking in, he had to have his checkup with the military doctor at Stadacona Hospital. Once the doctor saw how well Daniel was walking, he told him to stop taking the steroids cold turkey, without consulting with any of the other specialists! After his visit, we went to a nice café on Spring Garden Road, and afterwards we took a nice walk in the Public Gardens. Stopping cold turkey is not common practice when you are dealing with this drug. Steroids should be weaned off slowly, usually by twenty-five milligrams at a time. Within hours, Daniel began swaying back and forth, the back of his head swelled, and he became very dizzy. I managed to get him back into the truck. I took him immediately to the Victoria General

Hospital. He couldn't stand up. They wheeled him in, and within minutes, the head radiologist was at his side. I informed him that the Stadacona Military hospital told Daniel to stop taking the steroids. He was appalled. "Why would they do such a stupid thing? That is not proper procedure!" They kept Daniel in the hospital until the swelling was down and he could walk to some degree. By the time we arrived at the hotel, he was worn out.

The next afternoon, his parents had arrived. My heart went out to these people. They had already been through so much in their lives, and now this. We had arranged for them to stay with my parents, but that was short lived, as things got a little too hairy. For one thing, there wasn't the room to accommodate all these people. Each day, the walls were closing in. We were all on each other's nerves. It was the conflicting personalities that became hard to deal with. I already had enough on my plate without having to worry about the damn adults. There were times I felt like screaming at the top of my lungs, "For Christ's sake, *get over it*!"

As if that wasn't enough, Daniel decided to buy Adam a puppy dog. Daniel was convinced he was going to die, and in his heart, he thought every little boy should own a dog. I was too exhausted to argue with him. Give me a break people! Just picture this scenario: four elders, two up-tight kids, a sick husband, a strung out Tasmanian, and a puppy who pissed on every thing in sight all living in a two-bedroom bungalow with only one bathroom. Something had to give!

To give myself some sanity, the first thing I had to do was move his parents into a hotel. The puppy was next on my list. I was tired and sick to death of hospitals. When would this nightmare ever end? Finally, the treatments were over, and with a lot of will power and love, he managed to get on his feet rather quickly. The time had come for us to fly back to Gander. Even though it was a sad day, I personally was somewhat relieved.

When we arrived back at our house, it was a bittersweet moment. We had been gone for two and half months. As I walked by the refrigerator door, I eyed the newspaper clippings of my grand opening, a day that never happened. Yogo, the cat, was sure glad to see us. She leapt into Adam's arms and started purring right away. She gained about ten pounds. The treatments were just the beginning of that long battle. It was a sad return. I sat at the dining room table looking at what could have been a successful business. My business had gone down the tubes. It never had a chance! Goodbye house and investment! I couldn't worry about those things that were financial at that point, though. I was dealing with a much bigger issue—Daniel's health. One month later, we were posted to Halifax.

We moved into a PMQ (Private Military Quarters). We had lost all of our savings and RRSPs with the business, and Daniel's salary was reduced to general officer pay. We were broke. The quarters were very small and old. I think the last upgrade had been over forty years prior. The only thing that was good about the situation was that it kept a roof over our heads. Daniel started his new job at the Maritime Operation Centre in Halifax as a duty officer. It was shift work, and didn't he hate it! He was never meant to fly a desk. But for the time being, he had no choice but to take it. At least he still had a job. His main objective was to get well enough to return to flying. His hair began to grow back great. He lost his moon face and began to feel good about himself. Now all we needed was money. I needed to find a job and fast.

TEN

My brother Mark was building a new eighteen-hole golf course and was looking for labourers and employees to work for him. Even though Daniel's father was retired, he wanted to come down not only to work on the course, but also to spend time with his son. His mother was leery to leave British Columbia because their two daughters were there, and their young son, who had died of cancer a few years ago, was buried there. I totally understood how she felt. It was brave of her to leave not only her surroundings but her family and memories. They thought the change would be a breath of fresh air for them. At first I have to say I was a little skeptical of having them live with us since they really never accepted me as their daughter-in-law. Daniel's mom was a strict Roman Catholic, and I was a divorced woman with a kid and, to top it off, Baptist. Even though her religious views were old-fashioned, I still wanted to respect them. They didn't know anybody or the area where we lived, so we offered them a room in our home.

It was quite cozy at times in the jam-packed two-bedroom sardine can with six people and, soon to add to the confusion, another cat. I must have liked self-abuse. We converted our dining room into a bedroom. We sold off the set and purchased a double bed and dresser. His father went to work for the golf course. He was a farmer most of his life, and the thought of working again in the outdoors and with machinery pleased him greatly. He was right back into his realm. Two women in the same kitchen is not a good thing; it's like mixing baking soda with vinegar. At first, his mom and I didn't quite see eye to eye, but in time, we grew to get along better. Thank god Daniel worked shifts. He was around a lot to help out around the house. Since Daniel had left home early in his life, he didn't get to spend a lot of time with his father in his early adult years, so he certainly loved having his father around. There was so much laughter and kidding around in our home. Daniel is a bit like his Dad—they both have a sick but witty and dry sense of humour. There was one particular night that Daniel and his dad sat around the kitchen table getting pissed and talking about the days of yore on the farm. I guess it was a soul cleanser for the both of them. Of course, these actions really pissed off his mom!

Mealtime was quite an interesting event. Our tiny kitchen wasn't equipped for a large family. You could hardly open the fridge door without hitting the stove or a chair. One Saturday night, I had made some homemade beans in the pressure cooker. Between Alexandria tugging at my leg, Daniel and his parents speaking French behind me and the television blasting in my ear, I couldn't hear the pressure cooker dancing on the stove. It wasn't long before every one of us was covered in beans. There was complete silence as we stood there like beanpoles, dripping in brown gook. Finally, Daniel began to laugh to lighten up the situation. The lid had exploded, the beans hit the ceiling, and there was no place else for those beans to go but down. They were so hot and sticky. "What a mess!" Alexandria was hilarious. She sat her butt down right in the middle of the floor and started grabbing handfuls of beans off the floor and shoving them down her throat. It took the whole evening to clean up that mess.

I would often feed the kids first to make room for the adults. His mom tried to get me hooked on the soap opera *General Hospital*, but for only a short time! I had too many things going on in my life to start watching these depressing piano key-mouthed anorexic women sleeping with every Tom, Dick and Harry in town. And the most disturbing thing was they were getting paid good money for it.

The golf course was coming along great. Some of the fairways were starting to take shape. Banks were a little leery in loaning great amounts of money to golf courses, so the owners decided to have shareholders. In order to do this, they had to hire a licensed broker to sell these investments. The shares were a little pricey, but they were a really good investment. Once you purchased the share, you were a lifetime member of the course. If enough memberships were sold, it would generate enough revenue to complete the course. I needed a job, so they hired me on as a sales representative. I went out and bought myself an old secondhand car to get me there and back. Since I was working all the time, I placed Alexandria into a day care centre.

At first, Daniel's mom took care of her for me, but Alexandria had become bored. She needed little kids her own age to play with, so I put her into a day care close to home. The first day I walked into the office, I was introduced to the broker. He immediately reminded me of a slimy little weasel. I detected something from him right away. While we were out busting our butts off, drumming up business for the golf course, he'd be sitting in his posh leather chair working on his own business. We had names picked out for him like "bonehead," "prick," and "weasel."

Things finally seemed to be turning around for us. I was working long days and countless hours to promote and sell these memberships throughout Metro. Sometimes it was a little difficult convincing the public on an unfinished product. I put my heart and soul into that job; after all, I was a leading sales representative. The only drawback with that job was that there was little cash flow. I was paying for my car and day care expenses through my Visa card. Finally, after a few months, the golf course gave me some money, but I was so over my head in debt by then it just basically scratched the surface. I continued on plugging at it, hoping the next cheque would be better and not so long coming.

In front of the golf course, there were sixteen acres of land up for sale overlooking the ocean. I thought if I could find enough money to purchase it, I could put a summer resort adjacent to the course. After numerous meetings with the bank, I was finally convinced it was a great idea. There were several snags along the way. Besides working with the golf course, I was doing extensive research with major hotels throughout Canada and the United States, with prominent resorts and government programs to get funding for the project. I had to hire road engineers and surveyors to put a proper road plan in motion to please Department of Transportation. Even though the road would never be implemented, the county insisted the plans be properly drawn up and put into their files. It sounded like a money scam to me, but what could I do? I was dealing with the government. All they are is a bunch of legalized mafia.

These guys weren't cheap either. There was more money going out the back door. In my heart, I thought it was really going to work. I was burning the candle on both ends. Money was getting pretty scarce. The bills were piling up, and tension between all of us was mounting. The government took months and months to meet with me. I'd receive letters regarding the latest developments on their end. I phoned them so many times, it basically got down to harassment. The final straw was when I had to come up with a large amount of money to also invest my share into the project. At that point, my financial means were burnt to a pulp.

A couple of months passed, and the stress level was boiling on the home front. Between work, kids, money problems and lack of breathing room, someone or something was soon going to burst. It's not that we all didn't get along. It was the lack of space and the worry about money all the time! There were days I would come home from work, and before going into the kitchen, I would go down into the basement, stick my head into the dryer and scream. I would look up at the ceiling saying, "What did I ever do to you to piss you off so badly?" We moved Daniel's parents into a lovely apartment close to the golf course, but over time, his mom was getting depressed and homesick. She loved Alexandria and Daniel immensely, but that wasn't enough. She started missing her daughters a lot, plus she was stuck in an apartment all day by herself, lamenting about the past. It wasn't long that we were packing them up and sending them back to British Columbia. There were no hard feelings. It was sad to see them go. I was glad that Daniel had managed to spend a lot of time with his dad.

The golf course had shed some light on the situation. They called me at home and told me they finally received a huge sum of money. I was so happy I could finally pay off some bills. Daniel went out and bought a bottle of wine to celebrate. I ordered in a pizza and told the kids we could eat in the living room that night. That was a rarity in our home. I could see a light at the end of the tunnel, at last! I could hardly wait to get to work the next day. I just got my foot out the front door that morning, and the phone rang. I had a gut feeling it was going to be bad news. It was my brother Mark telling me not to go to the office that day. The office had been shut down. Apparently, the owners of the golf course gave the check to the manager the night before in good faith. He was suppose to distribute the money evenly among the employees the next morning, me being one of the employees. The dishonest little prick took the money and ran to the United States. I was beginning to develop a phone phobia! I met Mark at a coffee shop close to the closed-down office. There were hurricane winds and rain coming down in buckets as we sat in the coffee shop with both of our heads hanging into our shoulders. He knew I had worked very hard for the course and was saddened to tell me the news. I couldn't get mad at him since I knew it wasn't his fault. It was that untrustworthy little weasel. I swore to myself if I ever ran into that little low-life bastard that, without any hesitation, I'd kick him square in the nuts, and while he was down, I'd kick him again in the face. It certainly left me in a very difficult situation. I had no one to fall back on. I had debts up my ass, and if I was to look at another hotdog, I was going to puke. Really, with the luck I had been having, I should have expected it. Since the money was gone, I would never see a cent of what I had earned. It was only ten in the morning, and my plate was already full of spoiled food.

I left the shop to get soaked getting to my car. As I was turning the key, I kept repeating to myself, *Why, Why, Why?* and started to cry relentlessly. I was five minutes from the bridge when my car starting acting up. Between the rain beating in on the window and the smoke pouring out from the hood, I couldn't see two feet in front of me. The car took one last jump and died. *Great, now what do I do?* I had no money, my credit card was maxed out, and I was ten miles from home. I bit the bullet and walked to a garage. Oh to own a cell phone! I was soaked to the bone and shaking. The garage attendant took pity on me and poured me a hot cup of cocoa. I very nicely asked him if I could use his phone. My hands shook so badly I spilled the cocoa all over my hands and the phone. I knew there was no point in calling Daniel. He had no money either. I eventually got a hold of Dad for help. He gave the attendant his Visa number over the phone. I was so embarrassed, but at that point, being embarrassed was nothing for me to handle.

I had to wait an hour or more for the tow truck. I sat in this dirty chair that reeked of oil and gas, staring out the window. I had visualized that day to be totally different. *What did I ever do to deserve such continual misery?* As I watched the rain pouring down, I had a million thoughts going through my brain: the development, golf course, banks, Daniel, money, bills…the list kept growing and turning in my head and wouldn't stop. The tow truck picked up my wreck of a car, dropped it off at a salvage yard and drove me home. It wasn't a customary thing for me to pull out the bottle at two thirty in the afternoon, but at that point, I didn't give a shit. I poured myself a strong triple with no ice or mix and downed it.

I called Daniel to pick Alexandria up at the day care. I didn't dare show my face there that day. They thought they were getting paid. Little did they know! It wasn't long before they were home. Daniel was beaming with excitement. He couldn't wait to see my cheque. I greeted him at the door with a long, saddened face. He didn't even have to open his mouth. He knew it was once again bad news. I explained to him what happened over dinner. There was no one jumping for glee that evening in our house. He was so upset and pissed off with essentially everything, he took some of the grocery money and went out to buy a bottle of whiskey. He looked at me and said, "What do we have to lose? Tomorrow's Saturday. Let's put it behind us for tonight; the hell with it!"

That slime ball manager has still never been located. He left a lot of people penniless, miserable and hurt. As for my property, since my finances had gone to he dogs and were shit out onto every sidewalk in Metro, I had no other choice but to sell it. The money I made off of it barely paid the bills off. I ended up selling my car for parts. As far as I know, I never did square off with the day care. I honestly think they felt sorry for me. Another dive into the empty pool!

Daniel's health was continually on my mind. It was eating at me inch by inch. The worry of his cancer returning was troublesome. For the first couple of months after his surgery, my guts were always in a knot. It was always nagging at the back of my head. I knew he wouldn't be out of the woods for several years. We were told that for the first year after the surgery, he would need a CAT Scan every three months, for the second year every six months, and for the third year once a year, and finally, the fifth year was supposed to be the last. My goal was only to get him back to one hundred percent so he could return flying again. I spent my days researching his type of cancer, finding out what were the best foods for it, developing an exercise regiment, and figuring out what vitamins and minerals he should be taking. This cancer thing was new to me. The only time I could remember hearing the word "cancer" as a child was when my grandfather died of it. When anyone died back then, we never heard how or what happened. It was pretty cut and dry—they just got sick and died. There was never a big fuss over it either. I remember the wakes being pretty wild. My brothers and I would sit on the steps leading down into the dining room listening and watching them drink and talk about the good times they all had with the deceased. My family rarely got sick unless it was from an occasional hangover!

One of my passions in life is messing around with food. I think I missed my calling in life. Playing with different recipes and creating dishes was my escape from reality. When I used to get really stressed out with Daniel's situation or the kids getting on my nerves, I would head for the kitchen. I'd pour myself a glass of wine and bury all of my frustrations and worries by kneading them out into the dough. Sometimes the dough would be a little tough—it would depend on how stressed out I was that day. Making bread was my favourite. The kitchen was and still is my sanctuary. Little did I know at the time I would be spending the next six years of my life in the kitchen, being a mom, taking care of the house and Daniel's health. As each year went by, he became stronger and stronger. Daniel would spend the next six years working his way from Maritime Operation Centre to the Base Commander's Executive Assistant, all of which entitled him to fly a only a desk—or, as he called it—flying the mahogany bomber.

Three years after his operation, Daniel was not only capable, but also anxious to go back flying. He started inquiring and writing letters to headquarters in Ottawa to find out how to go about it. The wood on his desk was wearing thin, and so was his patience. He was getting itchy feet. He had his pilot's license before he had driven a car when he was seventeen years old. Flying was one of Daniel's passions. Flying to him was not only his dream, but it also gave him a sense of freedom, and we can all use a bit of that from time to time! He started inquiring on how to approach the topic with the military. The meetings, phone calls, letters and waiting were lengthy and extremely time-consuming. The wheels started to turn. The military began setting up medical appointments with specialists here in Halifax. Daniel had gone through so much extensive testing in Halifax and Toronto that he was getting sick to death with them. He gave up counting how many times they made him stand on one leg to touch his nose with his fingers.

It was around the third year of his recovery when the military scheduled him to go to Toronto to see some specialists. After examining him, they asked him to talk to doctors that were attending a Flight Surgeon Course, and Daniel agreed. They asked him to sit in the middle of the room where he could be observed by at least twenty white coats, who were sitting in a circle. They started asking him questions about his cancer, which he was glad to answer to help in future cases. Some of the doctors would approach him to examine his eyes, scar, and to once again do the one-legged stand. He was so humiliated, he felt he was being treated like a guinea pig. Daniel started putting his feelers out looking for another job. He started applying to everything from the Coast Guard to oil refineries throughout Canada.

The military held numerous boards trying to justify why he shouldn't return to flying. They were very apprehensive to put him back into the cockpit. They had no precedents of pilots returning to flying status after having a brain tumour. They had to be very careful in their judgement calls since they had nothing to base their decisions on. Therefore, they kept rejecting him, even though all of his tests he took in Canada were normal. They finally decided to send him to Brooks Air Force Base, located in San Antonio, Texas, for extensive testing. They specialized in aircrew who lost their category over medical or physiological reasons. He was tested medically, physically and physiologically. On one of the tests, he had to stand up on a platform that would tilt back and forth while he was blindfolded so they could test his balance. As part of his psychiatric evaluation, he was given quotes that he had to explain, such as, "People who live in glass houses should not throw stones." On the last day, he had an appointment with a US Air Force psychiatrist, who was very interested in knowing how he had coped with cancer, family, etcetera. He replied, "You know, Maj, there are a couple of things that have affected me."

The doctor looked at him with deep concern and asked, "What are your concerns, Daniel?" Daniel rubbed his finger up and down his scar.

"Well, I used to speak Spanish, but that was in the part of my brain that was removed, and on top of it, I now have a French accent!"

The psychiatrist gave him a strange look and said, "Whoa! You've got some sick sense of humour!"

Daniel replied, "Well, you have to!" All of the doctors in Canada and in the United States always remarked on his sense of humour and wit throughout the whole ordeal. It sometimes can be the best medicine money can't buy. You could say that he survived cancer with flying colours! They were so optimistic and impressed with Daniel's health and condition that they faxed all the reports immediately to the Shearwater doctor even before he arrived back to Halifax.

The military had no choice but to give him back his category. They offered him another flying tour in Gander, Newfoundland. His category was classified as with or as a co-pilot, which meant he had to fly in crew aircrafts. It took a total of six years from beginning to end to make it happen, but with his determination and willpower, he did it. When he received his posting message in late spring of that year, he was the happiest person I had ever seen. Meanwhile, he had received a phone call from an oil company in Alberta. They were sending a representative down to Halifax to do some interviewing of a couple of candidates they had for the position of senior pilot. It was an exciting flying position. He would fly the CEOs from different oil companies throughout the prairies. He would be flying the brass around on civvie street instead of the military.

He didn't know which way to turn. If he were to work for them, he would not only lose his seniority but his pension as well. Daniel decided he really had nothing to lose and went on to the interview. Once the oil company had the opportunity to meet with him, they were quite impressed not only with his flying experience, but also with his credentials, which were outstanding. Within a week, Daniel heard back from them. The offer was so overwhelming that he had to accept it. The company bought out his pension from the military. He graciously put in his release to the military. It was a huge lifetime change for all of us, associating with people on civvie street. He first beat brain cancer and then was able to go back flying. Now that's incredible! It was one hell of an accomplishment. Daniel is the only military or commercial pilot in North America to ever go back to flying who had such a life-threatening disease. It was certainly one of the most difficult times we ever had to go through.

We had been to hell and back. Between sickness, financial problems and being bounced around like a sac of potatoes, everything seemed to be on the up and up for a change. But something had changed within me while going through the turmoil. There was something missing inside of me. I loved Daniel so much but in a different way. It wasn't the type of love that I should have had. The best way to describe the feeling was that he was a best friend. That was it! I spent so much time worrying and taking care of him over the years, I became emotionally numb. The six years of downhill misery certainly did a toll on our marriage. I kept thinking, *Where's my life?* How selfish was I to think like that? I thought time would make those feelings go away. Our marriage was lacking romance and needed to be embellished. It wasn't so much Daniel, it was more me. I was the guilty party. He still enjoyed the romantic meals and loved to wine and dine me at expensive restaurants. I was the one who needed a kick in the ass. We had gone through so much in the past, you would think our love would have grown deeper and more intense. I felt time would heal all.

ELEVEN

Once the great news was absorbed, we had to get a grip on reality and start planning our trip. We decided to drive instead of flying. We had a beautiful cat named Yuppie. At the time, the trip would have been too long for her, so we gave her to a neighbor. It was heart-wrenching, but again, at the time, it seemed the right thing to do. The kids cried for days over that poor decision. I should have never done that to the kids. To my understanding, Yuppie is still alive today. God, the stupid things I did in my life. There were times I wish I would have slapped myself across the face before making a final decision on things. The drive was long but fun. It was the facelift I needed. It was around a twenty-five hundred mile trip. The kids had a ball. We always made sure we stayed in a hotel that had a pool. We spared no expense. It was our paid vacation, and we enjoyed every minute of it.

There were actually moments I was at peace with myself. Not many but a few. It's funny, peace of mind is a difficult thing to obtain and hang on to. I had experienced through my travels in life that when I had a moment of peace of mind, someone was right behind me to steal it away. There were times when the bottle and me became good friends. It was one way I could cope with some scary situations I wanted to forget about. I'd grab that bottle with a vengeance. *Come here, baby, let's suck you back so life can be a better place*. Isn't that a demented way of thinking? As awful as it sounds, it had its good moments. We always made sure we left the hotel early in the morning so we could have a fun-filled afternoon at the next stop. When we arrived in Quebec City, we met up with Daniel's best friends. Years ago, they were on the same flying course. We had a typical lunch in Old Quebec—lots of wine, bread and cheese. There is one particular dish that I can only get in Quebec, which is fondue parmesan. It is to die for! Every mouthful you shove down your throat is an ounce of fat on your butt, but it's worth every bit of it. Old Quebec is one of my favorite spots to visit. It is so unique! The boys spent the afternoon drinking beer and sharing memories of being on flying training together. The kids and I went shopping. There's one thing I can't stand, and that's mimes. The area we were shopping had one on each corner. They are so eerie and creepy! There was one mime who leapt in front of me. He scared the living crap out of me. It was a good thing there were lots of kids around, or I would have floored the mindless creep.

The day we arrived, it was so god awful hot. It was such a big ugly city. Thank god we bought our house in the suburbs. It was about a twenty-minute drive outside of the city. It was a peaceful, quiet, family town called Creek Well. Someone was thinking when they developed that town—they planted trees along the streets and behind the houses, and there was a beautiful man-made park right smack in the middle of the town. When we were driving into our street, there wasn't one green lawn. They were all burnt up to hell and flat! You could see for miles and miles. Our house was nestled in beautiful trees in front of a small man-made lake. As soon as I stepped out of the car, there was a lady standing in front of me with a jug of lemonade. Talk about friendly! I said to her, "Next time, I would appreciate a cold beer!" and started to laugh. She didn't take to kindly to that remark. I quickly said, "I was just kidding." That's the last thing I needed was to have a bad reputation right off the bat. God, I hoped she wasn't an example of the rest of women in town. Christ! Just what I need! We didn't have to worry about food or drinks the entire day. The neighbors had that all taken care of. They wanted to know all about us immediately. After the moving truck pulled out, we decided to take a drive around town. It had everything you wanted and more. I took in the surroundings—everything was so perfect. The properties were kept almost flawless. It was like driving through Pleasantville.

The kids were not long making new friends. I was always amazed by how quickly kids can make friends and adapt so fast to a new environment. On the other hand, the adults are the anti-social species. We would rather backstab and cause fights among one another. Before I knew it, the kids were having sleepovers, and we were having barbeques with our nosy neighbors. The gossip in that town was incredible. The word "private" was not in their vocabulary. Christ, the only thing missing seemed to be the white picket fence. Everybody liked everyone. Everyone had a smile permanently painted on their faces. It did not take long to get to know most of the town folks. They made it easy to know them. There was not a lot of opportunity for women to work, and the ones that were lucky enough to land a job were quite fortunate.

The town consisted of a small mall, a city hall—which was run by an obnoxious overweight mayor—and of course, the one and only general store. But just ten minutes outside of town was the huge oil refinery that employed over a thousand men. That is where Daniel would be doing most of his flying. That's what was keeping that lovely little haven afloat. My lovely nosy neighbor informed me about the town's Ladies' Club. It was called, Creek Well's Ladies' Best. These women took that club quite seriously. They had a president, secretary and a bookkeeper. Every now and then, I had to check the calendar to see what year I was living in because it appeared that I was re-living the fifties and sixties. Since I was new in town, I had received a written invitation to attend one of their meetings. At first I declined. I could not see myself socializing with a bunch of women. That would put me in the same category as an old woman rocking and knitting on the front porch, sipping on a cup of tea. I was more the type to lie back in a hammock sucking back on a can of cold beer. Male conversation and habits were more my style. But as time went on, I realized that if you were not a part of the club, you were left out of everything in the town. Also, curiosity did get the best of me.

When I walked in the door, I was the center of attraction. The younger women greeted me with handshakes and the elder with hugs. They gave me the red carpet welcome. I kept my guard up the entire evening. Initially, I found it to be quite amusing. All the ladies were dressed in beautiful suits and chatting about god knows what. When the president stood up and asked everyone to be seated, in a very robotic way, each person sat immediately. My good judgment told me to sit also. The president was a very poised lady but a tad nervous. Every now and then, her voice would crack.

There was something about her that I could not quite put my finger on it. While she was reading the minutes, she kept one eye on her paper and one on me. I knew she was dying to talk to me, being the new gal in town and all. After the meeting, the ladies served tea and coffee. I was bombarded with questions. I met each one of them individually. There wasn't much I didn't know when I left the hall that evening. The president came up to me and cordially introduced herself. Her handshake was cold and clammy. It gave me the sensation of shaking hands with a corpse! A quick chill ran up my back. Her conversation was short! She lit up with a nicotine smile and told me she had another appointment to attend to that evening. Christ, I looked at my watch, and it was ten thirty at night. *Where in hell do you go in a small town like this at this hour?* The only thing I knew that was open was the local sleaze joint or the hotel lounge. Anyway, that was her business.

I was in town the next day doing a few errands and noticed her in the general store. I went over to her to say hello. She immediately looked side to side and quickly flew out the door. Her purse caught onto the chip rack, which collapsed and spewed chips all over the floor. She said nervously, tugging at her purse, "That damn purse!" Everyone in the store froze in their tracks while she made a total butt out of herself. *What a strange lady!* Her word was powerful at these meetings. When she spoke, they listened! Once the president said her good evenings, welcomes and the latest town news, the floor was opened for discussion. Just picture a group of women all sitting around drinking tea and coffee trying to come up with a new concoction for the month. That just seemed too anal for me, but what else is there to do in a small town?

The events were quite elaborate at times. There was never a detail unnoticed. The president asked me at one of the meetings to offer any suggestions for an event. The first thing that popped into my mind was, "Let's have a dirty night." She didn't quite know what that meant, so she asked me stand up and explain it the other ladies. "We could all get together at one of our homes, bring a bunch of junk food and booze, hire a couple of male strippers and enjoy!" The more I said, the more their mouths remained open. *Well that didn't go over to good!* Truth be known, half of them would have totally enjoyed it! Bunch of up-tight prisses! They sure didn't know what they were missing out on in life. They were appalled that I could think of something so disgusting. The president never asked me again. That was one way to be ignored! They discovered my demented sense of humor very quickly and often ignored it. Needless to say, I really didn't give a damn. There was one rule they had, and that was they couldn't kick you out of the group unless you became rude or uncontrollable. As time went on, some of them found my foolishness and my sick way of thinking rather refreshing. I added a little spunk and excitement to the group.

I met one particular lady. Her name was Melanie Crooks. We clicked almost instantly. We had a lot in common. She had basically the same feelings toward the group as I did. She also thought there was something unusual about the president too. One way or another, we were going to find out. We hung out together getting groceries and swimming in her pool. Her pool was a great asset to have with kids, especially when it was thirty-five degrees outside. She lived three doors down from me. My kids had already discovered her kids and, of course, the pool. She had two young girls and an older boy. Melanie's husband worked in the oil refinery as well. He was one of the top executives. Every time I would go over to Melanie's, she had on an apron. I hadn't seen one of those since I was a little girl. There you go, like I said before, all I needed was the white picket fence, and life would be one rosy place to be in. But that blindfolded bitch was about to walk right into a bushel of thorns and didn't even know it.

The oil refinery wanted Daniel to go to Victoria, British Columbia, on a safety course for a couple of months. That was a great opportunity for him to visit his family for a while. Melanie's husband was also going but not on a course. He had to attend a convention. Since Daniel was flying him out there, they had the opportunity to get to know one another. He traveled quite extensively throughout North America. There were a lot of Friday and Saturday nights we would join up at either place and enjoy a bottle of wine around the pool. Over time, we became best friends. We became the shit disturbers at the Club. It was so bad that when I went into town without her, they would wonder where she was. You could hear the murmurs as they were shrugging their shoulders at me. "Where's the other rotten half?"

Those prissy, anal creatures never fazed me one bit. I added spice to a boring pit! We had our daily walks around the still lake and confided our secrets in each other. Her pool became our hangout. Many a night, we'd sit on the side of the pool and get hammered. Halfway through the night, it was guaranteed we'd be in the pool, clothes and all. You'd think after a while, we would have had brains enough to put on our bathing suits before cracking open a bottle. Hell, that would have been too easy! Once the wine level was higher than our blood level, we would sneak over to our neighbors houses and peek into their windows. I know what you're thinking. It sounds like something a bunch of teenagers would do. You have to keep in mind that our husbands were both away a lot, and there wasn't a lot of activity in that town. It was amazing the stuff we saw inside of people's homes. We learned who walked around in just their underwear scratching their nuts, who who drank continually, and saw which husbands often put a good beating on their drunkard wives. We saw whose darling little angels smoke not just cigarettes in the basement but pot. It made going to church and community events exciting.

There were times in church I would spot one of the men playing pool in his underwear and burst right out laughing. Once I had everyone's attention, I would quickly bury my head into the hymn book. That wasn't such a perfect little town after all. We had to take a vow never to repeat anything we ever saw to anybody. The president of the group lived two streets over from us.

Melanie and I were drinking some wine and were trying to decide what to do that evening. We were trying to find out what was making the president of our club so jumpy and uptight. Once the bottle of wine was gone, we knew exactly what we were going to do. We got her older son to watch the kids for us. We headed over to the president's house. We knew her husband was away, so the likelihood of her being home was good. We had to go through the back way so no one could spot us. As it was, we looked like idiots. We giggled the whole way there. Her car wasn't in the driveway, but there were a couple of lights on. Very quietly, we crept up the back deck on all fours. My god, how stupid we must have looked. The drapes were drawn in the dining room window, so we couldn't see anything, but we could hear voices. I said to Melanie, "It sounds like the mayor!" We decided to move to the side of the house.

The window was too high up. I carefully and quietly took one of the garbage cans and supported it with my legs so Melanie could get up to have a look inside. Next thing I knew, Melanie was on top of me. Her eyes were bulging out of her head, and she could hardly speak. "What are you doing? get off of me!" I had to shake her.

She finally murmured and whispered into my ear, "The mayor is having sex with the president on the dining room floor." I had to see this for myself.

"Holy shit!" I couldn't believe my eyes. That innocent, snobby, bony-butt bitch was doing it with that fat-ass mayor. If nothing else, it certainly was entertaining! I lost my grip on the windowsill. I tried to hold on but lost my balance. On my way down, my fingernails scratched the windowsill by accident. I briefly thought I saw the president look directly at the window. When I hit ground, we leapt into the bushes. We hid there for a while to see if she was going to come outside. She finally came out with a robe wrapped around her bony body, but she didn't leave the deck. Thank god she didn't notice the garbage can was missing.

I had thorns digging up my butt and ants crawling up my legs. The mayor came out behind her and, bravely enough, wrapped his arms around her and kissed her neck, than caressed her breast. That guy had more guts than he showed! How repulsive! I suddenly had to pee really bad. My back teeth were starting to float. Finally, that horny old bastard left the deck to go home. He couldn't wait to suck back on a cigarette. I guess it was good for him! We quickly put the can back and ran through those woods with hot pee running down my leg. I got ahead of Melanie, and she yelled at me, "Don't you dare put your pissy butt into my pool, I'll kill you!" She didn't have to worry. By the time I got to her house, I reeked of pee! That was the least of my worries. My concern was if she got a glimpse of me that night. I would soon find out at the next Ladies' meeting.

There were a couple of reasons I didn't want to go, one being that Daniel was away and I thought it would only be a couples thing. And that's enough to bore anybody silly! In addition, I knew the mayor, our president and their spouses would be attending. Wasn't that going to be a pretty picture? But Melanie convinced me to go. We thought we'd go as a "couple," and plus it was something to do. Besides, we thought it might be quite amusing to see what happened that night. Curiosity got me again! All the bigwigs from the oil refinery and the town would be attending accept for Daniel and Melanie's husband. We were like the two widows on the street. That didn't bother me any—I was totally enjoying myself. Don't get me wrong, I certainly missed

Daniel dearly. It was just the break I needed from him. It was an annual event the community organized to raise money for the needy and the homeless. Since I was such a strong contributor for the cause, I had no other choice but to go.

I didn't have anything classy enough to wear. I had forgotten the last time I had gone to such a formal affair. I headed into town to check out the latest fashions. It was a pretty sad sight. It took all of ten minutes since there were only two dress stores in the mall, one being a secondhand store. There was one hair parlor with pictures of hairstyles half-taped to the wall. They were so old that the pictures had turned yellow. The event gave the town their annual financial boost, given that everybody with a name or money would be invited. The tickets alone were one hundred dollars apiece. I headed to the West Edmonton Mall. It was about a forty-five minute drive, long and flat, but it was worth it! I had to the prettiest one there that evening, regardless of if Daniel was there or not. The scenery was nothing to brag about—the odd shack and barn. You could see for miles. About halfway in, I spotted a beautiful snowy white owl perched on a pole. I laid on my horn as I drove by him to get him to fly away. When he took off, he was elegant. His wingspan had to be twenty feet wide. I thought to myself, *Okay, I had my nature moment for the day!* The West Edmonton mall is one of largest malls in Canada. It even has a huge sliding pool, an amusement park and three submarines. People often remarked that hey had more submarines than the Canadian Navy. It's mind-boggling, it is so massive. If you don't remember what door you came in through, you could actually get lost. I wore my visa out that day buying the finest cocktail on the rack. I bought a slinky, backless, black dress. It slithered onto my body like skin peeling off a snake's back. I must say I looked rather stunning in that dress. Next was a pair of shoes, a purse and earrings. I wasn't leaving one detail out. Vanity runs pretty deep into my bones! I always had to be the belle of the ball or stay home.

Since the town was lacking in beauty essentials, we decided to do our own hair, nails and makeup. We kept the kids busy with movies and pizza. We began the makeover late in the afternoon. My dining room was converted into a cosmetics shop. To add some flair to the afternoon, we cracked open a bottle of wine. The babysitter arrived, and we left for the grand event. We hired a cab, knowing we were going to bury our heads into a wine vat. You talk about fancy. The event was red carpet treatment from the front steps right through to the back of the ballroom. The ladies were given a long stem rose when entering the foray, followed by a pleasant sweaty handshake from the mayor. That hand shake made me a little queasy. I knew where his hands had been! That was enough to make anybody gag. When I walked into the ballroom, it resembled a penguin farm. I don't know how the women distinguished who their husbands were that evening other then by the color of their hair, or lack thereof. The ladies all had up-does and were dressed to the nines. I'd like to know how many girdles were bought at WalMart that day. I knew most of these women, and there was no way they had flat guts up until now. The flower arrangements were drop-dead gorgeous. The one floral shop in town must have done extremely well! I guess that's why I always saw the owner driving around in a Mercedes. He must have drooled when he got wind of a wedding or funeral.

The single ladies were escorted into the ballroom by a nice tight-butt hunk. They had to have brought these guys in from Edmonton because I never saw them around town before. And trust me, I would have noticed those pieces of meat! We entered into the ballroom through an arbor tastefully decorated with red and white roses, with lace intertwined through the wicker. There was a quartet playing sonatas in the far corner. Each table was layered in antique linen and topped with fine lace. The tall waiters pranced around with their trays lined with champagne, wine and hors d'oeuvres. Every CEO from every major business was there, and of course, so was the mayor. Basically, anybody who liked kissing butt or liked to be kissed was there. I knew I was totally out of my league, but what the hell. I could bullshit as well as the next guy! The food and booze were free, so I went with the flow and enjoyed every minute of it. I knew people who took advantage of that sort of shit every day.

The first priority was to grab a glass of wine and hook up with Melanie. As soon as we had walked in through the front doors, I lost her. My eyes were designed to detect tight butts. I could easily bounce a quarter off their butts. Just the thought of it put a tickle up my leg. Just because I was married didn't mean I couldn't look. It was time to have some fun. I eyed the mayor at the bar standing next to our saintly president. I went up to them and boldly shook their hands. I tried to keep a straight face, but it was hard. His smile resembled the crack in his fat butt. I had to cut the conversation short seeing as my sides were ready to burst with laughter. I knew now she didn't see me in the window that night. At least I knew I could put that to bed.

I squeezed my butt onto a stool and began talking to the bartender. I wasn't sitting for more than thirty seconds when this drop-dead gorgeous man pulled up a stool beside me. His teeth were so white, I could see my face in them. I sensed he was undressing me with his steel blue eyes. He introduced himself as Stephen Marlow, owner of a huge computer chain in Regina. Since he had been in town on business with the oil company, he had been invited to attend this prestigious event. As he was putting his glass up to his sensual lips, he asked me, "What is such a beautiful woman doing here without an escort? Some guy is quite likely to sweep you off your pretty little feet this evening!" He went on about his investments around the world and other activities he was involved with throughout Canada. He was certainly a worldly gentleman. It appeared he was very good friends with the mayor. Before I knew it, we were involved in a heavy conversation. I was grinning from one ear to the other. He was a breath of fresh air. I was Cinderella again. I had to snap out of it, and fast. Flirting with eyes and smiles is fine, but when the tingling started that was a different thing. I was just about to excuse myself when a bony finger jabbed into the back of my shoulder. I quickly turned around, and there stood a very refined, angle-faced lady.

She introduced herself as Mrs. Janet Marlow, her finger pointed directly at his nose as she said, "His wife, darling!" If looks could have killed, I would have dropped dead! She drilled a hole through my forehead with her piecing, shark-like eyes. I felt like I had run head-on into a shark! I could hear the words that were never spoken aloud, *Get your Barbie doll butt off that stool before I kick it out from under you!* My Cinderella bubble was blasted into orbit. I excused myself very quickly and headed back to safe territory.

Melanie met me at the dinner table. I was so infatuated by that man, I couldn't wait to fill her in. Once she saw who he was, her mouth dropped to the floor. She gave me one warning and that was, "Stay clear of him." He was way out of my league, and there had been several stories about him regarding past relationships with women. He was one of the biggest of the bigwigs in society. Everybody and their dog knew him, not only in Canada, but also in the United States. He was a very powerful man not only in society, but also within the business world. When Melanie said that, it rang a bell. I actually remembered reading an article on him dealing with computers a few months prior. I felt there was no harm done. It was just simple conversation and a little flirtation. She knew more about the guy than she was letting on. I wanted her to tell me everything she knew about him, but she refused. "There is a lot of stuff about that guy you don't want to know about," she told me. What's more, I wasn't to go near him again! She gave me a "fear" warning!

The meal was delicious. It consisted of seven courses with a variety of wines. What a fairy tale evening. There was a long, narrow table draped with the finest of linen with gold-plated settings. That, of course, was for the heavy brass in town. There were swarms of gorgeous flower arrangements throughout the dining room. The tiers of candles gave the room a soft ambience. Stephen and his wife were sitting at the head table. During the entire dinner, we had made eye contact. Melanie kept kicking me in the shins to stop it. I thought nothing of it at the time, just having a little innocent fun.

There were long-winded speeches and the typical boring political jokes that we all had to laugh at even though they were dry. After dinner, we all returned to the ballroom to indulge in more wine. I could hear soft talking throughout the room with the occasional out burst of laughter. In the background, the band was tuning up their instruments. There was a lot of money floating around in that room—more than I'd ever see in a lifetime! By the time the music started, I was half in the bag. No damn wonder—every time I'd turn around, there would be a waiter with a tray of drinks. Humans are funny; anything free we will take full advantage of, never mind the consequences!

I spotted Stephen at the bar sipping on a scotch and chatting with the CEOs from the oil company. He noticed me instantaneously. Melanie threw herself in front of me to break the beam of light coming from the bar. She grabbed me by the arm and lead me to the washroom. She warned me once again, "He is nothing but trouble!" She told me that he had had affairs in the past and told me to look at who he was still with. In fact, one woman he dumped tried to commit suicide. "Take a good look! Don't be stupid. Think about it!!" She gave me a hug and flew out the door. When I came out of the washroom, Stephen was standing right outside of the door. He certainly took me by surprise. I took a couple of steps back. He handed me a glass of wine and offered me to have a dance with him. He told me how beautiful I looked and said it certainly would have been a pleasure if I would have had one dance with him. If I had one brain cell that was functioning properly, I would have said "No, but thank you anyway." That would have been too easy. Between the booze and his radiant eyes, I couldn't refuse him.

The question that came to mind was, "What about his wife?" I strutted out on that dance floor like one brazen bitch. I stuck my head up proud and was glowing from one end to the other. On the other hand, his wife was fuming. I could smell the smoke! She either was used to the behavior, or she tolerated it. I mean, after all, the guy was filthy rich and powerful. She wasn't going to let one dance destroy what she had going for her. I had a feeling she had witnessed that kind of action before. We were both being a little bold. Of course, we were both under the influence of god knows how many glasses of wine. He was such a wonderful dancer. He had all the moves. He swung me around that ballroom like I was a butterfly.

The little game of flirtation was going a bit too far. I was beginning to get the evil stares from every female in the room. When the song ended, I thanked him and left the dance floor. Being as bold as I was, I just ignored the looks and kept right on smiling. Melanie grabbed me from behind and escorted me quickly outside. She was furious with me. I knew I would be the talk of the town the next day.

My recollection of that evening was totally innocent until the phone started ringing. Melanie and others refreshed my memory quite quickly. Needless to say, I was slightly hungover. I sat outside and on the steps for hours, feeling guilty as hell. I pondered if I should tell Daniel when he arrived or just let the whole thing pass. I dug deep down inside, trying to justify my actions the night before. I was beating myself to death over it. Then I realized it wasn't like I had slept with him or kissed him in public. It was one innocent dance with a lot of jealous bitches making a mountain out of a molehill. A lot of them wished they had the guts to have a dance with one of most prominent man in society. The problem was that it happened in a small town where everyone knew everyone's business, and they basically had nothing better to do. What threw me for a loop was when the president phoned me up and invited me over for tea. Tea wasn't exactly what I had in mind, but she was a butt and that was to be expected.

She greeted me very coldly. The conversation was to the point and brief. She wanted me to dismiss myself from the ladies' club. I was a disgrace and an embarrassment to the club. I apparently had made a fool out of myself and was no longer welcomed. Now there was the pot calling the kettle black! When I left her place, I was livid. "The gall! The nerve of that bitch!" She was going to have her day, and it was going to be good! The town gossiping and exaggerating stopped over the next couple of weeks. Trust me, they had their fun at it while it lasted. I couldn't stop having these feelings for that man. It was eating at me every day. I wondered if I would ever see him again. I thought the odds were pretty slim since we didn't travel in the same circles of life. The women throughout the town shunned me. They ostracized me in the stores, on the sidewalks and in church. Melanie still remained my friend, at least for the time being. She knew as much about the president as I did. I needed her support in the matter. She was my only witness, and I had to keep it that way.

TWELVE

Christmas was just around the corner, and Daniel was finally due home in a couple of days. I tried to keep my mind busy with decorating and baking. Of course, the kids were bouncing off the walls given that Christmas and their dad were coming. Daniel arrived with bags of gifts, special wines and kisses. He loved Christmas as much as I did.

The town had a huge, beautiful tree standing in the middle of the park. It took every available man and woman to decorate it. I, of course, wasn't asked to participate, but I volunteered anyway. I was a little nervous attending the event in fear of what some small-minded bitch might say to Daniel. I had to stop beating myself to death over the issue. Christ, it was only a dance! Everybody and their dog were there for the lighting up of the tree. When that tree lit up, you could see it for miles. Afterwards, the Ladies' Club served hot chocolate, "spiked" cider and donuts. Of course, when they served me, they made sure they spilled it all over my mitts. Small minds! All of the children received candy canes from the local staggering, scotch-breathed, drunk, infested Santa Claus. His cheeks were beet red and not because of the cold wind!

I swear that man carried a mickey in every pocket. I didn't think I had ever seen that man sober. He was also the town's Easter Bunny and birthday or party clown. He was quite versatile! The town personnel had the streets decorated with beautiful wreaths and candles. They spared no expense! The event went over with no hitches. We had a beautiful Christmas. As time passed, my feelings had slowly subsided for Stephen. Daniel and I were getting on with our lives. We would take the kids swimming at the local indoor poor, and we tobogganed down the only man-made hill. Daniel arrived home one night from work with two tickets to a dinner and dance. The event was to raise money for a sick little boy who had cancer. The family was poor, so the community pulled together to help out as much as they could. Even though there were some people still a little bitter with me, they admired me for the devotion and hard work I put into raising money for the little boy and his family. The town wanted to send him and his family to Walt Disney World. I must say, I was a tad nervous going in for fear that I would run into Stephen. But what would be the likelihood of that happening? He lived in Regina. Daniel and I were getting ready for the evening. When he walked down the stairs in his tuxedo, he was truly handsome. It brought back such wonderful memories from the good old days. God, he looked so handsome that night!

I decked myself out in a long, navy blue silk gown. The kids were coming for the first part of the evening for the games. The organizing community had games, prizes and pizzas donated by one of the local pizza owners. The kids later were sent to Melanie's place to spend the night. I looked at myself in the mirror and said, "Self, be a good girl tonight!"

When we walked into the room, the mayor was greeting the guests one by one. As I was walking towards him, I muttered, "Why can't that fat butt drop dead of a heart attack?" smiled, then walked into the ballroom. Everyone had on their perfect smiles and were on their best behavior. If only I could have dropped a huge rotten fart in the middle of the room just to see their facial expressions. God forbid anyone would ever say anything to me in public. They'd rather dish it around the community behind my back. I noticed that the mayor snarled at me as I walked by him. I knew he would recognize me right away. I grabbed Daniel's arm abruptly, bypassed the mayor and headed right for the bar. Daniel, being so easygoing, never said a word. I never remained in one place too long. At that point, things had been going pretty smoothly. I received a few dirty looks from the local noted bitches and quickly shunned them with a dirty look.

I had expected that much would happen anyway. There was the occasional dagger bouncing off the back of my head. I certainly didn't have to put ice in my drink; the room was cold enough to chill anyone's drinks.

After all, by now I was the "Town Slut." The hall was decorated marvelously, as usual. The chef had hand-carved a large Mickey Mouse, which was on display in the middle of the ballroom. Some of the kids were being their destructive selves by chipping away at Mickey's feet and throwing food all over them.

Little demons! I thought. God, kids can be idiots sometimes. I often wonder why we have them. The sick little boy was sitting at a table full of stuffed animals and toys donated by the local department stores. We went over to talk with him. He was a sweet little fellow. He was hooked up to an IV. I put his tiny cold hands in mine and told him everything would be all right, just to remember one thing: that humour was the best medicine. Daniel told him that he was a cancer survivor, and told the boy could he be too. Daniel showed him the scar on back of his head. The little boy rubbed his fingers very gently up and down the scar. The boy, with a weak little voice, said, "Thank you," and put his thin little arm around Daniel's waist. I almost lost it! I needed a drink and fast. There was more emotion in that one minute than I'd had in an entire year. Later on that evening, there was to be a silent auction going on in one part of the building, turkey draws and a 50/50 draw at the bar. All of the proceeds were to go to the family. I looked over my shoulder to see a clown making up animal balloons.

I have detested clowns since I was a little girl. They belong in horror movies. There's nothing funny about a clown. To this day, I don't know what kids see in a big, red-nosed, oversized moron dressed in a ridiculous costume and topped with a head of red, tangled hair. The kids were scheduled to leave the party before the dinner was to commence. What a bunch of hyper, chocolate-overdosed, noisy brats there were running around! The establishment wasn't permitted to serve alcohol until the kids were out of the building. I knew the clown had his own private stash. In fact, he wasn't the only one. The parking lot had more men it in than cars, and there was a constant flow of ladies heading for the washroom. There were more town drunks than I realized! Once the kids left, there was a race to the bar.

Melanie noticed me and started waving her arm in the direction of the entrance. I looked over Daniel's shoulder to take a look. *Oh my god! It can't be!* Christ, there he was, chatting up a storm with the mayor. *What is he doing here? Doesn't this guy ever go home?! Why?* Within seconds, my heart was in my throat, and you could bounce a quarter off my butt. Every muscle and nerve ending tensed up. Before long, Stephen was inside, shaking hands and making idle conversation with the locals. I noticed his wife wasn't with him that time. I tried to keep low to the ground, basically out of sight. Daniel noticed I was being evasive but didn't say anything. It would just be a matter of time before Stephen had spotted me. I had seen him scanning the room. I excused myself and, like a snake, slithered to the ladies' room. I was pacing the floor and breathing like an oversized pig. *What is happening to me?* I was shaking my fingers back and forth in the air. Was I embarrassed, or did my feelings for him resurface? I didn't know if I could face him again. I knew one thing—I definitely wasn't going to make a butt out of myself this time. I definitely wasn't going to dance with him that night. Melanie came storming into the ladies' room with a drink. I grabbed it out of her hands and downed it. She told me that Daniel and Stephen were at the bar kicking up quite a conversation. It wasn't a pretty picture for me. *Great, now what?* Now what in hell was I going to do? I had to get a grip on the situation.

Really, I had nothing to hide. Stephen knew I was married and had a family. I looked into the mirror, straightened out my dress and took a deep breath. I got a grip on things and walked out the door. I walked directly toward them and reintroduced myself to Stephen. There was no sigh or gasp. He remained cool and quite poised. He acted as if we had never met before. That should have been a clue right there. He seemed to be a pro at that sort of thing. He was a little too smooth. My feelings for Stephen boomeranged right back into my face. When he smiled at me and offered for me to sit down beside him, I became weak all over. The conversation stopped instantly, and it was though, for a moment, everything in the room came to a stop. The room froze. We had our eyes fixed on each other, but just momentarily. Melanie tapped me from behind. Boy, did I jump! Daniel observed that there was something going on, but instead of asking any questions, he just offered anyone another drink. Daniel was never one for creating a scene. I think he did that to break the ice. Stephen had a smile that could knock the panties off any woman. He was charming, handsome and intelligent. Mind you, Daniel was nothing to kick out of bed either. I found out through his conversation that he was in town to close a huge computer deal with the oil company and that he would be flying in frequently to assure the equipment was properly installed. Just what I needed to hear! I quietly excused myself from the bar to attend to the children. I took a glimpse over my shoulder to see he had his eyes fixed on me.

Adam and Alexandria were full of pizza, ice cream and cotton candy. It would be amazing if they didn't throw their guts up on the way home. The mayor announced that dinner had been served. Like cattle, we plowed our way up the steps to the dining room. The dinner was tastefully elegant! Each table had a selection of red and white wines. The food was to die for. They served everything from French onion soup to two mouth-watering, suckling pigs topped with a rich brandy sauce and vegetables galore. The mayor, who was sitting next to Stephen, made the announcement that so far that evening, they had raised over five thousand dollars. The roars of glee and laughter brought down the roof. The sick little boy and his family would definitely be going to Walt Disney World. I never had a doubt they would be. That place stunk of money.

There wasn't a minute spent during dinner that Stephen and I weren't trying to have eye contact. There were times when he would even tilt his chair back to see me. Our table was noisy as hell. What else could I expect? I was surrounded by pilots and junior executives. I was so glad when that dinner was over. After dinner, we all retired to the ballroom for more drinks. The games were about to begin in more ways than one. It's funny how booze can make you bold and brave at the same time. I waited for Daniel to get into a lengthy flying story with his buddies before I excused myself. I took a good look around to see if Melanie was lurking about. Stephen was coming down the stairs from the dining room with his glass of scotch, chatting up a conversation with the mayor's wife. When they hit the bottom of the stairs, she left and headed for the ladies' room. I daringly and swiftly approached Stephen before someone else could grab him. The words that came out of his mouth threw me for a loop. I was just about to ask him for his work number, and he said, "How are you tonight, gorgeous?"

What else could I say other than, "Great, thank you!" Without any hesitation, he copied his private cellular number down on a napkin and tucked it into my hand.

Within an instant, the mayor came directly behind me to speak to Stephen. As Stephen walked by me, he gave me a quick wink as he muttered, "This is the safest way!" I figured if I could talk to him privately, I would get him out of my system once and for all. Guess what "figure" did. All that did was put another part of my body into a deeper pot of hot soup. The evening was coming to a close. As Daniel and I were walking towards the lobby to get into our cab, I detoured and headed for the washroom. When I came out, Stephen was standing by the archway, and he grabbed my arm and said, "I've got you under my skin, and I can't get you out! *Call me tomorrow*!" I was all flushed and confused. Daniel was in the lobby waiting for me.

Afterwards, I started questioning myself. What kind of person had I turned into? In a bizarre way, I felt it was something I had to do. It didn't appear to be dishonest or unfaithful. I looked upon it as being a little secret or game I was playing. I felt like a teenager again with the uncontrollable jitters. It put some excitement in my life. I found it to be intriguing that such a man had taken notice of me! It was a period in my life when I seemed empty and lonely. I was walking into something with visors glued to both sides of my head. I could hardly wait to tell Melanie that he gave me his phone number. When I did, I was sorry. She almost ripped my head off, she was so pissed off with me. Man, was she mad! She warned me several times not to call him. She was trying to reinforce my relationship with Daniel. I was so fortunate to have such a great guy and two wonderful kids. She told me to take a good look around at what I had before screwing it all up. I was basically asking for it if I was to pick up that phone. It would only open a whole can of worms, and I would probably regret it for the rest of my life. But I couldn't see that at the time. I was following my heart. I never even gave it a second thought that it could end up hurting a lot of people.

The following day, I called him at work. It took me hours to pick up that receiver. What in hell was I going to say when he answered the phone? And what in hell was I getting myself into? I was excited and nervous at the same time. When I heard his voice on the other end, I slammed the receiver down immediately. I was sweating like a pig. I ran outside to take in a deep breath of fresh air. I finally got my nerve up to call him again. This time I didn't hang up. We decided to meet the next day at a small restaurant sixty kilometres outside of town. We couldn't dare take the chance of someone seeing us from Creek Well. We'd be digging our own graves before we were shot down. My insides were dancing with excitement and guilt. My stomach became part of my tonsils. I was wearing down the kitchen tiles. I was trying to convince myself not to meet with him the next day. No matter how hard I tried, the curiosity was killing me. I finally convinced myself I'd meet with him just once, and that would be it. When I walked into the restaurant, our eyes met. I melted in my tracks. I was so jittery. I swear, I was smiling so much you could see my tonsils. The spark was put back into my life. His smile lit up the entire room. We kept the conservation pretty light at first. We basically talked about our interests and children. He had four children—two girls and two boys. He had been married twenty-one years and, from what I had gathered, most of it unhappily. I had met his wife, so I knew where he was coming from—a bit of a frump with a personality of stone. I gathered from the conversation that she too had a lot of money. She was originally from England. Stephen met her there on business. Apparently, her father owned quite a few wineries throughout England. After her father passed away, she, being the only daughter, inherited the wealth. The more he talked to me, the more I wanted to hear. I was enthralled by that man. I felt as though he put a spell over me. We only met for a short while because we had a long drive back into town. He escorted me back to my car and gave me a kiss on my cheek. I was sixteen again. I sang the entire trip back home. I smiled so much my cheeks hurt. Daniel swung the back door open wearing a big smile on his face. He gave me a tight squeeze and kissed me on the back of my neck. "Let's go out for supper tonight. I feel great!" Nothing like driving another guilty stick up my ass. That was the last thing I wanted to do. I finally persuaded him to have something delivered. Bags of food arrived at the door. It was so rarely that we had delivery, the two kids were at the window waiting for the delivery truck to pull up in our driveway. They ran in with the bags and sat in front of the television. Dinner was unusually quiet that night. Daniel was sitting back, having a cold beer and telling me about his day. I couldn't eat a bite of dinner. He asked if I was feeling alright. He told me I looked a little pale. *It's called the guilt look!* The worst look an unfaithful woman could have on her face. I wanted to jump off of the couch and tell him everything, but I didn't have the guts. The guilt was eating away each layer of my guts, tissue by tissue! My innards were in total turmoil. I had so many mixed feelings. I couldn't even look at Daniel that evening. Was I willing to jeopardize all of that? After dinner, Daniel played with Alexandria on the living room floor, then took her upstairs for her bath. I was a wreck! I was on the biggest guilt trip known to man. I had done something so terrible, *why*? Damn it, almighty I hadn't asked for it to happen, and I certainly wasn't looking for it. It just happened. Daniel knew something was wrong but didn't know what. While he was bathing Alexandria, I took a long walk, trying to gather my thoughts and make some sense out of them.

My evenings became fewer and fewer at home. I told Daniel I had joined an exercise club in town, which was partly true. While Daniel stayed home to take care of the kids, I was out galloping my butt off with another married man. I should have been shot! He never questioned me of my whereabouts. He trusted me with his life. Some nights were just for women and others co-ed. I often would meet Stephen after I had a thirty-minute workout. Other nights, we decided to meet inside the exercise room, and we would use some discretion and keep our distance. We were busy pedaling away on the bikes, and in walked his wife. I hadn't realized he had brought her on his business trips, and he never mentioned it! How stupid for him not to tell me. Not only that, how did she know where to find him? Her eyes were like a shark out for a kill, and mine were full of blood. Before she could come in for the kill, I hopped off the bike beelined it out of there. Apparently, Stephen told her he had a meeting with the CEOs of the oil company, which he did, but he cut the meeting short so he could meet up with me at the gym. Some nosy bitch from the gym spotted us and couldn't wait to call her at their penthouse suite at the hotel. As I ran down the hall, I could hear her screaming profanities at Stephen. He was definitely in the doghouse that night.

When I arrived home, Daniel had told me that Dustin had called and told Adam he had been married that past weekend to a lady from New Brunswick. Adam wasn't very thrilled over the news. I ran up to Adam's room and found him crying in his pillow. Christ, we were a fine bunch. Here his dad was married for the third time, and I was seeing another man. I don't know who was more demented!

Each day, it was becoming harder and harder to cope with everyday issues. The laughter had slowly faded away into the distance. There weren't many happy moments. The static between the two of us was very growing by the day and becoming very uncomfortable. I was feeling so bad for Daniel. I really didn't want it to happen. Every day, Stephen would call me. He was either on a plane or somewhere in Canada doing business a deal. We started taking more risks. We started meeting at places closer to town. Daniel was becoming more aware of what was happening. He was more suspicious by the day. I didn't know how to tell Daniel. It was tearing me to pieces. I was in love with another man. God, I never thought I would say that. In all honesty, I truly thought my infatuation for Stephen would die. The thought of hurting Daniel, especially in that way, was unforgiving and thoughtless. Even the kids became uptight. Alexandria would cry frequently, and Adam had lost his appetite. I had confided mostly everything to Melanie. She was my support blanket. As much as she hated the thought that I was seeing this guy, she still remained my dearest friend. Since she was my best friend, I assumed I could have trusted her. Sometimes I wouldn't know the location to meet Stephen, so Melanie, who knew the area, would help me find it. She promised me on numerous occasions that she would never breathe a word of any it to anybody, no matter what happened.

The situation at home was mounting. We couldn't look at each other without ripping each other's faces off. Our conversation was minimal. Something had to be said, or I was going to crack. I had become miserable with Daniel and started treating him like shit, and he was one guy who didn't deserve to be treated that way. There is a saying in the English language that should be removed: We need to talk! Those four words can drive anybody nuts, especially if it's said over the phone. Daniel called me up from work and said exactly those words. He walked in the front door very distant and sad. The happy-go-lucky, carefree person I married was so unhappy he looked like someone zapped the life right out of him. The air was thick with tension. He went to the fridge, grabbed a beer and sat down in the living room. He knew I was extremely unhappy and miserable. I sat down beside him with tears falling down my cheeks. I didn't want to mess with words. That was never my way of dealing with a situation. I had to come right out and say it. I held his hand and said, "I want a divorce, Daniel!" He put his head on my shoulder and began to cry. He felt he should have done more for me and been more supportive in our marriage. I, on the other hand, was sick to death with guilt. He asked me why, and I said with every ounce of energy I had left in my body, "I don't love you the way I should!" Why not just rip the guys heart out and feed it to the wolves. He probably would have felt better. I tried so hard to encourage him not to be so hard on himself. He didn't know it was because of another man. We were both bawling in each other's arms. Words can't explain how awful I felt at that moment. I wanted so hard to tell him the truth, but I didn't have the courage or guts to hurt him more than I already had. I watched that man almost die from cancer, we almost went bankrupt over sour business deals, we lived in crappy houses, and we still stayed together. It didn't make any sense to me. He assured me he would make sure I had enough money to take care of the kids decently. My god, how selfish and cruel could I be? When was I going to wake up and smell the coffee? How could I have done that to a man who had been through so much in his life. I had destroyed my entire family over a man I hardly knew. Daniel got up from his chair with his head hanging, took his beer and walked upstairs to our room. When I awoke the next morning, he was gone. He wasn't long moving out of the house. He moved into a bachelor apartment in town. The kids were shattered to see their dad leave. The day he left was terrible. As Daniel pulled out of the driveway, Alexandria with her little legs ran down the driveway crying out, "Daddy, Daddy, come back!" Adam ran to grab her. I held the kids in my arms, trying to convince them that everything was going to be alright. That evening, the house was cold. I truly missed Daniel's laughter throughout the house. There was one part of me that was happy, and the other was totally confused. I sat in a dark dining room grasping onto a glass of wine, watching my tears hit the side of my glass. I stared at that wine trying to come to grips with why I ever let it happen to such a wonderful, lovely person as Daniel.

Melanie came over a couple days later after things quieted down a bit to see how we all were doing. We were all a mess. I was a mess! I can't say she didn't warn me. All she did was shake her head back and forth. She grabbed a beer from the fridge, looked directly at me and said, "Are you proud of yourself? *I warned you, didn't I?*" She was right all along. I had hurt so many people. I told Melanie I didn't tell Daniel about Stephen. I told her it was best to let sleepy doggy lie! Bad mistake on my part. She downed that beer, and before I had a chance to say another word, her butt was out the door. I ran out to the driveway. "Where are you going?" I screamed to the top of my lungs. "Please don't tell Daniel, please! His heart is already broken into pieces!" She couldn't wait to tell Daniel about Stephen and I. He was shocked, hurt, and torn to pieces even more. I hope she lost some sleep over that little episode. As soon as the phone rang, I knew it was him. I picked up the receiver to hear nothing but every rotten thing you want to call someone that has broken your heart.

Now I really knew I was going to suffer major consequences, and I deserved every bit of it! In all the years I had known him, he had never once called me a terrible thing. He loved me so much, he would never ever hurt me. Obviously, that trait didn't rub off on me. During the evening, he called me a couple of times to apologize. He had no reason to apologize to me for his actions that night. It's a wonder he didn't beat the living shit out of me. I could tell by his voice that he was drinking quite heavily, and I became worried about him, so I called one of his friends to go check up on him. He wrangled up some of Daniel's friends and took a couple bottles of whiskey to the rescue. I received a phone call later on that evening that he had some comfort in a bottle of whiskey. I don't say I blame him. Even today, I don't know why she did that to Daniel and I. All she did was pour iodine into an open wound. Miserable bitch! The situation was bad enough as it was. So much for faithful, trustworthy friend. Within a blink of an eye, the news was all through town the next day. I now wasn't just the town slut, but a horrible, evil home-wrecker. Christ, it's a wonder they didn't hang me in town square or, even better, tie me up to a pole and let them throw rocks at me yelling, "Evil woman!" Excuse me, that was too good for me. It should have been, "Burn her at the stake!" That would have made them all happier! No matter where I went in town, I was looked upon as the town slut. I could hear people muttering, "She's the one," and they would even move their kids to the other side when I walked into a store or down the sidewalk. When I think back, they had pretty pathetic, small minds. I didn't have a friend in the world. I was alone with two kids who didn't know what to believe. The day I called my family was devastating. They thought the world of Daniel and never dreamt anything like that would ever happen. I think by now they realized they had given birth to a girl who had turned into a monster.

THIRTEEN

It wasn't long before Stephen's butt was kicked out of the penthouse suite. His wife had a third World War brewing in town. Basically, every woman within a two-hundred mile radius knew what had happened. The town congregated at City Hall to discuss the terrible things that had happened to her. The Creek Well's Ladies' Club held an event at the local hotel to have a fundraiser for the "poor" lonely, devastated wife. If she wanted to, she could have bought the entire town. That wasn't good enough. The president held a huge barbeque on her property, hosting Stephen's wife with all the dignitaries and shopkeepers in town. The president of the club was assigned as the campaign manager for the event. Boy, it was big-time news for Creek Well. After she did significant damage to him, Stephen's wife headed back to Regina. Stephen had a history of having affairs but never had ever once thought of leaving his wife. I, for some reason, broke the record. Great! I soon learned that a lot of Stephen's money was his wife's. I had heard through the grapevine that the president, in her speech to the local lady folk, was to warn them that that sort of thing could happen to any one of them. "Beware ladies! Protect yourselves against women like her! She's a defiant woman and can't be trusted. There's more out there than we know of!" Once I heard that, I knew if I was going down, then that horny two-faced bitch was going down too. Just how? I needed some leverage and fast! I had to figure out a way to nail that bitch to the wall. Another big obstacle against me was my star witness, Melanie. She switched sides on me. I bit the bullet and went to Melanie's to ask her to stand by me on this one, but I soon realized she had no backbone. She slammed the front door in my face, and if I said anything, she would deny it all. That bitch! Who would believe my story without a witness? I kept my strength through the ordeal and was determined to take her down. I was angry and pissed to the limit. I had a mission, and that mission was to ruin her and, if I could, take that fat-butt mayor down with her! The town needed some new news to take the pressure off of Stephen and I for a while. One rainy night, the mayor's son was killed in a automobile accident. It was unfortunate, but it took some relief off of us. The town knew he had a drinking problem, but it was constantly covered up because he was the mayor's son. The alcohol level in his blood was four times over the legal limit. That was not exactly what I was hoping for, but that did relieve us temporarily. Now the town focused all of their attention and energy on the funeral and support for the family. For the time being, I was put on the back burner. It was a nice change playing second fiddle.

The son's mother was the town's basic basket case. Trying to see her calm would be like waiting for the heavens to open up to see Christ himself wearing Bart Simpson's underwear. It wasn't long after when they had her butt in a straight jacket heading for the nearest loony bin. She was what you might call the Town Druggie. She ate pills like I'd eat pizza on a Friday night. No wonder, living with that fat butt pig all of her life. I would have had done him in years ago, and he would never have known what hit him. The word around town was that her bathroom medicine cabinet was loaded with more uppers and downers than the hospital. Christ, I wonder what doctor she was blowing. Those horny old doctors in that town would have given anybody a prescription for a lay or a blowjob. Those poor bastards! That wasn't a good time to bring up the mayor's affair. I had to wait until things quieted down a bit. The owner of the floral shop was in heaven! It would buy him a trip down south next winter. The funeral was enormous. People came from far and wide. I don't know where they found all the limos. They even closed down the oil company that day. It certainly was quite a funeral. I didn't go near the place. Stephen, on the other hand, being a businessman and friends with the mayor, felt obligated to attend. Plus, he had lost a lot of business over the breakup and needed to show good faith with his business buddies. In other words, it was kiss butt time! The wake was amazing. I never dreamed a town could damn near clean out a liquor store. They sure gave it a run for its money. The next morning, the town was a ghost town. The mayor called it a "civic holiday." Trust me, there were no complains from the locals. A couple of weeks passed, and the town was relatively quiet over not only the death but the affair. A lot of things went on in that town, but everything was kept very hush-hush. Now it was time for the next bombshell to hit. I was on my mission, my revenge for that backstabbing rich bitch. I discreetly went out to monitor every move she made. I drove into Edmonton to purchase a video camera. I didn't dare buy one in town. If I had, the next thing I would have heard was that we were now doing home porn movies to sell to the local kids in the neighborhood. Whereever I went, I carried it on me. It became my best friend.

That night was the usual ladies' night at the club. Stephen was due to fly in late that evening, so I knew I had some time. I sat outside the hall in my car, waiting for the meeting to end. I was crouched down in my car, waiting for that elusive bitch to leave the building. Of course, she would be the last to lock up the building. She got into her car and took a big swig of something, undoubtedly booze, and lit a cigarette. She really did have a secret side to her. Christ, you talk about a split personality! When she pulled out of the parking lot, I waited a couple of seconds before I started to tail her. There wasn't a star in the sky; it was pitch black. *Where in hell is she going?* She drove for forty minutes or so to a seedy, rundown, cheap motel. I never even knew the town existed. She parked her car away from the highway and streetlights. She discreetly and hastily ran to the furthest motel door. She obviously knew where she was going. The door wasn't even locked. I turned my headlights off and parked at the other end of the motel. I was as jumpy as a cat in heat! I didn't want to wait too long, so I grabbed the camera and quickly and quietly made my way over to the window. I had to keep looking over my shoulder for fear that someone would see me. I crept down low beneath the window. I took a quick peek, and sure enough, there was that fat-butt mayor in his jockeys, having a drink. The most disgusting part, though, was seeing the president lying on the bed naked, sucking back on a cigarette and holding a bottle of wine in her hand. What a way to lose a couple of pounds! I damn near got sick. Regardless of how ghastly it looked, I needed to get it on film. I took one last look around and started filming. It wasn't long before the two of them were getting right down dirty. It was good I had a strong stomach. The old flab on the mayor was just a bouncing that night. I couldn't for the life of me understand what that bony-butt bitch saw in that creep. Anyway, at that point I didn't care. I just needed their live performance on tape. The first episode of their show was enough for me, so I turned the camera off. When the words "my son's death" came into play, I started taping again. He started talking about the huge insurance cheque he received from his son's death. They were laughing their butts off while waving the check in the air, and the mayor said, "We're rich, babe, she's locked up, and he's dead." They were so glad there was no autopsy performed on his son's body, or the police would have detected the drugs in his blood that his own father planted into his drinks that night at the house before he went out. At the time of the boy's death, the mayor had waived off the autopsy, and of course, who was going to question or argue with the mayor? The boy did have a drinking problem but was never known to drink and drive. In other words, he wasn't careless. The story around town was that the mayor had paid the bartender off the night of the accident to convince the cops the boy had drunk too much. The mayor started playing down his son. "He was nothing but a drunk. He had a damn drug addict for a mother. His death was inevitable. He was a born loser right from day one." I couldn't believe my ears. It sounded as if the two of them had concocted it up from the start. It was too good to be true. What a rotten prick! And her, why, she was worse! You talk about your money hungry sluts! Christ, she was spread-eagle, smoking a cigarette and sucking back on a bottle of wine. How more of a slut could she be? What I had witnessed that night was unbelievable. My eyes ached from pure disbelief. You talk about evil people. All I did was wreck a family and have an affair with a guy, and for doing so, the town was crucifying me! These two creeps were murderers! I was dealing with a totally different ballgame here. I went from adultery to murder, all within five minutes. Evidently, the mayor was a high roller. He liked playing with the big boys in town. Between his wife's addictions and his elaborate spending habits, their money had been depleted. The townspeople knew it, they just kept their damn mouths shut. Truth be known, there were a lot of rich but terrified people in that town, a lot of them paid off by City Hall. They clinked their glasses and started right back into it again. I had heard and seen enough for the rest of my life. My stomach couldn't have taken much more. When I arrived home, I made three copies of the tape of the evening's colorful events. I put one in my safety deposit box, another in the attic, and the other one was on its way to the local television station.

Each time Stephen came into town, we became more public with our relationship. The town already had us blacklisted, tarred and feathered. What more could they do to us? I started spending every weekend at his penthouse suite. The kids loved it there. There was a heated indoor pool, a gym, and room service, but the penthouse was soon coming to an end. Stephen didn't own the penthouse—it belonged to his wife. As soon as she got wind that we were spending our weekends there, she changed the locks on the door and put it up for sale. He rented out another room in the hotel. It wasn't as lavish, but it was still quite posh. His trips were becoming fewer and fewer. His work at the oil company was coming to a close. He grew to love Alexandria very much, but Adam was a different story. Right from the beginning, I sensed a lot of tension between the two of them. Over time, the town became almost unbearable for the children, and I to live there. Adam was getting abused at school from the local bullies, and it was almost impossible to go into town without being verbally abused. One day he came running home and ran to his room crying hysterically. I was seconds behind him. He started screaming at me, "I hate you! I hate you, Mommy! You're a bad person! Don't you ever come near me." I was shattered. The closer I came to him, the more he screamed and yelled. "My life's ruined because of you!" I didn't know what to do. I loved him so much, and it was breaking my heart in two. I let him get it out of his system. After he cooled down, I tried to talk to him. He eventually fell asleep in my arms. The next morning, he was happy-go-lucky and bouncing around the house. Stephen and I couldn't even go to the movies, we were so ostracized. We loved each other so deeply we could overcome it. *To hell with them! We can do this!* It wasn't that we were banned from places, it was the way people treated us. It was like we had the plague! We had no other choice but to spend our time together between walls.

The entire situation grew utterly out of control. I really don't think we thought the affair was ever going to elevate to that level. Stephen found out through the grapevine that I had confided in Melanie. She knew so much on us, she could have written a book. He was furious with me. It took him days before he would speak with me, and I certainly didn't need that. He was spending a lot more time in Regina, cleaning up some of his misses and dealing with lawyers. He was the only support system I had going for me. The rumours and gossip were increasing daily. It was ridiculous! His wife was having a field day in Regina and throughout Canada telling everybody the news. What pissed her off was that I was the first to break the mold. He left me for her, and that was driving nails into her heart. What was so different from me than the others? She was always able to convince him that she was the one, but then along came me. If she had had the opportunity, she would have had my throat slit within seconds. I, for once, had the power over her, she wasn't in control. Even without the money, I was more appealing than her. It wasn't only my body but the way I mesmerized her husband had her in total limbo. She contacted every business partner he knew to discredit him. Over that, he had lost clients, since they thought he wasn't trustworthy anymore. That was like driving a nail through his belly button. I learned very quickly that Stephen's pupils often were shaped like dollar signs. Money meant an awful lot to him. Even though his wife was filthy rich, she still was going to take her share of the finances. In other words, she was taking him to the cleaners! Though there was only one child of legal age to receive child support, he was going to pay dearly.

That very week, the mayor held a town meeting. It was always advertised in the local paper what the agenda was going to be. It basically let the town know what was happening and let the locals know of any new developments. No one missed that event. Everybody and their dog attended. In fact, some people did bring their dogs. I don't think people attended so much to listen to his long-winded bullshit, but rather for the free food afterwards and to catch up on the town gossip. But that particular meeting would be different. The night before the meeting, I went to the local television station. They loved seeing me. I brought spice and dirt to the boring, so-called "innocent" town. They even had a column in the paper covering the affair. After all, I was the town slut. I went there to get some assistants in a film I was making, at least that's what they thought. I was there for only one reason. When I walked into the building, the receptionist was extremely busy filing her nails. She took one look at me and asked me for my autograph. She really needed a life! I needed to speak to a reporter, and since there was only one on board, that wasn't a difficult task. He wasn't in at that moment, so she asked me to sit in the lounge and wait. I sat for a while and waited for her to go to the washroom. I quickly ran down the hall to find the video room. Frantically, I started looking for the tape on the new development I read about in the paper. There it was, next to the computer. I switched it with my tape. I immediately got my butt out of there. When I arrived at the reception area, she had her head buried into some stupid romance magazine. The most surprising thing about her was that she wasn't even blonde! She hadn't even noticed that I'd left. I often wondered who she was doing in the office. Most businesses would fire a mindless twit like her.

The mayor had some promising news for the town. Just outside of town, there was a group of businessmen from the United States who had invested a lot of money in developing a new complex. The complex would consist of a luxury hotel with conference rooms, pools and ballrooms. There was even going to be a helicopter pad. The complex was going to generate new business, more revenue for the town businesses, and cause expansion. It was a very exciting thing for the town. Maybe down the road there would be more than one floral or beauty shop. Before the big meeting, the mayor had asked the local television crew to go to the new site to tape the bulldozer lifting the first truckload of dirt away, plus give the locals a look at the new infrastructure. It was going to be one explosive night. The parking lot was packed to capacity. The camera crew had set up inside, and the maintenance personnel installed a huge screen behind the podium. It was a big night for the town. The town could smell the new money even before it hit the bank. Once everyone was seated and the idle chatter stopped, the mayor very proudly stood up to welcome and introduce the developers, business folks and townspeople to the meeting. He got a standing ovation before they saw anything. I was in the far back of the room, next to the exit, dressed like a man so no one would recognize me. The anticipation was driving the crowd crazy. The group from the States, the president and her husband, and the other dignitaries of the town were all sitting in the front row. Usually, the mayor started the meeting with the town's business, but that night, he emerged into the main event. He stuck his chest out proudly, took a deep breath and, without any further delay, announced the new development with great pride and dignity. It was even harder to look at him with clothes on, his fat gut hanging over his belt and his rosy fat-cheeked face juggling with every word he spoke. He wanted the town's people to have the first glance at the plans of the new development. When the lights were shut off, that was my cue to sneak behind the curtain. The only thing you could hear in the room were sighs of anticipation. The excitement bounced off the walls. That moment was priceless. When I saw, "ten, nine, eight, seven, six, five, four" roll onto the screen, I leapt in front of the camera man, wrapped my arms around his neck and gave him a long, passionate kiss. He was enjoying every moment of it. As I was kissing him, I kept one eye on the screen and one eye on him. I had one hand on his nuts and the other on his butt. There wasn't an eyeball that wasn't glued to that screen. The first thing that appeared on the big screen was the mayor in his jockeys looking down at this naked lady lying on a bed sucking back on a cigarette and slurping back on a bottle of wine. The mayor jumped out of his chair and frantically asked the cameraman to stop the film immediately. "Stop it at once, now! At once! I'll have your job for this!" When the cameraman heard all of the commotion, he looked up to see a porn show. He was intrigued.

He said to me, "Finally, someone nailed that bastard," and kept right on watching. The audience was spellbound. They could not believe their eyes. They covered their children's ears and eyes and left the building. I didn't see one man get up from his chairs. It was hilarious to watch. The mayor ran down the aisle to try to stop the film. The townspeople wouldn't let him near it! It took six guys to bring him to the floor. The women were rustling their kids out of there as fast as they could.

The president of the club ran through the crowd, waving her hands in the air and screaming, "How could you? You've ruined me!" She was horrified when she watched herself being banged back on by the mayor. She ran down the aisles holding her hands over her ears, screaming, "I know who you are, you bitch!" That was the best movie that town had seen in years. If they threw me in jail for ten years, it would have been worth every minute. The look on their faces was priceless! I never told Stephen what I had intended to do that evening. I knew he would have put a stop to it. The next day, my phone rang of the wall. I warned the kids not to answer it. I knew all too well they were death threats from the mayor and his whore. There was only one cop I could trust in town. I figured he wasn't on the mayor's payroll, so I had previously told him what I was going to do. He was only too glad to see the mayor go down, and he too knew the mayor was sleeping with the president for years. So, the next couple of days, he was only too glad to hang around to keep an eye on me. The newspapers were full of the previous night's events. I imagine those printers were on fire that night. One of the headlines read, *Meet the New Couple in Town!* Under the caption, there was a picture displayed of the two of them in bed together smoking a cigarette. The best one of all read, *Put Your Hands in the Hands of the Man*, accompanied by a picture of them standing in the mirror with his hands cupped around her breasts. When I saw that, I laughed my butt off! When I went into town, the people looked at me from a different aspect. On every coffee shop and street corner, people had their heads buried in the newspaper. Even though the townspeople hated to admit it or show it to me, they were pretty happy over the whole ordeal. Stephen had flown in that afternoon and heard about the episode that went on at City Hall. It didn't take him too many guesses before he figured out who was behind the scheme. As for the airhead at the newsroom, she received a promotion for being so diligent in her work. If the truth be told, she probably received another pair of kneepads from the boss. Stephen called me as soon as he landed to confirm our dinner plans that evening. He never asked and I never mentioned anything about the night before.

As I walked by the local coffee shop, I caught a glimpse of the cameraman. It looked like someone beat the livin' crap out of him. It didn't seem to bother him too much. His eyes were black, and when he smiled, I noticed he was missing two front teeth. The size of that lump on the side of his head could have classified it as his buddy. Nasty! I popped my head in the door to ask him if he was all right. When he saw me, he gave me a thumbs up. Rumor had it that one of the mayor's hotheads put a nasty beating on him after the show. That goon was now holding hands with the mayor in jail. It wasn't long before the dirt started spewing out. The mayor was charged with obstruction of justice, fraud, stealing and embezzlement. He was involved in more scandals than you could count. Now that the authorities had verbal proof of the mayor plotting his son's death, he had also been charged with first-degree murder, and the president with second-degree murder. By the end of the day, he had enough charges to put him behind bars for a long, long time. The day the excavators showed up at the boy's gravesite was another eventful day. The camera crews and every nosy person in town gathered around that site that day. That little town of Creek Well had made national news—they were finally throughout Canada. The police needed solid evidence to put that pig in jail for once and for all. The mayor and the president's days were over.

Every dog has its day. For the first time in a long time I walked down that street proudly.

Daniel called me to ask if he could over to talk with me regarding Stephen. Seeing as Stephen was spending the day with clients in Edmonton playing squash and taking them out for dinner, I told him of course. When he walked into the door, he had a very concerned look on his face. He gave me a warm hug and said, "I miss you a lot, but I am not here to cry my guts out to you, I'm here for the sake of the kids!" I poured him a cup of coffee and sat at the table. Stephen's wife had called him up the other night. Her words were few but powerful.

She said, "Daniel, don't let your children live with that man. He was an awful father with his own! I'm forewarning you! There were times he was down right cruel with them!" She portrayed him as being some sort of monster.

I said to Daniel, "She is just jealous that he left her for me. Don't you see that it's just a game she's playing?"

Daniel replied, "I hope you are right on this one. If he lifts one finger, there will be war!" I assured him they would be fine. I wouldn't let anyone harm our kids. He just wanted to give me heads up on some of the things he too had heard through the grapevine. He had heard Stephen was once engaged to a woman while still married to his wife. Apparently, he got cold feet and left her high and dry. It appeared that when these relationships became too serious, he would back off and ditch his lovers. Most of his money belonged to his wife. He knew that if he lost his wife, he would lose a lot of his finances. He had other affairs, but Daniel didn't have a lot details. He was just warning me and telling me to be careful. I was dealing with a different breed here. He said, "Just remember, a leopard never changes its spots." There was still a part of me that loved Daniel. He was truly a genuine and kind person.

As he was leaving, I patted him on the back, looked into his saddened eyes and said, "Don't worry, okay!" It was nice seeing Daniel, though the conversation was a little peculiar. I didn't know whether I should have brought it up with Stephen or ignore it all together. After he left, I certainly did question myself, but obviously not enough. The more I heard about Stephen's adulterated past, the more I wanted to be with him. It gave me the satisfaction that I was the one he chose to leave his wife for. I was better than all the rest of them. I thought, *He must truly love me to do this*. In my sick, demented way of thinking, I won the contest! Where was my head, up my butt? Most women would have run from that guy if they heard all that shit. Our relationship was going great, and I wasn't going to let anything or anyone interfere or mess with it. The town no longer made bad judgement on me. I was able to walk into a store and be greeted kindly. The town was thriving with the new development. The mayor's trial had started. That trial was finished even before it started. The first day of the trial, they found him hanging from a rope in his cell. He did the town a favor, saved them some tax dollars. She had to do one year of community service and got a slap on the butt. She must have been delighted when she was sentenced to one year of community service. After all, she was a pro at it. There was a new election brewing in the air. I was considering putting my name into the hat. The town even had a new mall in the works.

Stephen had to attend this somewhat snobbish party at the hotel. It was quite the la-de-da affair. It had something to do with the new development with the Americans. I spent part of the evening making idle conversation with people I'd never even met. It was so boring. Stephen had disappeared into the crowd. One of the waiters noticed how bored I was from my facial expressions. He eyed me over to the kitchen door. He swung the door open and pushed me inside. There had to be at least thirty to forty servants running their butts off, preparing trays of elegant delectable foods. He introduced himself as Pierre, the head waiter at the hotel. He mentioned he had noticed me before at these functions. He was going on break and wanted me to join him in the servant's stairwell for a glass of wine. *Why not?* He grabbed a bottle of wine, left the glasses behind, and we quickly fled between the walls of the kitchen. It was fun! I felt like a little kid who just stole the last cookie from the jar. He started telling me the gossip from the hotel walls. He said, "If these walls could talk, the town would have to hire a truckload of lawyers just to handle the law suits." I think the waiter had the hots for me. I could tell by the way he kept staring at my breasts. He sure was a lot more fun than that bunch in the ballroom. We finished the bottle of wine off quite quickly since I had to get my butt back into that room before Stephen missed me. Before I left, he winked and said, "Come by next week and have lunch with me!"

I looked back at him and replied, "Do you know who I'm with this evening?"

Before he shut the kitchen door, I heard him mumble, "Yea, that miserable prick!" Before I had a chance to grab his arm, he fled behind the doors. I had heard a lot of incriminating things about Stephen that week. How did that waiter know Stephen? I had to find out. I started asking a lot of questions during the evening. Although I tried to be discreet, word got back to Pierre that I was asking too many questions. A waiter came up to me, and handed me a glass of wine with a little piece of paper wrapped inside the napkin. I put the glass down and went to the washroom. The suspense was killing me. I ran into one of the stalls and sat on the seat. What I was about to unfold took my breath away. *Oh my god, no. He can't be.* I kept reading on and on. The last sentence read, *You know how I know he's one miserable prick? He's my father. He disowned me years ago. He wouldn't recognize me if he fell over me, and that's the way I want to keep it*! That boy must have been lying; that couldn't have been true. I had to speak with him. I wrote him a note back and asked him to meet with me the next day at a little coffee shop just out of town. I handed it to one of the waiters to give to Pierre. I was starting to have my doubts about Stephen.

When I entered the ballroom, Stephen came to me to give me a kiss. I suddenly turned my head the other way. He asked me what was wrong. I told him I was a little under the weather and wanted to leave. The following day couldn't come quick enough. I sat at the coffee shop, having my third cup and eyeing my watch. I was just about to leave when Pierre walked in. He apologized for his tardiness and sat across from me. I understood why he hesitated in coming. I mean, after all, I was partially living with his so-called father. The waitress came with a pot of coffee, and he said, "No thank you. I'm not staying that long!" I could tell by the way he fiddled with the napkin that he was nervous. He said, "My dad and I used to be somewhat close—

that is, whenever he was home—until he caught me in bed with my lover, Frank, the guy who lived two doors down from us." Pierre couldn't even look me in the eye.

I rubbed his hand to comfort him and said, "I know this must be awfully difficult for you, you don't have to go on!"

"No, I want to get it off my chest. He ripped his belt off and beat us like a mad man! Every swing of his belt, he would yell out, 'You fucking, you fag, you fucking fag! You have shamed our family, you get out and never come back!'" My eyes filled with salty tears, and each drop fell into my shaking lap. My hands were trembling for fear of what that poor boy must have gone through. He told me he still had scars on his back from the beating. When he left home that night, he never returned. He came to that small town thinking there was no way his father would ever show up in a place like that. He told me he had to keep a low profile whenever he was in town. With much anger and pain, he whispered across the table, "I detest that man!" He warned me to be very careful. I promised Pierre I would never breathe a word of it to anybody, not even to Stephen. As he got up to leave, he looked down at me and said, "Don't ever cross him, or you'll be so sorry. And god forbid if you have children!" He left the restaurant with his head hanging, wiping his saddened eyes. I never laid eyes on that boy again. When I arrived home that afternoon, I sat in the living room and kept going over all of the things I'd heard lately about Stephen. It was as though they were talking about a totally different person. *Who am I in love with?* Stephen treated Alexandria and I like gold. I must say, I was somewhat troubled and bewildered over it all. I poured myself a glass of wine and tried to enjoy a hot bath. I convinced myself that a lot of things being said were exaggerated.

That following weekend, Stephen arranged for me to fly me to Regina to attend his company's tenth anniversary gala. The kids stayed with Daniel. It was my first time flying first class. What a treat! Normally, when I flew, I sat in the back with the rest of the cattle. Now I was living the high life. Stephen met me at the airport. We had so much fun that weekend that I totally forgot about all the terrible things I had previously heard. He wined and dined me the entire weekend. I was sad to leave but anxious to see Adam and Alexandria. He fulfilled every dream and desire I had. He bought me expensive jewelry and took me to live concerts. He was showing me a world

I'd never experienced before. I was enjoying every minute of it. That was about to come to an end, and quite rapidly. His wife became very vindictive and selfish. The axe was about to fall. You know the old saying "You can't judge a book by its cover." That quote came into my life a little too late!

FOURTEEN

Stephen gave me a call from Regina with some surprising news. He was considering opening another business in Victoria, British Columbia. He asked me if I would like to join him. I replied, "You mean move in with you?" I thought that was great—a new start, a fresh place and new people—that is what our relationship needed. The only problem was the kids. Adam and Stephen didn't get along that well. Truth be known, Stephen didn't want Adam to come with us at all. Right there, I should have packed up my things and left for Nova Scotia. There was a definite character conflict going on there. I didn't want to hurt Adam any more. Daniel was distraught knowing he wouldn't be able to see his children on a regular bases. I contacted Dustin, who was living in Dartmouth at the time, to let him know that we would be moving to British Columbia. He was totally against the idea. He bluntly said, "There is no way Adam is going anywhere with that man!" Dustin had dealt with Stephen in the past and had heard some pretty nasty rumors about him. Dustin wanted Adam to fly down to Nova Scotia to live with him and his new wife. That wasn't about to happen, at least not right away. Dustin was going to be gone for most of the summer, so it was best for Adam to live with my brother Mark and his wife Jackie. Then, in fall, he would move in move in with his dad. At the time, I could live with that, even though it broke my heart. I knew Dustin and Jackie loved Adam like a son, and their kids treated him like a brother. It was a good chance for Adam and his dad, too. They could spend quality time together. I knew I was trying to convince myself that it was a good plan. In reality, Adam was being torn apart piece by piece, and it was all my damn fault. There was only one thing that saved my sanity, and that was the fact that I knew he would be in great hands. Mark and Jackie adored him and treated him like a son.

That day I had been dreading finally came. Daniel brought Adam over to Stephen's suite the day he was leaving for Halifax. It was a day I would never want to have to go through again in my life. It was a heart-wrenching day. I tried so hard not to cry in front of Adam. I sure did enough of it when he left. Alexandria held onto him like glue. I promised Adam I would write to him every day and definitely see him in a couple of months. That was one of my saddest days in my life, watching my boy walk down that hallway with Daniel. Both of their heads were looking down at the floor. Thank god I still had Alexandria to hold on to. Stephen was very comforting and understanding at the time. Of course, why wouldn't he be? He had one less mouth to feed. I was missing Adam immediately. There wasn't a day or night that I didn't want him with me. I swore I would never do that ever again for any reason. It was plain selfishness and stupidity on my part. I was sick to my stomach for days after he left. He called me the minute he arrived in Halifax. Dustin met him at the airport. Just hearing Adam's voice made me a little happy. There were times I wanted to hop on a plane and be with him. Even today I regret that I didn't do that. I live with that pain every day!

We were packing up for the big trip to B.C. I was never so glad to leave a place in my life. I remember when we pulled out of the town, we held each other's hands and smiled. If it wasn't for the fact that Adam wasn't with us, I was almost at peace with myself. Alexandria was little, so she had adjusted quite well to the new situation, even though she sure did miss her dad a lot. The drive through the Rockies was fabulous. There were times I was a little nervous—heights weren't my thing. We didn't stop much because we were in a bit of a hurry to get there, and Stephen hated to waste money on hotels. There was a lot of work to do when we arrived. We couldn't afford to purchase a home right off the bat. Between the divorce lawyers and the new startup cost for the business, money was scarce. Even though money was tight, Stephen still had to maintain his image. The food and clothes were secondary. The house was loaded with all the bells and whistles. It was a long, low ranch surrounded with willow trees, and in the back was a heated kidney-shaped pool. Once again, I was Cinderella, and here was my new castle. It had four bedrooms and a huge kitchen overlooking a sunken living room. The dining room had windows galore facing the huge pool. Along the side of the pool were six colourful peach trees, six pear trees and a picture-perfect cherry tree. What a place to party! The master bedroom was equipped with a Jacuzzi and sauna. Alexandria's room was a dollhouse, every little girl's dream. The walls were covered in pink and pastel purple balloons. The windows were covered in a petite white lace that flowed from the ceiling to the floor. She had her own private bathroom. The house was partially furnished. That was a good thing because we didn't have near enough to fill the place. The lot was surrounded by six-foot hedges for privacy. The only thing missing from the picture was Adam. He would have loved it there. There was a part of me that hated Stephen for not wanting to bring Adam along. That should have been a big eye-opener for me.

We signed up as members at the prestigious local country club. If you were a resident of that community, you were advised to be a member, especially if you were involved in the business world. That place was something out of the movies. The mahogany staircase was endless. I remember walking up them and singing the song, "Stairway to Heaven." There was more mahogany in that place than in the entire forest. The bathrooms were incredible. The Italian marble and brass must have cost a fortune. The common bar had to be twenty-five feet long, covered with marble. There were squash and tennis courts, a health spa, an eighteen-hole professional golf course, board rooms and a private sitting area. I hated to imagine what Stephen paid for a membership. I knew he would have had to have maxed out his Visa to belong to that place. Just to say you were a member of that place got you into a lot of doors—a lot of doors that had money behind them. I guess you could have called it an investment. I never did ask where he got the money. He wouldn't have told me anyway. I looked at the foyer bulletin board to see the upcoming events. My good lord, I couldn't believe my eyes. That place rocked seven days a week. There either was a dinner party, wedding or some sort of social event every day and night of the week. Those people knew how to have a social life. The only problem was that, in order to participate in those events, you had to have the money along with it.

I noticed on the board that there was a golf tournament coming up in two weeks. It sounded like fun. There would be twenty sets of four in each team. It didn't matter if you were a terrible golfer or not since you would play best ball. I hadn't played golf in years, so I was so excited to tell Stephen about the event. Following the tournament was a buffet and dance, and to boot, if you were a gold member, it was reasonably priced. I finally influenced Stephen in to going. If you had a handicap, you had to put it on the entrance form. That way you wouldn't have a bunch of pros playing on one team. I figured it was one good way to meet some new people in our community. Also, the club had a list of reliable babysitters. That morning ,we were out the door headed for the club. The air was sweet with fruit and the sun was making its way through the clouds—a perfect day for golf. When we arrived at the club, we looked on the board to see who we were playing with. We noticed we weren't playing on the same team. I was actually relieved. I was going to have some fun! The prizes were listed at the top of the board. The winners would receive dinner for two at a plush restaurant totaling six hundred dollars, and second and third places got a bottle of wine of their choice. I played with some wonderful people. We laughed so hard we almost pissed our pants. There was myself, another lady, and two men. One of the men was a scotch drinker. Before he would take a swing at the ball, he'd take a swig of scotch. In all honesty, he thought it improved his game. By the time we reached hole number six, he was swinging at leaves. Of course, there was the faithful beer cart, though at six dollars a beer, I learned to sip it. We were one of the first teams to arrive back at the clubhouse. Shortly after, in walked Stephen's team. They were quite confident they would be in one of the standings. We were quite confident we won the booby prize. We all had a quick shower and met back at the bar. I noticed Stephen was chatting with the local business people, trying to drum up some business. He certainly wasn't paying any attention to me. I became second fiddle that evening. Some guy put five hundred dollars down on the bar, so drinks were free for at least thirty minutes. I wasn't long grabbing a couple of free beers. It was a good thing since they were so damn expensive. The buffet looked so appetizing. There was everything there from seafood to roast beef. There was no lack of money in that joint. I ended up eating with my teammates. As we were eating, they announced the winners. Stephen's team came in third.

I looked over at him and blew him a kiss to congratulate him. Bad move on my part! After, I tried to find him, but he was nowhere to be seen. I finally found him on the back deck talking to some tall slim bimbo. Her daddy owned the resort. That alone would have been enough to attract Stephen to her. At first, I didn't mind, but after a bit, it became quite irritating and embarrassing. I didn't want to spoil the evening, so I kept my mouth shut. I struck up a conversation with a marketing executive at a nearby publishing company. There was no place to sit in the lounge, so we ended up on the million-dollar steps in the hall. Before long, I had him convinced to give me a job in his business. He had on this really different necktie. I couldn't help but remark on it. It was a male golfer holding onto a golf club and mooning another female golfer. It was actually pretty funny. When you pressed the golfer's butt, it would say, "Fore!" That is a term used in golf to warn golfers ahead of you that there is a ball on the way. I liked it so much that the guy gave it to me. In exchange, I bought him a drink. Soon, we had quite a crew hanging around the staircase. We were bragging or basically lying through our teeth about the great drives we had that day. Of course, we all knew most of us sucked. All of a sudden, I felt knives being driven into my back. I looked over my shoulder and saw Stephen staring at me, and he wasn't smiling. Well, I'll be damned if he didn't finally realize I wasn't standing by his side that evening. He had no business being pissed off at me. He was the one ignoring me half the night talking to that spoiled little bitch. Stephen wasn't long getting to the stairs. He grabbed me by the arm and excused us. I quickly looked over my shoulder to see them all shrugging their shoulders. I could see their mouths moving, like, "What's his problem?" He didn't want to appear too rude because he was there drumming up new business He opened up my side of the car and threw me inside. The drive home was horrible. I was nothing but a vamp, a floozie and a drunk! And what nerve I had taking that man's tie. And furthermore, I'd better think twice before throwing him a kiss in public again. I was speechless. Christ, what could I have said? He said it all for me. I think he was pissed off at me because I was the centre of attention that evening. I had more businesspeople around me than he did. He was too busy making the moves on the owner's daughter.

Stephen started working extremely long hours, trying to get the business off the ground. It was a very competitive business, and he had to be on the ball constantly. There was a lot of money in the air, and Stephen wanted it. He began dealing with businesses in the United States. There was the odd occasion I was able to travel with him. My Cinderella life had taken a turn for the worse. I started seeing a different side of Stephen, at times terrifying and shocking. You've heard of Dr. Jekyll and Mr. Hyde? Well, as time went on, I started seeing more of Mr. Hyde within Stephen. One particular Saturday, he went to play his usual game of racquetball at the club with his colleagues. I had gone shopping and then met up with some of the girls at the club. It was a lovely sunny day, not a cloud in the sky. They came over to my place, and we had a couple of glasses of wine—nothing out of the ordinary. It was late in the afternoon, the girls had left, and Alexandria was down for her nap. I turned the stereo on and was dancing around the kitchen preparing dinner. He walked through the patio doors and gave me a warm welcome. The minute he smelled my breath, he freaked out. He turned the music off, grabbed me and shook me back and forth. He was furious with me. He started yelling at me, "Who was here with you, drinking my wine?" He kept shaking me back and forth. I was terrified. I tried to explain that a few of my friends had come over, but he wouldn't listen to one thing I had to say. There was only one thing I was glad of—that Alexandria was asleep upstairs and couldn't hear anything. He threw me against the cupboards and walked out. I had no idea what had snapped in that man's head, but whatever it was, it wasn't good. What was so strange was that an hour later he came back smiling and wanting to help me with dinner. I never said a word. He was a poor looser, and having good sportsmanship was not one of good traits. So maybe his game sucked that day. He'd never let on anyway. He was too superior to everyone else to admit to failing in anything.

As each day went by, I would notice more and more how much he was changing. I wasn't able to invite any guests over unless I had his approval. As well, I could never purchase anything unless it was not only approved but absolutely necessary. When Alexandria and I would go shopping, we used to hide the stuff in her closet. We would normally say we picked it up at a secondhand store or that it was a gift from my parents. Stephen rarely was home. If he wasn't working on a new deal, his butt was on a plane trying to find a deal. Alexandria and I spent a lot of time alone, but we made the best of it. In the evenings, we would fill the Jazzuci up and play in it for hours. When

Stephen was home, he had to make his usual appearance at the club at least once or twice a month. The club became our center of entertainment. When Stephen wasn't exhausted with work or frustrated with the divorce, we would have such a wonderful time together. There was one thing he never did in public, and that was let his guard down. He was an extremely private person. Sadly enough, those occasions became few and far between. There were moments when he became very irritable and testy, but in all honesty, I understood. I was going to stick by him no matter what. After all, he had a lot on his plate to deal with, and I knew that, in time, things would smooth out. At least I hoped they would. I was missing Adam something terrible. I wished we had electronic mail, that way I could have talked to Adam on a day-to-day basis. I was always at Stephen to have it installed. He raised his voice slightly and said, "It's nothing but a luxury, and until the divorce is finalized, there will be no unnecessary spending, understood?"

As I walked away from him, I uttered under my breath, "You cheap son of a bitch!" Boy, he sure portrayed a different image when was at the club. I was constantly calling Adam just to hear his voice. I wrote to him continually. There was always a piece of me missing. Even when things seemed to be somewhat pleasant at home, I still wasn't a whole person. Adam was part of me, and without him, I would never be completely happy.

I had arranged for Adam and my parents to come out to visit us for Christmas. I spent countless hours baking Adam's favorite foods. I had the freezer full to the top. That house needed some life in it. I don't think Stephen was really looking forward to the visit, but what choice did he have? He kept his mouth shut on that matter. Stephen wasn't very easy to live with. There were times I was living on eggshells. He was very demanding and controlling with everything. I never had a say in anything. It was his way or nothing! I was trying to put all that crap behind me to get in the festive mood. Decorating the tree was always a big event throughout my life. It symbolized the beginning of great family times ahead. A tree, to Stephen, was not only a waste of money but a mess in the house. After dinner one evening, we went out to buy a tree. He bought the cheapest tree on the lot. I swore it was half dead. Half the needles fell off in the trunk. Even though he wasn't overly excited about the event, I was determined to make it great for the kids. Alexandria and I dug out the decorations from storage and began distributing them around the tree. If Stephen had his way, he would have stood on a ladder and dumped the box over the tree. Adam and my parents were scheduled to arrive the following afternoon. I spent most of the day wrapping presents and putting the final touches on the decorations. My little elf, Alexandria, was in charge of the tape. I had Christmas music playing in the back ground with the fireplace crackling to the tunes. There was just enough snow on the ground to make it look Christmasy. Stephen was at work finalizing some loose ends. I took a look at our tree, and said to Alexandria, "That's one sick tree!"

She started giggling and replied, "Like Stephen!" I told her never to say that in front of him. She must have heard more around there than I thought. I went over to the tree to pick up a half a dozen ornaments that had fallen from the tree to put them back on. Alexandria came over to help me. In walked Stephen.

"Ho, Ho, Ho!" Boy, he was in a good mood.

We both looked at each other and whispered, "Let's keep it that way!" As he was taking his coat off, I simply mentioned to him that the ornaments wouldn't stay on the tree because the limbs were sagging. He plowed through the living room, shoved me out of his way, picked up the tree and tossed it out the back door, ornaments and all.

"There. You don't have to worry about that problem any more, do you?"

Alexandria began to cry, and with snot running down her lip, she looked up at me with those beautiful brown eyes, ran into my arms and said, "Mommy, we don't have no tree for Santa this year!"

I looked right at the bastard and, in a sharp, bitter tone, replied, "Oh, yes we will. Come with me!" I think Stephen realized after the fact that he had gone too far this time. I brushed by him with steam coming out my butt, picked up a box from the porch, and went outside to salvage the ornaments that made it through the craze. We got into the car and drove to the nearest tree stand. We picked out a beautiful big pine. She was gorgeous. It sure put a smile on Alexandria's face. Come hell or high water, I was going to make this a beautiful Christmas. When I arrived home, he was whistling to Christmas tunes. He had a bottle of wine breathing on the dining room table with a tray of hors d'oeuvres next to it. This was major sucking up! He knew he had made a complete butt out of himself earlier, but I wasn't going to bite until I heard him apologize to both of us. I asked him to help bring in the tree.

He said, "Gladly!" When he brought the tree in, I noticed that he had cleaned up the mess from the previous tree. I could smell something cooking. I went into the kitchen and opened the oven door to find a delicious roast cooking, surrounded by vegetables. He sure was on the right track. Now I needed to hear those magical words, something like, "I'm sorry for being such an idiot!" Well, he would never admit to the last part.

During dinner, I spoke very few words to him. Alexandria got up from the table, walked over to him and said, in a quiet fragile voice, "Are you ever going to say 'I'm sorry' to Mommy and I?"

He replied, "Did your mom put you up to this? And is this why I'm receiving the silent treatment?" He directed the questions at me. "You two have such small, petty minds. Look what I've done here! Don't I deserve some appreciation around here?" He certainly had a way with words, and those were his words of apology. I put some Christmas music on to get back into the festive mode. We had a tree to decorate and a few ornaments to put on it. Of course, I never said a word. Alexandria and I would make the best out it.

The next day, the house was bouncing with excitement. Alexandria and I spent the morning making ornamental Christmas cookies to hang on the tree. Adam and my parents were due to land at two thirty that afternoon. The time couldn't go by fast enough. Stephen spent the entire day watching sports on television. Every now and then, he would come crawling out of his hole for a cup of tea. By mid morning, the tree was completely finished. Alexandria called it the "Cookie Monster tree." She emphasized the word "monster" quite clearly. Truth be known, she wasn't too off base with that remark. Adam and my parents arrived bearing gifts and lots of hugs. I couldn't wait to get my arms around Adam. Alexandria and I cried with happiness when they walked through the front door. My parents at first weren't very comfortable around Stephen. My mom just basically had no time for him. Of course, Stephen had a natural talent for making people feel like that. Seeing Adam made Alexandria's and my Christmas that year. Adam had so many things to tell me. He didn't know where to start. We spent the afternoon doing a lot of catching up on everything from golf stories to what was going on in the family. The next morning was Christmas day. Adam and Alexandria were up with the birds, ripping the hell out of their stockings. That was one moment I wasn't going to miss. I sat on the top stairs looking down at the pair of them.

I put my chin in the palm of my hand and gave out a long peaceful sigh. Another Kodak moment!

The traditional Christmases in my home as a child were the large, artery-clogging breakfast, where dishes had to be done and beds made. That tradition remained with the family for at least forty or more years. Dad and I prepared the breakfast while Mom and the kids made the beds. So far, everything was going along smoothly. The kids inhaled their breakfast and sat by the tree, anxiously waiting for the adults. They grew to know that the next step to the family tradition was the opening of the gifts! One of the gifts my parents gave me was a check. I sure could use that. The gifts I had received from Stephen were either too small or downright useless. You know those fake diamond necklaces that little girls wear when they are pretending to be princesses? That's the kind of crap I got! I knew his new business had absorbed some of his money, and the divorce lawyer showed no mercy when it came to money matters. On the other hand, I spared no expense on the two kids or Stephen. Although I was disappointed with my gifts, I wasn't gong to let it ruin Christmas. The main thing was that I had my two great kids with me. Basically, everything he bought me had to be returned. After the gift ordeal, he gave me the receipts so I could exchange the items. I looked at them and noticed he bought all of my gifts at a secondhand store down the street. I looked right at him and said, "You cheap bastard!" It was a good thing there was no lingerie in one of those bags. This guy gave cheap a whole new meaning. I was appalled. He was actually proud of himself for getting such great deals.

He replied, "Now I feel dejected!" He walked downstairs. I went out on the back deck to get some air. What could I say? I had come to the conclusion that morning that his bolts were a little loose. My parents knew I was pissed off at him. The air in the house became cold and thick. Dad walked into the kitchen and started to pour himself a drink of rum and ginger.

He said in a humorous way, "It must be noon somewhere in the world!" I wanted to suck that bottle dry, but the terror I felt in my spine told me not to. Could you imagine him seeing me drink a rum and ginger at eleven thirty in the morning? I'd be history! Other than the morning's drawback, the rest of the day was as normal as it dared be. The Christmas dinner was the traditional oversized turkey with all the trimmings.

My parents wanted to do some sightseeing while visiting. Stephen had arranged for the assistant manager to take care of the business over the holidays. Since we had a barrel of turkey left over, he insisted we make sandwiches and fill the thermos with tea. The parks were all closed for the winter months, so where were we going to eat, in the car? Stephen could have insisted all he wanted, but there was no way my parents we going to brown bag it throughout Victoria for the next ten days or so. My mom bluntly said to him, "What's wrong with eating in a nice restaurant?" I could hear her mumble under her breath, "I'll throw that goddamn turkey out to the birds, that will fix him!" We had a conflict right off the bat. I had Mom and Stephen battling it out in the kitchen. This was cute. I had Dr. Jekyll and Mr. Hyde confronting one another. I would put my money on Dr. Jekyll. They hadn't traveled three thousand miles for nothing.

"Why waste money unnecessarily? Look at all the food we have!" He bucked immediately at my mom. There was no compromising between the two. Dad and I sat in the living room listening to the two of them. Dad laid back into the couch and, with his witty humor, said, "I find this rather entertaining, I can't wait to see what the outcome will be!" I warned the kids to keep their distance from the kitchen and surrounding areas. In the end, Mom won the battle. Now I was left to pick up the shattered ego in the kitchen. Every day, we chose a part to visit. Even though Mom won the battle, Dad lost in the end. He paid for every lunch and the tip. I knew Stephen would never cough up a dime. That would have shown weakness, and that would have meant, in his mind, that he lost the battle. Trust me, he never loses a battle! Dad often called him a cheap son of a bitch under his breath and more. Once we had toured most of the surrounding areas, there was time to spend some time around the house.

Before my parents had arrived, Stephen had already had New Year's Eve plans in motion. Stephen invited his business buddies and almost all of the club members. The party was easy for him—all he had to do was invite people. I was left with all the preparations and cost. The only thing he contributed was the champagne and some beer. Thank god Mom was there to help me with everything else. It took every cent I had plus a lot of my mom's money to supply the food and decorations for the event. He even told the guests that it was B.Y.O.B. that evening. I was surprised so many people showed up because of Stephen's arrogant ego. Some people had classified him as being a money hungry prick. He certainly was a business tycoon in more ways than one. When you live in that kind of a neighborhood, you don't ask people to bring anything to a party, but I couldn't tell him any differently. You know, what was so bothersome about it was that it never even fazed him. He was not only a control freak, but also one cheap son of bitch. It was becoming more prevalent everyday. Mom and I spent countless hours preparing food for that evening. Adam and Alexandria were having a ball putting up the decorations. The doorbell began to ring. I had just enough time to put on my earrings, slip into my shoes and run downstairs. Stephen greeted everyone with his handsome two-faced smile. Most of the ladies were generous enough to bring a dish. Thank god! The house was full of people. The guests were having a great time. I, on the other hand, was running my ass off refilling trays and drinks. When I had the opportunity, I would grab a glass of wine, sneak out on the deck and down it, take a deep breath and start right back at hosting our guests. I was a nervous wreck that evening. I knew he was watching every move I made. It was like I had a radar detector around my neck all night. People ate, drank and danced all hours of the night Plus, he watched every seep of wine I took. I could have killed him that night. I was in the kitchen refilling the trays, and my eyes caught site of the butcher knife lying on the counter. I kept staring at it. Adam tugged at my dress. "Are you alright, Mom?" He startled me.

I replied, "Oh, just fine, honey!" I had him dressed up in a white shirt and bow tie. He was my little helper in the kitchen that night. The thoughts that ran through my mind in that split second... There were times I only wished I had the guts to do it! From a distance, all I could hear was Stephen's voice bragging about his successful business and how well it had grown. I thought to myself, *Gee, maybe that's my cue to jump in on that conversation and remark on the lovely Christmas gifts the cheap bastard bought me!* The party was an enormous success for him and his phony friends. When everybody left, I looked around the room and saw nothing but half-filled glasses, a floor covered in crumbs and ashtrays overflowing with ashes. The house reeked of nicotine and booze. All I could see was a lot of work ahead of me. I was too exhausted to bother with it that night. Stephen never even offered to help. He quietly slithered up the stairs like a snake to go to bed.

I poured myself a brandy, kicked off my shoes off, and plunked my ass into a chair. Every sip of brandy brought a little comfort to my soul. All I wanted was peace and quiet for a couple of minutes.

Mom, the kids and I got up and moved around the house like church mice the next day, hoping not to wake Stephen. What goddamn mess it was. Adam and Alexandria were on glass and bottle patrol, and Mom and I cleaned the floors and tables. Dad was already busy frying ham and bacon for breakfast. We heard a rumble upstairs. It was Stephen on his way downstairs. Dad was singing to some crazy tune on the radio while Mom and I sat at the dining room table. The smell of the bacon and ham frying overtook the awful lingering smells of the night before. The kids were busy giggling their way through the mess and nibbling on the leftovers. There was actually a warm and happy feeling in the air that morning.

Stephen owned this stereo that he managed to salvage from his rotten marriage. You'd swear it was the only kind in the world. There was nothing special about it; it was just your basic run-of-the-mill stereo.

He came down the stairs, and instead of coming into the kitchen and saying good morning to everyone, he immediately took a right turn into the living room to examine any damage. We were all in the kitchen at a stand still. Dad was mimicking him through the walls. Thank god Stephen couldn't see or hear the antics that were going on in that kitchen. Adam and Alexandria wouldn't stop laughing at their grandfather until I immediately covered their mouths with my hands. It wasn't long before this red-eyed, vein-popping, miserable Mr. Hyde came racing into the kitchen and started ranting and raving at the top of his lungs. His face had turned purple, and the nerves in his face were ready to explode. His voice was vibrating off the walls. The night of the party, a lot of people were changing the music to their liking. No one said a word at the time. I mean, how can you keep an eye on the stereo? People were dancing and talking so loud, you couldn't hear yourself think. It had to be the last thing on anyone's mind that evening. A blanket of fear filled the room. Even the bacon stopped crackling. He grabbed a piece of toast and fled to the living room. He sat there staring out the window. This is how he started New Year's Day off.

Dad said, "Where is that bottle of rum? That man could turn the Pope into an alcoholic!" We all got a chuckle out of that. Dad certainly had a great sense of humor. My parents were very upset over his actions. We all looked at each other and shrugged our shoulders. He didn't speak to any of us for hours. We tiptoed around the house like mice. Dad went into the living room to try to break the chill on the inner walls.

Stephen turned around, looked at Dad, and with disturbed tone said, "Doesn't anybody respect other people's property anymore?" Dad was back in the kitchen within seconds. What do you say to some one like that? It's not like we were dealing with a car that got totaled or a window that was smashed. After a bit, we could hear him reorganizing the tapes and records. Once he was through organizing his treasured belongings, he said to everyone in the room, "This is a warning. No one, and I mean no, one is permitted to touch my stereo again. Understood?" He couldn't have made it any clearer than that. Mom and I went out in the kitchen to make a cup of tea.

Mom quietly said, "The first chance I get, I'm going to take a hammer and smash it to pieces!"

I looked at Mom, "Please, Mom, don't even think about it!" He even had my parents walking on eggshells. As soon as the kids heard him yelling, they tailed it upstairs. As the day went on, he eventually cooled down. Dad and he were in the den watching a movie. At least that kept him out of my hair for a while. Mom and I were on our way into the living room to find Adam and Alexandria playing a game with his stereo. They were taking turns touching the stereo then running under the dining room table. "Are you two insane? Go play in your room for awhile." Before leaving the living room, Adam had to quickly have one more touch, then the two of them flew up the stairs, giggling their butts off.

Even though I was working, money was always a welcome sight in that house. I took Mom and the kids in town to go shopping. I needed everything from dishes to clothes. I eyed a beautiful comforter. The one we had on our bed was from his first marriage, so I thought it was time for a change. Instead of buying something for me, I bought a new thing for the house. When I pulled into the driveway, I said to my mom, "I hope he is still downstairs watching that movie!"

She replied, "Why?" Dad and Stephen were sitting in the living room sipping on scotch. Stephen noticed I had a large bag in my arms. If looks could have killed, I would have dropped dead in the doorway. I was so excited that I got it for fifty percent off, and it was something new for the house. You could have cut the air with a knife, the tension was so heavy. Mom had her question answered quite quickly. Mom looked gave him a look from hell and sighed. She came up into my room to help me put the new comforter on. She said, "What is wrong with that man? It was your money to spend!" I started to cry, and my hands started to shake.

"He's just like that, Mom. He's a control freak!" I had to get my wits about me for fear he would walk into the room. The comforter did brighten up the room. He didn't think so. Since we had a perfectly good one already, it was a total waste of hard-earned money. He was a very bitter man over it. When we came downstairs, Dad joined me in the kitchen to help me make some cocktails before dinner.

Dad said, "Do you think we can down one in the process of making these?" I took two shooter glasses out of the cabinet.

"Why not? Fill those suckers to the top!" They went down so smoothly. "Let's have another, and make it quick!"

As we were making the drinks, Dad said with his demented sense of humor, "You know, those prostitutes on the street corners, they have to do it quick, or they would starve to death!" Dad was trying to take some pressure off of me, but when we entered the living room, the stare of death dampened that. Stephen had everybody so uptight. There was absolutely no need for it. As the days went on, Stephen realized that he had to relax a little, put down his guard and enjoy the moment. In other words, he had to take that rod out of his butt! My parents had really gone out of their way to help out with food and entertainment cost. In the evening, we would sometimes play cards, usually poker. Dad thought it would be a nice idea to order in some pizza. By now I was broke, so I couldn't pay for it. The pizza arrived at the door, and Stephen handed the bill directly to Dad, thirty-six dollars. For once in Dad's life, he knew to shut his mouth. He simply paid the bill and enjoyed every morsel of it. While he was there, he never ordered another pizza. Trust me, Stephen sure had his share of it!

We had a couple of warm, sunny days, so the club opened its course for gold members only. Stephen, Dad and Adam headed out for a game. When they arrived back, Dad headed right for the kitchen to pour a stiff drink. His eyeballs were hanging out of his head. I knew he had had a rough day. He said to me very quietly, "Don't you ever leave me alone with that man ever again." On the other side of the coin, the three of us had a ball. Mom took us shopping, and bought Alexandria and I a bunch of new clothes, treated us to a fabulous lunch, and bought Adam a Nintendo system.. Mom spared no expense. Her visa took an awful beating that day. So there would be no confrontation when we arrived home, she bought him a wool sweater and a bottle of scotch to shut him up. This would save me a lot of explaining. Stephen pulled the rod out of his butt and started to enjoy himself. Maybe it was because he had indulged in the bottle of scotch. I didn't care as long as everyone was enjoying themselves. Alexandria was parading around the house in her new clothes. Adam was busy playing Nintendo. For once, everything seemed normal. What a nice change! Mom and I were about to start dinner when Stephen brought in a bag of beautiful steaks. Stephen, much to my surprise, went out after the golf game and bought some decent steaks, and for once, I didn't have to marinate them for six to eight hours. He even bought wine to have with the dinner. It's funny; when things were good, it was great, but Jesus, when they were bad, look out! There was no in between. It was like living on a teeter-totter. Watching my two kids playing was priceless; if only it could stay that way. They loved each other so much. Adam and her spent most of their evenings playing in the huge tub upstairs or watching movies. They were clean! It was a good thing the water was included in the rent, or that scene never would have happened. The night before they left was a pretty emotional for me and Adam. I didn't want him to leave. The only thing that kept me from jumping off the back deck was the fact that I knew I was going to see him in a couple of months. We would be together again, and this time for a long, long time.

FIFTEEN

The day they left was sad. A lot of tears had fallen. I cried the entire way home from the airport. Stephen hadn't said too much to me on the return trip, but I sensed I was in shit for something. I learned to detect the horrible vibes he would give off. That something was the comforter. He still wasn't over the fact that I bought it without him and that I wasted all that money. The least I should have done was ask for his approval. We weren't five seconds in the doorway, and he started in on me. He grabbed me and literally threw me across the room. I could see his hand raising into the air, and within a second, I grabbed Alexandria and fled upstairs into her bedroom. Before escaping, he managed to nick my backside. Nothing like a backhand on the side of my butt to make me realize how stupid I was. I immediately locked the door. We both sat on the floor quiet as mice, holding each other so tightly. We were both scared. I heard the car pull out of the driveway. He flew down the driveway, and away he went. Thank god! I didn't know what to do. I had no money and no place to run. I called my sister-in-law crying so much she could hardly understand me. She was so sympathetic with me. She knew from past conversations what I was dealing with. She didn't know what do to for me other than try to comfort me. I felt a little better after talking with her. I brought Alexandria downstairs and made her some hot chocolate. The house was so quiet and empty without Adam. I poured myself a glass of wine and stared at Adam's picture on the mantel. I didn't care if he gave me shit for having a glass of wine. I was in no mood to put up with his bullshit today! We sat in front of the fireplace without saying a word to one another.

I didn't want to give up on this relationship. We had gone through so much together. I thought that, down the road, things would improve in time once his divorce was finalized and the business started making more money. It was only a temporary phase he was going through. I was constantly trying to convince myself of that, but it wasn't always awful. When he was nice, things were wonderful. We would play in the pool, have barbeques, curl up on the couch and watch movies. There were some pretty special moments we had. It was just when things went sour that Stephen came all undone. In the beginning, Stephen used to read to Alexandria every night and sometimes join us on our walks. Stephen was quite a swimmer, an overall outstanding athlete. Over time, he taught Alexandria to be an excellent swimmer, surprisingly enough for a man who really didn't have time for kids in genera, and I'm speaking even with his own. I was amazed that he took the time to do things with Alexandria.

Stephen's business was soaring. In fact, it was doing so well that we decided to go on a little trip with some friends from the club. It seemed like the Stephen I once knew was coming back, slowly. There were three couples going. We loaded our things in the van and headed for Lake Louise. I had arranged for Alexandria to stay with my girlfriend down the street. Lake Louise was breathtaking, the air so crisp and the scenery out of this world. We both needed that trip. The hotel looked amazing. It was hard to see it from the parking lot. It had been designed by a German. It was nestled high into the mountains. The only way to get there was by cable car. We parked the van and loaded our gear onto the next available car. It was terrifying for me since I hated heights. When we walked out of the car, there was a massive cedar building looking at us. We entered the building to see an incredibly large fireplace. It was massive! It went right to the ceiling. The aroma of the firewood burning and the smell of the food coming from the restaurant was enough to drive anyone crazy. What a place to lay back! It had every luxury item a person could need for a romantic weekend. It was a weekend to unwind and have some fun. No kids, no meals to prepare, just a great time to catch up on life. Fun, my butt! Stephen brought an uninvited guest with him—Mr. Hyde. We started the evening off with a couple of glasses of wine in front of the fireplace—the perfect evening! I'd look up at the ceiling and be astonished by the stars, how perfectly and quietly they lay in the sky. I didn't want to let my guard down for a minute. God forbid I relax. We met up with the rest of the couples at the bar to have a cocktail before dinner. The food and company were joyful and uneventful for a change. We wined and dined, and the conversation was delightful. During dinner, Stephen actually held my hand and would often kiss me on the cheek. It had to be that place. It was magical! That evening, I didn't have a care in the world. Life wasn't so bad after all. The first thing we ordered were king crab legs. What a messy dish, but they are so good! They were to die for. Stephen would take great pains to remove the meat and feed it to me with his fingers. He totally blew me out of the water that night. God, I loved him so much when he acted human. After dinner, the women decided to go to the pool to have a nightcap. The men chose to stay and drink their scotch around the fireplace at the bar. We were in full swing around the pool. One by one, we ended up in the pool. The more wine we drank, the sillier and the more personal we became. They started asking me a lot of personal questions, like how I could stand living with such a control freak and why I let him push me around so much. I hadn't realized that people noticed his behavior so much. My god, was I that blind? Was it that obvious? They saw things I had never seen. Oftentimes, Stephen would go to the club without me. Apparently, there were some incidents I never even heard about. One in particular was with the owner's daughter. She had quite a liking for Stephen and made it quite well known throughout the club. Even though Stephen probably had the desire to be with her, he couldn't afford any more scandals in his life. The more he tried to ignore her, the more he pissed her off. She was one spoiled bitch trying to take away the little bit of relationship I had left.

I walked into the room soaking, wringing wet, humming away to "What a Wonderful World" to find Stephen sitting on the edge of the bed, drinking a glass of scotch. I leapt onto the bed to wrap my arms around him and said, "I'm so happy this evening. We had such a lovely time!" When he turned around, his eyes were hollow and dark. I quickly jumped off the bed. Before I could say ask what was wrong and with one big thrust of his hands, I flew into the air and landed back onto the bed.

With his jaws moving back and forth, almost in the lock mode, he said, "You're nothing but an ingrate, a floozie, a drunk and a vamp!" I lay there in terror. As I tried to escape, he grabbed me by the shoulders and threw me back onto the bed. He held me down with such force and started shaking me back and forth so much that the circulation was leaving my arms. With all my might, I managed to push him to the floor. The only thing that kept him down there was the fact that he had a few scotches in him. I actually pissed my pants. Thank god I didn't lock the door when I came in. I opened the door so quickly, I banged the middle of my forehead. As I was running down the hall, I was praying the girls would still be at the pool. I was soaked to the hind, reeked of piss and my head was throbbing. I was scared shitless. My friends were still there, laughing their heads off and drinking cocktails around the pool. When they saw the condition I was in, they quickly sobered up. They came running to the rescue. They couldn't believe their eyes. I was crying hysterically.

They covered their noses, and one of them said, "Gee, did you piss yourself? You smell like a donkey."

As I was crying my eyes out, I looked at them and said, "Yes!" They took me back to their room and cleaned me up. They warned me to get away from him, telling me he was nuts. I finally fell asleep on the bed. It was dawn when I awoke. I crawled back to my room trembling. When I opened the door, I could hear him snoring. I was safe for now. I crawled into the spare bed very carefully and quietly. The last thing I wanted to do was wake Mr. Hyde up. When I woke up the next morning, I was disorientated and felt like I had been through a meat grinder. I shook my head a couple of times and stretched. When I raised my arms in the air to stretch, the pain was awful. I noticed he had already gone for the day. The men had some previous arrangements early in the hotel lobby the next day. I crept into the bathroom and looked into the mirror. I was astonished to see how badly I really looked. That bastard! I had bruises around my neck and parts of my shoulders. I was so sick I started dry heaving. I cried so much I was weak. I managed to get into the shower holding onto the walls so I wouldn't fall. I was exhausted! I had to wear a long-sleeved shirt and wrap a scarf around my neck to conceal the bruises. The phone rang. It was the girls wondering where in hell I was. I had been supposed to meet them at the restaurant thirty minutes prior. I applied a lot of makeup, more than usual, and headed for the elevator. They all greeted me with sympathetic hugs and kisses. One of the women came up behind me and ripped the scarf away from my neck. They couldn't believe their eyes. They covered their mouths with their hands. From that day on, they hated his guts. The stress-free weekend of fun turned into a horrendous time for me. I couldn't wait to get back home to hold Alexandria. When Stephen returned from his day trip, he acted like nothing happened at all. He entered the room, gave me a hug and a kiss, looked me the eyes and said, "I love you so much!"

He told me he had made reservations for us at this succulent seafood restaurant in town, just for the two of us. I thought to myself, *Great, just what I need—to be alone with a psycho!* Was he blind? Could he not see my bruises? In all honesty, I was totally confused. I began to get ready for dinner. I came out of the bathroom with a strapless dress on, hoping he would say something.

He looked at me and, as he was rubbing my shoulders, said, "Did you fall somewhere last night? Are you alright, love? You better put something on to cover those marks." That guy had a serious problem, and it didn't take any rocket scientist to figure that one out. I never said a word. My heart and body ached enough as is was. The rest of the group went their separate ways that evening. Christ, no wonder why! I'm sure once the wives told their husbands what happened to me the night before, the men probably felt like beating the shit out of him. Stephen went to no expense that evening. We drank expensive wine and had mouth-watering lobster. He treated me like gold! I didn't know which way to turn. My emotions were being torn from one end to the other. You talk about mixed emotions! After dinner, we went back to the hotel and had cocktails in front of the fireplace. We talked about everything that night. We actually talked about opening up a bed and breakfast somewhere in Kenora. Stephen had a way about him that could conveniently make circumstances disappear. When we arrived home, he said we would contact a real estate agency to start looking at places. See, in his mind, the overwhelming news could erase the bad, but I don't forget or erase that behavior easily. We had a wonderful evening. While sitting between his legs, he would rub my shoulders and smooth my hair. It was a night I would cherish for a long time.

It was time to head back home. We arrived in the lobby to meet up with everybody. There was no one in sight. We called their rooms, but there were no answers. Stephen went up to the bellboy, and he told us they had left several hours ago. Stephen was beside himself. He yelled, "They did what?!" All he could think of was his perfect image being destroyed at the club. I came to his side to see what the problem was. He looked at me and said, "It's all your fault! You're to blame for this!" I had no business running out of our hotel room that night. I should of stayed put. He looked at me and spat out, "It's no one's business what we do behind closed doors!"

I grabbed my suitcase and muttered behind his back, "Yeah, that's right, Stephen. Even if you're shaking the living daylights out of me!" I shrieked and went outside. I must have been sick in the head as him for staying with him as long as I did. We loaded our stuff onto the cable car. The silence was torturous. One minute we were madly in love with each other, and the next he could cut my throat. What was keeping me hanging on to this relationship? When it came right down to it, I didn't want to face failure again. I had already gone through two divorces. I was trapped inside of a cocoon and couldn't get out. I knew I could have picked up the phone at any time, and my parents or Daniel would have gotten me out of there. That's what I didn't want to do. I wanted to prove not only to myself, but also to my family and to the people back in Creek Well that this was going to work, no matter what the consequences were. I know that is one selfish way of thinking. My determination was driving me to stay. That unforgiving drive home was endless and chilling. He would only stop if I had to piss, and even then, he would make damn sure I was in agony. There was no stopping at a restaurant. When we arrived home, the house was cold. I couldn't wait to go pick up Alexandria. It would be nice to have some civil conversation with someone. He was exhausted and pissed off to the limit. He poured himself a drink of scotch and went upstairs to have a soak in the hot tub. I put on some classical music and poured myself a glass of wine. I was only glad to be home for one reason—to be with Alexandria again. The next time we attended the club for an event, the members were very cold towards him. It didn't take long before the news traveled throughout the clubhouse. I actually felt a tad sorry for him that evening, even though he deserved every bit of the brush off. I stuck by his side, playing the typical happy role. I wanted to come across like everything was okay at home. Stephen had a business to operate, and a lot of those people had methods of making or breaking him.

Stephen came home from work one night dancing ten feet off the floor.

He had a bottle of wine in his hand and bags of Chinese food in the other. He put his arms around me and swung me around the room. He started saying, "Finally, I finally landed the biggest contract ever in Mexico!" It was the break he was waiting for. He cracked opened the wine, and we toasted to his victory. He mentioned that some of the wives would be attending but never elaborated on it. Over dinner, I casually brought it up that maybe I could go along too. In fact, it took every nerve in my body to ask him. He abruptly flat out replied with, "No way, I won't hear of it. Besides, do you know how much money that would cost me?" That was all the guy thought about—money! I knew I could arrange for Alexandria to stay with our friends down the street. . He made it quite clear that it was strictly a business trip, not pleasure. I couldn't understand why some of the other wives could go and I couldn't. I didn't want to push it that evening. He was in too good of a mood. The phone rang right after dinner. My friends, asking me if I was joining them in Mexico. They were so pissed off at him.

They replied, "What's wrong with him? You won't interfere with his business dealings. We'll be having too much fun!" I ran up to the bedroom and bawled my eyes out. Alexandria came in and rubbed my back with her little fingers.

She said to me in a low, gentle voice, "Mommy, I have twenty dollars that I can give you for the trip!"

I replied, "Thank you, honey, but that's really not the issue!" I looked at this beautiful creature, patted her on the backside, held her tightly in my arms and assured her we would have a great time while he was gone. "We will have the time our lives, I promise!" Every morning before he would leave for the office, I pleaded with him to let me go. I told him I could buy my own airline ticket.

He looked around at the door and said, "And how would you be able to do that, my dear?" I didn't expect him to respond. I hesitated for a moment because I wanted to say the right thing.

With a cheery voice, I replied, "I don't know, but I'll find a way!" He came back into the kitchen and looked me straight in the eyes, waving his finger in my face.

"If your way of getting money is through your parents, *forget it*! I won't hear of it! Understood?" With every word he spoke, I moved back an inch.

At that point, I wanted to melt into the floorboards. In other words, he would have been embarrassed if I asked them for financial assistance, especially for a vacation.

He flew down the hall and slammed the door, and I kicked the front door and yelled out, "Yeah, you know damn well you're cheap, and so do my parents, you son of a bitch!" I smashed my big toe all to hell. Alexandria came running down the stairs to see me lying by the door with blood spurting out of my toe. She helped me into the bathroom to get it cleaned up.

Alexandria looked up at me and said, "If you used it on him, it was well worth it, Mommy!" Stephen never gave me any money for anything, and I never asked for any. I had a part-time job with a publishing firm and the children's allowance from Daniel. By the time I bought the food, paid the phone bill and bought clothes for us, I barely had a cent left at the end of the month, so there wasn't a lot left over for pleasure trips or entertainment.

Stephen was busy packing for his trip to Mexico. I totally ignored him. Alexandria and I stayed in the den to watch a movie. The next morning, I never even bothered to make him breakfast. There were very few words exchanged. Alexandria and I sat on the living room couch, watching him put his coat on. It was a miserable, rainy, windy day, as if the day wasn't gloomy enough already. The scene was beyond words. He knew I had no money, there was hardly any gas in the car, and there was very little food in the fridge. In spite of it all, he walked out that door and never even said goodbye. He called me that night from Mexico to see how we were doing. I could hardly speak to him. He knew the situation before he left the house. For once and only once, he truly felt guilty for what he had done. I could hear it in his voice. He assured me he would wire me some money the next day. He said, "I'm sorry, love. I guess I left too hastily!" They are cheap words through telephone wires. The next day, I went to the bank at least three or four times, and nothing! At closing time, I phoned the bank, and still nothing! *That son of a bitch!* The money transfer never happened! I had about a hundred dollars left on my visa and roughly forty dollars in my checking account. There was no way that was going to last us for three weeks. I bit the bullet, called Mom and asked her to wire me up a couple hundred dollars to get me through until payday. She was more than delighted to help out. I knew I could always count on her. Sure enough, the next morning, the money was there. Now I could relax a bit. My girlfriend down the street knew he was away, so she came up to visit us. She wouldn't come near the place while he was there. She was one of the nicest ladies I had ever met. She was a secretary for the local elementary school who had a daughter Alexandria's age. She was also going through a nasty divorce. For the next three weeks, we hung out together every day. We developed a program while he was away. When the phone rang, it was Alexandria's duty to run to the stereo to turn it down. It was my friend's job to throw a glass of water over my face to sober me up, and her little girl had to maintain total silence throughout the house. We had the drill down pat! While I was on the phone with Stephen, my girlfriend was in the background pointing her middle finger to the phone. He would go on and on with his irritating voice about how successful everything had turned out. At that point, I really didn't give a rat's butt. As he was bragging on, I took the receiver, pointed it to my butt, and said to him, "Well, this is what I think of your business deal!" I could hear fabulous music playing in the background and lots of voices. I knew damn well he was in a lounge partying. I had learned another side of Stephen—he was extremely self-centered and egotistical. As soon as I hung up that phone, we cranked up the music once again. She helped out with food, and oftentimes they would spend the night. Our house was alive again. Hearing the two girls playing and giggling was a wonderful sound. The girls spent time playing with their dolls and watching movies. We enjoyed the sun and drank wine around the pool, thinking of a conspiracy on how to get rid of our men. I'd have the stereo just blasting to good old rock and roll. Our house was nestled into the woods, so the trees silenced the noise. One night, we decided to make a big pot of good old spicy meat sauce and spaghetti.

She dumped the pasta into the sieve, but before running water over it, she said, "Let's see if it is done or not!" She took a handful and threw it up against the sterile, blinding white wall. It slid to the bottom of the floor quite rapidly. She had put too much oil in the water. The girls were getting a charge out of this. She ran a lot of water over it and attempted to do it again. Another handful hit the wall. That time it stuck! *What a mess!* I thought to myself. *If he could see this kitchen, there would be war!* The funniest part was neither one of us cleaned it up until the next day. There were no limitations that night. She despised Stephen with a great passion. She had witnessed too many examples of his crazy ways. Some mornings, we woke with sore and pounding heads, but it was well worth every Tylenol we shoved down our throats. We did very little cooking. Most of the time it was takeout. The eggshells we were all walking on just turned into hard-boiled eggs. We all raised hell for three weeks, and what a time we had! The only time I lifted a finger other than at work was to lift a glass of wine to my lips.

My friend was our guardian angel. I never forgot what she did for us. The only disappointing thing was that the three weeks were coming to an end. The day before he arrived home, we had to clean up the house. My friend took all of the garbage and wine bottles to her place so he couldn't trace anything. The girls were responsible for empty junk food bags, and I had the nasty job of washing the kitchen walls down.

We all made a vow never to breathe a word of it to anybody. The community was too tight, and if one word got out, it definitely would have made it back to Stephen. We weren't really bad; it was more of being devilish and letting some steam off. I never forgot her. Someday I hope I will run into her again. If he knew how I behaved, he more than likely would have kicked both me and Alexandria out on the street. I still can't believe a man who claimed he loved me so much could leave me and a small child in a house with no money and little to no food. Did he not have a conscience?

When he was scheduled to return home, I made it a point not to be home. There was a birthday party at the club that day for one of the members' children. I had to put the brat's birthday party and the prick's returning home on a scale of one to ten. The brat won. It was not only the fact that I couldn't look at him, but I also didn't know if I could tolerate his ego. I arrived home late in the afternoon, and I noticed all of these pretty bags on the dining room table. That wasn't a sign of a guilt trip or nothing. I almost went into a state of shock. It had been several months since I'd seen him buy us anything. He came out of the kitchen full of hugs and kisses and couldn't tell me how much he loved Alexandria and I. He swung me into the air. For a moment there, I thought he was doing crack. He was too nice almost to the point that I was a little suspicious. I thought maybe the trip was what he needed, that possibly the business trip paid off in more ways than one. He bought me a beautiful pair of earrings that were still in the original box—in other words, they were new—and Alexandria a gorgeous handmade "new" doll. He had earlier arranged for a sitter so he could take me out to dinner. We went to the most expensive restaurant in town. During the dinner, he was unusually quiet. I had to strike up most of the conversation, which I had a talent for anyway. He ordered a very expensive bottle of champagne. Now I became downright worried. He started going on about all the hard times we had and the good ones. He spoke in a sensual, smooth tone as he was pouring me a glass of wine. He said, "Even though I was a little rough on you at times, I never once stopped loving you! You have helped me get through some pretty tough times and—"

Before he could say another word, I intervened. "Answer me this, Stephen. If you claim you love me so much, why did you leave Alexandria and I alone for three weeks with nothing? What were you thinking?"

He took his hands and cupped them over mine. With a sad puppy face look, he said, "I guess I wasn't thinking clearly. I...I...I was too overwhelmed with the new deal I had just landed!"

Under my breath, I said, "You meant to say you were just plain selfish!" He reached into his pocket and pulled out this velvet box. The cheeks of my butt had lost all feeling and tensed up so they joined forces with my belly button. Trust me, there was no way I had anticipated any of this. He opened the box, and there stood a one carat solitaire diamond ring.

He looked at me with those handsome, unforgiving blue eyes and said, "Will you marry me? Of course, that is, once the divorce is finalized?" I don't know if I was captured up into the moment or taken aback by his kindness. He really startled me. He put the ring on my finger and said, "I love you more than you'll ever know!" I leaned back into my chair, admiring the size and brilliance of the ring. I was skeptical, scared to death and excited all at once. My mind was turning a hundred miles an hour.

I finally reached across the table, took his hand and said, "Yes, I'll marry you!" The next day at the breakfast table, I showed Alexandria my ring. She showed absolutely no enthusiasm at all.

She was motionless, and in fact, she said, "If you marry him, Mommy, I will move in with Dad.." I certainly didn't expect that remark.

I gave her a hug and replied, "We'll see what happens!" Now I was put into another awkward position. Alexandria had always hoped that I would eventually get back with Daniel. Stephen's and my relationship had slowly gotten back on track. If there was nothing going on at the club, he would spend the money on a movie rental. It was never a new release; that was too expensive! The ranting episodes were seldom, and my nerves didn't dance as much. Finally, things were looking up. Maybe the deal in Mexico was what he needed to get his confidence level back up to par. Everything was going alright until one evening, right after dinner, when I received a phone call from my sister-in-law, Jackie. She told me Dustin's plane went down that afternoon, and there was no trace of it. No one was speculating anything at that moment. Even though we were divorced, I still thought a lot of him. He was one great guy, he just wasn't marriage material. A huge lump came into my throat, and I began to cry. All I could say was, "Oh my god! How's Adam?" I needed to speak with him right away. That poor boy! His mom was three thousand miles away from him, and that was when he needed me the most. Alexandria was so upset for her brother. She climbed into my arms and cried. I maxed out my visa making plane reservations. I didn't care; I only wanted to be with Adam. He must have been totally lost and frightened. I must say, Stephen was very compassionate about the whole situation. He even agreed to come down with me. I had my girlfriend take care of the house for us. We flew out early the next morning. The flight seemed so long. We had to stop and wait in Toronto. For three long hours, I paced that floor and kept staring at the schedule, hoping our flight would, for some reason, leave earlier. My patience was running thin. I just wanted to get there, and fast. We got to Halifax International Airport, quickly rented out a car and headed to Jackie's place.

SIXTEEN

We arrived to find my entire family sitting on the deck, sipping on beers and making idle conversation. Daniel walked out with a beer to join the family. I actually was not surprised. He was very close to Adam. He felt this is where he belonged. After all, he had raised Adam for several years. I was so thankful and grateful to see him. Adam flew into my arms and began to cry. The search and rescue team had no news Dustin's whereabouts. We all had tremendous hope he was still alive. There was nothing I could say or do at that point except be there for Adam. It was day three now, and Dustin was still missing. The tension was mounting among all of the families, the community and, of course, the press. The coverage of his disappearance was incredible. The search teams came from far and wide. There wasn't a moment of escaping the image of Dustin; his picture was on every newspaper and television station. It even made the national news three nights in a row. Adam wouldn't leave my side. The men took Adam for a game of golf to ease up the emotions and to take his mind off of the whole ordeal. We all hoped and prayed that Dustin would still be alive but feared the worse. The only thing good about that day was the weather it—was a picture-perfect day. The sun was hot, and there wasn't a cloud in the sky. My mom and I went to Jackie's to see if she needed some help with the food. I had just come out of the kitchen door with a glass of juice. The phone rang, and I froze in my tracks. Jackie took the call. All we heard was, "Yes...oh no...I will!" I knew just by sound of her voice that it was extremely bad news. She hung up the receiver and walked over to me to gave me a warm hug of comfort. It was the minister who had called to tell us that they found Dustin's body in a wooded area. The search team found the cockpit first, then moments later, a mangled body and a parachute wrapped around trees. It was quite an emotional moment for all of us. We got most of our tears out before calling the golf course to have them notify the men to come home immediately. I had to be strong for Adam. He flew out of the van and came running towards us. I still recall the look in his eyes. His eyes were full of tears and fright. He could tell by the look on my face that it was devastating news. We all decided to go down to our parents home. I took him into bedroom to talk with him. It was one of the hardest things I ever had to say to that boy in my life. I hugged him with all my might. At first, he tried to be brave by holding back the tears, but he had so much love for his father that he finally broke down. All I could do was comfort him and tell him how much I loved him. Here in my arms was this little boy who felt so empty and alone. He would never see his father ever again. It took every bone in my body not to break down in front of him.

By now, the rest of the family were on the deck conversing and crying over the tremendous loss. My parents had arranged a huge steak barbeque with all the trimmings. Adam was holding out quite well. Heather and Linda, his first cousins, were his support team then and even today. Adam tended to relate to them better than to adults. It was a very sad day in Mussel Cove. I think the booze mellowed out a lot of the pain that evening. Everybody who knew me or my family called. The phone rang so much, we started taking turns. Daniel and Stephen remained cordial to each other. In fact, they both shared in barbequing the steaks that evening. There was no time for animosity between the adults that night. We were all there because most of us loved and adored Adam, and he needed all of our support.

The funeral was massive. People came from both coasts. Dustin had a lot of friends throughout Canada. There were people there I hadn't seen for years. It certainly wasn't the place to catch up on old news. All three of Dustin's wives were present with the children. It could have been classified as a disturbing soap opera, and I wished I could have…at least then it wouldn't have been real. Adam handled himself quite bravely through the whole thing. While holding his hand very tightly, I would look down at him to find him fighting back the tears. I came to the conclusion that Adam blocked his father's death out, at least for the time being. It wasn't until several years afterwards that Adam exposed his feelings over his father's death. We walked outside of the church to see hundreds of people standing around with reporters and cameras, trying to get that sick glimpse at the grieving families. All I wanted to do was get the hell out of there with the children and head back to my parents' home. I was hoping that Adam would want to come to back to B.C. with us, but he hated Stephen so much he wouldn't budge. When Adam looked at Stephen, I could see sparks coming from Adam's eyes. I ignored his opinion for once and still tried to convince him to come live with me in British Columbia. There was nothing I could do to change his mind. He decided to remain at my brother's home until school ended. It broke my heart. Thinking back, I should have stayed as well. I was heartbroken that Adam wouldn't come with us, but at the same time, I understood. I knew Jackie and Mark loved him dearly and would take good care of him. I really wanted him to be with me, but because of the circumstances, it was not possible, at least for now. Leaving Adam again was not in my plans.

The flight back was long and sad. I don't think I spoke to Stephen the entire trip. We arrived in British Columbia and stepped right back into reality. Stephen was so glad to be back. The only thing on Stephen's mind was his damn business.

The following Friday, we were invited to this tuxedo event at the country club. Stephen's business was so successful, he had donated money to a fund for the new hockey rink for the town. Truth be known, his accountant warned him to invest in something or he was going to get nailed at income tax time. He was a very prominent businessman. Stephen's business had generated a lot of new money in town. I started to get dressed for the gala and asked Stephen to help me hook my pearl necklace around my neck. He had purchased it at a yard sale several months ago. As he was putting the necklace around my neck, I casually mentioned that, since his business had taken off so well, maybe some day he could buy me a new pearl necklace from a jewelry store. It was the wrong time and wrong place to say that. He grabbed the necklace and ripped it off my neck. The pearls flew into the air and bounced off the floor. Then he grabbed me and threw me up against the bedroom wall. I was terrified. I ran down to the kitchen to phone for help. He ripped the phone out of my hand, grabbed my chin and said, "Don't you ever do that again!" He took the receiver from my hand and slammed it onto the phone. The doorbell rang. It was the baby sitter. Thank god! That was perfect timing on her part. I always meant to thank her for showing up when she did. Stephen went to the door and greeted her with a handsome smile. In the meantime, I was trying to compose myself. My makeup had run down my cheek, and my eyes were red from crying. I swiftly ran by the babysitter and went upstairs.

The babysitter said, "Is everything alright?"

Stephen replied, "Oh she got something in her eye. She'll be fine!" I popped into Alexandria's room to give her a quick kiss on the cheek, and I asked her to pick up my pearls for me. She never even asked why I was crying. As young as she was, she knew not to ask what happened. Inside, she already knew. I put myself together again and returned downstairs. Stephen looked at me and remarked on how lovely I looked. Stephen escorted me to the car as if nothing had happened. Lately, the only thing that came out of the guy's mouth was business or money. He began to talk about the new business he was opening up in Calgary. He already had the wheels in motion. Like, thanks for letting me know! Since he hadn't said anything before, I just figured he was going to hire new management to operate it. But that wasn't so. He was going to be running it himself. He left me speechless. Then he threw another brick into my face. Just as we were driving into the club, he informed me that the party was in his honour that night, and it was a going away party for the both of us. When the valet opened my door, my mouth was still open. I kept staring at Stephen, trying to figure out what went on in that head of his. The president of the club greeted me at the door with a beautiful bouquet of flowers. He escorted me in to the lounge. A lot of women would have envied the moment. I personally thought it was bullshit! Even though I was totally pissed off at Stephen, I had to put on a smile and pretend to enjoy myself. I finally grabbed Stephen by the arm, took him aside and asked him why he didn't tell me before that night. He had a lame excuse. It was something along the lines of, "I wanted to wait until everything was finalized before I told you. I wanted it to be a surprise for you tonight."

Yeah right! It's interesting how quickly the country club organized a party all within twenty minutes! "I wasn't born yesterday, Stephen. I'd like to know what other things you kept in the closet from me."

I found out that evening through the channels that he had known for weeks. It didn't matter what I thought anyway; either way, we were moving to Calgary. I guess the day the moving truck pulled in the yard would have been a hint. I always found that in our relationship, there was very little compromising. I basically was the last person to know, and that burned my butt. I kept my mouth shut, put on a painted smile and bullshitted my way through the evening. If I opened my mouth, I took the chance of waking up Mr. Hyde. Since I didn't want to look like the stupid one, I had to act like I knew all along. Stephen had already hired a new manager to operate the business here and had the movers arranged to come in for the end of June. The grand opening was scheduled for the second week of July. The speeches began. The president started on all of Stephen's accomplishments and all the contributions he had made in the community in such a short while he was there. He presented him with a town key, along with a picture of the Rockies signed by all the male members of the club. Now that was one biased gift! The ladies presented me with a putter. At least my gift was useful. As I was accepting the gift, I took the putter, held it up into the air and began to say, "I wonder if I can use this as a self de—"

Before I could finish my remark, Stephen blurted out, "Drinks are on me tonight!" As I was walking off the stage, I knew I would eat those words later on that night. Stephen approached me and said, "How dare you, you…"

As he was saying this to me, he was smiling to the crowd. I replied, spitting words between my teeth. "You don't know even what I was going to say, so let go of my arm, *now*!" The president announced that dinner was being served. It would be my last trip up those elegant steps to the dining room. They seated us at the head table. Now that was an honor! They really did know how to present a beautiful meal. Everything was prepared to perfection. During the dinner, I didn't speak to Stephen once. I was so furious with him. He knew it too. He kept putting his hand on my leg and smoothing my thigh. I would hate to see what he would do to me if I did that to him in a public place. The dinner was scrumptious, as usual. Each of the members gave me a warm hug and kiss on the cheek upon leaving that night. Before I left the club, I stood in the middle of the entrance to take one last look at this beautiful establishment. I wanted to remember this room forever. Even though I was so ticked at him, I was glad we were moving. When we arrived home, I lit into him like there was no tomorrow. I very seldom had the opportunity or guts to do it, but that time he deserved it. He didn't listen to one word I said. He went to the bar and poured himself a scotch. As he walked by me, he had balls enough to bend over and kiss me on the cheek, continuing downstairs to watch television. That made me even more livid. I threw my hands up in the air. By the time I got through yelling at him, it was too late to call Adam to tell him that we would be moving to Calgary that summer. It would have to wait until morning. I called him the next evening. It was so nice hearing his voice.

Before I had a chance to open my mouth, he blurted through the phone, "Mom, I want to come live with you. I miss you and Alexandria." I could hardly speak, I was so elated. For once, I was crying for joy!

"Oh Adam I'm so glad to hear such wonderful news! Soon as school is out, I'll fly you out to Calgary!" I didn't care what Stephen said either. That was the best news I had heard in a long while, and no matter what, Adam was going to be living with us. Since his father's death, he was missing me something terrible. He just wanted to be with Alexandria and I.

This time, Stephen wanted to purchase a home. We flew down to Calgary to go on a house-hunting trip. We hunted for a house for almost a week. We finally found *the* house. The outside needed a lot of work, but other than that, it was beautiful. It was huge. There was a large, oval pool in the back, surrounded by weeds and rotten wood. There was a clothesline covered in bushes. I don't think it had been used in years. The next strong windstorm would take the fence down. The inside was remarkable! There was a long, open staircase to the front entrance. The kitchen was a masterpiece—every cooks dream—with everything built into brick! Off the kitchen was a huge living room with a fireplace that went straight to the ceiling. The den had two large country doors leading out to a filthy, dirty backyard. The master bedroom had a private deck overlooking the pool. The window coverings were tastefully and elegantly designed to compliment the house. There were five bedrooms, five bathrooms and two living rooms. It was a house for a family of at least ten, but Stephen's surroundings reflected the amount of success in his life. The bigger the better! Stephen asked me, "What do you think, love? Do you like it?"

I replied, "Yes, of course I love it, though it's more than what we need!"

We went back to the hotel to discuss the house. We were so excited. We discussed what colours we would paint certain rooms, and how we would redesign the pool area and maybe change some of the flooring. Once we talked ourselves to a conclusion, he called the real estate agent over to draw up the contract. It was a day to rejoice and celebrate—our first house together. The agent arrived and organized the paperwork on the table. While the agent was preparing the quote, Alexandria and I went in to the kitchen to prepare some iced tea. We were in the kitchen singing and acting silly. I could hear them discussing a price. I served the tea and stood behind Stephen, rubbing his shoulders. He cupped one of my hands and looked up at me and smiled. I said to the agent, smiling from ear to ear, "Isn't it a beautiful home?"

He replied, "Yes, you'll certainly love the area!" The agent took his pen, looked at me and said, "How do I spell your last name?"

I never got to speak. Stephen cut me off and said, "The house will only be in my name!" The agent swiftly turned to Stephen and said, "Stephen, are you sure about this?" I couldn't help myself. I started crying immediately. I ripped my hands away from him. My jaw dropped to the floor. I grabbed Alexandria and flew out the door. I was shattered. We walked the streets for hours. I called Dad up collect from a pay phone. He advised me to get the hell out of there and fast. Everything I owned was in storage with his stuff. If I only I had thought beyond my nose. Dad said I could have my things shipped out later on. I was a sucker for punishment. I knew he was right, but I just couldn't give up, not now. I wish now I would had listened to Dad. There was something that kept drawing me to that guy. I felt quite confident that once Adam moved in with us, everything would be great. We sure had our arguments over that issue! Stephen still was reluctant to have Adam move in with us. I took Alexandria to Wendy's for a burger. I can only thank god that she was too young to understand all of that. On the other hand, she was a very bright little girl. When we returned back to the hotel, he was shuffling through all of the papers from the house sale. The room was silent! I bathed Alexandria and off to bed we went. When we awoke the next morning, he was gone. He returned later with a bottle of red wine and flowers. He tried to convince me to understand that it was the right thing to do. He said he had a home before, and he lost fifty percent of everything. He wasn't going to do that again, at least not for a while. It would still be "our" home, I just wouldn't own any of it. After all I had been through with that man, that was how he thought. He took selfish to a whole new level! We flew back to Victoria to make the final moving arrangements. The drive to Calgary was tedious. The house issue was still on my mind. It just didn't sit well with me. I had invested a couple of hard years with him, not to mention I was engaged to be married to him. I couldn't for the life of me understand why he did what he did. To this day, I still don't understand. My heart had been torn in so many ways, and the most outlandish thing about it all was that I still loved him.

The day I picked Adam up from the airport was one of the best days of my life. He was and still is my pride and joy. Alexandria and I were elated when we saw him walking through those terminal doors. Now I felt complete with my two children with me. I knew Stephen would be at work when we arrived home. I was glad because it gave us time to catch up. He looked so great, I couldn't stop hugging him. We showed him the house and his new room. His room also overlooked the pool. I had prepared Adam's all-time favorite meal for dinner that night: steak, potatoes, and homemade apple pie! It was so wonderful to have my boy with me again.

That summer, the heat was intense. Luckily enough, we had a huge pool in the backyard that we all thoroughly enjoyed. We had lots of barbeques and started mingling with the neighbors. One of our neighbors was giving away kittens. The kids fell instantly in love with them. I finally convinced Stephen to have a look at them. There were only two left. The woman said she wouldn't split them up because they were identical twins. We ended up with the two of them. We named them Kit and Kat. They were so adorable. They chewed, peed and climbed on anything and everything for the first while. We had so much fun with them. They actually brought warmth into the house. The house finally had some life in it! Stephen showed compassion towards those two furry creatures. Stephen was constantly at Adam's throat about getting a summer job. Since I had found a full-time work with the local newspaper, I thought Adam could stay home and take care of the house and Alexandria for me. There was no way that was going to happen. Adam finally managed to get a job doing landscape work with a local business in town. He enjoyed it very much, plus it got him out of the house away from Stephen. There were times when they did see eye to eye, but they were few and far between.

Things had been going along quite nicely until one summer night. I arrived home from work and started to prepare dinner. Before diving into the shower, I took the steaks out of the fridge and brushed some barbeque sauce on each steak. Stephen walked into the kitchen and gave me a hug. While he was hugging me, he saw the steaks on the cupboard. He threw me up against the cupboards. He kept staring at the steaks and started yelling at me, "You destroyed the steaks. You never put sauce on them! Don't you ever do that again!" He grabbed his steak, threw it into the sink and washed it off immediately. Mr. Hyde had returned. God, it had been nice around there without him! It had been a while since I'd had a visit from him. I sped by him, grabbed Alexandria and ran upstairs to Adam's room. I slammed the door and locked it. He was a little bewildered. He hadn't witnessed too much of this stuff in his life. All three of us watched him cook his steak from the bedroom window. As he was eating his precious steak, we quietly went down the steps and quickly got into the car. There was a moment when I had hoped he would have choked to death on it. I took the kids to MacDonald's. When we arrived home, he was sitting by the pool sipping on a glass of wine. It was so hot that evening that we wanted to go for a swim to cool off. As we walked out onto the deck, he sat there like a piece of deck furniture.

I said to the kids, "Ignore him and have some fun." As soon as he saw the kids, he left the deck and went inside.

The property was in need of some landscaping. That was to be our late summer project. One sunny day, Alexandria and I decided to start working on the front of the house. It had to be at least thirty-five degrees out. The front entrance had to be groomed and weeded. It took us most of the day to complete this task. We dug, carried, pulled, planted and dragged for hours. We were covered with dirt from head to toe, our hands were covered in bleeding, sore blisters, and we were totally sunburnt. When we were through, it looked beautiful. Even the neighbors came over with lemonade and complemented us on the diligent and beautiful work we did. It seemed that the previous owners weren't much into keeping the grounds up. We were so proud of ourselves. We sat on the front step admiring it and sipping on homemade lemonade. We washed up and dove into the pool to cool off. It was a great day, and I was going to reward Alexandria and Adam by treating them to supper at Pizza Hut. Adam had come home early and joined us in the pool. I went in the kitchen to get us all a cold drink. I turned around to see an enraged man flying through the patio doors with veins ready to burst and eyes fuming with fire. He grabbed me and started yelling at the top of his lungs, "Who did that to the front of my *house*? Was it *you*? Did you ask my permission? Don't you ever, ever do anything to my house again without my full approval!" He released his hands from my shoulders. The kids heard the shouting and came running in through the patio doors. I told them to run to their room at once. Mr. Hyde once again appeared at the scene. Stephen stood there with his fist clutched, breathing heavily. I managed to make it out of the kitchen before he exploded again. Every bone in my body trembled.

I turned around in the hall and said, "We were only trying to *help*!"

He replied, "I don't want to hear any of your lame *excuses*!" I ran upstairs. When I opened the door, the both of them were crouched down on the floor, crying in each other's arms. They were afraid for me. The next time I decided to do something to "his" house, I would have to get full approval from him. Once again, I saw the control freak lose his mind. Once he was over his little tantrum, he went outside and dove into the pool. We all watched him swim through the window.

Adam said, "We can always hope he has a heart attack, Mom!"

Alexandria replied, "That would be too good for him!" I hugged them and assured them everything would get better; soon, I hoped. The person I was living with seemed to have different personalities, and certain things just made him lose it.

Our neighbors Jeff and Linda were great people. They were so friendly and hospitable. I got to know Linda very well. Often, we would sit around their pool and enjoy a glass of their homemade wine. It was so relaxing and peaceful in their home. There was never anyone watching over my shoulders, and there was no one to answer to. They had a wine cellar with an array of wines, as, in time, so did Stephen. Someone else couldn't dare have something that he didn't. He finally acquired a hobby. I had to hand it to Stephen, his wine was quite nice. Jeff was a riot, easygoing and full of fun. One evening, we invited them over for a couple of games of cards. They arrived with a few bottles of wine. The evening was going along pretty smoothly until Stephen noticed that I was filling the wine glasses over half full. Linda thought that was great. She said with laughter in her voice, "It saves time going back to the bottle!" Jeff and I got a kick out of that, but Stephen didn't even crack a smile. He made it quite clear to me in front of Linda and Jeff not to do that. It was improper to fill a glass over half full! I was so embarrassed. I could have cracked the bottle top off and cut his throat open. Every hair stood up on my back. *Here we go again.* Before long, the air was so thick you could have cut it with a knife. Stephen's unpleasant looks had discouraged any hope of fun that evening. They soon left for home and never returned. Trust me, I didn't want them to leave. I knew I was in shit. I made him look bad in front of them. At least in his eyes, it was all my fault. For once, he didn't go crazy. He simply took his glass of wine and went downstairs. If looks could have killed, I would have dropped dead. I must have been a cat with all of those lives! For the first time, I believe he felt embarrassed for opening his mouth, and that was rare.

The fall approached, and I had to get the children ready for school. Stephen's business had taken off. Things at the moment were fine. I had put Adam into Boy Scouts and Alexandria in Brownies. Our social life was a little dull, but that was too be expected. Stephen was so busy with his new clients that he didn't have much time for us. I missed having Linda and Jeff over. Linda thought Stephen was such an anal butt. They always welcomed the kids and I at their place anytime. Thank god. There were times their home was my salvation. Between the house, the children and my job, I kept quite busy. My financial responsibilities were to buy all the food and pay the phone bill, over and above taking care of all the children's needs. Plus, I helped with the cost of the landscaping and home décor items. Trust me, I paid my share. Our weekends consisted of watching an old release rental, because it was cheaper, or just watching television.

In the late fall, my family phoned to ask if they could come up to spend Christmas with us. They wanted to see our house...excuse me, his house. I still had difficulties dealing with that issue. I was delighted that they wanted to come for a visit, but I was a little concerned over Stephen. He was a tad anal and somewhat uptight. I had become a pro in dealing with some of Stephen's uproars and learned to handle them delicately. On the other hand, my family just went with the flow and enjoyed life as it came to them. Mind you, I hadn't mastered all of his quirks! That would have taken a lifetime. The news was refreshing and something to look forward to. If nothing else, it would be interesting. There was a lot to do. In the evening, Alexandria and I would make cookies and pies to freeze. Adam was our sampler. Two weeks before they arrived, the kids and I decorated the entire first floor. My kids didn't need chocolate to make them bounce off the walls. Just the mere thought of seeing their relatives put them on a natural high.

SEVENTEEN

They brought bags of presents, booze and food. Now that was Christmas! The entire house lit up when they arrived. That house never saw so much excitement. It was wonderful to see them all. We once again had a pissy little tree. The only thing I could say about it was that it was alive. There were twelve of us in total. I had to buy and prepare all of the food for the crowd. Stephen never gave me one cent toward anything while they were there. I walked on eggshells the entire time they were in our home. In fact, I know I wasn't the only one walking gently. He gave the kids a hard time with their rooms. They became a little untidy because they were having so much fun with their cousins. They had better things to do than worry about their rooms, and I couldn't blame them. He was always at Mom for one thing or another. The first day they arrived, they were drinking tea in the living room. That made me very nervous. Stephen had bought a gorgeous white rug a couple of weeks prior, and he didn't bother to spend the extra money to have it Scotchguarded. Within five minutes, Mom had spilled tea on the carpet. Everyone's eyes focused on that two-inch square. Stephen immediately walked over to it, holding his tea very carefully, and examined the spill. No one said a word. He very delicately took a tiny brush and warm soapy water, went down on his knees, and began the process. On another occasion, she got nailed for wearing her wet boots through the laundry room, down the hall and into the den. He was going to throw her out onto a snow bank for that one. Of course, Mom said to him, "I'll slap your butt if you don't stop complaining about it!"

He replied, "That would be the day!" The two of them never saw eye to eye. I don't imagine most people did with him. He basically complained about everything from the number of beer bottles mounting in the garage to the constant lack of manners. You have to understand that he wrote the book on manners, and if you didn't comply under his rules, then you were basically a rude individual. One morning, Mark put a muffin onto a teacup saucer.

Stephen said with a snappy voice, "That is not the proper plate for a muffin!"

Mark replied, "See that little circle in the middle of the plate? That was designed for a muffin! The muffin fits perfectly into that hole!" He was saying this to Stephen while demonstrating. Mark knew better; he was just trying to drive Stephen crazier than he already was. Stephen had lost control of his home. My family would humor and mimic him—mind you, not in front him. A lot of it was between walls. He kept a close eye on me too. The first night, everyone was pretty tired except Jackie and I. We were and still are best friends. We were so excited to see each other and had so much news to catch up on that we decided to stay up for a while. We sat in front of the fireplace, laughing and enjoying a couple of glasses of wine. Jackie looked over her shoulder to find Stephen standing halfway up the staircase, staring down at the two of us.

Jackie gave me a funny kind of nervous look and said, "Don't look now, but...we're being watched!" A cold chill went up my back. Once he was noticed, he quickly continued up the stairs. That kind of ended the moment for us. The next morning was the moment the kids were waiting for: Christmas Day. The excitement that morning was exhilarating. What a Christmas we had. Stephen managed to bottle up his anal behavior that day and put it into the cupboard.

Their visit was great, but it had taken a toll on Stephen. I knew he was ready to blow up by looking at the size of the veins in his neck. It was a wonder he didn't have a heart attack. Somehow he managed to control himself. One morning, we had boiled eggs for breakfast, and there were two left over. The next day, Jackie had noticed that the eggs were still on the countertop, so she threw them into the garbage. She knew what Stephen was like, so she buried them deep down into the garbage and made sure they were totally hidden. That evening, I was making a spinach salad. He thought he had put the eggs in the fridge, but we knew he didn't, and none of us were going to argue with him. He opened the fridge and got on his knees to find those eggs. Meanwhile, in the den, the gang were all playing a game of Trivial Pursuit. I could hear the laughter bouncing off the walls. They were having such a grand time. On the other side of the wall was this persistent, crazed man looking for a pair of eggs. Boy, he was determined he was going to find those eggs. Sheri and I walked into the kitchen to witness the scene of stupidity. His next move was the garbage can. We both looked at each other with fear. He was about to come across the eggs. Luckily enough, earlier I had thrown out some old noodles and lemon sponge. Stephen hated to get his hands dirty. Finally, he gave up the egg quest and started to boil some fresh ones. We took a deep sigh and returned to the den. When he joined us in the den, he still was on some sort of mission and asked everybody if they had eaten or seen the eggs that day. All I could hear were low-lying murmurs throughout the room. In other words, *get over it*. Jackie thought he was nuts. During the days, the men took the kids sleigh riding and sometimes to a movie. We were all so glad to be with one another. Some of the time we would go to the malls, but mostly we would relax around the house, sitting in front of the fire, laughing about old times. It took some time to prepare the meals since there were so many of us. Elsie, Justin's wife, was a hoot. I swear, she spent every waking moment in the kitchen making cookies and pies. She was in the kitchen making some kind of orange glaze for these cookies. Jackie and I were sitting in the living room chatting up a storm. All of a sudden, I could hear a terrible grinding noise coming from the kitchen. I heard Elsie yelling, "Get in here and help me!" I ran into the kitchen, and she was standing there by the sink with her hand down the garbage disposal.

"What are you doing, Elsie?"

She replied, laughing out loud, "I was grinding up the orange peelings when the f…top of the grinder fell in!" Jackie, by now, had joined us in the kitchen. We were all laughing. Elsie said, "What's Stephen going to say when he goes to make his precious juice in the morning?" Jackie and I never said a word. Our faces went blank. Elsie said, "He's right behind me, isn't he?" We both nodded our heads. Elsie took her hand out of the garbage disposal with the chewed up grinder in it. Stephen walked over to the sink and kindly asked her to move away. With great patience, he removed every piece of that top from the garbage disposal. He placed it onto the counter and tried to piece it back together. Jackie looked at me.

"I'm out of here!" Elsie and I weren't far behind her. There was one thing about Elsie—she always had a smile on her face. The three of went into the living room to chill out in front of the fire.

Elsie said, "I know where I'd like to shove that grinder!" When Jackie and I were together, we would do an awful lot of laughing, much of the time over the least little thing. The night before they, left we had a party. We danced, drank and ate. The house was full of laughter. Since their flight was leaving early the next morning, we couldn't stay up too late. It was eerie how quiet the house was after they left. The kids and I sat on the couch with two cats with long faces. Stephen didn't spend a long time at work that day. I mean, after all, it still was the Christmas season. When he arrived home, he was tired, cranky and pissy. We exchanged very few words, and the ones that were said weren't pleasant. In his opinion, I was raised by a bunch of hillbillies. My parents were classified as Ma and Pa Kettle. As for my brothers, I won't even go there. He added that he had never seen so many cases of beer being consumed in such a short time in his entire life. I wished he would shut his mouth. The more he muttered, the more he was ruining a completely wonderful time. I didn't know what he was griping about anyway—he had enjoyed himself too. I think the fun he had scared him a little. He saw another side of life, not too mention that he had indulged in his fair share of wine, beer and scotch. We spent the rest of the day shadowing each other. The kids and I started to put some of the decorations away. There was no point in leaving them up.

Stephen's divorce had taken a turn for the worse. Between his wife getting greedier by the week, his lawyer's cost and the cost of maintaining that huge house, there wasn't a lot of money left over. At least he didn't let me think there was anything left over. He was so frugal in everything he bought. I'm definitely sure he had a stash somewhere hidden away. One Sunday, we went for a drive. I said, "Stop so I can grab a couple of coffees for the road!" How stupid of me to even suggest such a thing!

He replied, "Instead of spending your hard-earned money on coffee, you should consider investing it." He went on and on. "If every time you wanted to buy a coffee you invested it instead, just think how much money you'd have saved in a year." I looked at him with a disgusted look. *Give me a break!* I hardly had enough money to feed the kids and clothe them decently; there wasn't a hell of a lot left over for investing. When we arrived home from the countryside trip, I checked for messages. There was one from Daniel. I waited until evening to return his call, mainly for the discount. He told me he was taking a transfer to the oil rigs in Halifax. I was so happy for him; he had a lot of friends there. There was only one drawback, and that was that he would be further away from the kids.

March break was just around the corner. I had suggested to Stephen to take a couple of days off so we could do something with the children. My boss was kind enough to give me the week off. He understood since he also had children. Stephen agreed to take time off but not to spend it with us. He was going to visit his son in Winnipeg. That was news to me. I suggested we all go to make it a family trip, and I could meet his son. There was no question that we were not going with him. It was a rainy, windy day when he left for the airport. I said to him, "Let me take you to the airport? It will save you some cab money!" I had just assumed he was leaving the car for us. Next thing I knew, he was packing the car up and heading down the driveway. I stood in the kitchen with the children, thinking, *Why in hell is he doing this?* Here I am with the kids, no car and hardly any money. Great! My god, he was self-centered. It rained for three continuous days nonstop. We would put our rain gear on and walk to the corner store to rent movies. I managed to scrape up enough money to treat them to a pizza the first night he was gone. The following day, a card came delivered to the door. It was a birthday card from my parents. Seeing as I had to sign for it, there had to be money in it. I shouted to the kids, "Come here!" We gathered around the table while I opened the card. There it was, a sight for sore eyes—a check for two hundred dollars. It couldn't have come at a better time. I told the kids to get their coats on. Since we didn't want to waste cab fare, we decided to walk to the mall. Trust me, that was one long walk, especially when it was pouring rain out. We spent the entire afternoon at the mall. We stopped on the way home to pick up some goodies, movies and wine for the evening. I didn't dare touch his precious wine. I think that due to the circumstances, the kids had had a pretty good time so far. Stephen never called me once. I tried to get a hold of his son's phone number, but it was unlisted. He had one awful mean streak in him! He arrived home and was so loving it was almost sickening. It was like he was on a guilt trip of some sort. He was one tough cookie to figure out.

Stephen's business was now making a huge profit, so things weren't so tight around the house anymore. Instead of old releases on Friday night, he was now renting new releases. Sometimes he and I would play crib tournaments on Saturday. It was rather fun. He'd crack open a bottle of his cherished wine, and we'd sit playing by the hour, seeing who was going to be the champ in crib. In most cases, the games were pretty close. Stephen had to leave on another business trip to Mexico. He would be gone for a couple of weeks. I didn't even bother to ask if I could go since I knew he wouldn't allow me anyway. To be honest, I really didn't want to go with him in the first place. I was too happy to be with my kids. It would be a nice break for me. The children and I had a ball. We raised hell while he was away. I needed some wine to calm the old nerves down and relax a bit. At least with him gone, I knew I could sit back and enjoy it! We would invite our friends over and have pool parties and sleepovers. I swept the eggshells in the corner while he was gone. When he returned home, he was so glad to see and me and, surprisingly enough, even the kids. He had bought gifts for us all. These trips were making a better person out of him. The only problem was that they were short-lived. That following weekend, my friends from work were having a barbeque. It was bring your own everything, from food to wine and even the kids. The kids didn't want to go. They were content in staying home without Stephen around. It gave them a night to raise hell and run wild in that huge place. It was a casual affair. A lot of them had never met Stephen. The women all thought he was extremely handsome and quite a conversationalist. I knew all to well how he behaved in public. *Here we go, the "perfect gentleman" act!* One of the guys at work made wicked potent wine. The girls and I grabbed a bottle and went outside on the deck. Every now and then, I would look inside the patio door, and to much of my surprise, one of the women started to flirt with Stephen. Of course, he was lapping it up. It boosted his ego even more. She knew we were engaged, but for some reason, that never bothered either one of them. The thing that really ticked me off was that he was enjoying it! So I started drinking more wine. I was getting hammered, and I didn't care! My girlfriend took me down to the basement to sober me up. She had met Stephen before, so she knew how he would respond to that sort of behavior, even though his wasn't much better. I was so sick. That homemade wine was tasty but brutal. She laid me down on an old couch, hoping I would be able to sleep some of it off before Stephen realized I was missing.

I kept saying to her, "Why is he such a prick? What's he doing with that bitch in the kitchen?" She told me to be quiet and try to get some sleep.

She said, "I'm going to keep my eye on him for a while. I'll be back!" The minute she noticed him looking for me, she would dive into a conversation with him. It wasn't long before he detected something was up. He found me passed out. Later, I blamed it on the wine and all the stress I had been under. In his eyes, there were no explanations.

The next day, I thought I was going to die. I hugged that toilet bowl most of the day. He never once asked if I was okay. He would walk into the bathroom and say, "You deserve every bit of this!" He showed no mercy whatsoever. That wine must have been bad because I wasn't the only one sick. The girls called that afternoon, and they too were pretty sick puppies. I didn't even drink a lot of wine that night, and I was quite capable of drinking a liter at least. Once again, I was in the doghouse, and he, on the other hand, was totally innocent.

That summer, Daniel flew the kids down to visit him for a month. They were so happy to get out of that house for a while. The only things the kids missed were me, the cats, and the pool. The month they were gone, I missed them terribly. I couldn't fret over it. I knew they would have a wonderful time with their dad. Daniel never spared his love or money with those two. While they were gone, I enjoyed the pool and the hot sun. Stephen and I had some wonderful times that month the kids were gone. We attended some concerts and live plays and enjoyed the pool. It was a peaceful month. It brought harmony back into our relationship. I'm not suggesting that the kids brought tension into our relationship, but I personally believe that they did in Stephen's eyes. My phone bill was incredible. Before long, they were back home. We worked on the house all summer, inside and out. The kids returned home just in time to get ready for school.

One evening, Stephen came home from work and, much to my surprise, told me to get a dress on because we were going out for dinner. I immediately fed the kids and got dressed in a stunning blue dress. It was a treat for me. I hadn't been anywhere in months. I was wondering what brought it on. He first took me to the symphony. The music was splendid. After, we headed for a seafood restaurant around the corner. The meal was superb; not only the food, but also the company. The conversation was cheerful and hopeful. The evening was going so smoothly, I thought it would be the perfect opportunity to bring up New Year's Eve. I told him that one of the wives from his office had called me and asked if we were going to attend the lavish ball. She had also mentioned that we were the only couple who hadn't bought tickets. I wished I would have eaten those words. I had released Mr. Hyde!

He said, "Waiter bring the check now. At once!" He put his coat on and headed for the car. Our meals hadn't been touched. That was one way to lose weight! He lay into me like a bull's butt was on fire. I should have known better than to open my mouth. I jumped into the car, and before I had the door closed, he started in on me. He started yelling, "By the time my wife gets through ripping out my jugular, I'll be lucky to breath. Don't you understand that?"

I quietly replied, "I should be so lucky!"

He muttered the whole way home. "Woman, damn woman!" When we arrived home, he poured himself a glass of scotch and went to our room. I could hear him yelling at someone on the phone. "Well, next time when you get an idea, run it by me first. Is that understood? And I'd appreciate it if you wouldn't call my home!" That poor bastard! I figured it had to be someone from work. It was about time someone else got a piece of his tongue. I would imagine that person from work packed his bags and headed for a third-world country, never to be seen again. There was no way I was sleeping with Mr. Hyde that night. In fact, I didn't even want to go upstairs to sleep. The kids were watching television in the den, so I joined them. They could tell by my voice that things weren't great. I went to the fridge to see if we had a bottle of wine open. I didn't dare open a new one. I wasn't sure if he counted them or not, so I didn't want to take the chance. But he had a vat of wine brewing in the basement, ready to be bottled off in a couple of days.

I took a bowl from the kitchen and said, "Adam, come downstairs to help me get a couple of glasses of wine out of the vat." Adam was more than happy to do anything against Stephen. I lifted the little tube from the top of the vat, and with everything we had, we managed to lift the vat and pour not only a couple of glasses of wine but several. Holy shit! There was wine everywhere. We must have spilled over half of it over the cement floor.

Adam looked at me. "We're dead, Mom. You know that!" One good thing was that the bowl was sure filled to capacity. We started giggling our heads off. We could hear footsteps as someone was coming down the stairs. We almost pissed our pants. That really would have been game over in more ways than one. We both held our breath, froze in our tracks, and our eyes were glued to the door. The door opened slowly. It was dark on the other side, so we couldn't see who it was. There was a little hand on the doorknob. Luckily enough, it was Alexandria! She stood there laughing really loudly.

"Alexandria, be quiet! Don't wake up Mr. Hyde, or we're history!" All she could see was a wine trail and two people standing at the end of it. Since we didn't want to walk through the wine, we had Alexandria bring down all the towels in the laundry room. What a terrible mess! I had put Alexandria on Mr. Hyde watch while we cleaned up the mess. It took several towels and a lot of mopping to clean up that awful mishap. Adam and I were covered in wine. We looked at each other and took a swig of wine. "Good job, mate!" But now we were in another dilemma—the vat was half full..

Adam whispered, "Mom, what are we going to do?" He knew that if we didn't do something, there would be a death sentence for their mom. I decided to fill it up with cold water from the tap. What other choice did we have? We hid all of the towels in black garbage bags and hid them under the deck. We made sure everything was perfect before we went upstairs. I thought afterwards that I could have siphoned it out with our tube! It wasn't so much needing a drink of wine that night, it was more taking something that belonged to him and getting away with it. We had one hell of a good laugh over it. The day he bottled that wine was pretty nerve-wracking. He went downstairs to prepare to bottle. The three of us stayed upstairs. I thought for sure the batch would have gone bad. The three of us watched the clock, counting the minutes. Each minute that passed gave us another breath of air.

He opened up the door with the tester in his hand, brought it into the kitchen and said, "Give me two glasses!" I could hardly keep my hand still,

I was so nervous. He swirled the wine around in his glass and put it up to the light to test the clarity of it. When he put the glass to his lips, I was ready to make a run for it. The kids had already had their cue to hide in their rooms. I waited in anticipation to see his reaction. As he lowered his glass, he said, it was the best batch he'd ever made—so smooth and sharp, perfect! It took everything I had not to blow my mouthful of wine all over him. After he bottled the batch off, he started in on the next one. I swear, I wasn't going near that one. Once again, we could breath again. I began my chores for the day. Stephen was busy cutting out a new piece of cardboard for the lid for his new batch. He laid it on the ironing board while preparing the ingredients. I had asked Adam to bring in the clothes that needed ironing. He put the cardboard down on the floor so he had room to put down the clothes. Adam didn't know what that cardboard was for. I was ironing Stephen's shirts, humming away with relief, and the kids were playing Nintendo in the den. He walked into the room and picked the cardboard up off the floor. His eyes went blank, and his face reddened. I put the iron down.

"What's wrong, Stephen? Are you alright?" There was a brief moment when I thought he was having a heart attack or some kind of seizure. He picked up the piece of cardboard.

He came directly at me, yelling, "It's *ruined*! Who did this? Now it's full of dust particulars! Why?"

I yelled back at him, "What are you, some kind of a psycho?" Bad choice of words on my part. The only thing between Mr. Hyde and me was the ironing board. His face spanned across the board.

It was within an inch of my face, and with this terrifying, chilling voice, he yelled, "*Don't you ever call me that again*!" He was so close to my face, I could see the hair up his nose. He turned very slowly, took the piece of cardboard and snorted his way downstairs. He sounded like an overheated bulldog. I kept my hand on that iron with every ounce of strength I had. I was prepared to use it if I had to. The kids hid behind the chairs in the den. So much for a lovely day! I grabbed the kids and fled upstairs. We hid upstairs for a couple of hours. I wanted to call Daniel for help but didn't have the courage. I didn't want to think I'd failed again in yet another relationship. The kids begged me to call him.

I said to them, "Do you think your father is going to help me after what

I did to him? Think about it! There's got to be another way!" Alexandria was crying in Adam's arms, sobbing.

"Mommy I hate that man, he's mean!"

Adam looked at me and said, "I'm with her, Mom, all the way, and Mom, look at the way he treats you! Come on, Mom!" I was torn. If only I had had some money. I hated to commit to failure once again in my life. The three of us hurdled in a corner of the closet until we heard the car pull out of the driveway. We ran down the stairs to fill up on food. As each one of us showered, the other one was on window watch for Stephen's return. We quickly got dressed and headed over to Linda's place. She greeted us with open arms. We didn't come home until later on that night. We quietly crept into the back door to find Stephen asleep in his chair with the television blasting. The three of us tiptoed to the basement, curled up in balls and fell asleep.

When I awoke the next morning, I could smell breakfast cooking. I jumped up to see if the kids had gone upstairs to make breakfast, but they were still nestled beside me. I quietly walked up the stairs and peeked around the corner. *My god, he is making breakfast!* When I came into the kitchen, the table was set for four, the coffee brewing, and he was whistling. I said under my breath, "Well, it's good to see Dr. Jekyll dropped in this morning!"

He looked at me. "Oh good morning, love. How are you today? Would you like a cup of freshly perked coffee?" I looked at him as if he were crazy. *Christ, what am I dealing with here?* He was quite chatty and humming to a Roger Whittaker song. I think he felt a little ridiculous and childish about his previous actions over the cardboard. He said, "Get the kids up! We'll have a nice breakfast and then head to the airplane museum." I thought to myself, *Is this guy totally insane or what?* I couldn't understand his behavioral pattern at all, but who really knew what made him tick? I often thought the devil! The kids were hesitant to eat with him, so I told them they could eat downstairs in the den while watching cartoons. That suited Stephen fine. After breakfast, we headed into museum. It was fascinating to see the huge displays of airplanes. Adam was enjoying himself immensely. He loved everything and anything to do with planes. We were all getting a little hungry, so Stephen said he would treat us to lunch at one of the fast food chains. The kids were right in their glory. In the back seat of the car, I could hear them chatting about what they were going to order from the menu.

Adam said to Alexandria, "Everything!"

Alexandria replied, "You can't do that, he won't let you!" The place was packed. Each one of us ordered what we wanted. We sat at a table, and Adam, being a boy, just grabbed the first burger in sight and took a huge bite out of it. Well, when Stephen opened his burger, it was Adam's.

He grabbed the burger out of Adam's hand and yelled out, "You stupid brat, that's my burger! Didn't you look at it before you bit into it?" Adam's face hit the floor with embarrassment. The entire restaurant came to a stand still, and the looks of pity filled the room. Stephen took his burger and drink, got into the car and drove off. The three of us got up slowly, packed up our food and went outside. We sat on a ledge in the parking lot eating our cold burgers. I had five dollars on me, and that wasn't enough to get us home. A nice couple came out of the restaurant and asked us where we lived. Without any hesitation, they drove us home. I warned the kids as soon as they walked in the door to run to their room and lock the doors. He met me in the hall.

"How did you get home?" I never answered him. I swept by him to go into the kitchen. "I'm speaking to you!"

I turned around, "He's only a kid! Don't you have any kind of a heart?" He put his head down and went downstairs. I never saw him for the rest of the day. Thank god!

After that day, the kids learned very quickly to avoid, elude and ignore Stephen. I was trying to cope with the situation and made every attempt to make the relationship work, but my nerves were running thinner by the day. I was a nervous wreck!

Christmas was there before I knew it. Daniel had arranged to fly to Calgary and take Alexandria skiing over the holidays. Since Alexandria was going to be gone for a week, she had one of her dear friends over to spend the night with her so they could exchange gifts before she left. That morning, I was making a deluxe breakfast for everybody. The kids were chatting away at the table and giggling their little heads off. Adam was swooping forks in the air pretending they were airplanes. I, on the other hand, wasn't as cheerful as the kids. I was a little worried because I couldn't hear any whistling coming from upstairs. I was quickly going through my thoughts. *What could he possibly be upset about? Nothing unusual happened yesterday, the kids behaved! Christ what could it be?* I was getting prepared for the worst-case scenario. I was soon about to find out. Mr. Hyde came storming into the kitchen waving a belt in the air. Everyone in that kitchen froze in their tracks. My stomach went into one big twist tie. We all held our breath waiting for the big explosion. The veins in his neck were flowing with lava-hot blood. That was the calm before the storm. The room went silent. With one big thrust, he slammed the leather belt down on the table. Forks, spoons, milk and plates flew into the air. I could see the kids trembling in their seats. The palm of my hand was sweating around the handle of the bread knife. If I had to use it to protect my kids, then I was ready. He screamed to the top of his lungs and looked directly at Adam. "Who put holes into my good leather belt? Who? I want an answer and *now* !" His words echoed off the kitchen walls and pierced through my back. Alexandria and her friend started to cry hysterically. Adam's eyes kept on getting bigger and bigger. He was terrified. He knew who put the holes in the belt.

I said, "Stephen, Stephen, get a grip! I put those wholes in your belt."

Before he gave me a chance to explain, he took one big step toward me. "Why, may I ask?" He was staring right down my throat.

Trembling, I responded,"Because…'cause…I bought Adam a new pair of pants for a Boy Scout luncheon and couldn't afford a belt."

Adam spoke up. "That's right, Stephen, the luncheon you were too busy to attend!" I was afraid for him now.

"Adam, you and the girls go upstairs, *now*!" They flew as fast as speeding bullets up those stairs.

I continued on explaining to him. "So I took the liberty of making two small holes in your belt because it was too big for him!" He yelled at me so loud I started trembling in my sleepers. With his vein-infested face and overpowering arms, he shook me back and forth.

"Stop that excessive crying, stop it!" He finally stopped shaking me and shouted, "You are not permitted to use any of my things ever, especially for the kids!" He emphasized that quite strongly. I managed to get away from him and ran upstairs to make sure the kids were okay. As I was going up the stairs, I heard the phone ring. Adam answered it.

"Hi, Daniel, it's so good hearing your voice!"

I took the phone. "Hi, Daniel. Merry Christmas!" I was shaking so hard I could hardly keep the receiver in my hands. I had the two kids clinging to my housecoat. "It's so good to hear from you."

He said, "Is everything alright?" He could tell by my voice that something was wrong. My voice was shaky.

I replied, "Oh, everything is just fine!" He knew differently. He told me he would be there in thirty minutes or so. I asked Daniel if he would consider taking Adam along with him over the holidays. I didn't want Adam to be in that kind of environment over the Christmas holidays or, for that matter, anytime. Daniel knew for sure something definitely was wrong. Alexandria's little friend called her mom up to come and get her. She also knew something was up. Her mother wasn't long getting to the house. She met me at the door with swollen red eyes, trembling. "Are you alright?" She knew from previous experiences that things were bad.

She gave me a hug and said, "If there is anything at all you need, I'm here for you. Don't forget that!" He wasn't long getting there. I had the two kids packed up in minutes. If I had thought about it, I should have packed and left too. Daniel met three sad, watery-eyed, trembling people at the door. Stephen was in the den reading a book and enjoying the deluxe breakfast I made for the kids. If only I had had time to put some rat poison in those scrambled eggs. Daniel was hungry and asked if I minded cooking him up a few slices of toast.

"Of course not, Daniel. Come on in and have a seat." You could have cut the air with a knife, and Daniel sensed that. Daniel wasn't long shoving those pieces of toast away. He left with the two kids, leaving me at the door scared and panicky, with my eyes full of tears. I knew he felt bad for me but didn't think it was his place to interfere. I went into the dining room and cried and cried. I cried relentlessly until I couldn't cry anymore.

It was an tremendously cold day, thirty-five below with the wind chill. The wind was howling and whistling around the house. I hastily got dressed and stormed out the door. I walked for hours in the freezing cold. The snowdrifts were piled four feet high. The wind was so strong, the snow felt like nails being driven into my face. I had no choice but to return home. It was either that or die in a snow bank. When I returned home, the car was gone. I didn't give a damn where he went. I was numb to the bone. It was as cold on the inside as the outside. That was one thing about that house—it was never warm. He was too mean to keep it at a decent temperature. I had a long hot shower to thaw out. I couldn't turn the heat up because he had it programmed to his liking, and I could never find the instruction manual. I wrapped myself in a warm blanket, made a fire and enjoyed a cup of hot tea. Several hours later, he arrived home. At first, I couldn't look at him. I went into the hell-risen kitchen to see plates full of food on the counter, hard and cold. The only plate empty was Stephen's. He never had the decency to clean up that morning's mess. He came up behind me and put his arms around me. He scared the hell out of me! My body had turned into ice once again. Then the phone rang, and I jumped out of sheer nervousness. It was Daniel letting me know they were safe and sound at the chalet. I envied them. I would have given anything to be there with them. My eyes were sore from crying, I couldn't stop my body from shaking. What a way to spend Christmas day. Once again, he tried to smooth things over, trying to explain to me it took him years to gather all of his possessions and belongings. He said to me, "I value each and every thing I own; it took me years to accumulate! You learned a valuable lesson today. Now, let's move on and start preparing Christmas dinner!" That was the only thing he valued. It certainly wasn't people's feelings or emotions.

He left the kitchen to stoke the wood in the fireplace. He put some relaxing music on and sat by the fire. I looked outside the kitchen window, questioning myself. It took me more than one glass of wine to put those nerves back in place. I had wised up and started buying my own private stash. I spent the entire afternoon in the kitchen making the traditional turkey dinner. Trust me, I took my time. The last place I wanted to be was in that room with him. Every now and then, he would come in to give me a hug. My arms hung to my sides. I didn't have the energy or emotion to hug such a monster. I dressed the dining room table with the bone china and crystal. We both sat on opposite ends of the table with very few words spoken. I didn't have much of an appetite for food. It sure didn't stop him from eating. He enjoyed every morsel of it with his domestic wine. I went upstairs to call the kids at the hotel. I was concerned about what had happened earlier on that day. It was such a relief to hear their voices. They filled Daniel in on all the details. It was a wonder he even brought the kids back to me. The only reason he did was because he knew he could trust my best judgement, at least when it came to the kids. Stephen retired early that night, probably due to all the physical activity! I remained downstairs by the fire sipping my wine and second-guessing the decisions I had made. The week the kids were gone was horrible. He spent most of his time at the office while I stayed home with the cats. The kids finally arrived home, and I was never so glad to see them. That was one Christmas I wanted to forget. I didn't know how much more abuse I was going to take from that bastard. I was running out of patience and strength. I became so run down I had to see my doctor. She couldn't believe the sight of me. I had lost a tremendous amount of weight, and my nerves were shot.

I explained to her, "Every morning I get up, and the tub is full of hair. I can't hold a cup of coffee without spilling it all over myself. I can't think straight!" She thought I was on my way to having a nervous breakdown. She prescribed some pills to calm me down and recommended I think about different living arrangements. I was slowly but surely losing it! I couldn't wait to return to work. At least I had a bit of peace! I think the kids felt the same way about returning back to school. I made a promise to myself that I wasn't going to put up with his foolishness much longer. The relationship had once again taken a turn for the worst. But being stubborn and strong-minded, I was determined to give it another chance.

EIGHTEEN

Stephen's birthday was approaching, and I was determined to make it a fabulous birthday. I came home early from work that day and started in the kitchen. I have a passion for cooking, so I was in my realm. I had prepared a seven-course dinner with everything from soup, salad, and jumbo shrimp to filet mignon. I selected some delectable wines to have with each course. It cost me a fortune! Surprisingly enough, the dinner went off effortlessly. The kids had been quietly playing in their rooms that evening. I actually bribed them with treats to keep them upstairs. The classical music was softly playing in the background as we were enjoying a passionate, quiet evening. I bought Stephen a very expensive painting of a moose done by Robert Bateman.

"Oh, you shouldn't have! It's priceless!" He adored it. He couldn't thank me enough. He swung his arms around me and held me tightly. As he was looking into my eyes, he said, "Do you know how much I love you? I couldn't live without you." He was so passionate that evening. Finally, a peaceful evening! I thought nothing was going to spoil that evening until I heard a knock on the door.

It was our next door neighbor. I greeted him and, being neighborly, invited him in. I mentioned to him, "It's Stephen's birthday, come in and have a glass of wine with us!"

He sat at the table and said, as I was pouring him a glass of wine, "How would you two like to join my wife and I on a trip with the canoe club this summer?"

I stood up. "That sounds marvelous!"

Stephen put his glass up to the light and replied, "Isn't that wine clear?" He took a swig of it. He never even responded to the trip. "Oh yes, about the trip. It's too early to commit myself right now. I have too many things on the go right now!" I began clearing the table. Our neighbor chatted up a storm with Stephen, enjoyed a few glasses of wine and then left. I ran upstairs and offered the kids five dollars each if they helped clean up the kitchen. They were thrilled! Five dollars to them was a lot of money. I went into the den to put another log on the fire, and as I turned around, there was Mr. Hyde in full attire. I didn't realize I had invited him to dinner! He threw me into the chair and slapped me across the face. "What did you do that for?" he yelled. "Don't you think one bottle of wine was enough to bring up from the basement? You didn't have to give him two glasses of wine! What's wrong with you, you lush?" I laid in the chair, shaking and crying. There was not a sound to be heard in the kitchen. Stephen grabbed his wine, stormed upstairs and slammed the bedroom door.

Within seconds, the kids came to my rescue. They held me and smoothed my back. God, I don't know what I would have done without those two. They were two amazing kids for putting up with that shit and seeing their mom constantly upset! We could hear him laughing on the phone upstairs.

"I had a great birthday, great gifts, and the dinner was fabulous!" I often wondered who he talked to that night. We went in to the kitchen and looked at the piles of dishes. He certainly was not worth the effort, the cost, nor the trouble. He deserved a boiled hot dog, and even that was too good for him.

Adam said, "Mom, you should have made him pâté out of dog food!" I had to hand it to the kids, they kept a pretty good sense of humor over some of the situations. Stephen was off to work early the next morning, probably out of pure shame. I ate supper alone with the kids that night. I didn't even bother to make him anything. He wasn't worthy. I didn't speak to him for days. He finally broke the ice.

"Let's go to your favorite steakhouse in town! I'll order in some pizza for the kids, my treat!" It was a rather expensive restaurant. When I looked at the menu, I ordered the most expensive thing. I not only loved the food there, but also the people were so warm and friendly, and I sure needed that. The conversation was light in the beginning. The meal was delicious as usual. I was just about to cut into my steak when, right out of the blue, he said, "I think you should consider getting your own place!" I dropped my fork, and my eyes filled up with water. I had no response. Speechless might be a better term.

Finally, I got the courage, and with a shaky voice, replied, "What did you just say?"

He replied, "You heard what I said." Why would he go to all this expense to tell me to get my own place to live? It didn't make any sense to me. He could have done that at home. At least I could have screamed at him. Once he saw my reaction, he immediately apologized for saying that. He said, "I think I just need a break from the kids. They tend to get on my nerves." I thought that was strange since they avoid him at all cost. They wouldn't even stay in the same room with him for more than a minute. He turned a romantic dinner into a guessing game. I don't know who I had dinner with that evening, Dr. Jekyll or Mr. Hyde.

That evening, I slept in the guest room down the hall. During the night, I heard a terrible noise coming from his bedroom. I ran in to find him lying on the floor, sweating like a pig with his hands over his chest. I ran to get Adam and Alexandria. The three of us stood there looking over his body. Every now and then, Stephen's eyes would roll around in their sockets. He went into the fetal position and complained about severe chest pains. We looked at one another, not saying a word. Finally, I said, "What do you think, should I call 911?" Adam and Alexandria both looked at one another.

"It's up to you Mom!" In all honesty, when I picked up that phone, the kids were disappointed in me. They rushed him to the hospital and diagnosed him with hypertension. Within a few days of bed rest, he would be fine. When I arrived back from the hospital, the kids were sorry to hear he was still alive. I brought him home in a couple of days. He was sweet as pie for the next while. I think he had a touch of death and was making up for lost time. He'd need ten lifetimes to make up for the misery he caused people over the years.

He wasn't long getting back to himself. Over the next couple of months, the tension between Stephen and the kids mounted. He totally ignored them. He would spend endless hours reading books and eating chocolate in the den. After every supper, he formed a habit of going directly into the den, sitting by the fire and ignoring anything or anybody around him.

One Friday night, I had it. Alexandria was at a friend's place for a sleepover. Adam and I were playing cards in the kitchen. I had bought myself a bottle of wine on the way home from work to enjoy the evening. Several hours had passed. We were having a ball laughing, playing crib and eating popcorn. Stephen walked into the kitchen. "What are you two doing out here?"

I looked up at him. "We have been playing cards out here for hours. What have you been doing?"

He looked down at me. "You think you're smart sitting there drinking wine—" Before he said another word, I got up, picked up the glass fruit bowl full of fruit, and threw it at him as hard as I could. I aimed it right for his head.

I said, "Adam, duck!" He flew underneath the table and covered his head. The only thing I regretted was that I missed that son of a bitch's head. That night, Adam and I slept downstairs. Mealtimes were uncomfortable and tense. If he caught an elbow on the table or improper English was used, he would bat the elbow off the table and be constantly correcting their English. Mealtime was not an enjoyable event anymore in that house. Even though things were deteriorating, I still wanted to hang in there. I wanted that relationship to work one way or another. I knew that sounded outrageous and selfish of me considering all that we had been through, but I tried so hard to win his love back I didn't want to lose what little we had left. I wasn't a quitter!

It was a snowy, wintry Friday night. That night still haunts me to this day. I had returned home from work early due to the storm. The city was basically shutting down since the roads were getting rather icy. I had put a cozy, warm fire on and chilled a bottle of wine to have with our supper. I put a prime rib roast in the oven with all the trimmings. The smell from succulent meat drippings made me hungry. The storm was worsening by the minute. While Alexandria and I were preparing dinner, I kept watching the clock click on to each hour of the evening. There was no sign of Stephen, nor did I receive a phone call from him. Adam had left a few hours earlier to go to a friend's house for a sleepover. It was getting rather late, so we ate in the den in front of the fireplace. We started watching the movie *Peter Pan*. It wasn't long when we heard the back door open. I greeted him with a hug and kiss. I knew by the smell of his breath that he had been at some office function. I didn't open my mouth to ask any questions or comment on his tardiness or lack of respect. I knew if I opened my mouth, the weekend would have been destroyed. I didn't have the strength to face Mr. Hyde that evening. I gave him some dinner and poured him a glass of wine. He sat by the fire enjoying his dinner. Alexandria was quietly sitting on the couch watching her movie and eating some popcorn. We started making idle conversation about our day. The more I spoke, the colder the room became. Every hair on my arms stood up. I sensed something was about to happen. He continually stared at the fire. He looked at me. "Thank you for the beautiful supper. It was delicious!" I could have cut the air with a knife. I knew something was up his sleeve, but I didn't know exactly what. It was like I was in my doctor's office waiting to hear my test results. The fire was crackling, and the snow was falling quite rapidly. In most homes, that evening would have been a perfectly cozy, romantic winter night, but that house had turned into one big sheet of frozen glass Within a second, it was about to shatter right in front of our eyes.

Without any warning, he swung his chair around, looked me square in the eye and said, "I want you to leave."

I looked at him. "What do you mean, leave?" At first I presumed he meant leave the room. Boy was I wrong. He meant leave his house. His words were, "I want you and the kids to leave." He turned his eyes away from me immediately and glared at the fire. Every muscle in my body tensed up. I couldn't say one word to him. What could I say? My eyes filled up with tears. He got up from the chair with his glass of wine and walked upstairs to our bedroom. We sat there in shock, staring at one another. I gave myself a couple of minutes and took some deep breaths. We were both in a daze. I composed myself and called Linda to come over. As I did, I was crying, "He wants me to leave, me and the kids!" She was reluctant at first, but I convinced her that Stephen was upstairs for the night. She could hear my voice cracking on the phone. She brought over a bottle of wine. She walked in the front door and gave Alexandria and I big hugs.

She said, "Why did you give him the satisfaction of ending this goddamn relationship? That's what I don't understand!" I should have done it months before. It was an issue of security and stubbornness on my part.

I said to her, "To be honest with you, I was afraid to leave him. I didn't know where to go. Don't you see I didn't want to fail again? I'm such a failure! Why is he so awful? Is there another woman?" I was crying into my hands. After I'd spent several months doubting, being skeptical and living on eggshells, he had finally made the decision for me.

Now I had absolutely no choice in the matter. She tried to be sympathetic and console me. She made an effort to convince me it was better in the long run for the kids and I. She told me to remember all the terrible things he had put me and the kids through, all the sleepless worrisome nights I'd had. She said she knew I was scared, but that it was for the best. She said I should have been glad to be rid of the beast! I knew deep down she was right. In the last couple of months I had been living on Adavan to get through my day, trying to cope with him and his moods. He had the kids and me half crazy.

I was lost, scared and frantic. She shoved a couple of pills down my throat to slow my heart rate down. She wanted to know where Adam was so she could go get him. Within minutes, she had returned with him. The kids hated to see me crying. I sure had my share of it, living with Stephen. Adam wrapped his arms around me, pointed his baby blue eyes at me and said, "Mom, I love you very much!" Linda thought it was pretty selfish and prickish the way he ended it. There were more civil ways to handle those types of delicate situations. She never gave him the time of day anyway. In her eyes, he was nothing but a cold-hearted, egotistical bastard. If I had had half a brain, I would have called my parents to fly us all home, but I didn't! For one thing, I couldn't think straight, especially not that night. I didn't know what in hell I was going to do. I knew one thing—I wanted the kids to finish out their school year before moving them home. Another part of me wanted to live close to Stephen in hopes that he would change his mind in time. I must have been mad to think like that! I began to shake uncontrollably. Linda took me into the den and sat me by the fire. The kids wrapped a blanket around me to comfort me. They were crying, but not for the reason that I was. They were upset seeing their mom so wounded and scarred. Adam and I put another log on the fire to keep at the least one room warm in the house. One of the burning logs rolled out and landed on the rug. We forgot to close the protective gate. I almost burnt my hands off trying to get it back into the fireplace. The rug had at least four or five burnt holes in it. I was sick! While Linda was putting ointment onto the burns, I thought, *What more can he do to us?* That would be a little memento for him to remember us by. Once I had calmed down, Linda left to go home.

The kids and I huddled together in the guest room and held each other all night. I was dreading the next morning. I knew when he saw that rug he would go wild. I awoke the next morning to an awfully cold house. My teeth were chattering. The kids looked peaceful, so I let them sleep. Not only that, I didn't know what to expect when I went downstairs. I went to the washroom first to see if I looked as bad as I felt. Sure enough, I looked horrible. My eyes were red and sore from crying, my guts were in knots, and my hands trembling with fear. To sum it up, I looked like a junkie who was having ghastly withdrawal symptoms. I found him with his coffee in the den, staring at the smoldering holes in the rug. Chills rapidly went down my back like a roaring waterfall grabbing onto every nerve ending I had left. He turned around very swiftly to see nothing but a waif standing before him and started yelling, "Another accident! Explain this one you *mindless ingrate*! Just look what you've *done*. The rug is *ruined*!" His words spitted between his teeth. Every word threw daggers into my chest. I was being bombarded with one brick after another. My frail body could hardly stand the abuse. As if I didn't already have enough scars to remember him by! After he was through displaying his warm affection for me, he swept by me and flew out the door. It was the sound of music hearing his car pull out of the driveway.

At once, I got the kids up to feed them a wholesome breakfast. I told them, "Eat until you drop!" When they were through stuffing their faces, we began taking cans and dry food out of the cupboards and hiding them underneath the kids' beds. I paid for it, and I was taking it with me.

Stephen offered to let me to stay in his house until the kids were through school. That was so kind of him! One thing he didn't do was offer me money. At work, I became a waste product. Thank god I had great friends. They did a lot of covering up for me. At night, the three of us crawled into one bed together to comfort one another. I would cry myself to sleep. I was afraid of the unknown. Adam would say to me, "Mom, he's not worth all of those tears!" I knew he was right. I moved all of my belongings into the guest room. Adam and Alexandria were so glad we were moving out of his house. He tolerated them, and they detested him! The anxiety and stress levels between Stephen and I had reached their boiling points. I had to start making some decisions. It was time to get the hell out of that place once and for all. I just didn't know how, when or where. I called work just to give them a heads-up. They were totally understanding over the whole thing. I began looking at apartments. My main concern was to find one close to the kids' school. I had very little money, so it wasn't going to be any five-star accommodation. You know the old saying, "It never rains 'til it pours"? Well, it was pouring. The same time Stephen asked us to leave, I lost my job. The company had gone bankrupt.

A few nights later, I received a very distressing phone call from home. My brother Mark had been in a terrible, life-threatening car accident. I put the move on hold, and we frantically headed for home. My dad forked over the money for our trip. Upon my arrival, I also became ill. I was so run down and thin, I came down with a terrible cold. Once Mark was out of the woods, I returned to Calgary. Now when I think about it, I should have stayed home and had our things sent down, but I wasn't thinking clearly. All of our personal belongings were in his house, and I wasn't letting him have them. I also felt that deep down in my heart I would someday get back with Stephen. My god, I was so blind with love for this guy it was sickening . When I was home, I brought my family up to date on the situation in Calgary. They were all relieved I was finally leaving him and wanted me to come home. I told them as soon as the kids were through school, I would consider that option. Mom was generous enough to give me a few hundred dollars to help me out.

When I landed at the airport, Stephen was nowhere to be found. I was sick, tired and poor. I had called him the night before to give him my arrival times. I thought for sure he would have had a little bit of pity to pick us up. It cost me thirty-eight dollars to get us home just because that selfish guy didn't have an ounce of heart to pick us up. When we walked into the house, it was bitter cold. We could actually see our breath. He wasted no time in reconstructing the house. He had already started painting all the walls white. It reminded me of a hospital ward. We were so cold, we had to leave our coats on and put our shoes back on. I still don't know why the pipes didn't burst. He was so cheap, he hated to turn the heat up past eighteen degrees.

As the days went on, my health deteriorated to the point that I had to be seen by a doctor immediately. I was taken to the hospital for x-rays of my lungs. I had developed double pneumonia. The doctor put me on over four hundred and fifty dollars worth of medications. Stephen never offered once to help pay even a portion of it. Again, the move was put on hold. I was sick in bed literally for a month. I was unable to stand for more than a minute. I would spend my mornings vomiting until the dry heaves set in. I was burning up with fever. I was just so grateful to have two wonderful kids. They waited on me hand and foot. In the evenings, they would take turns applying cold cloths to my forehead. They were genuinely marvelous kids.

Stephen, out of pure guilt, took a week off to help me. He only did that to get me better so I could get out of his house quicker. I wasn't stupid! He would bring me in fresh fruit all cut up perfectly and hot tea. Christ, why couldn't he act that way in our relationship? I did enough waiting on him over the years! He was being too nice for my liking! I knew what he was up to—no good! Every night I would say, "God bless his goddamned soul because no one else would!"

One morning, I found the strength to walk downstairs to make a cup of tea. He asked me to sit down and go over a couple of financial details for the move. Of course, I thought he was going to offer me some money. Oh no, that would have been too nice. How stupid could I be? Here I was in dire straights, my life a calamity, listening to this prick talk to me about how much money I was going to need to move out. He had it broken down to the last penny, even as far as how much each kid used for water, electricity and heat while living in his house. I looked at him. "You're simply incredible! You're beyond comprehension!" All I could do was gaze into his eyes, trying to find a glimpse of compassion. Instead, I found the devil looking at me through his hollow greedy eyes.

I had heard enough and returned to bed. I not only was physically ill, but was also torn to pieces. He had turned into a greedy, money-hungry, evil prick! Once my health started to improve, I had to get motivated for the move. It was definitely inevitable, so I dug my heels in and got at it. I called at least twenty or more moving companies to get the cheapest boxes I could. They were all too expensive for me. I picked up the phone to try the last guy on my list. I told him with a very dry, cold voice, "The prick I am living with is kicking me and kids out in the middle of the winter with no money, no place to live, no car, no job and very little furniture. *What are you going to charge me for boxes?*" There was silence on the other end. I didn't know if he hung up on me or if I left him speechless.

His reply was, "What is your address and phone number? I'll see you tomorrow morning."

He arrived the next morning with a truckload of boxes and paper, something I never even asked for. He charged me twenty dollars for the load. There was no paperwork drawn up, just word of mouth. Before he left the house, he put his hand on my shoulder and said, "Would you like me to beat the shit out of him for ya? I'll do it for free!" If I knew I could have done it without going to jail, it sounded like a pretty good offer and was well deserved. We both got quite a chuckle over that. That brightened up my day! After all, that guy saw what kind of house Stephen was living in. I think it totally pissed him off.

After dinner, the kids and I would spend hours packing up our things. He would go into the den and read the entire time. The only time he would move off his butt was if he wanted a cup of tea or a glass of wine. It used to annoy me to the limit knowing he was sitting in that comfortable chair reading his precious books. Night after night, he continually did that. He wouldn't even help assemble the boxes for us. It was a good thing Adam was strong. It took me a couple of weeks looking for a place that was affordable, suitable and convenient for both kids' schools. I finally landed a place. It seemed okay but was nothing to write home about. It had a pool. Mind you, it needed a lot of work, but it was still classified as a pool. Little did I know it, but the rental agent never informed me that it was full of welfare recipients. I soon learned that the couple above me screwed their brains out all night, the couple to the left of me listened to heavy metal all hours of the night, and the man in the couple on the right side had serious drinking problems and liked beating up his wife. Lovely neighbourhood to raise two small children!

NINETEEN

The day of the move were sweet and sour in more ways than one. The kids were glad to be rid of him, and there was a part of me that was glad too. Stephen had been gracious enough to pay for the rental truck and eventually, out of sheer guilt, he had cable installed. He never gave me one dime to support myself or the kids. Here was a man making a lot of money and living in an elaborate house, and he didn't have the decency to even ask if I wanted financial help. I seriously don't know how he could look himself in the mirror and live with that image every day. All the utility hook-ups, groceries, and draperies I had to cough up! What a merciless prick! Between my child allowance from Daniel and Adam's pension money from his father's death, I was able to pay the rent for that rundown, seedy apartment. The night before we moved out, I heard Stephen come in through the back door cursing and swearing over the mess in the laundry room. What did he expect? We were moving out the next morning. He said loud and clear, "One more night, thank god!"

I yelled at him, "I heard that, you asshole!"

The night we moved into the apartment, I made sure it was going to be fun for the kids. They had been through enough shit to last them a lifetime. The last couple of weeks staying at Stephen's place, I hardly bought any food, only what we needed to survive. I didn't give a damn what he wanted to eat. To boot, I never paid the final phone bill either. At that point in my life, every penny counted. I ordered in pizza, donairs and even treated myself to a nice bottle of wine. We ate and giggled until late hours of the night. That night, we all slept together with the cats lying on top of us on the living room in blankets looking out the window at the stars. The place was a mess the next morning, and we didn't care. At least there was no one to yell at us. We were at peace and without fear.

When I viewed the apartment, I noticed it had a antique fireplace. Of course, the rental agent never said a word about it not working. I took for granted that the thing worked. I thought we could finally be warm for a change. We were tired of being cold. We always had to wear heavy sweaters and wool socks plus slippers so we literally wouldn't freeze. Stepping out of that damn shower with icicles hanging off my nipples wasn't a great way to start my morning. After breakfast, we started unpacking some boxes. I had the radio on in the kitchen while preparing breakfast. We were going to be hit with a huge snowstorm that night with powerful winds. Before we did any more unpacking, we all got our winter gear on to go gather some sprigs and wood from the nearby park to burn that evening. If nothing else, we would be warm that night.

We dropped the wood off at the apartment, then headed to the local grocery store to stock up on some essentials before the storm hit us. Last but not least, we rented out a new release. Alexandria bounced her way back to the apartment, she was so excited. Adam was so keen to get back to get the firewood in place. Those two kids had high expectations that night. We spent the remainder of the day unpacking. After supper, the storm was coming in hard and fast. Adam took great pleasure in getting all the sprigs and wood arranged inside the fireplace. Boy Scouts paid off after all! We put our pajamas on and put the treats, pop, pillows and wine around the fireplace. Adam and Alexandria's eyes were full of happiness and no fear—something I hadn't seen in them in months. They had their sticks for marshmallows all sharpened up for later on that evening. The two of them nestled their butts into the big fluffy pillows. The closer the match came to the fireplace, the wider their eyes got. It was a *Home and Gardens* moment! As I put the match onto the twigs, black smoke poured out of every crack and brick within seconds. The room was full of smoke. While they covered their mouths, they grabbed their coats and boots and ran outdoors into the cold blizzard. I threw the cats into their kennel and put them with the kids. By the time I got to the deck, I had almost passed out. Once I got my breath, I ran back inside, grabbed a bucket from the closet, filled it with water and threw it into the fireplace. Even the fire detector didn't go off. Every window and door had to be opened. The entire apartment was full of smoke, and what a smell! So much for that idea! What a mess! Fluffy pillows turned into wet, soggy mats, and the walls were covered in black, dirty smoke. The place was wrecked! Once I cleared some of the smoke out, the kids came in with the cats. They were covered in snow and cold. I felt so sorry for them.

We all had a hot bath and put it behind us that night. We managed to salvage the junk food since it was still in its packaging. We moved the television and VCR into the kitchen, wrapped ourselves in the only remaining two blankets and watched the movie. For what we had been through before, that was nothing. We actually laughed it off over breakfast the next day. I found out the next day through my half-wacked-out neighbour that I could have burnt the entire complex down. I probably would have done the provincial government a favour. The neighbors had smelled the smoke, but they were too drunk to get up. I had it out with the rental office, but they didn't seem to care very much. They said they would "look into it." By law, they had to replace the fire detector, which they did in their own good time.

The only other source of heat we had was electric, and that was expensive. The wind used to blow in through that fire hole continually. We froze to death half the time. I had to nail an old blanket against the wall to keep some of the wind off. Now we were really living in style! The only things missing in that picture were the gang fights and the gunshots on the streets.

We ate a lot of cheap macaroni and cheese dishes and cheap ninety-nine-cents-per-pound hot dogs. To eat an all beef hot dog would have been a luxury meal. Today, if I look at a bowl of any kind of macaroni, I want to puke. My health began to worsen again. I was thirty pounds below my normal weight. In other words, I was skin and bones. The only thing keeping me from going crazy were the few strong nerves I had left hiding behind my back muscles. Linda rushed me into the doctor's again. I suffered from acute anxiety and panic attacks. Again I was put on heavy medication.

Since my health had deteriorated so much and I had lost so much weight, I was unable to look for work. I was a total wreck physically and mentally. My medications were costing me so much money I had to ask my parents for financial assistance. They often paid for the high electrical bills and kept us in food for most of the winter. I started missing Stephen terribly. Don't ask me why. I think it was because I was so physically weak, sick and dreadfully lonely, plus I was totally insecure. I don't think it was so much Stephen I was missing, it was more the comfort of a beautiful home and some security. After several phone conversations hearing me crying for help and me saying I missed him, you would think he would have taken some responsibility and compassion in some part of the breakup. Instead, he turned a blind eye. One night he invited us over to his place for dinner out of sheer guilt and pity. We were reluctant to go. The kids saw how miserable and sad he had made me and couldn't understand why we should go near him for anything. The only way I could convince them to go was by reminding them it was a free hot meal. At least, I thought it was going to be.

When we arrived, he was full of smiles. "How are you, love?" he asked and gave me a big hug. He offered me a glass of his homemade wine and the kids some watered-down Kool-Aid. In no time at all, dinner was on the table. There were four tiny little cold lobsters called "canners." There is about a quarter of a cup of lobster meat in each one, if that. In the middle of the table was a medium-sized store-bought container of potato salad. He had a few slices of bread on the table with a tub of cheap margarine. How generous of him! He started talking about his work and how successful it was. His words were so distant to me. His lips were moving, but to my ears, there was no sound. I couldn't stop looking around at his huge house that had turned so cold, even in the summertime!

When we sat down to eat, I was staring out the window at the gleaming, inviting pool. It hurt my eyes to look at it. There was not a soul around to enjoy it. He had painted every room brilliant white. The little bit of warmth the house had was gone. You could have performed surgery in that place. The house was just one big parcel never to be opened and enjoyed! We were so hungry that it didn't take long to eat the meal. We didn't hang around long. The kids were nervous, so we left. He offered to drive us home, but we walked instead. I mean, after all, we had to walk off that huge meal! Generosity was not one of his greatest attributes! When we arrived back to our apartment, Adam said to me, "Mom, don't make us go back there again. There are too many awful memories!" I rubbed his face and gave him a hug.

The nights were so long and lonely. I didn't know where my life was headed. I was scared for the kids. I would look around at my surroundings and think, *Is this what my life is supposed to be?* Something was bound to change. I couldn't continue going through life living on anxiety pills and hoping that one day we would get back together again. Linda would often come over to comfort me and give me a shoulder to cry on. She said, "Every night his house only has one little light on." I remembered that was where he would sit and read continually night after night. There was never any sign of life or lights inside or outside except for that little beam from that corner of the house. She said it was almost eerie. She watched him come home from work with his head down.. He had become a miserable old man! She came over to the apartment one evening to see how the kids and I were doing. She brought over a couple bags of food and two bottles of their homemade wine. After she left, I was down in the dumps. I hopped onto my bike and drove over to Stephen's place.

I must have been crazy. I rode through a wooded area in the pouring rain. Even though it was late, I didn't care. I just wanted to see him. I pounded on his front door soaked to the bone. He finally opened the door. He stood there in a worn-out housecoat, unshaved and beat-up. He was furious! He didn't even have to open his mouth before I realized that Mr. Hyde was standing before me. It was a horrifying moment. What was I thinking? It had to have been the homemade wine and the anxiety pill that drove me to do that. No one in their right mind would have inflicted that kind of agony upon themselves. I was crying hysterically and uncontrollably. I stood in the doorway soaking wet, crying and shaking. He looked down at me and said, "If you ever do this again, I will call the *cops*. What in hell is wrong with you?" He eventually took pity on me and pulled me into the house. He pulled me into his arms. He held me until I stopped crying. He pushed me away and said, "Leave. And remember, next time I'm calling the cops!" Now there's a guy with a heart. On my way back home, I did a lot of cursing and swearing at myself for being so stupid. I never did that again. But it wasn't me reacting that way. My whole system was screwed up. Between the pills, wine, stress and no sleep, I was totally messed up! If I had to point a finger on who was to blame it definitely would have been him.

On one rainy Saturday evening, it poured rain all day. We didn't even bother to get dressed. We lay around playing with the cats and watching cartoons. We noticed someone was moving across the street. They were two bums that partied up their welfare checks every week. We had some entertainment for the day! They were a real pair of idiots. The only things we ever saw them bringing into their apartment were beer and cheap whores. Since we didn't have a lot of things, we constantly kept our eyes peeled to the window to see what "goods" people were going to get rid of. Even the cats Kit and Kat patrolled the window with us.

One particular item caught our eyes. We noticed they laid a twin bed with mattresses on the sidewalk. For the longest time, that bed sat on the sidewalk getting dredged. They took so long packing that truck. For every two boxes on the truck, they would drink a beer. The rain was beginning to taper off. We weren't sure if they were leaving or taking the bed. As they were putting the last box into the truck, they turned around and threw the bed mattress into one of those large rotten garbage bins. Since I was sleeping with Alexandria in her twin bed, I thought, *Why not?* Alexandria and I shared one bed and Adam the other. As disgusting as the thought was, we waited for the evening to become a little darker. The rain had picked up again. It was bouncing off the sidewalks. In our pajamas, we put on our hotel shower caps and headed for the garbage bins. The three of us looked liked prowlers in the night. We crept with embarrassment to the garbage bin, hoping, of course, no one would spot us. Adam stood on my back so he could jump inside to get a hold of the mattress. By now, we were soaking wet, and so was the mattress. He managed to push one end up so I could grab it over the side. I gave it one big tug, it flew out of the bin, landed on top of Alexandria, pushed us into the mud and covered us in garbage. God, it reeked!

Adam crawled out of the bin and pushed the mattress that laid on top of us. We shook the debris off the pissy-smelling mattress in the pouring rain and began dragging it to the apartment over the rough, beat-up sidewalk. Just before we hit the stairs, we could see headlights facing right towards us. I wiped the rain from my eyes so I could see. "Oh my god, it's Stephen!" Great, just what I needed! Now that was perfect timing on his part! These next few words that I am about to write have been etched into my brain for my entire life. I still, to this day, lose sleep over these words. He ran up to the three of us.

"Hello, what in earth are you guys doing out here in the pouring rain? What do we have here? Let me give you a hand with that!" The three of us moved back from him.

"It's okay, I have it!"

He looked directly at me and the kids in the rain as we were stinking of garbage and said, "I must commend you guys on being so resourceful!." I remember Adam and Alexandria standing there in the rain, stinking like rats, soaked to the bone looking down at the ground. I felt such pity for my two kids. In reality, I should have taken pity on that prickish beast for being such an ignorant pig. What kind of person would have said that in any circumstances? I swear, to this day, if I had had a knife in my hand, I would have slit his throat and happily done life in prison for it. At least I would have had the satisfaction of knowing he was dead. With the hell he put me through, I personally think the judge would have showed mercy on me.

He followed behind with his hands in his pocket and said, "Do you mind if I come in?" He offered his help to assemble the soaking, pissy bed. I didn't want his buttery, worthless, greedy little mitts touching the already soiled wet mattress. I'd rather have had the filthy hands that threw it into the garbage bin on it than his. He knew he wasn't welcome and soon left. The three of us stood in the living room, cold, dripping wet, stinking to high heavens and were once again humiliated by this man. It took a couple of days for the mattress to dry out. I poured a bunch of baking soda on it to take some of the smell away. After a couple of days, Adam and I assembled the bed. As nauseating as it was, I slept on it. It wasn't so bad. There had to be worse off people than me. A couple of days had passed.

Without any warning one evening, Stephen was standing at my door. He looked so handsome. He gave me that breathtaking smile, and for a moment, I briefly forgot of all the miserable things that had happened. He had a way of doing that to women. To be civil, I invited him in for a cup of iced tea. I was in the kitchen wondering what in hell he was doing here. I gave him his tea and sat beside him. He blurted out, "I am reconsidering having you and the kids move back in with me. We could get a nice apartment and give it another try!" I poured the tea all over the counter.

"Really, are you serious? What changed your mind?" I didn't know if I should believe him or boot his ass out the door. To be honest, at first I was elated, beyond words, in fact.

As he was drinking his iced tea, he said, "I'm lonely without you. I miss you terribly! You know I never stopped loving you! What do you think about the idea?"

I took a long look at him and said, "Well, let me think about it!" He finished his tea and got up to leave. Before he left, he told me we would go out for dinner the following night to discuss it in more detail. He bent down and gave me a kiss on the cheek.

"I miss you!"

Once he left, I called up Linda to ask her if she could take care of the kids for me. She was very glad to do it, but she hoped it wasn't because of Stephen. Deep down, she knew, but she never interfered. I spent the entire day getting ready for that dinner. Linda came over early to take the kids to Wendy's for supper. She told me she didn't want to be there to see what she didn't want to see. I must have been mad to want to go back with such a horrible creature! I kept thinking maybe he'd changed. He seemed sincere when he talked about it.

He showed up at the door dressed to kill. We hugged each other crazily. It felt so wonderful to be in his arms again. The dinner was exquisite. We talked about moving back in together with the two kids. He had found this attractive apartment with a heated swimming pool. The schools were just around the corner, so the kids could walk to school. I looked across the table at him. "This is so very exciting, Stephen, but before I make my final decision, I'll have to discuss it with the kids!" He totally understood. I knew I was grinning from ear to ear. The more wine we drank, the more we talked about our future together. My hopes and dreams with Stephen were back in motion. He reached over and grabbed my hands.

"I do love you, you know. I love you very much!" He treated me with such respect, love and kindness that night. That was the man I fell so deeply in love with a couple of years prior. He finally was back! I was floating on cloud nine.

After dinner, we went back to his place for a nightcap. We made extraordinary love that night. It had been so long since he had been so compassionate and loving. Afterwards, we went back to his place and sat in the living room looking at old pictures of me and the kids. I lay in his arms for hours. I was so content and at peace. As magnificent the evening was, I had to break up the moment to go back to my apartment that night to take care of the kids. He gave me a long, sensual kiss at the door and said, "We will talk more on the subject tomorrow." The kids were both sleeping, and Linda was sitting at the table, twirling her fingers around a glass of wine. I knew she was pissed off at me. I couldn't blame her. After all, look what he had put us through. And on top of it, I had thrown her into that same dirty laundry basket.

She said to me in a harsh tone, "Stay away from him, he already has you half crazy! Do you want him to finish you off so I can commit you to a loony bin?" I told her what he proposed to me over dinner. She replied, "He is nothing but poison to your blood, and trust me, he is up to no good!" Before she slammed the door, she said, "What is it going to take for you to realize he is a monster?" Her words meant nothing to me that night. I sang myself to sleep that night. The next day, I was singing away in the kitchen, making the kids breakfast. They never asked me about the night before.

As I was giving them their plates, I asked, "Would you guys consider going back to live with Stephen again if things were different?" There was silence around the table. Their forks hit their plates.

"Are you crazy, Mom?" Adam yelled out. "Are you insane? How could you even think of it?! That guy is nuts! *No way*, and I'm sure Alexandria feels the same way!"

I looked down at the two of them, "But Adam, it would be different this time. We wouldn't be living on eggshells like before."

He replied, "Yeah, how long would that last? A week? A month? *No way*, and if you make us, we will move in with Daniel!" He grabbed his school bag and stormed out the door.

Alexandria just sat there picking at her pancakes. I got her ready for school and walked her to her bus stop. I returned back to the apartment, leaned up against the door and slid slowly to the floor. In one way, I was happy, but in another, I was totally confused over the whole thing. I thought, *What changed his mind?* I hoped it wasn't some sort of game he was playing. Was he actually feeling guilty over the whole thing? Needless to say,

I glowed all day. I cleaned the entire apartment, made cookies and sang to the tunes on the radio. I hadn't done that in so long. I felt refreshed and happy again. I did my nails and had a soothing bubble bath. I felt alive! When the phone rang, I jumped over cats, chairs and anything that was in my way to get to the phone in time. He never called me all day. Each minute turned into an hour. Before I knew it, the kids were home from school. Neither one of them mentioned the conversation we had over breakfast.

I was in the kitchen cleaning up the mess when Adam came running in and yelled, "Mom, he's at the front door!"

I looked at him. "Who is it?" I peeked around the corner to see Stephen standing at the door. He was standing there with his hands in his pocket, swaying back and worth. I welcomed him in with open arms. I buried my head into his chest and gave him a warm hug. I wrapped my arms around his neck and gave him a big kiss. "Come in, Stephen. It's so good to see you again!" Adam and Alexandria beelined it outdoors. They couldn't stand the sight of him. I put on some nice quiet music and made some iced tea. He walked into the living room and took a seat. Through the walls, I heard him muttering, "You know, about last night..."

I replied, "Yes, darling, it was marvelous! Thank you so much for the lovely meal!" I walked into the living room with a tray of iced tea and homemade cookies.

As I was placing the tray on the table, he looked up at me and said, "When I went home last night, I gave some more thought to what we had discussed over dinner. I don't think it is such a good idea after all. I think it would be best that we remain separated."

I dropped the tray on the floor. "What do you mean? You had it all worked out...the apartment and the schools. What, what...changed your mind?" I was sick to my stomach, my knees became weak, and I fell to the floor. I looked up at him, tears falling down my cheeks. Shaking my head, in a very low voice, I said to him, "It's not going to happen, is it, Stephen?"

He looked down at me. "No, I can' t see myself living with you and the two kids. It just isn't going to happen."

As I was sobbing, I said, "But what about last night? It was so beautiful, and we shared so much love for one another. Didn't that mean anything to you?"

He said, "I love you dearly, but it will never work!" He stood up and walked out the door. I put my head between my legs and screamed hysterically. The two kids were playing outside.

They saw him leave rather quickly and heard me screaming, "Why, why, why did you do this to me? That fucking bastard!" Within seconds, they were by my side, holding me as tight as they could.

I could hear Adam say quietly under his breath, "I hate that man. He'll have his day, Mom, don't you worry!" I couldn't control my crying. Adam was getting worried, so he called Linda over to take care of the situation. I was beyond! What a brutal, unmentionable thing to do to any human being, especially when I was so vulnerable and fragile. That was one terrible night.

Linda was there in minutes. She took one look at this frail thin waif of a human being and said, "He is the devil!" She couldn't for the life of her understand why he would do something so cruel to me. I became so out of control, she thought she was going to have to take me to the hospital. After a couple of Atavans and a glass of wine, I started to simmer down. Now that's a bad combination.

For several hours, I lay in her lap, shaking and shivering. I finally fell to sleep. There were times I didn't know what I would have done without her. She spent the night with me for fear that I might kill myself. She knew I was distraught and wounded. Of course, Stephen didn't help any. He was always keeping me hanging. One minute I was up, the next minute down. I was one sorry-looking being. I looked into the mirror to see what that bastard had done to me, again! I must have been strong because I had the ammunition in my apartment to do myself in at any time, but that would have been the weak and selfish way out. Deep down, I was a much stronger person than that. Not only that, it would have been too easy for him. How could anybody on the face of the earth do what he did?

A couple of days later, he had the nerve to come over to tell me he was putting the house up for sale. He was moving to Winnipeg. He couldn't even look me in the face. I had three words for him: "You gutless bastard!" He knew by looking at me that I'd had a rough couple of days. He never even said he was sorry for what he had done. He promised me he would give me a few thousand dollars upon the closing day of the sale. For him to say that must have meant he felt somewhat guilty because he never gave anybody anything! Maybe it was the mattress scene or the getting back together scene that got to him. Who in hell knows, there could have been a thousand reasons. The devil himself would only know that one!

The only good thing about the whole conversation was that I possibly was going to see some money from him eventually. Anything at this stage in my life would have helped. For some reason beyond any explanation, I was saddened he was leaving, most likely because I knew it was really finally over. Another chapter was about to close in my life. As he stood there in the doorway telling me about his plans, my mind went into a fast-rewind mode. I relived my life with him all over in seconds. If only I had the remote control to stop it in certain places to change some of the things that had occurred. It's funny about life—you can't change the past, but there's always hope for the future!

Our relationship had been through a lot. Our mountain had soared to the sky and come down like an avalanche. And how many people we hurt along the way! His house sold within days. Of course it would have; it was in a secluded, beautifully wooded area. The house was completely renovated from top to bottom and landscaped to perfection. It had my golden touch. A lot of long hours of my hard work and sweat went into that house—a house I tried to make into a home. He, on the other hand, had made it into a showcase. That home had sterile values, meaningless morals, and little to no emotions. It was a place to rest your head but awaken tired. It could make a tear to turn to ice and a heart become numb. The outer walls shut out the love and warmth of people and the house's surroundings. It was simply a house and nothing more than a house!

Stephen gave me a call the night before he left for Winnipeg. He was leaving on the nine ten morning flight. A huge lump came into my throat, and I began to cry frantically. I became totally helpless. My entire body filled up with confusion and other emotions. He tried to soothe me with his soft-spoken words, but that didn't help. Those words were only to make me feel better for the moment. They would ease some of the guilty pain he felt. In one way, I was petrified that he was leaving. The last bit of cord snapped from the rope. Even though he had those terrible, selfish, controlling moments, there was a part of me that was surely going to miss him. I asked Linda if she could come over to the apartment early that morning to watch the kids for me. I had a very important errand to run. She didn't ask any questions, she just showed up with two coffees. The cab driver was right on time. I grabbed a handful of money from the emergency jar and hopped into the cab. I had ordered the cab the night before so he would be on time.

The drive to the airport was full of mixed emotions. My fists were holding down a bunch of crumpled up old money. Why was I wasting money on a cab to say goodbye to such a dreadful person who left the kids and me out in the cold with nothing?

He had made a ton of money on the house sale, and as of yet, I hadn't seen a cent of it. I cried the whole trip in. The only explanation I can give to myself is that I was still in love with him and totally confused. When I arrived, I took a long pause before entering the airport. I looked at the flight departures to see that his flight was on time. I headed for his gate to find him looking out the window, drinking a coffee. He was very handsomely dressed. I walked up to him very slowly and nervously. From behind, I tapped him on the shoulder. He turned around, looked down and saw a red-eyed, skinny waif looking up at him. His eyes filled up with tears. He wrapped his arms around me tightly. There were no words spoken. We had constant eye contact, and there were a lot of tears hitting the floor. For the longest time, I looked deep into his sky blue eyes, trying to figure out what made him into such a terrible person. For a brief moment, I saw a scared little boy running from something. The more I looked into his eyes, the shallower they became, like a shark in the deep waters. I got a chill up my back. The image remained with me for a long long time. The man who once was the man of my dreams, my true love in life, was now slowly removing his arms from me and walking through the security gate. He never took his eyes off me until he could no longer see me. I was paralyzed! I wanted to capture that moment for the rest of my life. The further he went, the more I cried. I hastily ran out of the airport. The cab drive home was sad. I cried until I couldn't cry any more.

TWENTY

When I arrived at the apartment, the kids were up eating breakfast. Linda knew where I had gone but never said a word. Maybe she thought it was for the best. I had to end that thing my way and put some kind of closure to it. That never happened. She reached out and gave me a big, comforting hug. For days after that, I rode my bike to his house, paused and then rode on. One day while I rode by, I could hear the new owners' kids laughing and carrying on in the yard. I put a smile on my face as finally that house had found love and harmony! I went on my way with a warm feeling in my heart.

We were all so happy to see the summer come. It was warm at last. Daniel was on his way up to visit the kids for a couple of weeks. He had booked a cottage several months ago in the deep woods high up in the hills. He was so glad that we weren't living with Stephen anymore. He remembered that terrible Christmas where everyone was upset but Stephen. He heard so many war stories from the kids and from colleagues that it was a relief for him to know they were out of there. It was a beautiful, sunny, warm summer evening, and I knew Daniel was flying in that afternoon. Alexandria was sitting outside playing with the two cats on their leashes. The cats were rolling around in the sun while she was tickling their bellies. She loved those cats. Daniel had telephoned me from a phone booth to tell me he was only minutes away from the apartment. He said, "Keep your eyes open for an old, dark green Mazda!" But I wasn't to tell Alexandria.

She adored her father. There wasn't a day that passed by that she didn't think of him. Every day, she would draw pictures and write numerous letters to send to him. He was never a forgotten image in her mind. No matter where we moved, there was always that very close bond between the two of them. From the living room window, I could see his car pulling in around the corner. Alexandria wasn't long seeing him either. She dropped the leashes and ran to the parking lot. I had to quickly run out to rescue the cats. All I could hear was, "Papa, Papa!" Another Kodak moment. If only I owned a camera! Adam was at his buddy's down the street. I soon got a hold of him to tell him the good news. He was home in a flash. Daniel carried Alexandria into the apartment. There were a lot of tears of joy and happiness. Adam was right behind them just dying to get his little mitts on him too. What a moment.

Daniel took a look at the surroundings. He remarked on how clean and quaint it was. I knew he wasn't truly honest, but he would never say anything bad. As far as the furniture, it was pretty basic. What could he expect? It was all old, secondhand furniture. The tables had cigarette burns on them, and the chair and the futon were stained with god knows what. He was dying for a beer. I looked at him like he was crazy. I told him, "Help yourself. There's a ton of it two streets over!" Christ, beer? I was lucky to have milk in the fridge. He went into the kitchen and couldn't believe that there was hardly anything to eat in the kitchen. He was quite perturbed over that. He opened the cupboards to find the same thing.

He also was stunned by my appearance. I was a ninety-pound waif with black hollow eyes. The kids didn't look too bad because I made sure they had most of the food, plus they weren't on anti-depression pills either. He didn't have kind words to say about Stephen. We knew damn well he wasn't going hungry or sitting on stained, old, beat-up furniture. That was above him! Of course, the kids couldn't wait to show Daniel the dirty, pissy mattress I was sleeping on. He was appalled that I had been sleeping on such a disgraceful thing. It actually smelled of piss, and trust me, it wasn't mine. He ignored that issue for the time being. His main concern was to get some food and beer into the place.

He took us all to the grocery store. It was like winning the lottery. We could buy any thing we wanted, there was no limit. We took our time going up each aisle, being very selective with the food we put in to the basket. Christ, even Stephen didn't care if we had food when he kicked us out.

Daniel let us buy the fancy cereals, chocolate milk and the finest steaks money could buy. He even bought us a portable barbeque to cook the steaks on. Then we went to buy some fine wines and cold beer. What a treat for all of us! The kids headed for the video store to pick out whatever they wanted to watch. They kept calling Daniel "Santa." You know, it's funny—you never know what you have until it's gone. I sure learned fast that the grass certainly wasn't greener on the other side. The light bulb in the fridge had company, and lots of it! The kids thought they had died and gone to heaven. I felt so guilty for depriving them of so many nice things in life, as well as for keeping those kids in that environment for so long.

I hadn't realized it until that moment how miserable they really both were. They both loved Daniel so much. It had been so long since I had seen my kids so happy and content. I had forgotten the last time we had a decent piece of meat to eat. When Daniel threw those steaks on the grill, the two kids sat on our makeshift lawn chairs (plastic milk cartons) and watched the steaks cook. Alexandria clapped her hands and danced around the milk cartons, and Adam stayed in a state of awe, licking his chops. When those steaks hit their plates, you could see sparks flying. They were like a pair of starving hyenas devouring the body of an antelope. We belonged in one of the *Beverly Hillbilly* shows. *Hee Haw*! What a fun-filled night we all had. For once, I didn't worry about anything. After dinner, we all went for a long walk along the river. The birds were truly singing that night. Usually they shit all over me! I had begun second-guessing my good judgement. It obviously wasn't good keeping the kids and myself in such an environment for so long. Those two kids must have truly loved me for putting them in such an unpleasant, tense living environment. They watched movies until they both passed out on the floor. Daniel and I sat on the steps drinking wine and beer, talking about the days when we were first married. We talked about the whys and the "how comes," and the more we drank, the more we analyzed everything to death. It's amazing how a couple of bottles of wine and a few cans of beer can solve the world's problems in one night. We not only slept well that night, but so did the rest of the world!

The resort gave Daniel a call the next day to reconfirm his reservations. At the time, he only anticipated having the two kids with him, but as my life came crashing down over the months, I somehow became part of the plans.

He invited me to come along with them. I was overjoyed. I had absolutely nothing keeping me there. Besides, all I would do home was cry over Stephen and throw darts at his picture. We were scheduled to arrive at the cottage within the following few days. We loaded up the car with food, beer and the two cats. The weather couldn't have been better—sun and more sun. We headed out really early in the morning. I normally sleep a lot in a car, but that trip was different. I didn't want to miss one thing. I wanted to take in as much as I could. Even stopping at the gas station was exciting! That has to tell you how sheltered and benign my life had become. I would stick my head out the window and just let the wind blow through my hair, breathing in as much air as I could. Now I knew what a convict felt like when released from prison. Freedom! I hadn't had that sensation for such a long time, and what a feeling! That's something money can't buy everybody: freedom. As we were approaching the cottage, the car started to act up a little. We never thought anything of it until the engine caught on fire. We were about twenty miles from the cottage. The nearest town was a good thirty-minute drive. Since neither of us had a cell phone, we had to hitch a ride into town. An old man with an old, rusty pickup truck stopped. We all hopped into the back, cats and all! What a ride! Thank god the cats were on leashes, or we would have lost them several times. We bounced around like popcorn. Just picture a cat on a motorcycle going full speed. Of course, the kids thought it was great. They were on a circus ride. I swear the old boy was drinking because we surfed down that mountain road on extremely high waves. He had his radio just blasting on the local country and western station, and to boot, he was trying to sing along with them. We arrived in town with sore butts and two wild-eyed cats.

The heat was incredible. There was not a breath of fresh air. Since the cats were now wind-burnt for life, they wouldn't step foot on the ground. In other words, they were scared to death, so Daniel and I had to carry them. Every time a car would zoom by, Kit, who had always had an extremely nervous disposition, would piss all over me. I had become an overheated walking toilet bowl. It was not a good start to the vacation. We finally reached a garage, and being as it was Saturday, there was no mechanic on duty. Great! Now what would we do! We had to get the car towed down the hill to be looked at by a mechanic on Monday. Even to find a tow truck in that town was difficult. We managed to find one guy with a high price tag to do the job. Have you ever tried to find a rental car in a small hick town in the middle of nowhere? Good luck! The only thing rented out in that town was a U-Haul truck owned by the manager of the garage. He showed us mercy and let us rent it until the car could be repaired. We all jumped into the truck. The smell was dreadful! The fact that I was saturated in cat piss, mixed with the heat and sweat, didn't help matters.

That was just a mild setback. We weren't going to let that ruin our vacation. We arrived at the cottage with bags of food, beer and wine. The picture of the cottage they had mailed him was totally different than what we were standing in front of. A good windstorm would have taken that place out easily. The last time that place saw paint was in World War II. It was a tad rundown. I couldn't even call it cozy. It was your basic, ugly, seedy cottage, and they were charging an arm and a leg for that place. But you know, we really didn't care. We were there to have fun and enjoy the moment. We didn't give a damn that the curtains were barely hanging on the rods or that the kitchen only had one pot and no condiments. The drains in the bathroom were full of hair, but hey—it was a vacation, and we were going to enjoy it! When you sat on the beds, your butt hit the floor. The bathroom was the size of a closet. It had that nice Lysol smell to it.

As far as recreation, well, that was another story. They said there was a sandy beach, and yes, there was a beach, but you had to walk through piles of rocks to get to it. The evening entertainment was having a bonfire on the so-called "beach." We still made the best of it. We weren't there to have luxury living anyway, though Daniel paid for luxury. The day after we arrived, the rain came down, and I mean rain. The devil was beating on his mother again. I could only thank god we brought the VCR with us. The only problem was that we didn't have any movies to watch. But in the brochure, the resort's store was fully equipped with all the necessities of life. Adam and I headed for the store in the rain. The only thing they had were cigarettes, pop, chips, ice cream and bars. They didn't even have milk. We ran back to the cottage to tell Daniel we would have to go to town to find a video store, if any existed. We drove into town in the pouring rain in that old rusty U-Haul truck. It would have been easier driving an elephant. The shocks were shot, and the tires were tread bared. We managed to find one corner store with a small video rental section. Their new releases were beyond old. At this point, we weren't going to be too picky. Of course, the guy wanted my Visa number, driver's license, and a picture ID card. The only thing he didn't want was the skin off my mother's butt. He was incredible. My Visa was so overdrawn, it was to the point where I was waiting for the shackles to swing out from the bank door when I walked by.

I explained to the moron behind the counter what had taken place that day. That guy was on an ego trip. I had cash on me, but he still wanted to push me to the limit. I looked at him square in the eye and said, "We need movies." I assured him they would be returned to him the next day. I had to give him the name and number of the garage the car was in before he would consider giving us some movies. The little bastard knew the owner of the garage and called him at home to verify the information.

I grabbed Adam by the shoulder and was just ready to leave the store when he finally yelled out, "You're okay folks, come back!" It's a good thing he couldn't read my mind. What a jerk off! We had a long haul up that horrible mountain with that gutless truck. I grinded the gears until the smoke was just a-pumpin' out of it. When we arrived back at the cottage, I was ready for a brew and a warm dry blanket. We didn't picture our first night at the cottage watching old movies, but at least we were safe and happy. Even though we kept busy with hiking and swimming, I still missed Stephen terribly. Thoughts of him gnawed at my guts every day. I couldn't come to grips with the fact that the relationship had failed. That was the part that was bothering me more than anything. A couple of times I had to look in the mirror to see if I looked as crazy and I felt.

Daniel and I were enjoying a nice glass of wine, sitting around the fire. For some stupid reason, I started crying. Daniel put his arms around me. "It will be okay. Give it some time. I know you are hurting inside. He did a terrible thing to you!" I looked at Daniel thinking what a wonderful guy he was and how he was so understanding.

I said to Daniel, "I need to talk to Stephen." I frantically said, "Daniel, I really need to talk to Stephen. Please take me to a phone now." I began to panic and sweat. "Please, Daniel!" I don't know what happened to me. Poor Daniel had done so much for the kids and I. I couldn't help myself. Daniel understandably felt a little awkward with my actions. He put his emotions on the back burner and took me to the phone booth.

I managed to get a hold of his new telephone number in Winnipeg. When he picked up the receiver, there was silence. I didn't know what to say other than, "Hi, it's me." He knew from my voice I was upset. I was crying to the point that he couldn't understand what I was saying. At first, he was surprised to hear my voice.

"Where are you? Are you all right? Calm down!" He was trying to sound compassionate. I could sense a bit of concern in his voice. Just hearing his voice put me at ease. I started to breath normally again. I guess you could call it a temporary fix. Poor Daniel patiently waited outside the phone booth, throwing stones into the ditch. I felt so sorry for him. And why in hell was he putting up with my actions? Most ex-husbands would have left me high and dry long ago. I should have kissed the ground he walked on. Instead, I acted like a heartbroken, shattered basket case. I think Stephan finally realized that he had truly broken by heart. After the phone conversation, Daniel and I walked back to the cottage. Daniel was a little ticked with me.

"Do you feel better now hearing that freak's voice?" We arrived at the cottage to see the kids sound asleep on the floor. Daniel was put off by that evening's events, especially after all of the things he had done for us. He wasn't long going to bed. But at the time, I wasn't thinking straight.

As Daniel tucked me into bed, he looked down at me. "Things will get better, trust me! You have to forget about that selfish creep, put him behind you! Look what he's done to you!" He was my reinforcement blanket. I knew in time that that horrible pain I had would subside. I just had to be patient. The next day I woke up to the smell of maple bacon. Daniel was a fabulous cook. On that morning, for the first time in a long time, I sensed that everything was going to be alright!

After breakfast, we packed a picnic and scouted out the area. Did you ever notice how brochures show a different picture? They basically lied through their teeth. I guess that's why they call those places tourist traps. Once they have your credit card number over the phone and your scheduled dates, you're trapped! One way or another, we were going to make the best of this trip. We walked the shoreline to gather up firewood for the night so we could have a bondfire on the beach at night. I saw a whole new light in the kid's eyes. They were happy again. As far as swimming went, good luck! Somehow, we managed to get to the water after crawling over rocks and debris. We had to be careful since the rocks were slippery with slime. I had a funny feeling that the slime wasn't algae either. The evenings were simple but totally relaxing. We would sit around the fire eating marshmallows and drinking beer. The lake was so peaceful at night. The lights of all the surrounding cottages reflected on the lake. You could often hear the occasional screech from an owl off in the distance. The fireflies were so entertaining to watch. Alexandria had a fun time trying to catch a couple. The smiles on the kids' faces were priceless. They were filled with love and happiness. They certainly deserved it!

The first thing we had to do on Monday was head into town to find out the problem with the car. Apparently, a part had to be sent up from Toronto, and it was a sweet eight hundred dollars to have it fixed! We just were glad to have a vehicle to drive around in, although that poor old U-Haul was ready for the grave. We spent the entire morning doing the tourist thing. We visited the local rip-off shops and had lunch at the only restaurant in town. That guy had it made! He could have served cheap hotdogs or eel every day and probably got away with it. The only other choice we had was to drive a couple of hours to the next restaurant. At that point, we weren't in the mood. What pissed me off was that those guys got away with that stuff everyday. He certainly gouged the public.

It got so hot, we cut the tourist scene short and headed back to the cottage. Without any hesitation, we headed for the beach to cool off. It was so quiet and serene, just what the doctor ordered. Between pigging out on great steaks and burgers, swimming and lying around like lazy dogs, the week flew by so quickly. We really hated to leave. It was called reality! The last night at the cottage, we had the big party. The grill was full of an assortment of meats, and the table was lined with salads. We invited the neighbors over to help eat all of the food. The next morning, we were on our way home. During the trip back home, Daniel tried to convince me to return to Halifax. He remarked, "There is nothing keeping you here anymore." It actually wasn't a bad idea. By the time we arrived to the apartment, I had decided that we would leave. The only things that remained there were bad memories. It was time to move on with my life. The kids didn't need any convincing at all. The only problem was money—I didn't have any. Daniel said, "If it's money you're worried about, I'll take care of it. Don't you worry about anything. You have been through enough!" He was just so glad to know Adam and Alexandria would be living in his backyard again. It was best for everybody. It was one of the best decisions I had made in several months.

The first thing I had to do was unload the crap in the apartment. Daniel's first plan of action was to burn the filthy mattress. That night, we hauled it down to the river and poured gasoline over it. We didn't even want to roast hot dogs over it. God knows what disease we would have caught. The smell was incredibly disgusting! Over the next couple of days, we organized a huge yard sale. It was quite successful. We made over four hundred dollars. After the sale, we began packing. Daniel had to take an extended holiday until I could get everything organized for the move. One thing I didn't sell at the yard sale was my freezer, so I advertised it at the local grocery store. A young couple from town bought it. We made arrangements the day we left for Nova Scotia to drop it off on the way. I made a terrible mistake. I didn't get any cash from them. They told me they would give me a check when we arrived. The check they gave me bounced to kingdom come!

The moving day arrived. Daniel went up to the garage to pick up the U-Haul truck for the move. Within hours, the truck was loaded. That was one place I certainly wasn't sorry to leave! I drove the Mazda with Adam and the cats, and Daniel took Alexandria in the U-Haul. It was a long, tiring trip for all of us. I suffered terribly with my panic attacks, which meant several stops, plus, highway driving was not for me. I am a country girl and used to Sunday drives. Adam and I took our time and finally made it to Nova Scotia in nine days. Daniel had given up on me and made it home in six days. He made sure that I had enough money for gas, food and lodging, though. The one thing he did forget to give me was the cat's litter box. It was in back of the U-Haul. When we pulled up to the motel, the cats were pretty anxious and antsy. I found an old carton in the dumpster, and we filled it with dirt from the motel garden.

For the first while, the cats didn't know what to do with it because they were indoor cats. They have never smelled dirt before. I had to take them and rub their noses in the dirt. They finally got sick of crossing their legs and used it. I didn't have a clue what I was going to do when I arrived in Dartmouth, Nova Scotia.

We were exhausted when we finally arrived. Daniel had agreed to let me and the kids stay at his place for the duration of the summer, but in the fall, I would have to find my own place. I wasn't looking forward to that, but he wanted his own space, and I couldn't blame him for that. He had a beautiful old character home. You could feel the warmth and love the minute you walked in the front door. I could tell he had spent a lot of time and money on that place. Both the living and dining rooms had outstanding views of the ocean. It was so inviting. The yard was huge. Even though I knew my visit was going to be short, it still didn't stop me from putting the "woman's touch" on it. Daniel didn't mind as long as there was nothing pink. In a joking manner, he said, "No pink, or you are out of here!" The kids were in heaven. What a peaceful place. It wasn't enough that Daniel had paid for the entire move and trip down. The following night, he went the extra mile and bought fresh jumbo lobsters for supper. We sat on the deck enjoying cold beer, looking at the ocean and digging our teeth into succulent Nova Scotia lobsters. It was good to be back home.

As he was boiling up the lobsters, I was out on the deck listening to the music floating across the harbour from the outdoor pubs. He took care of everything for me. He even put my belongings into storage. The next day, the sun shone brilliantly. I hung out a huge load of laundry. My folks called and invited us out for a barbeque that night. As soon as we got organized, we hit the road. Everyone was so glad to see us. They met us with open arms. I was laughing and crying at the same time. The deck was covered with food, beer and wine. My mom never held back when it came to a party. It was a treat being around my family again. That was one thing about my family—they never seemed to have any worries. At least, they never showed it. I could tell they had a million questions for me, but with Daniel there, they didn't want to say anything. Jackie, on the other hand, being so inquisitive, nailed me a couple of times in the kitchen, and whispered, "Have you heard from the beast lately? Did that prick ever give you any money?" As she was leaving the kitchen, chuckling, she said, "You must admit, he was one piece of work!" When we arrived back to Daniel's place, I noticed the clothesline was empty. I jumped out of the car.

"My god, where are all of our clothes?" I couldn't believe my eyes. I ran onto the deck and looked over the side, thinking that maybe a strong wind came up and blew them down. They were nowhere in site. Somebody had the nerve to come into the backyard and steal all of our clothes. "Great!"

I was constantly on the phone with Stephen, literally begging him for money. My life had gone to the dogs. The pills the doctor had me on were deadly. I was either wired for sound or extremely tired. There were days I doubled up on them just so I could cope with everyday living. Even though Daniel's generosity and patience were overwhelming, I still couldn't stop thinking about Stephen. After numerous calls, he finally said, "I will send you ten thousand dollars in the next couple of days!" Every day I went to the mailbox, waiting in anticipation. It never happened! I called him continually and got nothing but an answering machine. He was totally avoiding me. I called him relentlessly every night until I finally got a hold of him.

"Where is the ten thousand dollars you promised me?" He never even answered me. The last thing I heard was him slamming the receiver down.

The summer was coming to a close, and I had to make other living arrangements. I needed that money to help me get started again in life. I started threatening Stephen. I had no choice in the matter. I was going to take the story to the press and let the rest of world know how he miserably treated the kids and I. He said, "If you do that, I will remove your name from my will." He was quite convincing. In fact, he was so convincing that I never carried out my threats. I was naïve enough at the time to think he really meant that I was actually still in his will. There were nights I'd spend crying myself to sleep. Out of all the calls I had made to him, there was one that stuck with me over the years. He actually confessed in a low voice, "I feel so guilty for what I did to you. I truly mean that!"

The only response I could think of was, "Guilty as charged! Now where is my money?" Oh to have that statement on tape! Words can be cheap sometimes, and he was good using them.

I became so ill I had to be taken to the hospital several times. My whole system was out of whack. The doctor changed my medications, and after several visits, I was slowly coming around. Even though I was frail and unable to return to work, I still bugged him to help me. My nerves and stress were becoming my best friends. I don't know how Daniel put up with it. He would comfort me in nights where I was hysterical. He would hold me in his arms, rubbing my back and telling me, "Cry it out, cry it out. You'll feel better. He'll have his day in hell!" He knew it was not easy for the kids and me. It was going to take a lot of time and support to get me back to myself again. I hadn't realized how sick I had become over this break up. My emotions were torn to pieces. I was heartbroken. The only thing I had on my side was Daniel. He took such great care of me. There were more than a few times he drug my butt to the hospital over severe panic attacks. All because of one man, my life was torn upside down, physically and emotionally. The sad part about it all was that I knew he wasn't suffering one bit.

It was time to start looking for an apartment. I had saved enough money to pay for the first and last months' rent plus the damage deposit. That basically left me penniless. I found a nice cozy apartment in Halifax, across the harbour. It was small but clean and warm. At least the heat and water was included in the rent. Once I had the apartment, I needed things to put in it. Daniel and I went furniture shopping. Since I had depleted all of my cash, I couldn't go to a second-hand store because those bastards want cash up front. I ended up buying new furniture at one of those places where you don't pay for a year. It was sad to leave Daniel's place. It was so comfortable. I found some sort of peace and relief staying at his home. It was good therapy for me. Regardless, I still had to move out.

Daniel's friends and my brothers moved us into my new place. They did a lot of cursing at me. It was all stairs. After the truck was unloaded, they had a feast of beer and pizza, again on Daniel. From that day on, they gave me a nickname, "En Route." I was the only member of the family who had done so much moving around the countryside. That name has been with me for several years. The first night in our new apartment was rather exciting. Daniel stayed for the evening to help assemble the beds and tables. My new furniture was beautiful. At least I knew the mattresses were clean. Within a day or two, I had the place looking like we had lived there for years, but my life had gone from riches to rags. The money I was getting from Daniel's and Adam's income was not enough to keep us going. My medications were costing me a fortune, and the cost of living was much higher than it was in Calgary. There were times when food was scarce. When it came right down to it, I wouldn't eat so the kids would have more food. The fact was, living like that was eating my guts out every day. There was no need of it! If Stephen had kept his promise and sent me that money, I wouldn't have been in that predicament. It was certainly a blow to my ego. I wasn't used to that way of life. I knew damn well that bastard wasn't going hungry. If my health hadn't been so bad,

I could have taken any job just until I could land something decent. I had to bite the bullet, swallow my pride and apply for social assistance.

That was the biggest slap in the face of my entire life. It was one of most difficult things I ever had to do. Not only that, it was extremely embarrassing. I phoned Stephen to let him know how badly I had deteriorated.

"I had to go on welfare today!"

His only remark to that was, "You gotta do what you gotta do!" I thought to myself, *You rotten selfish prick. How can you look at yourself in the mirror in the morning?* I slammed the receiver down and called him every name in the book. It never even fazed him that I had to go on welfare. He didn't give a damn! As far as he was concerned, I was dead. The love I had for him slowly but surely changed into severe hatred. I only wished for him a painful horrible death. My family saw what he had done to me. There were times when my brothers were going to fly to Winnipeg and literally beat the living shit out of him. He was not only hated by my family, but also by our friends throughout the community. They lost all respect for that man. I don't know what I would have done without my parents. I had very little of everything, so my parents were there when I needed them. I would wake up in the morning with so much hatred for that man my bones ached for revenge. My blood was boiling with anger!

I always said, "What goes around comes around. That monster will have his day." That was my only salvation—that hopefully one day he would have his day!

TWENTY-ONE

Fall once again fell upon us, and school started. I hadn't looked forward to it, knowing I didn't have the means or hardly the strength to get the kids ready. But my darling mom was always there to come to the rescue. My dad brought her in to my place. Mom and I would hit the town. Again, Mom's Visa took a good beating. At the time, they were my money and help line. They knew I was barely making ends meet. My parents were furious with that bastard. That creep actually had the gall to write my parents a letter and tell them about our personal life. I didn't waste any time calling him up. I never even gave him the opportunity to say hello. I blurted out to him, "Where in hell do you get off writing a letter to my parents? The nerve! How would you like it if I wrote your parents a letter telling them how you abused me?" He agreed that it wasn't a very nice thing he had done and actually apologized. I don't know how many times I asked Stephen to help me out. I was stressed out to the limit, poor and vulnerable. My health had deteriorated again for the worst. Once again, I had pneumonia. I spent weeks in bed. I was deathly ill. I was able to send the kids off to school and had the strength to crawl back into bed. Beyond that I was useless. My health deteriorated rapidly. My mom basically lived with me until I was on my feet. My medications were costly. My mom even paid for those. Adam tried to take over the kitchen duty. One night he came into my room and tapped me on my back.

"Mom, I have supper on the table." With every ounce of strength in my body, I got out of bed and went to the table. I had to keep in mind that the only thing he had ever cooked in his life was either a Kraft dinner or a hot dog, so I was in for a treat. I walked in our tiny dining room to see the table all set, even with place mats. He had a plate in the middle of the table. On it was a piece of round steak burnt to a crisp that I had bought for a stew, and around it were a bunch of boiled potatoes. What could I say? It was priceless what he had done. As sick as I was, I made myself eat some of that horrible, tough meal. It was like chewing on an old boot. He was so proud of himself, and I of him. Alexandria was put on laundry patrol. That poor little creature would carry the laundry down three long flights of stairs and carry them all the way back. That basket full of clothes was bigger than her.

I became so distraught with the whole situation that I threatened to sue Stephen. After my health started to improve, I obtained legal advise from two different lawyers. They both advised me that, in order to sue him, I would have to move back to Calgary to file suit on him. They asked me why I never pursued a legal suit while I was living there before. To be honest, I didn't know. I think I was so confused and bewildered. For one thing, I was too sick to even give it a thought. I trusted him. I kept thinking he was eventually going to give me some sort of financial help. He kept me on a string while living there. He would offer his car so I could run errands, and take me out to dinner the odd time. He always remained very pleasant with me while living there. He basically sucked me in. He knew damn well I had legal rights, but being in the frame of mind I was in, suing him was the last thing on my mind. I started looking for work even though it was strongly advised not to until my health improved. But regardless, I did. Finally, I landed a job working as an administrator for a local real estate company. I couldn't afford a car right away, so I had to use the bus system.

That sucked big time! I remember those cold days walking to the bus stop, and every step I took was a reminder of how much I hated that terrible, selfish, egotistical beast. I knew that bastard in Winnipeg wasn't living in some low-life apartment. For the last time, I called Stephen and begged and pleaded with him to send down some money. I came home from work one day, opened my mailbox, and to much of my surprise, there was a letter from Stephen. Enclosed in the letter was a check for eight hundred dollars. I almost pissed my pants. If I didn't need the money so badly, I would have framed it.

Daniel was great with us. He was taking care of a situation he didn't have to. We always looked forward to Friday nights. He would show up at the door with steaks, treats for the kids, beer, wine and movies. Since he lived quite a distance from us, he would often spend the night. I would feel so sorry for him because I had two love seats in the living room. It didn't seem to bother him at all. He would curl up in a ball and fall fast to sleep. Even though I was working, he still wanted to help out as much as possible. On Saturdays, he would take us grocery shopping. He would always put the most expensive stuff in the cart—the fancy cereals, best cuts of meat, oh, and fresh fruit! The first time he did that, I didn't know he intended to pay, and he knew I didn't have the money to buy the brand name products. So, he just kept putting stuff in the cart like steaks, chocolate milk, etcetera. I kept thinking, *How am I going to pay for this?* He would wait until the very last thing was rung in before he would whisper into my ear, "I'll get this one." That bugger! He sure had a heart of gold and a wonderfully refreshing sense of humour. Jackie came over to see how things were going. The minute she walked in the door, the laughter started. We had so much fun together. We took nothing seriously and were constantly joking around with each other. I noticed her arm was quite red and swollen. She said, "Something bit me today while I was playing golf." She didn't seem to be worried about it, but as the evening went on her arm worsened. We continued to drink wine and carried on throughout the evening. By the time she left for home, her arm was in pretty rough shape.

She wasn't home long. She became very sick during the night and had to be rushed to the hospital. The bite was very severe. There wasn't a day I wasn't at her bedside. Her prognosis worsened over the next couple of days. They called in a specialist to find out what in hell bit her. They found out that it was a spider that probably came off one of those foreign ships and made its way to the golf course on a box of fruit. She was so sick, it was sinful. She called me up early one morning, crying frantically, "Could you come in right away, please? I'm scared." I arranged for the lady across the hall to keep an eye on the kids for me. She was kind enough to loan me her car. I was there in a flash. She was lying there crying her eyes out. Her helpless, red, infected arm lay there covered in markings so the doctors could determine how quickly the poison had spread. She was beside herself! They told her that morning that if the antibiotics didn't start to kick in, they might have to amputate her arm. She was hysterical! They could have at least let her have a cup of tea before sharing such lovely news to her. All I could do was hug her. As the morning hours went by, I swear a little guardian angel landed on her shoulder. Her arm started to improve. Not a lot, but enough to keep the knives away. The doctors started marking the downhill slide. That was a good thing. They increased her drip and hoped for the best. By nightfall, things were more promising. The arm would remain. She was one lucky individual. She was the only person in North America who had been bitten by that particular spider bite who hadn't lost a limb over it. I was exhausted when I got home that night. My neighbor, who lived directly across the hall, was sweet enough to feed the kids their supper. She was quite the character. She had an old guy that lived with her. He too was quite the character. He had a serious heart problem, smoked like a trooper and drank wine like a fish. They had a bedroom converted into a winery. There was never a shortage of wine on our floor. That woman had a heart of gold. She would go to any limit to please anybody. She had more energy than a horny old tomcat. She was sure full of piss and vinegar. She always sat in a big old La-z-boy, sipping on a glass of wine and smoking a cigarette. Everybody on our floor loved her. No wonder—she kept half the floor in homemade wine.

I had gone over to her place after dinner one night to bring them some homemade apple pie. They were sitting there drinking their wine and playing poker. The room was so full of smoke, you could cut it with a knife. I opened up the patio door to let some air in. No matter if guests wanted a glass of wine or not, they got it. I didn't stay long because Daniel was on his way over to take us all to the IMAX theatre that evening. I had a glass of wine with them and left. She said, "When you come back, come on over and have a game of cards with us." We went across the hall to join in on a game of poker. I knocked on the door, but there wasn't any answer. The door wasn't locked, so we walked in. The smoke was incredible. She was sitting in her chair, passed out with a cigarette smoldering its way into the fabric. The smoke was incredible. I don't know why the fire alarm didn't go off. Daniel opened the patio door. He drenched the chair. We carried her over to my place and put her into my bed. Her boyfriend was passed out on the couch. She could have burnt the entire building down that night. Once we had her in bed, we went back to her place to make sure everything was okay.

One night, Daniel called me up out of the blue and asked me, "Do you think the kids would like to have a computer for homework and to play games on?" I was speechless.

"Why, of course they would love to have a computer, but it's a little out of my league right now!" It wasn't long after the conversation that my intercom was buzzing. It was Daniel.

He said, "Can you come down and help me with something?" I was so excited. What had he bought now? I flew down those stairs. There he was, standing surrounded in boxes. Leave it to Daniel. We carried them upstairs and started unpacking the boxes. Santa came early that year! Daniel and I were sitting at the table having a cup of tea just waiting for the kids to come home from school. I knew they were going to go crazy. Daniel told them he had a surprise for them. Of course, they thought it was some kind of food. He made them shut their eyes, then he lead them into Adam's bedroom, where we had it installed. "Open wide." They were both speechless. They pawed over it like it was an animal. I had no idea they would be so excited. Adam loved it for the games, and Alexandria was more into the learning aspect of it.

One Friday night, I was bored to tears. There was one pint of beer in the fridge and a package of popcorn in the cupboards. We sat there watching the cats' heads go up and down as they watched the snowflakes hitting the deck. Now that's boredom! We started a game of crazy eights to kill some time. The phone rang. It was Daniel. He wanted me to take me out for a couple of beers downtown. I couldn't believe my ears. The kids were sitting at the kitchen table watching their mom going ballistic over a phone call. I wasn't long getting my ass into the shower and getting dressed. We visited our favorite places, met some of his friends, danced, talked, and drank a bunch of beer and wine. Boy, did I need that! My life was in such a turmoil, and it sure was nice to forget about all of the worries for one night. My soul needed cleansing. We hadn't anticipated drinking that much wine and beer, but what the hell. We ended up leaving the car downtown and taking a cab back to my place.

The next morning, we awoke to a lot of snow. Most of the city had shut down, at least for the morning. As we were sitting at the table watching the snow fall, a huge seagull landed on the deck. The kids ran to the window.

Daniel went out, trying to free him, but its wing span was so massive that he had to come back inside. The poor bird was terrified. The cats were hissing at the window, dreaming of sinking their teeth into him. He tried escaping by putting his beak through the rails. He was frantic. The blood was flying everywhere. I called the landlord to help.

He arrived with a large broom and long rubber gloves that went up to his elbows. Unsuccessful in his attempts, he left and returned with a saw. He managed to saw off some of the front rails so the bird could fly off the deck. We took buckets of hot water to wash the blood off the deck. I don't know if that bird survived or not. His beak was in pretty rough shape. What are the odds of that happening? The landlord said he had been there for over twenty years and had never witnessed such a thing. Once the weather cleared, Daniel called a cab so he could pick up his car downtown. I really hated to see him go.

I hadn't called Stephen in awhile. By now, he was nothing more than a horrible nightmare and someone who ripped away a huge piece of me that was once filled with love and emotion. My loving dreams of him became schemes and ways of murdering him in the most brutal ways no one could imagine. I was certainly better off without him. I became very cold and bitter person over that breakup. My friend called me to tell me Stephen had the balls to come over and visit one weekend. He showed up with a younger version of me. My friend wouldn't even let him in the door. He knew I must have spoken with her and filled her in on the horrible situation he put me in. He was definitely not wanted on her doorstep. The sight of him made her sick to her stomach. He never returned. One of the last times I talked with him was that Christmas. I called to wish him a Merry Christmas. While talking with him, I could hear a female in the background. There was one thing about Stephen—he never cared whose heart he broke. I asked him if he was seeing anybody. He bluntly said, "Well, of course. You're not the only fish in the sea." She was probably one of his office twits. Even though Christmas was just around the corner, he showed absolutely no remorse. He was one cold-hearted bastard! As far as Christmas went, that was his worse time of year. It meant he had to spend money unnecessarily.

It was a cold, wintry Friday night. We had just finished dinner. The buzzer rang. It was Daniel. I kept buzzing him to come up, but he kept buzzing me back. He finally said, "Look out your patio door." We ran to the window, went out on the deck, looked down and saw this six-foot-man standing there with this huge tree. At the top of the tree was a beautiful star. I yelled down to him, "You're incredible! We'll be right down!" He sure was full of surprises. Adam and Alexandria flew down those steps so fast to help him bring it up. Daniel was always a kid at heart, then and now. The tree was so big, it could hardly fit through the door. It took up a quarter of the living room. It was absolutely beautiful. I stood in the dining room watching the three of them putting that massive tree into its stand. It brought joyful tears to my eyes. It had been so long since I had a decent tree to look at, and so long since I'd seen that joy on our kids' faces. That moment was Christmas for me.

Alexandria and I dug out the decorations while they finished balancing out the tree. We spent the evening decorating, listening to Christmas music and eating pizza. The tree was gorgeous. The tree was fresh and alive. The smell brought life back into my life. After the kids went to bed, I poured us glasses of wine. We sat in front of the tree. We looked at each other. There was silence. We slowly looked up at this beautiful tree that we had created, and I looked right into Daniel's eyes as I lifted my wine glass and said, "Thank you for giving me back my life again." He held me in his arms until I fell asleep. The next morning, we were both still lying by the tree in each other's arms. The two kids were in their glory. They were like mice in the kitchen. They made us breakfast, as scary as that might sound. The table was covered in food—everything from sliced pepperoni to oranges. The eggs, well…I know they didn't use milk in them. Either way, they were delicious!

Daniel and I started seeing a lot of one another. The kids were thrilled seeing us together again. That Christmas was the best one we had in years. After Christmas, Daniel had to go away for a month. He asked me to take care of his house while he was gone. I was delighted. Every weekend, we would pack up the car, throw the cats in the back seat, and off we'd go. What a weekend escape. I spent endless hours in the hot tub listening to classical music. The kids amused themselves with videos and lots of pizzas. We hated to see Sunday come. The month flew by quickly. My medications were cut in half. I not only began looking better, but also started feeling like my old self again. When he arrived home, he noticed a big change in me for the better. He was weighed down with gifts for the kids. He gave me a hug and looked down at me. "I missed you so much, you and the kids. It's great to be back!" We started making plans for spring break. We both took a week off so we could do things with the kids. We would choose a different hotel around the area every night that had a pool. That was one thing about Daniel—he wasn't mean with his money. His motto was, "Either go all the way or stay home." What a splendid week! During that week, Daniel asked me a couple of times to move back in with him when the kids were through school. I had to give it some serious consideration. It wasn't that I didn't love him, I just couldn't stand another relationship to go sour. It would finish me physically and emotionally. When I asked the kids about it, there wasn't an ounce of hesitation on their part. On the whole, they were going whether I went or not. I decided it was best for everyone. We were spending all of our time together anyway. Why pay for two places? I put my notice in to the landlord. Adam's grade twelve graduation was coming up. We were so proud of him that day. He found high school to be a pain in the butt, and he made sure I knew it. Adam's idea of high school was going to Tim Horton's drinking coffee. Homework was a dirty word in his mind. I remember going to one of the parent-teacher nights. I confronted his English teacher.

"What is it going to take to get Adam to pass?"

He laughed. "Do you have your checkbook on you?" It was a constant battle getting him through grade twelve. With a lot of threats, tutoring and pulling my hair out, he finally did it. Seeing him standing in the living room with his tuxedo on made it all worthwhile.

We were scheduled to move out at the end of July. That gave us one month to pack. That wasn't a problem for me; I was becoming a pro at packing. The only predicament I had was that I hadn't found anybody to sublet the apartment. That meant I had to pay for the month of August. That pissed me off! Despite it all, I was tickled pink to be moving back in with Daniel. By the time we got everything organized into his house, there wasn't a lot of room to move around. We made the best of it. We spent endless hours sitting in the sunroom, looking at the lights reflecting off the water and watching the big ships roll down the harbor. What a priceless view! Daniel loved buying me things, especially jewelry. One evening, he was busy in the kitchen making an array of finger foods. He had the wine chilling in the fridge and Beethoven playing in the background. I was nestled into the love seat in the sunroom, content and, for once, at peace with myself. He yelled out from the kitchen, "Shut your eyes and don't peek!" I did what he asked, like a kid. "Open wide!" He was standing behind me putting a stunning emerald and diamond necklace around my neck.

He whispered into my ear, "Will you marry me? Again?" I was at a lost for words, and that was rare.

I turned around and, without any uncertainty, said, "Yes, of course I will!" The kids were playing upstairs. I shouted to them, "Come here, quick!" They could tell by my voice it was good news. They ran in the room and saw the necklace.

"Wow! It's beautiful, Mom!"

I looked at the two of them, smiling from ear to ear. "He asked me to marry him, again!" He opened up a corked bottle of wine to celebrate the occasion.

The house was getting a little to cramped. We thought about redoing the basement, but it wouldn't have been worth it. It was a gorgeous old house, but it lacked space. The two cats loved the old place. It was warm and cozy. They spent ninety percent of their time in the sunroom soaking up the rays. One morning, Kit escaped through the back door. Within seconds, he was out of sight. We spent the entire morning looking for him. By nightfall, we wrote him off as dead. It was devastating for Alexandria. She loved those cats so much it was incredible. Alexandria wouldn't eat for days. She'd sit on the back deck with her chin drooping into her chest. We even bought her a little pool to play in. That turned out to be a place for her to drop her tears. We became quite worried over her.

We took her to the pet store at the mall. There lay, in a little grey ball, an adorable kitten. As soon as I picked her up, she began to purr. I put her into Alexandria's little hands. That kitten never saw that cage again. She named her Lamby. Alexandria made it quite clear that the kitten would never replace Kit. I was a little apprehensive at first with the bigger cat at home, but the kitten showed her stuff the minute she walked in the door. She was an amazing cat. When I threw a tin foil ball up into the air, she would do somersaults in midair to catch it and then bring it back to me. I was in the kitchen preparing supper and could hear a strange noise coming from the back door. I opened the door and in leapt Kit. He was coal black and reeked of garbage. I yelled to Alexandria, "Come here, you have a visitor!" Even though he was filthy dirty, she didn't care. She picked him up and hugged him so tight he cried. We gave him a hot bath and a big bowl of warm milk. That cat to this day hasn't seen the outdoors other than through a window pane or a screen door. His face is permanently molded into the screen.

When Daniel went away with the rigs, Jackie would often spend the night with me. We would think nothing of going to the local fisherman and spending seventy or a hundred dollars on a couple lobsters and indulging in a couple bottles of wine. We'd drink our faces off and talk about the first things that would pop into our minds. No matter what we talked about, I usually twisted the conversation directly into the gutter. Most of our conversations regarded Stephen. At least now I could joke about him. The names we called that man. I imagine there were nights his ears were burning off the side of his head. The next morning, our bodies would crave good old greasy eggs and bacon. There was a diner up the street from us that had the greasiest food in the world. The food was so greasy that the waitress had to do a balancing act with the plates so the food wouldn't slip off. You could feel your chest tighten with each mouthful of food. If I were to do that today, my body would self destruct!

Daniel had gone away for a couple of weeks. I decided to start spring cleaning the place. I loaded the washer full of curtains. Alexandria and Adam started cleaning all the windows. Within a couple of minutes, I heard a terrible bang and then a thrust of water. I ran downstairs to find the entire floor covered in water and soap. The drum in the washer had rusted out and fallen to the floor. It took us most of the day to clean up all the water damage. There was one bright side to it—the floors were clean. Alexandria and I wrung out the curtains as best we could and put them into the dryer. I was too tired to cook, so I took the kids out for pizza. I went to get the curtains out of the dryer to find that the dryer door had fallen off. *Isn't this cute! What's next?* I called my neighbor over to see if he could put it back on for me. It was hopeless. The hinges had rusted off. I called Daniel that night to tell him about my day's adventures. He couldn't believe what he was hearing. Of course, who would? That wasn't good enough. The next morning, we got up to find water all over the kitchen and dining room floor. The fridge had died during the night. I lost most of the freezer stuff. I stood in the middle of the room and began to laugh. That black cloud continually followed me where ever I went. I looked at the stove, pointed and shook my finger at it, and said, "You're next, aren't you, you son of a bitch?" I went over to it and kicked it. I had no washer, no dryer and now no fridge.

Jackie had popped in to have a cup of tea with me. I put the kettle on the stove and basically forgot about it. Jackie reminded me, "Where's that tea?" I went to the stove, and the kettle was ice cold. I checked all of the fuses and turned on all the knobs and the oven. The stove was cold. I stood there in total amazement. Jackie was behind me laughing her butt off. I turned around.

"Do you know I have no appliances left? There's a dead fridge behind you, two at the curb, and now this! Do you believe this?"

The only thing she could say was, "It could only happen to you!" As she continued to laugh, I knew now I was jinxed! That afternoon, we went out to buy four new appliances. The sales clerk asked if I wanted the extended warranties.

My reply was, "Yeah, lifetime!" When I told him what happened to me, he couldn't believe it. Daniel explained to me that he had previously bought the four appliances at the same time from a second-hand store, but still, that was no reason for them all to die on me within twenty-four hours. Christ, what luck I had.

It was a foggy night. Daniel was away but was due home later on that night. Adam was visiting his buddies down the street. Alexandria and I were cuddled up on the couch watching a movie. The doorbell rang, so I got up to see who it was. Thank god there were two doors to get to the main front door. The closer I came to the second door, the more visible the object was on the other side. It was a gang of teenagers with masks on. I damn near pissed my pants. They hadn't seen me yet. I dropped to the floor, crawled into the living room, put my hand on Alexandria's mouth and crawled through the dining room to the back door. I only prayed they weren't in the backyard also. I opened the door very quietly, jumped off the deck and fled to my neighbors'. I never knocked, I just walked right into their kitchen. He came running out of the living room. We were trembling all over, whispering, "It's me, it's okay." I called the cops, and without any delay, our neighbor grabbed a golf club and a flashlight. We watched anxiously by the window. By the time he got out the front door, the car was speeding up the street.

When the coast was clear, he waved to me. I walked up to the front of the house to see that the bastards had spray painted the front screen door bright red and ripped the mailbox off. The cops were there in a couple of minutes. There wasn't much I could tell them other than that they were tall and wore face masks. Within minutes, Daniel rolled in behind the cops in a cab. That was not a pleasant incident. I never felt comfortable in the house ever again. Every time I heard a creak or anything, I jumped out of bed.

Over time, the house went up for sale. It was sold within a couple of weeks. The day of the house inspection was nerve-wracking. We had to upgrade the power. We had an electrician come in to give us a quote—fifteen hundred dollars. I ran up the hill to the Royal Bank in a panic without any appointment, burst into Louise's office totally out of breath, holding onto the door handle and saying, "I need fifteen hundred dollars by tomorrow, can you help me?"

She replied, "Would you like to sit down first?" It was a good thing she didn't have a client with her. It was heartbreaking to see that house go. We had so many marvelous times and warm memories in that place. Our new home was huge. It didn't have the fabulous view, but it was classy and roomy. We didn't have enough furniture to fill some of the rooms, and one in particular—the dining room. We didn't have a dining room suite. One Saturday, we spent the day looking for a suite. That was one of my favorite pastimes other than getting divorced and moving.

Finally, at the end of the day, I found a rugged Canadian-made oak set, a new bed for Alexandria and a large mirror for the foyer. Buying new stuff was so exhilarating. It was one of those don't pay for a year events. The furniture was delivered within a couple of days. We immediately started ripping out walls and painting, giving it our special touches. We eventually put a pool in the back. We held a large housewarming party. Everyone and their dog was there, even the neighbours who I hadn't really gotten to know showed up. I became the street event coordinator. I organized everything from yard sales to street barbeques to Oktoberfest. I loved that neighborhood. On one of the street barbeques, I noticed a guy I used to go out with in high school. He recognized me, came over and gave me a big hug. The only thing that had changed on him was his weight. Other than that, he was still the same good-looking guy. I could tell by the way he looked at me that he still carried a spark for me. He was dating my next door neighbor's daughter. He too had gone through a divorce. It seemed an awful lot of us had gone through that drill in life. They should teach that drill in high school, after all they teach us the fire drill. Why not the divorce drill?

One morning, I was heading out for work. I walked down the hall steps and could hear water running. I looked over the railing to see not water but sewer coming out of the den, down the hall and into the bathroom. "Oh my god!" The smell knocked me backwards. The sewer pipe on our street had backed up, and of course, why not back up in my home? I ran outdoors, gagging my guts out on the lawn. I couldn't go back into the house. The neighbours came over to see what was going on. I finally reached Daniel at work. "Get your butt home, now!" My neighbor called a company that dealt with those kinds of disasters. By the time they arrived, the sewer line had raised to about a foot up the wall. The entire downstairs was sewer. It was devastating! I covered my mouth to grab the cats and put them into my car. Since all of our suitcases were covered in sewer, I had to use a garbage bag to put some clothes in.

The men weren't long ripping out the walls, floors and carpet. Our driveway turned into a dumpster. It was impossible to live there. We contacted our insurance company at once. They weren't long sending out an agent. He estimated eight to ten thousand dollars worth of damages. *Great, just what I needed!* I thought. I stood on the lawn shaking my head. It was a good thing Adam was at a sleepover the night before, since he normally slept in the den. He would have woken up in a shitty mood! Alexandria was across the street playing with her girlfriend. Here I was trying to get the wedding plans finalized, and that shit happened, literally! The best of part of the ordeal was that we got to spend a week in a hotel with three cats. I would never want to live through that episode again.

Adam didn't now what he wanted to do with his life. He was working odd jobs here and there but nothing with a future. Daniel brought home some brochures from the local recruiting office to give him a few options. The next day, without any warning, Daniel walked in the front door, went into Adam's room and told him to get his coat on.

"We're going for a ride." He took him over to the recruiting office to speak with a recruiting sergeant. Adam came home with apprehension written all over his face. They phoned him a week later to come in and write the necessary test. He passed them all with flying colours. Within a month, he received his papers from the military. He was accepted in as an aviation technician. We were so proud of him. Even though he got the trade he wanted, he was still reluctant to go.

Before Adam was due to fly out to start his basic training, Daniel wanted to spend an evening with him. I had gone out earlier and purchased some beer and junk food. They planted their butts in the living room. I had a very expensive vase worth over five thousand dollars sitting in the middle of the living room table. Alexandria and I went out for dinner and a movie that evening. When I arrived home, the two of them were feeling no pain. Led Zeppelin was roaring down the driveway. When we walked in the front door, all I could hear was the two of them burping like pigs and chowing down on pizza and donairs. Men can be such animals at times. I guess that's why I love them so. I went into the living room to find that my vase had been used as a garbage can. It was full of cans of beer and chip bags. I could have brained the pair of them. Since Adam was only home for a couple more days, I took it easy on him. We had a quiet family going-away party for him at the house.

The day finally came when Adam had to leave. He was very quiet that day. I couldn't look at him, or I would have broken down and cried. He certainly didn't give me any indication that he wanted to leave. When we arrived at the airport, the ticket agent told Adam his flight had left five hours prior. My dad was standing right behind him, and within seconds, there was a Visa card slapped down in front of the agent. He said, "Put him on the next available flight. He is not going back home!" In the end, dad didn't have to pay anything. The ticket was not an excursion, so he was able to get the next flight out. It was sad to see him go, but it was time he left home to start his new career. When we returned home, it was so quiet. There was no crazy music bouncing off the walls, and the kitchen was left with no air conditioning system. It took me along time to learn to cook for the three of us. Adam ate enough food for three, so I had to make some major adjustments in my cooking habits. My birds became very fat over the next couple of months.

We had a beautiful pool in the back with an enormous deck basically covering the entire backyard. I decided to put leashes on the cats to tie them to the deck. Dad and Mom were in visiting, so they helped me take them onto the deck. I no sooner turned around then Dad started yelling, "Get out on the deck, now!" I looked out the patio door and saw three cats dangling and swinging back and forth. I leapt over the fence, damn near broke my ankle, and grabbed all three of them at once. Dad was lying on his stomach trying to reach each cat as I was pushing them up from the side. Luckily enough, none of them were hurt. I still don't know to this day why they didn't break their necks. I had to wrap my ankle in ice for the remainder of the day thanks to those stupid furballs! That evening, we had a barbeque on the deck. By the time the men started to barbeque, it was getting pretty dark. The men were drinking some beer, and Mom and I were enjoying some wine. Whenever we were outside, the cats would have their heads glued to the screen window, crying to get out. They did it so often their faces were imprinted into the screen. Usually when Daniel entered the house, he would tap on the screen with his foot to scare the cats away. That time he didn't. The beer had absorbed too many of his brain cells. Kit was the sneaky one. He flew between Daniel's legs and beelined it up the tallest tree we had. Daniel got the ladder out, and Dad and I secured it while he climbed up. There were moments I thought for sure he was going to fall. After all, he was half in the bag. He reached as far as he could with his arms. He finally had to start climbing the limbs. I was visualizing headlines the next day: Man Falls to his Death Rescuing Cat. After several attempts, he managed to grab Kit's tail. The sounds that cat made on his journey down were sinful. He landed right on my shoulder. If not, he would have landed on a huge rock. That cat really did have nine lives. I saved his life!

Alexandria and I often took walks down by the lake. It was a beautiful lake to look at, and that was all. It reeked of sewer. I should know—I developed a nose for that smell. Along the beach were a bunch of boats all lined up in a row and upside down. As I was walking by one of them, I could hear the noise of a kitten crying. I tried to lift it up, but the boat was stuck into the icy sand. I called Alexandria over to help me. We found a piece of wood on the beach. I pried it under the sand and gently stepped on it. Since Alexandria had little hands, I said to her, "As soon as the boat lifts, grab the kitten!" When her hands came up from underneath the boat, she had two kittens. Someone had put them there to die. They were so tiny that the two of them fit in the palm of one hand. They were wet and cold but adorable.

We rushed them home to feed them. While I was making them some hot cereal, Alexandria was busy deciding on names for them. She named them Bonnie and Clyde. Once you name an animal, it's yours. They buried not only their little fury faces, but also their front paws into that bowl. I took them to a friend of mine who was a veterinarian. She cleaned their ears up and gave them their first shots. When we arrived home, we gave them each a bath and wrapped them in a warm heavy towel. Daniel was not thrilled over the idea at all. In fact, he was opposed to it right away. He kept saying, walking from room to room, "No, no, no, no way. Five is too many. Most people don't have five kids. No! People are going to think you are certifiable!" Once I told him I had just spent two hundred dollars on them, he looked at me with a half smile. "You're nuts, you know that? Plain, simple nuts!" The no's didn't last too long. He fell in love with them instantly.

TWENTY-TWO

The wedding was just around the corner. I had pretty much everything organized. We each had three people standing for us. So much for a small wedding party. They named me the "Supreme Allied Commander." Of course, I found that out after the wedding. I am very particular with attention to detail and accuracy. As a wedding gift from Mark and Jackie, it was being held on the deck overlooking fairway number two. I could not have asked for a better day. There wasn't a cloud in the sky nor a breath of wind. The day of the event was grand. I had chosen blue and white balloons for the decorations. Some of our friends that flew in stayed at our place. You talk about a party. The week before and right up to the wedding day was one big party. The night before the wedding, the bridal party had to stay somewhat sober because we had to attend the rehearsal party. Christ, I didn't need to rehearse anything. I could have done it with my eyes closed, and I'm sure Dad had become quite experienced in walking me down the aisle. We were pros at that stuff! I had hired a private catering company to prepare the food. We invited over a hundred people.

There was only one drawback the day of the wedding: Adam was unable to attend. He was halfway through his course and couldn't get time off to fly down. Other than that, everything else was perfect. The girls met me at my place. We had hair and nail appointments and the final fittings for our dresses. There was no way I was going to buy a white dress. The crowd would have thrown stones at me. I almost went black, but my mom told me she wouldn't attend the wedding if I did, so I went navy blue. We had friends and relatives who flew in from all over Canada. My bridal party spent the remainder of the day at the hotel suite Daniel had reserved for that night. I wasn't a place that I would recommend to anybody. It was a Victorian-style building with absolutely no facilities to offer. Of course, he didn't know until he arrived there that evening. There was no room service, or for that matter, even a bar. It was one big room with a luxury bathroom and king-size bed. It would have been the ideal place if this was the first time around for me. When you had as many weddings as I had, you wanted to see lounges with booze and room service. The king-size bed had lost its glow fifteen or more years ago. The limo arrived. There is something special about a limo. The minute I stepped my foot in it, I felt rich all over. The driver had a bottle of wine chilling for us. He gracefully poured us all a drink and headed for the golf course.

We came in through the kitchen I picked out to have a look at the reception area. I was awed by how beautiful the clubhouse looked. One thing that was perturbing me was the fact that the caterers had arrived and started setting up the food too early. They were supposed to set the food up once the ceremony started. By the time the ceremony was over, half of the food was gone. The place was packed with friends and neighbors. I think some people wanted to attend just to be a part of my soap-opera life. Their smiles and charm filled the air with love. Screw the love part, I needed some good luck more than love! We had chosen an untraditional wedding song: "You Are My Best Friend" by Queen. I could see Daniel out on the deck with the boys having a beer. Everyone seemed quite comfortable. The temperature was just right. The music started, and that was my cue to start to walk towards the minister. I had a flower girl who walked in front of me throwing red petals into the air. I was grinning from ear to ear. Alexandria approached the deck first, and when her father saw her, he shed a tear. She was so elegantly dressed and looked very much a grown-up with the up-do and makeup. He couldn't believe his eyes. Dad and I walked out, and when we reached the minister, he kissed me on the cheek and, with a smile and a wink, whispered in my ear, "Let's make this the last trip!" The ceremony went off without a hitch. It wasn't long before people were indulging in wine and food. The music started and, the traditional rule of thumb, we had the first dance. Adam called us to congratulate us on our marriage. He had a gang of his friends in the background shouting, "Congratulations, Mom!" That was a very special moment that evening. We noticed the limo outside the clubhouse, so we thanked everybody for coming and left quickly. There were champagne and canapés laid out for us inside the limo. The driver gave us a tour of downtown Halifax to view the boats in the harbor that were all lit up, as if I never saw the lights at night before. The champagne was of more interest to me at that point. We were in the mood for partying. The day of carrying the bride over the threshold was definitely past for me. The only place I wanted to be carried into was a lounge with lots of loud music and wine. With the get-up I was wearing, I would have looked like a cheap whore being escorted by my pimp, so the only alternative was to head back to the suite, drink some cheap wine and try to have sex.

The next day, we arrived home to a house full of gifts and friends. We spent the day lounging around the pool, indulging in more beer and wine. It was time to do the opening of the gifts. Normally, that is a happy event, but when you've been around the block a couple of times, its really no big deal. After the tenth gift, I figured there must have been a huge candle sale in every mall in town. I got sick of counting the number of candles I opened. I guess it was better than toasters or kettles. Who needs electricity? Just get married for the third time! One particular gift was rather funny. It was a wine holder without the bottle of wine. Another was a wine decanter, an ugly one at that, again without a bottle of wine. I knew what had happened—the had purchased the wine, but when wrapping up the gift, they realized it was so pathetic that they ended up drinking the other half of the gift. Some people have no imagination any more. Once the wedding flair was out of the air, it was time to return to reality.

Since we had the only house on the street with a pool, it made us quite popular. There were times when there were kids in the pool we didn't even know, but it was okay since we knew their parents. I had turned into the street babysitter, and that was pissing me off. The screaming and yelling in the pool used to drive me nuts sometimes. There were days when if I heard "Marco Polo" one more time, there was going to be a drowning. I used to go out on my deck with my iced tea, watching those brats through the glass, visualizing strangling a couple of them. There would be a moment of joy, but then I would have to suffer the consequences. So instead of doing twenty to life, I put up with the noise. We had one obnoxious neighbor. He was always dressed up like he had somewhere to go all the time. I found out through the grapevine that he was a stay-at-home dad. There isn't anything wrong with that, but he certainly gave the impression that he was doing something very important. I could never understand why he was always dressed up in designer clothing. He would never shut his mouth; bragging was his talent. He had two little girls that brought screaming to an all new level. Alexandria could barely tolerate them. They were not only loud, but also spoiled rotten. Even their innocent sweat smelt of roses. Their father was standing by the poolside talking with Daniel with his hands in his pocket. I was headed to the table with my iced tea. As I walked by him, I casually pushed him into the pool. I proceeded to the table to read my paper. In other words, I totally ignored what I had just done. He got out of the pool, screaming, "What did you do that for? You ruined my clothes! Look at my watch!" He stood there yelling at me like an idiot. The kids in the pool were laughing their butts off at him. He immediately pulled the girls out of the pool and left. He was pissed! I never saw him again. Rumor had it on the street that I humiliated and embarrassed him in front of his girls. Poor prick! That taught him to brag around my pool.

The rigs gave Daniel a new promotion, which meant he would be away a lot more. With Adam gone, the house seemed so big and empty. We decided we would sell the house at the end of the summer and move into something smaller. There was a couple who loved our house. They had heard through one of our nosy neighbors that we had a problem with the sewer system. We assured them the problem was rectified. He insisted we hire a sewer specialist to take photos of the sewer lines that came in through our home. They came back three times to have a look at it. After going through the house with a fine-toothed comb and two different building inspectors, they finally put an offer in. I was sad to see it go, but I knew I would enjoy condo living much more. We started looking at condos. It would be the perfect and safest route for us since Daniel was away a lot. We ended up buying this luxury three-bedroom condo in Halifax. It had all the bells and whistles. We had a view of a crystal clear pool

We weren't in the condo for more than a month when Daniel had gone on the rigs. The condo living was great. My kitchen had every appliance you could imagine. That was luxury living. The only thing that bothered me was that one of my neighbors was a little strange. Whenever I would run into him in the hall, he'd give me this haunting look and, with a creepy voice, say, "Hi, how are you doing today?" I could almost see him drooling, and I knew when I walked by him he was still looking at my butt. He just wasn't all there. I always made sure I double-bolted my door. One day I came home, and there were a dozen long stem roses by my door. There was no note. At first I thought they were from Daniel. I put them in a vase and never really thought any more of it.

The next day, I was coming home from work, and I noticed a note on my door. It said, *Did you enjoy your flowers?* A chill ran up my back. I opened that door so fast. "Alexandria, Alexandria!" She came running out of her room. I had a terrified look on my face. "Did anybody knock at the door this afternoon?"

She replied, "No, Mommy, why?" Daniel called me that evening. It was good to hear his voice. I told him about the flowers and the note and about how I was a little uncomfortable. He never thought anything of it. He basically said with a chuckle, "Maybe you have a secret admirer!" A couple of weeks passed before the next episode. There were a dozen long stem white roses that time. That gave me the creeps! White roses symbolize death. I opened the door rather cautiously. I very quietly peeked around the corner. All of a sudden, someone tapped on my shoulder from behind. I jumped so quickly I banged my head between the door and the wall. When I turned around, I saw the door at the end of the hall swinging. I ran into the condo, locked the door, grabbed a bag of frozen peas to soothe my head and called the cops. When they arrived, there wasn't much I could tell them. They warned me not to open the door without looking first and said that if there was an article placed by the door that I was not to touch it, and I was to make sure I kept my door locked at all times.

I asked them if they could do me a favor. I had managed to get my creepy neighbor's name from the mailbox. I wrote it down and gave it to the cops. I asked them, "Do you think you could run a check on this guy for me?" I explained that he lived across the hall and that there was something odd about him. I knew Alexandria wasn't going to be home that evening because she was spending the night with her friend. That meant I was going to be alone. I called up Jackie, but she had made other plans for that night. I decided to go out and grab a couple of rentals and a burger. Upon arriving back home, I noticed a bag lying in front of my door. I bent over to see what it was. "Oh my god!" I threw up my burger all over the carpet in the hall. It was a bird with its head cut off. I ran out of the building and to my truck. I drove to the nearest phone booth and called the cops again. Luckily enough, I managed to get a hold of the same detective. He met me at the condo. I asked him if he had found out anything about my neighbor. He told me he was just about to do that when I called. I was getting pretty upset over this. He took the headless bird to hopefully find a fingerprint and recommended I stay with friends that night. He also asked me which condo the creep lived in. I asked him to stay long enough for me to get a suitcase packed. I also had to get in touch with Alexandria to warn her not to come home. I ended up staying at a hotel.

The next morning when I arrived home, there was a message on my answering machine. It was the detective. "I couldn't detect any fingerprints from the bag or the bird. Also, I should have some information for you later on today about your neighbor!" That was a relief to hear. Alexandria came running in the door.

"Mommy, Mommy, go look at our truck!" Someone had engraved on my door, *Piss off!* I stood there waving my hands in the air.

"Who in hell is doing this to me?" I called the detective up again.

While I was on the phone with him, he said, "I was just about to call you. I have some news for you." I went inside and anxiously paced the floor. When he arrived, he didn't have the kind of news I wanted to hear. The detective looked at me with great disappointment. "The guy I did a trace on apparently doesn't exist anywhere. I even doubled-checked! That causes me to be a little concerned!"

The detective went over to his condo to ask him some questions, but he wasn't home. Either that, or he wasn't answering the door. In fact, when I thought about it for a minute, I hadn't seen him around in a while. There wasn't much the detective could do. He warned me, "Be careful!" I was really worried now. I managed to reach Daniel on the rig to tell him what was going on. He was so tied up with his work, there was no way he could have come home, but he advised me to have a security system installed. After supper, I took the truck up to the dealer to see how much it was going to cost me to have the truck repaired. There was no way I was putting it through my insurance. While I was there, I took the opportunity to shop around at maybe buying something new. The truck was going on six years old. Maybe it was time for a change. It wasn't long before Phil, the sales representative I had dealt with for several years, was trying to put a deal together for me. I always wanted a van, so that was the perfect time to do it. I drove home in a beautiful silver van. I was a little skeptical going back to the condo that evening.

I made a bed up in front of the door. Alexandria thought that was great. "It's like camping, Mommy!" I only wished we were camping. I'd be more at ease. Before I curled up beside her, I dug out the baseball bat from the storage closet. I kept one eye on her and the other on the door. I somehow fell to sleep, but not for long. I heard a noise out in the hall. I quickly jumped up and looked through the peephole. *It's him, he's back!* I looked at the clock on the kitchen wall. *My god, it's three o'clock in the morning!* He put the key into his door lock, but before he opened it, he quickly turned around and started walking towards my door.

It was as if he knew I was watching him. I instantly crouched down to the floor and held my breath. I was terrified. There was only two inches keeping us apart. I then heard him shut his door, so I knew I was safe. The next morning, I was beat, but my nerves overpowered the tiredness. I called the detective to inform him of what happened the night before. I could almost have called it borderline harassment, but with no evidence, the detective couldn't charge him with anything. Since I knew he was home, it was a good time to question him. The detective went directly to his condo. I could hear him pounding on the door. I opened up my door and said, "Hello, you don't really think he is going to let you in, do you?" I said under my breath, "The only way you're getting in there is with an axe!" The detective got discouraged and came over for a coffee. He was getting a little concerned over the situation.

He looked at me. "I'm off duty tonight around nine. I'll pop over to see how you two are doing and try to speak with him." I mentioned to him that I had a security company coming over that afternoon to install a security system. I was getting the best high-tech system known to man. A fly couldn't escape it.

After he left, I took Alexandria out for supper and did some shopping. I had to take my mind off the situation. If only Daniel were home. We arrived home around eight o'clock. We were loaded down with bags. I walked up to my door, and there was a note taped to the knob. I didn't want to touch it, so I used my keys to pry it open. It was all sticky with goo; it was disgusting! It was hard to read as the goo had blurred some of the words. It was something like, *You...Bit...stop wha...you're doing!* I grabbed Alexandria and got the hell out of there. I phoned the detective to go to my condo and have a look at what was on my front door. When he arrived, there was no note. He phoned me on my cell phone.

"Whoever put the note there removed it," I said. *Great, now I'm dealing with a psycho.* Just what I needed! I was fuming. I yelled at the detective, "Can't you do anything about this? Come on, break down that creep's door and find some answers! What's it going to take, someone to get hurt or killed?" He sounded very sympathetic, but his hands were tied. Without proof, he couldn't do anything. I hung up the phone pissed off as hell. "I'll find him proof one way or another!" I said to myself.

I took an entire week off work just to monitor his patterns. By midweek, I noticed every afternoon he left around two o'clock and returned around six. I went to the condos' main office and said to the girl at the desk, "I'm taking care of my neighbour's cat, and I misplaced his key this morning. I can hear the cat crying. Could you be a doll and loan me a key? I'll just be five minutes." She knew damn well he never gave me a key. She also knew that guy was a "little" unusual. With a wink in her eyes, she handed me the key.

"You have ten minutes!" she said. "If anyone comes around asking questions, I know nothing, understood?" I knew she wouldn't say anything. I must say, I was really nervous going into his condo. I didn't know what to expect.

The first thing I smelled was a rotten litter box. His cat was purring her heart out to me. The place was a mess. He must have had a hundred newspapers stacked up in the living room. There were dirty dishes everywhere. I walked up to the bedroom door and opened it very slowly. The floor was covered with porn magazines. The sheets looked like they hadn't been changed in months. The cat leapt on the bed. It startled me. When I opened the bathroom door, it was filthy. I covered my nose and walked in. "My god, hasn't this guy ever heard of Comet or Javex?" So far,

I hadn't found anything to nail this bastard with. I went into the kitchen and opened up his garbage can. Way in the bottom was a receipt from the local florist down the street. On it read, *One dozen white roses, forty nine dollars*! That was better than nothing, but I needed something concrete. I went back into his bedroom and started shuffling through his dresser drawers. I found way in back of his bottom drawer newspaper clippings of rape victims from Toronto, Calgary and even British Columbia. Alongside them was a plastic bag with a couple of pairs of panties. *Ugh, this guy is sicker than I thought.*

There was a picture alongside the newspaper articles. It was his picture. The article read, "Police had their suspicions on a suspect but didn't have the evidence to charge the man. Anyone with any clues or evidence pertaining to these crimes, please contact your local authorities immediately!" The more I read, the sicker I became. My forehead broke out into a sweat. I quickly closed the dresser drawer and flew out that door. I didn't waste any time calling up the detective. That time, he didn't come alone. He had a search warrant and a crew of eight men with him.

While they were stripping the place from one end to the other, the owner walked in. "What in hell are you doing in here? This is private property!"

The detective approached him, "Yeah, pal. You're under arrest for the following rape charges that string from one end of Canada to the other!"

The man replied, "You've got nothing on me. This is harassment!" The detective lifted up the plastic bag of little girls' panties and shoved it into his face.

"Do these belong to you?" he asked.

"They're not mine!"

The detective said, "You're damn right, they're not!"

They confiscated boxes of evidence from his condo. The detective came up to me. "I know what you did was illegal, but I am going to turn a blind eye to it. And by the way, do you think you might want to change careers?" That evening, I was finally at peace. Alexandria and I curled up on the couch and eventually fell asleep watching television. The detective called me later on that week. They nailed my neighbor with five counts of rape and eight counts of sexual abuse. His final words were, "I have enough evidence to put him away for a very long, long time. My worries were over."

TWENTY- THREE

Daniel was due home any day. He sure missed a lot of excitement while he was gone. I had come home from work to see I had numerous messages on my answering machine. Whoever it was didn't leave any messages. I never thought much about it. If it was important, they would call back! After dinner, I drew myself a nice hot bath, poured myself a glass of wine and put on some classical music. Alexandria was busy doing her homework in her room. Before I went into the tub, I popped my head into her room. "Alexandria, please get the phone for me!" As soon as I got into the tub, the phone rang. I could hear Alexandria, saying, "Hello? Hello? Is anybody there?" She ran into the bathroom to tell me the person hung up.

It wasn't five minutes that passed and the phone rang again. I yelled at Alexandria, "Bring the remote in here. I'll get it!" I picked up the phone and sat up in the tub. "Hello? hello? Who is this?"

I was just about to hang up when a feeble voice said, "Hi, it's me. Stephen!" I almost dropped the phone into the tub.

"Stephen? Stephen who? Is this some kind of sick joke? Oh my god, is that really you, Stephen?" Every muscle and nerve ending froze. The water had turned to ice. I didn't know what to say to him. It had been years since I had heard from him. "What are you calling me for and where are you?" I got out of the tub and started drying myself off. His response was slow. "I'm here in Halifax. I would really appreciate it if you could come and see me. I'm at the Queen Elizabeth Hospital on the sixth floor. Don't ask any questions.

I'll explain it all when I see you." I told him I would be there sometime tomorrow afternoon. He had me baffled. I never slept a wink that night. I left work early the next day to head to the hospital. I had mixed emotions. I really didn't know what to expect when I entered his room. I opened the door slowly and peeked around the corner. I couldn't believe my eyes when I saw him. I gasped at the sight of him. He was so thin and pale. His mouth had white crust formed on the corners. His eyes were black and hollow. I walked over to his bed to hold his hand. His eyes were fluttering. When he felt my hands, his eyes opened fully. He was so weak he could hardly speak.

He looked up at me, smiled and said, "You look as beautiful as ever!" I ran my hand over his cheek.

"What's wrong with you?" It took every bit of energy he had to explain how he ended up here.

He had been on a cruise ship, and one of the stops was in Halifax. He knew before he took the cruise that he was dying of terminal cancer. He became so ill he had to cut the cruise short. He held my hand against his hollow chest. "You know, love, I never stopped loving you, not for one moment!" I couldn't fight back the tears any longer. It was such a riveting moment. I apologized for crying in front of him. He reached under the sheets and pulled out a hand-carved wooden box. The workmanship in that box was detailed to perfection. It had a brass lock on it. With his shaking, feeble hands, he handed me the key and said, "I wanted you to have this." I gently removed it from his hands.

"What is this?" Before he had a chance to answer, his eyes closed, and his head fell to the side of his pillow. I quietly got up, took one last look at the man I once was so in love with and walked away.

Printed in the United States
39440LVS00004B/16